THE HEALING OATH

ANDRÉ SOUBIRAN

The Healing Oath

TRANSLATED BY OLIVER COBURN

So81 h

G. P. PUTNAM'S SONS NEW YORK

This book is dedicated to Dr. Pierre Richard, of Saint Céré, and to all my friends born in towns, who have been willing to become doctors in the country, in order to rebuild an elite group there and save "the green valleys."

ANDRÉ SOUBIRAN

THE HEALING OATH

Part 1

MONTH IN THE AUVERGNE

Chapter One

Feb. 27th

"Time it, if you like; I'll bet you won't find a faster elevator in all Paris." This was Henri Philippon's usual boast when you set foot on his landing for the first time, still somewhat stunned at having arrived there so quickly. The elevator slowed down gradually, of course, in the last few yards, but I was not really used to it even after three years, and this abrupt form of propulsion still left me slightly dizzy. Through seven floors I was made unpleasantly aware of my stomach, and was always relieved to land safely once more on the thick woollen carpet of his landing. It was naturally a very luxurious apartment house, or Henri would never have chosen to set up his abode there.

I rang twice, as was customary for Henri's real friends. He came to open the door clad in an elegant dressing-gown, and then left me immediately, saying: "Come in. I'm phoning."

Coming out of the Metro, I had been caught by a sudden heavy shower and my overcoat was soaked. I took it off and joined Henri in his office, where I found him lying back in a deep armchair, carelessly balancing a red leather slipper on the toes of a bare foot. There was a look of keen pleasure on his face as he watched me come in, but the pleasure, as I gathered from a little face he made, was not caused by the voice at the other end of the wire. While he continued to grunt out comments and criticisms which did not concern me, his free hand was indicating to me the ivory receiver at his ear. On the desk

1

was a sturdy stand in the same immaculate hue. They had re-placed the gloomy old-fashioned telephone apparatus with its high base, which I had seen in the same position the night be-fore. This change marked the gratification of a childish whim which had been in his mind about a week. "White will be a bit more cheerful," he had explained to me. "The telephone is my chief working tool. It's as if I were buying myself the latest Medical Encyclopedia."

But now I saw the smile abruptly wiped out on his face. He straightened up, planted both feet solidly on the ground, bent his brow and broad shoulders aggressively forward, and said:

"Hello, yes...we are in 1936...quite so. Thank you for re-minding me...to be precise, the 27th of February 1936. But what, might I ask, is the relevance of the date?...Hello! The crisis? Yes, of course I've heard something about the new crisis. But crises, my dear sir, only affect third-rate commercial trav-elers, you must agree, while my champagne is a first-class extra-dry brand...No, the deal's off...No, of course not, if that's all you can offer. I'd rather keep it...Oh well, can't be helped. If I have any more of it, I'll drink your health in it next New Year's Eve... *Good* day to you."

He hung up the receiver, stretched himself, then flung him-self back in the armchair again, exclaiming with deep satisfac-tion: "My God, Jean, my new telephone brings better luck than any horseshoe. I could have paid for it a dozen times with any one of this morning's calls; it hasn't stopped ringing since ten o'clock. Just these few bottles of champagne, you know, and I've already been offered two francs more per bottle—that was what that was all about. I was right not to listen to you, you see, and to hold out a bit longer...."

Suddenly he seemed to remember that he was not just a wine salesman, but was also, unfortunately, supposed to be studying medicine. "Just back from the hospital?" he asked, but without showing any anxiety. "No roll call to-day?"

"Yes, there was, actually, and Barrière couldn't answer in your place today, the Chief was looking at him. But I made a cross in front of your name when Sister had her back turned. The list was in her drawer."

Henri listened absently to these details, and barely thanked me, he had become so used to my doing these things. He frequented the hospital only spasmodically, while I, being still a "dresser," was obliged to be in the wards for my work every day. Already he was thinking of something else.

"I was told just now of a rather interesting deal at Tattersall's. A Citroen in perfect condition which will be arriving tomorrow afternoon. I can't get down there then. Be a good fellow and go and see what it's like."

The embarrassing moment had come. I replied with an attempt at casualness: "I'm afraid I can't, Henri. I'm leaving Paris this evening to act as substitute for an old country doctor. I was asked to go by my old pal, Lucien Clément."

Henri looked up at me in astonishment: "That's very tiresome —what's the matter with you all of a sudden? At least I hope it's somewhere near Nice you're going to."

"It isn't. I'm going to Peyrac-le-Château, near Aurillac."

"Peyrac? Why, I know it very well. It's not so far from Mur-de-Barrez, where I was born. You're not really going to *Peyrac*, my poor Jean?" His expression and tone contained a boundless pity.

"My dear boy," he went on patronizingly, "I do wish you luck, but it's a completely one-horse town in the Cantal, miles and miles from the nearest city, in fact it might be the end of the world. You can't even get near it by train. You have to get out at Aurillac, and then take an asthmatic old bus for at least thirty-five miles...."

He showed even greater consternation when I admitted to him that I had already wired the date of my arrival there.

"Then listen to the advice of a friend who knows the dump well. Send off another telegram at once saying you're terribly sorry. 'Just broken leg now in plaster'—you know the sort of thing. And as a matter of fact it would be far better to spend forty days in a plaster cast in nice warm Paris than one week of winter in the Cantal. Particularly as there'll be a good layer of icy snow on the roads, so you'll probably get frost-bite and break your leg anyway...."

A ring on the telephone interrupted him. He had only to stretch out his arm to reach it. Then, recognizing the voice, he sank comfortably back in the armchair. "It's Buisson," he announced for my benefit.

I guessed the conversation might be a long one. Buisson was

a former dealer in second-hand cars, who had gone broke after a run of bad luck at the tracks. In the afternoons he continued to take an interest in the horses, but when his unlucky period lasted too long, he would try to keep body and soul together by dashing back to Paris to tell Henri about some promising cars for sale, in return for a small share in the eventual profits.

It was nearly one o'clock, and I was hungry. As always after a morning at the hospital, I also felt tired and drained of all my energy. Henri, his ear to the receiver, was writing down addresses in a leisurely way. He was freshly shaved, had just had a bath, looked rested and refreshed. With no hospital post, and confident that for the hospital lectures someone would answer his name at the roll call, he could stay in bed till noon. I, on the other hand, had arrived in the ward a little late, as always, and out of breath from having run. I had then made a preliminary round of the beds, to deal with new admissions and find out which cases had become worse during the night and which if any had died. I also had to give injections, put on dressings, take blood specimens, note developments in all my cases, prepare myself for going round the ward with the interne, and finally be present during the solemn visit of the Chief, facing the chance of being questioned at each bed.

So, while waiting for Buisson to finish giving his list, I was quite pleased to be able to go and sit down on the divan. Since the first year of my friendship with Henri, I had appreciated its comfort in more than one context. In those days I had not yet shown any inclination to participate in his car deals and other rackets, and I was still living at the Cité Universitaire, instead of in the more expensive hotel room in the Latin Quarter which I was later able to afford. The rules of the Jules Ferry Hostel strictly forbade bringing in women, and Henri, so often my companion in the evenings, had often lent me his office divan for the night. But the next day, while he could linger indolently in bed all morning with his girl, I had sometimes felt myself a martyr because I had to leave mine, as well as the soft divan, about nine o'clock. I would rise blearily, my head heavy, my flesh exhausted after a night of so-called pleasure, and would find myself on the street, my eyes hurt by the light of the outside world, half an hour late, but nevertheless on my way to the hospital.

4

"No, no coupés...no, it's too early in the year. We want a quick turnover. If we bought them now, we'd have them on our hands for weeks and weeks.... Hello! Yes, of course, except for something really good. That's right, not more than twelve thousand francs...."

For three years now, since I had first come to Paris as a medical student, I had been seeing Henri almost every day and we had been going around together regularly. How often I had admired him for that forcefulness, that air of authority and self-confidence, that instinct for the right move, the successful gamble, the profitable risk. I envied him too his facility for excluding from his mind anything which concerned the long-term future. Life at his side flowed smoothly and comfortably on; there were no periods of tedium or monotony.

During the distant summer when we had become friends, I had first of all despised him for his sensuality, his taste for money, his laziness and cynicism. But I had been right to suspect in my scorn a secret core of jealousy; and very soon I myself acquired a taste for the atmosphere of comfort and pleasure which he revealed to me. I knew now how far habitual physical well-being could insidiously take hold of a man, could impregnate his being so completely that in the end he was bound to it hand and foot. I could never have put on again the absurd ready-made clothes I was wearing when I first left Toulouse for Paris. To realize the impossibility of such a thing, I only had to remember my excitement when I ordered my first made-to-measure suit from the first-class tailor Henri had recommended. Till then, to come anywhere near the level of elegance set by my new friend, I had privately altered some old suits he had given me, and added to my wardrobe some ties he had stopped wearing. This was in the year when I was still living at the Cité Universitaire.

One evening on returning to the hostel I found a note from the Dean saying that he wished to see me. Perhaps he was going to expel me for sleeping out too often, or else he had seen me coming back to the hostel after midnight, I thought. I was therefore rather nervous when I knocked at his door; but good news awaited me. Lamine Diouf, a medical student from Gorée, in Africa, who had a substantial scholarship from the government of Senegal, had just died of tuberculosis in the

Students' Sanatorium. Since I had been born at Dakar, and since my father had been killed in the war, I had all the qualifications to become beneficiary of this scholarship in his place. I emerged from the Dean's office completely dazzled.

All at once I had become, if not rich, at least very well off in comparison with most of my fellow students. Of course, compared with Henri, I had always felt almost a pauper; and to go on enjoying his company I had to let him pay for everything. He did this without any trouble, as he hated being alone and I served him very adequately as a confidant. To remain on good terms with himself, he seemed to have a constant need for approval and admiration—which I was quite prepared to give him, although at times I was secretly disgusted at his vanity. Anyhow, on the very first day of my new wealth, I went to his tailor, who glanced at the jacket I was wearing and then, infuriatingly, showed me first of all some of his inferior material. I wanted the best, I told him, and even greater than the thrill of ordering it was the joy a few weeks afterwards of putting on my new suit for the first time and comparing it to the ill-fitting monstrosity I had on my back when I came to Paris three years earlier.

At the same time, until the award of this unexpected scholarship, I had really been quite indifferent to questions of money. I had been living on Henri shamelessly, but without envy. These small beginnings of financial good fortune overwhelmed me as much as my first sexual intimacy with a woman. From that time I took an increasing interest in Henri's financial operations, his sales of cars, for instance; and he, amused by my unexpected ardor as a business man, let me share in the profits on some of his deals. Without even waiting for these profits, I opened a bank account; and when I slipped my first checkbook into my pocket I felt I was beginning a new life of gilded ease. This was the life, in fact, which I had been leading in Henri's company the last three years. Now that I had money and could buy smart clothes and eat in comfortable restaurants, I could no more imagine myself returning to the modest existence of my first two years than I could think of going back to the Cité's self-service restaurant to swallow mediocre meals lugged about on a greasy aluminum tray. A few sporadic bursts of work enabled me to pass my University exams by a very

6

narrow margin, so that apart from my military service and submitting my thesis I was almost qualified as a doctor. Henri, two or three years older than I was, was taking his time over the end-of-year University exams, having failed several of them; he seemed to think about the future not at all. I imitated him in this as much as I could; once qualified, I meant to enjoy life and felt pretty confident of being able to "manage somehow" as far as my profession went.

"Yes, Buisson...at that price it sounds fair enough...How about the tires . . . and the body . . . ? Good, I'll just put that down...right, we'll go and look it over...."

The list of possibles seemed to continue indefinitely, and I thought to myself that Buisson must have had great disappointments over his horses of late to be taking so much trouble over the cars. Henri went on listening to him attentively, lolling comfortably in his armchair, receiver in one hand, fountain pen in the other. He must have regretted not having a third hand so that he could have lit one of the cigarettes lying within reach, on a low table, in a fine pigskin cigarette case.

When he had finished with Buisson, we could still not go to lunch right away; I had to wait for him to dress. So I slipped a thick velvet cushion under my head, and relaxed on the divan. I was beginning to feel very hungry and wanted a smoke. I did not even have to stand up in order to find a cigarette; that would have been unappreciative of Henri's sense of comfort, which was unfailing in every detail. At the head of the divan, almost under my fingers, I found cigarettes and matches in another expensive box.

It was pleasantly warm in the little room, though heavy rain was beating down on the large bay windows, which seemed to open directly onto a sky thick with lowering storm clouds. I shut my eyes so that I could better savor the contrast of the room's peaceful atmosphere. In this blissful state, I wondered for a moment whether instead of braving the rigors of winter in the Cantal region, I would not simply send a second telegram, as Henri suggested, apologizing for not being able to come after all.

For several minutes I tried to think of an excuse which would sound plausible to Lucien Clément. He had left Paris

7

three years ago to do a year as house physician at the hospital in Aurillac before setting up in general practice at Peyrac-le-Château. I had not seen him since he left Paris, and we had long since stopped writing to each other. In the letter I had received the evening before, he asked me if I could come and help him for two or three weeks, as the other doctor in the village, an oldish man, had had a very bad attack of angina pectoris a few days ago and was forced to remain in bed. I could live in the old doctor's house and look after his patients.

"Do try and come," Lucien had written. "I don't know anyone else at the Cité or at Aurillac Hospital whom I could ask to help me out at such short notice. Dr. Delpuech, for whom you'd be acting as locum, didn't want a stranger who wasn't even qualified, but when I told him we had been very close friends, he said it was good enough for him. I'm quite sure you wouldn't be wasting your time. You'll see here a side of medicine which I should imagine would be completely new to you. You must be just about through with your thesis now, and before you start on your own in practice, coming here as locum will give you some very useful experience. You know I'm not much good at expressing myself, Jean, but I can't tell you how pleased and grateful I'd be if you *could* come. And if you can, the sooner the better."

The careful regular writing, simple and purposeful, was so much like Lucien himself, that I was quite stirred to see it again. How often I had encountered it in lecture notes and notebooks I had borrowed! Without proper reflection, in an impulse of sincere friendship I had at once telegraphed that I could come. Well then: it was now much too late to go back on it. Lucien was counting on me, and I could not let him down.

"Hey there, Jean, you can't start going to sleep now, we've a lot of work to do. Buisson sounds as if he'd got his hands on two or three really sensational deals. This afternoon we'll go and see the one at the Porte de Vincennes, and tomorrow I'll get you to go over to the Porte de Champerret...."

Standing there in front of me, Henri was rubbing his hands at the prospect of handsome profits. He had obviously forgotten all about my departure for Peyrac.

"Well, it's all right for this afternoon, of course," I said, "but tomorrow as you know I shan't be here."

Henri at once looked irritated and exclaimed in an impatient tone, "Oh, look here now, you're not going to let me down on a couple of nice little deals like this. Your pal Clément can manage all right by himself with his yokels."

"I've been thinking while you were on the phone. I like old Clément a lot, and it's far too late to go back on my promise now. I can't possibly leave him in the lurch for your good business, which probably isn't so wonderful after all. With that old faker Buisson you never really know how good a car is till you see it."

Henri tried another line of argument: "Does Vicky know you're leaving?"

"No, she doesn't. We had a quarrel yesterday afternoon and she walked out on me. I found Clément's letter after dinner when I went home. I won't say that getting away from Vicky is my only reason for leaving, but it will certainly do me good to have a little change of air."

"Honeymoon over, what? Not been very long, has it?"

"Well, I don't know—it's nearly six months now. In fact, that's what scares me: she's beginning to get her claws in. I'm afraid she may even be beginning to think about marriage—and I don't like that idea one little bit."

"You see now, don't you? Women always think doctors are stupider than lawyers, more often inclined to marry their mistresses. You've never believed me, but one day you'll get caught. Let me tell you again, if you want to avoid trouble in the future, stick to married women. Like me with Denise, for instance—I'm quite free from all that kind of worry. Only if it's your quarrels with Vicky that you find disagreeable, I hope you won't mind my pointing out that you two have always quarreled, from the word go."

"Yes, of course we have. But at first I used to find it rather amusing, and we always finished by making it all up in bed."

"Whereas now?"

"She bores me stiff. I'm fed up with her tantrums and insinuations and nagging. And her lies! She lies as naturally as she breathes. She's just as made up and artificial as her Christian name."

"If she told nothing but the truth, poor girl, she might have trouble making conversation. And how do you expect her to

9

get anywhere in the theatre if she calls herself Victoria? I've no doubt her parents' intentions were very good when they gave her such a dignified name, but you must admit that Vicky looks a whole lot better on a poster."

"If she only had some talent. But you've only to hear her pulling everybody else at the dramatic school to pieces—and that's all she talks about—to be quite sure she'll never get anywhere herself. A pretentious, conceited little cat, that's all she is."

"She may not have any talent," remarked Henri soothingly, "but she *is* pretty, and she's willing, which compensates for a lot of other things, don't you think?"

Realizing I had made up my mind to leave, however, he gave me the benefit of the doubt. "After all, you're probably right to be on your guard. If you're beginning to feel you've had enough of her, this little trip is an admirable excuse for getting rid of her."

He went into his room, and I heard him humming as he dressed.

On my own again, I realized that I had not dared give Henri all my real reasons. He was quite able to see that I no longer wanted Vicky, that my body no longer demanded her body as it had done at the beginning of our love affair. Then I had dragged her about with me all the time, like a dog with its bone. In that respect, in spite of all my good intentions I had become like Henri, always chasing after something new. Six months, as far as love went, seemed to me a long time; after that, pale with irritation and boredom, I felt a panic desire for escape. All this was quite comprehensible to Henri, but the rest was harder to express, unless I had been willing to forfeit his good opinion altogether. He would only have laughed if I had tried to explain to him my reaction on opening Lucien's letter after the quarrel with Vicky. After our six months' affair I suddenly found Vicky falser and shallower, more stupid and more vicious than ever before. I felt such disgust for her that I hoped I would never see her again. All evening I had felt depressed and unhappy, vaguely disgusted with myself, my wasted years, and this hedonistic life which never seemed to lead to anything clean and worthwhile. I began to guess now that in wiring my answer to Lucien I was not only escaping from Vicky; I was unconsciously seizing a chance for a breath of good clean country air, far from the sordid and tarnished pleasures of Paris.

"Coming?" asked Henri, as he appeared in the room, ready to leave. "It's after half past one."

I rose rather listlessly, and he tapped me on the shoulder. "Don't look so glum, old fellow. I'll tell you—since I've had a good morning, you shall be my guest at the Tour d'Argent. Before steeping yourself in the manure piles of the Auvergne, you must taste civilized food just once more."

As I was putting on my coat, he added: "Talking of manure, if you're thinking of having a roll in the hay with some of the local dairymaids, I'd take a douche with you. Very useful invention...."

Chapter Two

Feb. 28th

NEXT DAY the pallid light of early morning found me squelching in the mud, suitcase in hand, outside Aurillac station. All night since leaving Paris I had stifled in the overheated railway compartment, and now that I was out of it I found myself shivering under a treacherous north wind. Still half asleep, I waited for the Peyrac bus, which a red-nosed railway official, not deigning to take his hands out of his pockets, had vaguely indicated to me with his chin.

At the bus station a herd of cows had just come to a standstill between two sturdy farmhands with drooping moustaches, who wore round black hats and dark blue smocks; they might, I thought, have come down from their mountain specially attired for a folklore festival. A dog was bringing up a straggling cow by snapping at its hams; the frightened beast trotted up heavily, feet splayed, dewlaps flapping, and buttocks in the air, covered right to the belly with patches of brown dung. I looked at the manure-colored puddles in the turnaround in front of the station, and the rustic-looking houses opposite with their pink-tiled roofs. The yard was certainly providing plenty of the powerful odors for which Henri had tried to prepare me; it smelled as high as an ill-kept farmyard.

Several times during the night I had looked out at the landscape. The train had puffed and panted as it dragged us through precipitous gorges, hollows full of black shadows, at the foot of mountains which stood out in icy outline against a sky swarming with stars. These magnificent views sustained my enthusiasm; but in the gray morning, in front of this station with its mud-spattered walls, I began to feel uneasy. If a sizeable country town was as squalid as this, what on earth would the meaner surrounding villages be like?

Stimulated by oaths and harassed by the dog, the herd eventually proceeded slowly to the entrance of the station stockyard, leaving behind it a trail of steaming dung. In its place a boxlike bus arrived and jolted to a stop. It was splashed with clay right to the roof and painted a dirty yellow, almost the shade of the excreta of the cows. With rustic slowness the passengers who were waiting with me on the pavement moved towards the doors and started climbing into the bus; there was much maneuvering of baskets filled with poultry. Almost before he had sat down my neighbor, a man in a black smock, opened his haversack and extracted a greasy piece of ham sandwiched in a thick hunk of bread. He began cutting this into large cubes, which he then swallowed with considerable concentration between long draughts of red wine. At last the bus started up with a sharp crackling of dry wood and metal, as if firecrackers were being set off underneath it.

Almost immediately, after passing through a drab suburb, the road entered flat muddy country, with ditches full of yellowish water which appeared from a distance to be dammed by ridges of snow. We seemed to have been traveling for some while before the coach started on the slow continuous ascent towards the mountains and Peyrac-le-Château. According to the milestones this would go on for thirty miles.

Already the farms became rarer, and instead of tiles most of the roofs seemed to be made of a flaky coarse gray slate. Then snow appeared on the crests of the hills, and very soon it came right down to the ditches. The dismal road began to slope upwards through a wide deep valley, grim and white, though the

12

whiteness was broken at times by a clump of dark trees or a huge vertical rock. The villages were spaced out further and further. When we stopped at a café-halt, you could imagine animals and humans huddled shivering inside each squat narrow-windowed house, trying to foster as much warmth as they could.

Apart from a few months in the summer I had always lived in a town, and the country in winter—any country—seemed to me by definition a terrifying place, not fit to be lived in, with its narrow deserted crossroads and muddy lanes which never seemed to lead anywhere. But the dismal scene revealed to me this morning was an even more sinister waste land than I had imagined. The only things that moved in these bare white expanses sparkling with snow were a few crows digging for worms. Henri's phrase was all too apt, I thought to myself: this place is really the end of the world. Apart from my companions in the crowded bus, I might have been exploring some uninhabited country.

My neighbor with the ham sandwich got out, and his place was taken by a big red-faced countrywoman. She spent a long while putting down her baskets under my bench and against my knees, then made an effort to sit quiet. But very soon she began moving about again, sighing, bringing out a handkerchief, and mopping her brow; she had gone very pale. Then suddenly she gave an abrupt hiccough, bent over, and after carefully pulling in her skirt began bringing up her breakfast on the floor between her legs. The driver stopped, and all the passengers comforted her in a harsh *patois;* someone offered her a nip of local brandy on some sugar, and this treatment appeared to be effective.

Till then I had been sitting near a window which was slightly open, gaining a thin jet of fresh air; this helped me to endure the pervading stench, more animal than human, mingling with the reek of gasoline and hot oil. I felt obliged to give up my own seat to the ailing woman, and sat down in her place, hurriedly covering the mess on the floor with a newspaper.

I had taken good care, of course, not to say I was a doctor, although this vomiting patient would have presented no great problem. My ingenious friend Paul Chavasse—"the great M. Chavasse" as one of the surgeons had sarcastically referred to him in our first year of study—had equipped me with several handy stock prescriptions for emergency use. He had also made other valuable contributions to my success, not least of them the example of optimism and self-confidence he had given me from the times when he had acted as locum himself. According to Paul, judging from his own experience, everything usually went off well both for the novice doctor and for the patients, given reasonable goodwill on both sides.

Suddenly the climb became steep. The engine attacked it with a terrifying noise and an increased reek of warm oil and burning grease. My neighbor began to go green again; she leaned over toward me to groan, her breath still smelling of bile: "It's lucky we're coming to Peyrac. I'm beginning to feel bad again."

In a last explosive effort the bus passed under an old stone gateway. Immediately afterwards it turned into a dark narrow street till it came to a small square where the driver stopped and the passengers began to get out.

When I reached the door myself, I looked for Lucien's solid figure outside; but he was not there. Before going off to find him, I would have plenty of time to examine my surroundings. Henri had not exaggerated, Peyrac certainly looked distinctly dismal. It was not even a small town, it was only a large village perched on the back of a lowering white mountain. Round its narrow slushy square, dominated by a gaunt square tower and a Romanesque church which looked like a fortress, stood a huddled collection of old stone houses with thick walls and low doors, doubtless intended to keep out the wind and the cold. In this meager rural county seat, scorned by the railroad and highways, time seemed to have stood still. You had only to forget a few slightly modernized buildings with shops or cafés on their ground floors to think yourself some five centuries back at the end of the Middle Ages.

On the side of the dark square facing the mountain a few rows of trees formed a sort of terrace. This opened out onto an endless range of rugged snow-covered hills, which seemed weighted down under vast banks of storm-clouds.

I turned up my coat collar, took up my suitcase, and following the bus driver's directions went grimly off towards Lucien's house. Almost at the end of the village it was—a stone building, poor enough but at least without any mud on it. The front door

14

had a shining new bronze plate on it, next to the night bell, saying *Docteur Lucien Clément*. The maid who opened the door offered me Lucien's apologies for not being there. He had just been called out, apparently, and had said he would come and see me at Dr. Delpuech's house as soon as he got back.

I went back to the square. Dr. Delpuech's house, the maid had said, was half way down the main street; this was easy enough to find because it started at the foot of the old tower with the pointed roof. Squelching through the slush I dragged my valise, now feeling unpleasantly heavy, as far as a fine-looking old house which was conspicuous among a row of impoverished shop-fronts. Under the knocker on the double-leaved front door a doctor's plate, almost worn out by years of polishing, told me I had reached my destination. I rang several times before hearing inside a clatter of clogs on the tiles, and then some steps which were drowned in a great rustle of skirts. The double doors came ajar, and through the opening appeared a suspicious eye and the corner of a wizened cheek, while a woman's voice declared with authority:

"Doctor Delpuech is ill, and not seeing any patients. If it's about the laboratory, come again next year."

But before I could answer the voice went on much more cordially: "Oh, please excuse me, sir. I didn't see your case. People here just don't seem to be able to understand that Dr. Delpuech is really very ill. You must be Dr. Clément's friend, aren't you? I must have kept you waiting for ages. I was at the back of the house and pretended to be deaf. And now I'm keeping you outside catching your death of cold. Do come in at once. Dr. Delpuech will be delighted to see you."

The door had opened wide to show a little old woman, her white hair caught up in a sort of black coif. The ends of her woollen neckerchief crossed under a curious sort of corset which covered her bodice; this formed a place in which to stow her handkerchief and spectacles. Above this severe costume, all black and without any embellishment, the face had lost its first suspicious expression. It was now smiling at me with the rough kindness of a bustling and motherly old countrywoman.

"My name's Félicie," said the old housekeeper, as I guessed her to be; and we crossed together a big dark flagstoned hall to the first steps of a fine stone staircase. On the first floor, having pushed open a door, she stood back and announced: "Here is Dr. Clément's friend, who's just arrived from Paris."

I went into the room, which was high-ceilinged and spacious. The curtains were open, but all the same I found the room dark. The sky outside was gray and heavy despite the snow, and there was nothing in the dull light coming in through the window to enliven the gloom. In the bed all I could see at first was a figure sitting half upright, propped on a pile of pillows.

"I'm very glad to see you, my young colleague," said a rather dim and muffled voice. "Félicie, please bring up a chair for the Doctor so that we can make our acquaintance in comfort."

When I reached the bed I saw a sick and aged face, pale and worn and thin; but it lit up at once with a friendly smile which I found extremely warm and heartening.

"It's most kind of you to come to my rescue at a time like this," said the voice. "Up to now we've not had too bad a winter, but it certainly has been terrible weather the last few days."

"You can always rely on the winters here," put in Félicie. "If we don't get our bad spell early, it'll come later, never fear." She had remained standing near the bed and was looking at her master with obvious affection.

"That's the inconvenient part of our profession," the old doctor went on. "We always get either too many patients or too few. In the summer farmers don't bother much about their health because they're too busy in the fields. In winter they've often got nothing much to do, so they all get bored and call in the doctor at the same time. I chose a very bad time to be ill, and your friend Lucien has been rushed off his feet. I didn't want him to bother you, for something so out-of-the-way. I must give you an idea of the position: I've been practising here for forty years and my patients are used to me. A young locum they don't know, instead of their own old doctor—well, it's bound to frighten them a bit. So you mustn't be too upset if they're not very friendly with you just at first. Lucien certainly needs to have some of the work taken off his hands, and as I'm so much better, I've told him I'll gradually begin seeing patients again in a few days' time."

"He's crazy," cried Félicie. "Him see patients when he's far more ill than they are! Just because they keep ringing the door-bell all day. I tell you honestly, if you hadn't come, I'd have

16

cut off the bell and the phone, and barricaded myself in front of the door so that his wretched patients wouldn't succeed in killing him altogether. They all refuse to believe he's in bed. They all tell you a doctor's never ill, specially a good strong man like Dr. Delpuech. My goodness, he's certainly spoiled them badly these last forty years. He's too kind, and the people are plain tough in these parts. You've got to protect yourself, or else. . . ."

She paused to recover her breath, but the gesture she made towards Dr. Delpuech showed eloquently the fate of those who allowed themselves to be exploited. The doctor took advantage of the silence to suggest gently: "While you're letting your tongue wag, Félicie, Dr. Nérac may not have had anything to eat."

This idea seemed to stagger the old housekeeper; she raised her arms and exclaimed: "Dear-oh-dear, the poor boy. You quite upset me, the stupid way you go on—you and your being so much better and starting to see patients!"

She disappeared towards the kitchen, and Dr. Delpuech went on: "Excuse my having used you to effect that diversion. I lost my wife and our only son seventeen years ago in an epidemic, and Félicie has been in control ever since. I no longer dare to make a frontal attack on her authority, still less would I dream of trying to shut her up. Even my patients have got used to finding her between them and me, as a power they have to come to terms with or else get round, somehow. Of course, she's been talking to me so long I don't really listen any more. We're quite used to each other, but I'm afraid you may not find it so easy. It's a sad house for a young man to come to, what with a garrulous old housekeeper, and an impossible old invalid doctor."

I protested politely, but he stopped me.

"Oh no, it's true enough, as you'll see for yourself. Any illness in itself brings on an acute attack of selfishness as well—your own pain becomes the only thing that's important. And there are no more selfish, difficult, finicky, distrustful, disappointing patients than the old. They're the greatest danger a young doctor can have for his future reputation. He'll never cure them, he'll have only disillusionments, for you can't make an old man young again. To gain their confidence I recommend two little pieces of strategy: one, always listen patiently to all

17

the minor complaints, even when they are intermingled with idle gossip and irrelevant details. Two, always sound as if you set great store by their opinions. Anyway, you can practise the technique on me."

Then he gave me his charming smile, and finished: "Still, knowing all these weaknesses in others, I'll try and behave myself a bit better."

The door opened abruptly, and Félicie told us from the entrance: "What a terrible crowd! They can't even let Dr. Nérac have his lunch in peace. The little girl from the Café Albignac has come to look for him. It's for a man from Farlat who's at the wedding of young Rouquerolle. He's had a stroke or something—the girl doesn't seem to know just what's happened."

"You'd better go at once," said Dr. Delpuech. "Félicie will give you the bag. The instruments and syringes in the case have been sterilized."

A little girl of twelve was waiting for me in the hall. Félicie put the emergency bag in my hands, and came to the door with me. The child, her hands wrapped in her muffler, trotted along near me. On the way I tried to gather some information about the case awaiting me, but she could help me very little. She hadn't seen anything, she was helping her mother with the girdles, she said, in the kitchen and afterwards there were too many people round the man to see him. She thought they had said something about a stroke.

Rather than risk a direct question about the exact meaning of "a stroke" in these parts, I asked first of all what "girdles" were. "Why, girdle-cakes, of course," replied the girl in scornful surprise, as if I had been trying to make fun of her by asking such an obvious question.

At this precise moment, for no very clear reason, the whole adventure on which I was now embarking suddenly struck me as a nightmare transposed into real life. I could not walk fast enough to shake off my extreme depression, nor avoid the icy fog slipping disagreeably down my neck, and the mud and slush which were softening up my shoes. I was hungry and tired and cold. I should have liked to return at once to a good meal and a good fire, to forget all about this benighted countryside, these rustics who were all alike with their bovine faces, their drooping moustaches, the filth under their smocks, and all their ailments and "strokes."

Here was I hurrying towards some idiot who, merely to annoy me, might quite well have chosen to burst a meningeal artery or get a clot on his silly brain. In the middle of the café, I thought somewhat hysterically, before hundreds of wedding guests, all spying on the young doctor just arrived from Paris that very morning, I would have to make my local debut. A fine chance to make a good impression.

"It's just over there," said the little girl as we came out on to the square. She need scarcely have told me, for I could read on the windows *Café Albignac*. Outside a crowd of bystanders was trying to peer through the curtains. Inside the guests were waiting for me. They all turned and watched my arrival passively, without moving or speaking. Only those standing round the door made a vague movement to clear it. Exaggerating my haste, I took some pleasure in pushing them unceremoniously aside.

But as soon as I was in the room, everything inside me changed at once. My heart was beating furiously, but it was more from a sense of challenge than from rage. As sometimes happens when confronted by an obstacle hard to surmount or remove, I at once registered everything in the room quite clearly: the marble tables, the playing cards lying on the ground, a couple of overturned chairs, some hideous colored posters on the walls advertising various wines and spirits; the glasses of aperitifs left half drunk; and the circle of rustics dressed in their Sunday best, with paper roses in their buttonholes, standing watching me. All that remained of my anger suddenly became deflated. However unimaginative my "audience," I realized that they expected something of me. I was a doctor—the man from whom alone, in an emergency, miracles could be demanded.

Already the café proprietor was exclaiming: "Get out of the way, all of you. Give the doctor a little room."

At the end of the room, against the wall, some men were making efforts to hold the struggling patient on a narrow bench of imitation leather. They turned round to watch me approaching, then scattered. I saw a big peasant trying to sit up, thrusting out his head in search of a gulp of air. It was a terrifying sight.

His face was dark blue and swollen, with globulous eyes and slate-colored lips. The lips were gaping wide, as if he were trying to utter a scream of terror. Dazed from his asphyxia, the patient was clenching clumsy hands on his throat in an attempt to pull away an invisible tourniquet. Nothing came out of his mouth but a bubbling, gurgling hiss, and at each corner of the lips there was a froth tinged with blood.

Suddenly I felt isolated in the middle of all these people. There were only two protagonists in this drama, the patient and myself. All hesitation, all anger disappeared. I was alone, really alone, and without my even having to bend over to auscultate the chest, the pinkish foam on the lips indicated a diagnosis of pulmonary edema, and dictated to me the necessary treatment. I was no longer cold or hungry or tired. I gave clear orders: "Remove his coat and waistcoat, open up his shirt and vest, roll up his sleeves and bring me another basin."

My hands meanwhile were obeying me with a precision I had never known in them before, opening the bag and finding there the knife and tourniquet and syringe and ampules and alcohol. Marveling at my skill, I felt inspired by a superb energy and joyfulness. I had an infinite affection for all these people who acknowledged my authority while I struggled to save this poor unfortunate who had accidentally been confided to my care. In this struggle I possessed full powers, with only God above me, and I was about to make my own independent decision. For the first time in my medical life, I was entirely alone, and responsible for a life. This life I knew I could save.

Two sturdy hands held the basin for me. I had had the patient stretched out on the bench, and now I placed the tourniquet on his bare arm. The skin was already dark blue, but with the tourniquet the knots of the vein swelled out at once, so that finding it presented no difficulty.

This man would have died without a doctor's aid, yet having him as my first patient I was in luck. I had all the luck: I could see diagnosis, treatment, and prognosis with equal certainty. With many other emergency cases I might have floundered hopelessly. But here there could be no mistakes, no hesitation, no doubts; I was completely sure of myself, as if at this very moment I had only just finished listening to Dr. Debel in the tutoring classes at St. Luke's: "You will diagnose acute pulmonary edema by the three signs I have just described to you, and immediately afterwards you must take swift decisive action. It is the most typical emergency case for the doctor. The life of the patient is literally in your hands."

In spite of three years of comparative idleness, thanks to Jean Debel I was still ready for this dramatic confrontation. Yes, really, I was in luck. Then I smiled inwardly and corrected the phrase: rather, the patient was in luck.

With a sharp stroke of the point of the knife I broke through the skin and opened the vein. Blood started rushing in torrents down both sides of the metal. It was not enough; I applied the knife obliquely with more force. Immediately the vein gaped wide, and I only just had time to incline the arm to one side in order to avoid the thick jet of blood, almost black, which suddenly began to fall into the basin in a rapid splashing rain.

These men and women were used to cutting pigs' throats and bleeding poultry every day; often they must have handled blood by the bucketful. But as they came nearer, I felt all around me murmurs of distress and hot gasping breaths. They were impressed and silent, as if fascinated by this dark red stream, this human blood I was letting in a sort of scientific exorcism. This magical rescue was like a modern Black Mass, for already the suffocating man began to grow calmer and recover his breath. While the blood began bespattering the basin, I did not scruple to enjoy this respectful silence for a few moments more. Then letting the vein flow freely, I filled a syringe of morphia and prepared by its side a second syringe of a cardiac tonic. Finally I removed the tourniquet. Where the incision had been made the blood again began flowing fast; I quickly bent the patient's arm over a plug of cotton wool, and passing to the other arm made the two injections slowly and carefully. The man already seemed less blue; he breathed with less difficulty, in very short panting breaths. He uttered a few sighs, and then, still dazed, repeated in a voice thick and hesitating, yet still distinct: "Ah, that's better, that's better."

I felt as if he had publicly proclaimed to the world the achievement of a miracle.

After that came the careful transport of the patient to a bed, the dressing, the return to the main room where there was an

21

abrupt silence, the aperitif offered me by the proprietor at the bar; I went through it all in a blissful state, overflowing with energy and affection and happiness for all mankind. I should like to have gone up to each one of these people, spoken to them, pressed their hands, given them friendly taps on their sturdy shoulders. I should like to have had the whole village needing my treatment there and then, needing me to save their lives. But in fact I merely collected the syringes and instruments in the bag with an offhand air; they had been left near the basin full of blood, which no one had dared to touch and which still, for each newcomer, testified to my triumph. On leaving, I casually tossed the black bag under my arm, and with an equally careless gesture of the hand, indicated that they should clean up the basin. I then went out as the groups of people scattered respectfully right to the door.

Outside the café a vague winter sunshine, distant and yellow-ish, had at last succeeded in piercing the fog; and under the sky the bare church, the old tower, and the dark houses on the square no longer seemed to me so forbidding. As I walked home I looked at them affectionately, and regarded solicitously all the passers-by who did not yet know me, who did not know that their lives, their worries, their sorrows and pain, might perhaps from now on be confided to my care.

Félicie must have been watching for my return, and she im-mediately asked: "Was everything all right?" I told her it had been, and she went on: "Go up quick and tell Dr. Delpuech, then lunch will be ready."

I tried to give the old doctor as modest an account as I could of my actions; but I could not keep a note of triumph out of my voice, and I am sure he guessed how I was feeling.

"That's splendid," he said, when I had finished. "As I didn't know exactly what was wrong, I don't mind telling you I was a bit worried while I was waiting for you. I know my compatriots all too well; they might just as well have expected you to put someone with complete paralysis on his feet again there and then. When I first came to the village they expected miracles of me too. I treated people as best I could, but they wanted to be positively cured, no matter what the complaint was—a simple misunderstanding between the doctor and his patients, but a misunderstanding which goes a long way back. It's almost as if they had nostalgic memories of the mythical time when Aesculapius was able to resurrect anybody he had inadvertently allowed to die. Of course the patients here got used to me in time, and it's a long time since they stopped taking me for God Almighty. Nowadays they are prepared to forgive me my failures. But with each new doctor their primitive appetite for miracles starts up again. He's a lucky man who manages to satisfy this appetite as early as you have."

Félicie, with a white apron over her black skirt, came to interrupt Dr. Delpuech and lead me away, telling him I would never get fat on his fine words. In a rather solemn-looking dining room, full of old Renaissance furniture lovingly polished, and before a fine wood fire, I sat down at table in front of a golden brown soup. "A good broth keeps the stomach up like a brace," declared Félicie as she poured me out a second plateful. The soup was followed by a fine roast chicken—it was the chicken which had given the soup its succulent flavor—stuffed with delicious chestnuts.

"Enjoy your meal," I was instructed by Félicie, who stood with her hands on her hips, supervising me. "In city restaurants you have to be careful what you eat, but everything goes down well here, you'll find, and you need plenty of food and drink to keep body and soul together. It would be very sad if you left Peyrac thinner than you are now, which is too thin for my liking already."

She scrutinized me with the same keen judgment as she must have used when assessing the weight of a capon. At the end of lunch, which I enjoyed according to her instructions, I completed her delight by asking her what the famous "girdle-cakes" were, and how they were made.

I had just gone up again to Dr. Delpuech to find out about the afternoon's program, when I heard a regular step on the stone staircase. There was a knock, and Lucien came in, looking just the same as ever, sturdy, calm, imperturbable. He shook Dr. Delpuech's hand and then mine in the easy way I remembered—as if we had only left each other the night before. He looked at me a moment in silence, with his frank penetrating eyes; then he said simply: "You've changed, Jean."

But it was not said in the tone of an ordinary statement; I

felt in his voice a slight note of disappointment and reproach. Without answering, I turned my head away. Dr. Delpuech had certainly divined my embarrassment, for he came at once to my aid: "But good heavens, of course he's changed. How long is it since you've seen each other?"

"Over three years," answered Lucien, and I said: "It's your fault, old chap; you promised to come and see me some time in Paris."

"And do you imagine," remarked Dr. Delpuech, "that his patients would have agreed to his deserting his post? A doctor just starting up isn't expected to take holidays. It's quite true," he added with a smile, "that I've got them into bad habits. This is my first leave for forty years."

Lucien told the old doctor briefly how some of his patients were doing, patients Lucien had taken over for the time being. Then he said he would go to lunch if we would excuse him, as there would probably be some patients waiting to see him. He left us, promising to return in the evening. I too was departing, thinking I should be starting work, when Dr. Delpuech said: "Just a moment, Jean—I've heard so much about you from Lucien, you won't mind my calling you Jean?"

I said I would be very pleased if he did.

"Well then," he went on, "you've surmounted the first obstacle very happily all by yourself, but there'll be others to come. May I offer you a little useful advice?"

"Of course, I'd be extremely grateful," I said. "I'm still feeling a little nervous, as you can imagine."

"All right," said the old man. "The first thing is that in a practice everything is completely different from at hospital. The difficulties here are usually far less technical than psychological. You are about to pass suddenly from the complaints of all mankind to the complaints of the individual man and woman, from the hospital ward to the family interior. You'll find it's quite a different atmosphere. Priority advice: let the patient talk, it's the only way of putting him at his ease. Listen to him attentively; what he wants above all is to be taken seriously. You'll see that as you go on. In hospital he's so impressed by everything that he hasn't got much to say for himself and accepts what he's told almost unquestioningly, but here he'll never stop telling you all about it and what he thinks himself. You'll

24

need a great deal of skill and gentleness to bring him to the essential questions without ever seeming in a hurry or bored. The countryman is an egoist, he won't try to put himself in your place or cut a single detail, even though it may be late in the evening and you've still got a long round ahead of you. The great art of the country doctor is to let each patient think that you've plenty of other patients to look after, but that at present you're concerned only with him. This is the price you must pay if you want to be effective and successful.

"Well, that's certainly new advice to me, sir," I commented. "At hospital, if I ever let patients run on too long, they stray from the point very quickly, and if you're to get through your work properly I don't see how you can afford to waste all that time listening to completely irrelevant details."

"Ah, but you won't really be wasting your time, Jean," Dr. Delpuech replied. "As I said, things are *quite* different here. By telling you minutely about his pain and discomfort, as he has experienced them directly, not as you've read them in textbooks, the patient will teach you the infinite difficulties of your profession. Day by day he'll be your true teacher. So what you need is patience and ever more patience. Explain your orders and prescriptions carefully, for sick people, like blotting paper, absorb everything the wrong way round. When you hear from their mouths the most startling medical absurdities, don't flinch or contradict them; you will only shock a family, to no purpose, who were getting ready to give you their confidence. Bacon recommended destroying a popular error at once on meeting it, as one cuts through a bramble on a walk— but then Bacon probably didn't have rustic patients to look after. Besides, you needn't think that stupid medical ideas are confined to the country. If you want to hear the most highly educated of men utter the most monumental stupidities, the recipe is easy: get them to talk about Medicine."

I smiled, but the old doctor insisted: "Try it, and you'll see I'm not joking. At the same time, with your patients here it's best to lose once for all the hospital habit of making high-sounding and complicated diagnoses. What matters to the people you're dealing with is the prognosis, not the diagnosis. Unscrupulous doctors are very well aware that in case of uncertainty they risk less by forecasting fatal results from an illness than by expressing hopes of a cure. They are proved right if the patient dies, and if by good luck he's cured, theirs will be the honor of having saved him. Finally, as surely as you'll sometimes make mistakes, don't lose heart—they happen even to the greatest specialists. If you are of a philosophic turn of mind, the only thing that will worry you in the long run is to know how often you will make the same mistake over again. But if you really love your patients, you'll suffer from these mistakes to the very last day of your career, as the cruel price paid for practising a difficult art."

He dismissed me with a smile. Before going out of the room, I began trying to thank him; but he interrupted me at once: "Oh yes, and just one more piece of advice—when God made lying a sin, He had immediately to make an exception for doctors. Learn to tell lies well so that you can console people better. And now I am making you late," he concluded. "Go down quickly and see your first patients. It was La Rochefoucauld, wasn't it, who said that one gives nothing as freely as advice?"

Crossing the hall I glanced quickly at the waiting room; and saw there only four people. I was half relieved, half disappointed.

I went into the office, and having shut the door went straight to the desk. All was in order, prescription book, case records, clippings from medical journals, samples of new drugs, reflex hammer, blood pressure apparatus, stethoscope. It was a good time to scatter round the writing pad some of those little cards covered with handy formulas, which I had brought from Paris. They were easy enough to consult at a glance right under the eyes of the patient.

To equip myself against every eventuality, I decided to be cautious and to place my precious notebook of prescriptions near the wash-basin in Dr. Delpuech's dispensary, where I could get it in an emergency. After that, somewhat stirred by the thought of having my first patient in to consult me, I sat down in the old doctor's armchair and looked round this room in which forty years of his life had rolled by. I examined in turn the old divan covered with peeling moleskin; the bookshelves filled with a collection of finely bound old books; the cupboard well stocked with medical samples; a little glass case for instruments, and some pictures on the walls. Over the fireplace there was a frame full of photographs of a child at different ages and a young woman; and these faces I also saw, in a smaller miniature opposite me near the inkpot.

It was a very different atmosphere from the bleak bureaucratic consulting rooms of a hospital, with their clatter of students and nurses, impersonal right down to their standardized furniture, the polished table, the doctor's wooden armchair, the iron chair for the patient, the dirty yellow pad for prescriptions. Owing to his stroke Dr. Delpuech had had to leave things in some disorder, and the effect of so many personal objects scattered over the room was to recall their owner very vividly. It was somehow touching, and I could not help feeling myself intruding on something very private, to be sitting in this office between whose walls so many painful confidences had been passed, seeing the outward signs of a man's whole life work —a life, moreover, which seemed likely to be brought to a premature end as a result of that work.

After these reflections I stood up, gave an extra comb to my hair, inspected my nails, and straightened my tie. I coughed like an actor about to make his first entrance in a play, and before opening the door to call in the first patient, I screwed my face into an expression which I hoped might suggest the skillful and experienced practitioner.

The young man who rose and came into the office first had his right hand inside his jacket, with the thumb hastily wrapped in an old handkerchief knotted round the wrist. Beneath this improvised dressing I was astonished to see a sort of hard brownish matter making a hood over the end of the thumb. The big horny hand was tremendously inflamed and swollen, while the forearm was beginning to swell up too. It took me several seconds to take in fully the nature of the brown stuff. While cutting wood, the man told me, he had run a splinter into his thumb. When a whitlow began, he had tried to bring it to a head with an ointment made from lard, yolk of egg, and lily bulbs; but it had not come up, so he had gone to the shoemaker and asked him to put on a layer of cobblers' wax as dressing. The purpose, at least as far as I could understand it, was to bring the splinter out of the wound and meanwhile protect

27

the finger. Unfortunately the resin beneath this shell had done nothing but increase the infection. Eventually, in some anxiety, the man had decided for the knife. With a forceps and surgical scissors, I freed the thumb from its wax shell; it was high time. The tiny operation to be made on this thumb did not seem to me above my surgical abilities. Half an hour later the man swaggered out, much relieved, wearing his hand in a sling with a clean white bandage on.

The second patient who came out of the waiting room was an old woman. She did not know about Dr. Delpuech's illness and seemed very disappointed to find me in his place. For years, she told me, she came once every winter from a remote mountain farm "for a check-up" by Dr. Delpuech.

"Such a fine doctor he is, and so kind," she said, "always ready to put himself out for you day or night. Seems very queer to me to think of such a strong man being ill, specially when he's a doctor."

Still, she went on, since she had come all this way and was here anyhow, she might just as well tell me all her troubles. She had always had "fallen stomach," but since Doctor had last seen her it was "coming right out." While she was undressing, I had considerable leisure to reflect on this unusual case, for the process was a lengthy one. One by one the old woman shed an impressive string of shawls, bodices, corsets, undervests, belts and combinations—after undoing a proportionate quantity of clasps, ribbons, buttons and pins.

When she was stretched out on the divan and could eventually show me this disturbing stomach, which she feared was beginning to leave its abdomen altogether, I observed with some relief that it was only a question of the uterus beginning to point down between her thighs. I almost told her this, but a few supplementary questions made me realize that for this Auvergnat countrywoman the stomach was less a distinct organ than a whole region of the body, extending (according to her anatomical conceptions) from the point of the sternum to the bottom of the abdomen. She gave me her view of her case, which was that her stomach had dropped so far it had probably become completely loose and disconnected from her other organs. She shook her head very knowingly and I did the same (recalling Dr. Delpuech's advice) while

28

prescribing for her a solid pessary to put this "stomach" back in place. Before being able to show her to the door again, I had to wait till she had put the finishing touches to her re-attirement, and had patted the bottom of her skirt with the back of her hand, taking out its creases with a most unexpected coquettishness.

My third patient was a man of some fifty years who complained of pains in the back. Here again I had some difficulty in discovering from him the precise region of the complaint, for pains in an Auvergnat back, as I eventually realized, might be located anywhere between the occiput and the coccyx, including lungs, vertebral column, pelvis and kidneys. When the man, to show me his back, had extracted his shirt from baggy corduroy trousers held up by a wide belt and solid braces, I found I could give these mysterious pains the more exact diagnosis of lumbago; and the patient departed with a fine prescription for *Meth. Sal*, surreptitiously gathered from my notebook while he was dressing.

I looked at the clock. It was half past four. The three first patients had taken nearly two hours, and I had one more to see. I was worried to have kept him waiting so long, but when I opened the door I found him motionless in the same chair, waiting for me with the patience of a cow in its stall. He stood up, a thin, bony, oldish farmer wearing a black hat with wide rims, clamped very firmly on his head. He had a tanned face with small hard suspicious eyes blinking beneath bushy eyebrows. Removing the hat, he nodded his head at me in greeting and came to the point straight away. He was at the Café Albignac this morning; he had seen me at my job and wanted me to "have a look at him."

I had him sit down in an armchair in front of me, and I waited for him to go on with his story. Instead of this, he now scrutinized me in silence, and finally I said: "Well, I'm listening. Tell me where the trouble is."

"Oh no," replied the man, "it's not for me to tell you, it's for you to find out."

I thought first of all that he was joking, and tried to explain that he must put me on the right track a bit, at least tell me what sort of pain he had and where. He refused to listen, and repeated: "It's not for me to tell you, it's for you to find out."

Each time he said this, he shook his head obstinately from side to side, like a cow being teased by a horse-fly.

With his narrow little sunken eyes and calculating air, the man did not look at all like one of the village buffoons trying to amuse himself at the expense of a new doctor, so that he could later recount in all the cafés of the main square the picturesque details of this memorable consultation. I felt he was quite firm in his resolution to say nothing. But since he was the last patient, and I had plenty of time, there seemed no reason why I should not act as a sort of vet, examining this dumb human as I would have had to examine one of his animals.

I asked him to undress, which he slowly proceeded to do. While he was taking off his shirt, a newspaper, which had been slipped over his chest like a dicky, fell to the ground. He picked it up, put it carefully on one side, and then with his trunk bare awaited my examination. I thought I saw a clue in this partial undressing: the trouble was thoracic. The trunk on which I now gazed was that of a thin tough bony old man. The dirty gray skin suggested that ablutions were not a daily habit. I looked hard for some sign which would have prompted an immediate diagnosis; but in vain. I decided to auscultate the lungs, then the heart, without finding anything abnormal there either. I tested his blood pressure and found it satisfactory for a man of that age. I worked the articulations of his arms, then those of the vertebral column. I inspected eyes and ears and the stumps of his teeth without making any noteworthy discoveries.

So far as the upper half of his body went, the man seemed destined to live to a hundred.

I asked him to take off his trousers and shoes, and meanwhile went to my desk on which I pretended to be turning over some papers. When I raised my head the man was naked; he stood modestly behind the armchair. I came towards him and, glancing at his feet, said: "Take off your socks too." He looked at me in astonishment; "But...but they're off," he stammered. I leaned over. In the shadow of the armchair I had been deceived by the uniform blackness of the feet right up the ankles. "Oh yes, that's fine. I didn't quite see," I added hastily, trying to cover over my *gaffe*.

I resumed my examination. Liver, stomach, intestines, hernial openings, all were in order. The calves were not varicose. I tapped the knee-caps with the reflex hammer and scratched with a pin the crusts on the soles of the feet without making any rewarding observations. I asked the man to urinate in a glass, and this he performed after turning away discreetly. I disappeared in the little dispensary to look for sugar or albumen; the urine was free from both.

The man had let all this be done in silence, observing my investigations with attentive respect. If I had caught the faintest sign of mockery, I should have thrown him out at once. But he remained passively polite, giving absolutely no excuse for any such action; and I could see no way of ending this disconcerting examination without losing face.

For me at least the man was not ill at all, and I was just preparing to tell him so, when I suddenly remembered an axiom delivered by one of the surgeons in my first year. In front of our group of students he had symbolically raised a forefinger, in a rubber fingerstall glistening with vaseline, and repeated: "Remember this, gentlemen. You cannot claim to have got to the bottom of an examination till you have in fact investigated a patient's bottom."

I made the man lie on the divan, intending to have a preliminary look. But because of the color of his feet, which had plainly not seen a footbath for many long years, I had considerable doubts about the use of baths and other details of rustic hygiene. I therefore prudently covered my two forefingers with fingerstalls before separating my patient's buttocks. Right at the bottom of the groove, among sediments of a dubious nature, I saw an oozing red crust. It was more than I had hoped for, and I at once straightened up to declare, with a note of triumph in my voice: "Well, I've at least found something wrong with you. You've got eczema."

But even before I had been able to resume my examination, the man jumped up and was back on his feet. As if right from the beginning he had only waited for this diagnosis in order to count the ordeal over, he started dressing again in lively fashion. He only slowed up after putting on his shoes and trousers. He seemed delighted.

31

"So that's it, Doctor, is it?" he asked. "Eczema is the only thing you can find wrong with me?"

"Nothing at all except that. But I must warn you at once that it won't be very easy to cure."

"Oh, as to that," said the man, "I don't want it cured. Dr. Delpuech always tells me that a good eczema is a sign of long life and that it's better to let it run as much as it likes, that it's all the bad stuff coming out of me, and stops me having something much worse."

I was flabbergasted. This man had demanded an examination to hear me offer a diagnosis which he already knew; and what is more, he was refusing to have any treatment from me. Then why had he come to see me?

Our looks met. The man observed me from beneath his bushy eyebrows with obvious admiration. Finally he declared: "Ah, you can claim to be a good doctor, all right. It's not every doctor who can find my eczema up there!"

He shook his head sententiously, and went on: "Oh yes, I'm very glad to have come and got myself examined. I don't regret my money with you. You certainly make a thorough examination."

After which he concluded, with an air of contentment and conviction: "Well, well, so you've found nothing else the matter. Just as well really, there's far too much trouble around already. Only doctors often tell you there's nothing the matter with you because they just haven't been able to find it. But you're different, you're a good doctor, and what you say can be trusted."

At last I understood: his eczema was his private test of the knowledge possessed by any doctor he came to see for the first time. In his suspicious old rustic brain he must often have said to himself that when a doctor claimed to find him in perfect health, he was obliged to take the doctor's word for it, without anything to prove that a thorough examination had been made. He would even be prepared to hear the doctor say: "There's nothing wrong with you"—and pay the fee, exactly as if the doctor had discovered him to be suffering from some serious illness. This would certainly seem to him a sort of swindle; whereas by declaring himself to be ill and then saying nothing about his eczema right to the end, he forced the doctor to

32

make a minute examination of all his organs. But supposing the practitioner, after having vainly explored everything else, ended up by glancing conscientiously between the buttocks, the chances of error became minimal if he then asserted that all the rest of the body was in reasonable condition.

I now regarded the patient curiously myself. Pushed to this point, avarice, distrust, and low cunning left the level of common minor failings, and almost compelled a certain admiration.

As he was going through the door the man turned to remark: "So it's like that, is it? Dr. Delpuech isn't too well. 'Course he always tried to do too much. On the road all the time he was. To think of all the money he must have collected with that job, these forty years, him and his father before him. Why," he concluded in a hoarse voice, "he must be rich!"

Beneath his bushy eyebrows the small eyes shone with unlimited admiration. They shone too with the fiercest envy. I almost made some answer, but confronted by this greedy face obsessed by money, with its frown of primitive covetousness, I decided it would be quite useless to explain that men were not always activated solely by self-interest. Without saying anything, I pushed the man towards the door.

I was finishing tidying the office before going up to see Dr. Delpuech, when there was a ring at the front door.

Félicie went to open it, and I heard her talking in the entrance; almost at once she came to tell me that the son of my patient in the Café Albignac wanted to see me. The man was waiting behind her in the hall; I called him in. He was wearing a leather jacket and a beret which made him look less of a rustic than his father. He told me he had come to settle with me for my call, before taking the patient off with him in his van to Farlat, a village about ten miles from Peyrac.

"It's not worth having the expenses of stamp and postal order, I might just as well pay you straight away. So about how much would it be, Doctor?"

He waited for me to name a figure, obviously uneasy and worried despite the prudent phrase "about how much," which was doubtless designed to introduce a possibility of bargaining. I too felt somewhat embarrassed. During the afternoon I had simply written down each patient in Dr. Delpuech's little appointment book without asking any fees; he would collect their fees in due course according to whatever arrangements he had with them. Being used to the free treatment of hospitals, I found it more agreeable not to mix up questions of money with my first activities in general practice. I had hardly glanced in passing at a board nailed on the door of the waiting room; it was the professional tariff of the doctors in the region. The board indicated: *Office: 10 francs. Call at patient's home: 15 francs.*

The man therefore owed me fifteen francs. He would certainly be aware of this customary tariff. But then, I thought, he had seen his father almost choking to death; he must be wondering very uneasily how much a doctor from Paris would charge for this piece of indubitable life-saving.

I found a certain pleasure in prolonging his uncertainty. Before answering, I explained to him the very serious condition of the patient's heart, the precautions to be observed during his transport back to Farlat, and the risks of a relapse; I also wrote a note which I gave him for the Farlat doctor.

During all this time the man listened to me without saying a word. He watched me with a look of anguish and suspense, sometimes violently swallowing his saliva. So much beating about the bush, such a wealth of verbiage, would lead him to expect a demand for some vast amount, as for some prize beast in a country market. After a little while, unable to restrain himself further he asked again: "Well, about how much does that come to, Doctor?"

I delayed my reply a few seconds more. I had never before had the occasion to reflect exactly on the difference between a regular salary and, as it were, payment for piece work; between work for which fixed fees could be charged and work which was essentially not to be priced. At this moment the difference seemed to me very striking. I would have liked all the wedding guests at the Café Albignac to have been there, and especially the old farmer who a few minutes earlier had been talking of Dr. Delpuech as of a tradesman simply out for his own profit. I would like them to have heard me say, with all due solemnity: "Counting it as a call at the patient's home, you owe me fifteen francs."

I looked at the man to savor his sigh of relief before a sum

34

so absurdly small. Fifteen francs! Could there be a common measurement between the saving of a life and this insignificant sum which left my whole dramatic intervention almost out of account? I was about to earn my first fee, and surely, as he handed it to me, the man would press my hands in gratitude, putting into that gesture his shame at having ever doubted me for a moment.

But the son of this patient so miraculously saved did not seize my hands at all. He was busy unbuttoning his jacket very deliberately. Then he opened his jacket and took out a huge purse with worn corners held by a chain. He began taking two greasy five-franc notes out of the purse, and then, one by one, five one-franc pieces held in the hollow of his hand. When he had finished, he carefully replaced the purse in his pocket, did up his jacket, counted out the money and handed it to me, saying: "There you are, Doctor, you'll find that's right."

I did not move to pick it up, and so, looking very surprised at my apparent indifference, he placed the mean little pile on the corner of my desk with as much care as if paying out a handful of gold.

Félicie had a list of calls for me to make before dinner, and she advised me to get clear of them without delay.

Thanks to my notebook, I felt I had come quite honorably out of my first consultations, but calls at patients' homes might prove a more formidable ordeal. Even when leaning over with an air of extreme concentration (as if making a very long auscultation) it would be difficult, I thought, to consult the famous notebook effectively under the attentive eyes of the family, and to extract a few necessary tips therefrom. But I had foreseen this complication, and had prepared a little diary on which appointments were replaced by formulas for prescriptions. I could thus refresh my memory by skimming through the diary, with the preoccupied air of an overworked doctor looking for a free date to write down a future call.

On leaving I slipped the precious prescription-diary in my pocket; but I did not have to use it. In a house on the main street I dealt with a German measles case, and in the square with an ordinary bronchitis. The hardest thing was to find my last patient at the end of a very dark alley, smelling of drains and the farmyard, where I slipped on a pile of ordures covered with snow and almost lost a shoe. My patient, when finally discovered, was a child suffering from so mild an attack of tonsillitis that I did not need to worry for a moment about the specter of diphtheria.

As I crossed the main square again, I noticed the colored bottles of a druggist's shop, like two reassuring harbor lights at night. One piece of advice I had been given by Paul Chavasse before my departure.

"Above all, don't forget to call on the local apothecary. In case you should make some awful break in your prescriptions, give him a warning that you're only just starting in and ask him to cover it up discreetly. After that you'll feel easier."

I went up to the door and read the golden letters saying: *René Mandaroux, First Class Pharmacist, Diploma of Pharmacy (Montpélier)*. On each side of the door, throned in the two windows, majestic and mysterious as science for the laymen, isolated from all neighboring commercial commodities, sat the two huge cut-glass spheres which had attracted my attention. The one on the right was filled with a red liquid, the one on the left had a green liquid; both had huge corks shaped like a pyramid. The door with the golden letters clanged, as you opened it and entered a fine old-fashioned pharmacy. Between the oak beams with rows of earthenware pots ranging right to the ceiling, a plump little man with a ruddy cherubic face rose from the back shop. He held out one of his short arms, and at once extended a fat little hand, saying: "Very glad you've come, Doctor."

I must have looked rather surprised when returning his handshake, for he added with a friendly smile: "I saw you this morning when you passed here on your way to the Café Al-bignac, and since noon the whole town has been singing your praises. So I was anxious to get to know you myself, and hoped you'd drop in to see me."

To confess the weaknesses in my pharmaceutical knowledge, as Paul had recommended, was rather humiliating, but I decided to get it over straight away. As soon as I had spoken, the little chemist hastened to put me at my ease:

"Of course I'll keep a look-out, Doctor. At the start you

36

can't be expected to have all the posologies in your head. Besides I've already seen two of your prescriptions, and I think you're being too modest. You know your stuff very well, and I find it very meritorious in one so young to take the trouble to write out prescriptions instead of relying on made-up medicines and drugs."

I smiled inwardly as he went on benignly: "With Dr. Delpuech we're back in the old school—only the time-honored classical drugs. And with me only the preparations of my own dispensary. Pharmacists from father to son since 1682. If it would amuse you, I'll show you the theriac made up by my great-grandfather. I keep up the old traditions, and each year I myself make up all my own mixtures and extracts."

He bustled me into the back-shop while continuing to talk: "Come this way, Doctor, we'll be less likely to be disturbed. I hope you'll accept a little aperitif—I make that too myself, of course. A very old recipe: St. John's Wort, Meadowsweet, Tansy and Erythraea, with the peel of bitter orange, ground up in a good white wine. You know your pharmacopoeia so well, I'm sure you'll appreciate that. Nothing but good ingredients, just you taste it, Doctor."

Without ceasing the flow of his conversation, he had drawn a bottle from a cupboard. He now greedily filled two glasses and raised his own to drink to my future success. He then swallowed a large draught from his home-brewed mixture, and concluded complacently: "It's no worse than anything else, and at least it's beneficial."

After having drunk a second glass, we parted, each delighted with the other, and in my case free of any fear of poisoning somebody through prescribing the wrong dose.

"Come along to dinner right away," said Félicie as she opened the door to me, and she led me at once to a good beef broth waiting for me in the soup-tureen. As I was sitting down, she told me someone had come to ask me to call in the country:

"Dr. Delpuech had me phone Dr. Clément, so he should be the one to go. It was up on the plains by Pierrefiche, and in the dark, with the fog and two feet of snow on the roads, you probably would never have gotten there at all. Dr. Clément also told me to let him know if anyone should ask for you tonight. So enjoy your food, it's not every night you'll be sure of dining and sleeping in peace."

"Enjoy your food" seemed to be Félicie's special motto.

When I went up to bid him goodnight, I found Dr. Delpuech reading by the light of a small lamp placed at the corner of the bed; apart from this the huge room was sunk in darkness. The old doctor put down his book as he saw me coming in, and looked up at me from his pile of pillows. There was several days' growth of beard on his cheeks, and only the forehead, catching all the reflection of the light, was still full of wisdom and serenity.

"Everything go off all right?" he asked with a smile. "They haven't been too troublesome?"

"Oh not at all. Though I must say I had a bit of difficulty trying to understand about their fallen stomachs and mysterious pains in the back."

"Aha, so you have seriously started on your initiation into Auvergnat anatomy and pathology."

"Will I have to begin all my studies right from the beginning again?" I asked with a laugh.

"No, just finish them. Now you've learned the essential about diseases in five or six years, you still have to learn what the patients think about them themselves. And I assure you that the patients make a far more formidable board of examiners than your medical school officials. Their decisions are almost without right of appeal; for those who flunk there's very little hope of a second try. You have to pass the first time."

I gave a detailed account of the patients I had seen, and Dr. Delpuech nodded approval of what I had done. When I came to the man from Farlat, I could not help expressing disappointment at such ingratitude; but the old doctor protested gently: "Ingratitude—that's a very big word in a doctor's mouth. Surely you've heard this description of the heart—a hollow muscle incapable of holding anything for long? That definition is not only local and regional, it has universal validity. And haven't they ever told you that the brain does not retain all its memories indefinitely? Ingratitude! Why, Fiessinger has clearly shown it to be a physiological reaction—to unburden the memory and relieve the heart. People think that doctors are there to cure, as tobacconists are there to sell cigarettes. Once cured, why should your patients remember your cure as an exceptional service, outside other normal occurrences?"

"All the same, between noon and five o'clock in the evening, for a life saved, I thought I could have expected a small residuum of gratitude."

"Not at all, Jean. Between noon and five o'clock today you have turned from a life-saver into a creditor, and no farmer thinks of his creditors without odium. Here's exactly how the son worked things out in his mind: 'After all, they don't die young in my family, and Dad's still fairly strong. It didn't give the doctor much trouble to pull him out of his trouble. We're not from this town, and the doctor isn't even from this part of the world. Why should I waste my time being so grateful to a man I'll probably never see again?' You'll gradually learn that gratitude, when it exists, is often based less on what you have done in the past, than on what the patient thinks you may be likely to do for him in the future."

He looked at me a moment before adding: "You find me cynical, I dare say. You'll think the practice of medicine is quite hard enough already without extra troubles caused by our patients in their apathy and malice and disloyalty. But that's the point: Medicine is truly great just because our devotion almost always goes unrecognized and unrewarded. Do you remember the famous dialogue: 'I have dressed his wounds,' begins the doctor humbly, and the patient finishes off with a sneer: 'And God has cured me.' My young friend, if every devoted action we performed were reciprocated not even by an action but by merely a single sentiment of true gratitude, it would be far too good to be true. We should lose all merit, we should be overpaid a hundred times over."

Félicie opened the door abruptly and interrupted him: "And they say women talk too much! Aren't you ashamed of keeping Dr. Nérac from going to bed? He must be dead tired, the poor boy. At his age it's not like at yours, he needs all the sleep he can get. For wakeful young or slumbering old, Death can most surely be foretold."

"Well, that's encouraging at least," said the old doctor with a smile. "It's months now since I've been able to sleep."

39

Chapter Three

Next morning, at about a quarter to nine, freshly shaved and in the best of spirits, I sat down in the big dining room with a healthy appetite, before a steaming cup of chocolate, a plate of bread and butter, and a pot of honey. I felt an appetite for activity, too, and a powerful urge to be on the move and at work all day.

Framed in the windows were the endless ranges of hills and valleys, spotless and sparkling beneath the sun. Sunlight played over the china cup, the white tablecloth, the heavy old furniture and the silver on the sideboard. This second day was certainly beginning well.

A clock in the hall grated before emitting from its antiquated mechanism a harsh nine strokes. At the last stroke, like one of those figures coming out of a clock, Lucien Clément, having promised to be there at nine o'clock, punctually appeared. He came in without hurrying, solid and serene, as if he had all the time in the world to tackle his day's work. I could not refrain from saying with a laugh: "Ah, these country doctors who can start their day off so comfortably and steadily at nine o'clock. No wonder you look well on this sort of routine."

"I saw my first patient at seven o'clock this morning," answered Lucien.

"An emergency call, I suppose?"

"No, a small dressing to be renewed."

"Then why at seven o'clock?" I asked in bewilderment.

"I don't know. It's no use my being curious," said Lucien, "about a patient's reason for coming at an unusual hour. During my first month in practice, in the summer it was, one farmer arrived in a horse and cart at four o'clock in the morning, for something which could quite well have waited five hours longer. That time I was really angry, but the man evidently couldn't at all see why. He explained to me, as something quite natural, that he had come before daybreak because his horse had trouble with flies when it was hot. A week later I was called again before dawn to a village in the heart of the mountains. It was the mayor, and he had no particular medical reason for wanting me. He was simply finding out whether I was likely to turn out at once when his constituents called me."

"And you said nothing?"

"What could I have said? You can't really blame these people for being as hard to others as they are to themselves. You have to put up with things in the country, they say, and it's certainly a pretty grim life for them. Before calling you in at all, they've probably been trying for several days to save the expense of a doctor. Just to try, they'll have given sudations, herbal mixtures, hot poultices, purges; but once they've decided to squander their money on a doctor, if the messenger doesn't find you in and ready to drop everything and follow him at once, you'll be accused of not caring and they'll remember it against you. Countryfolk are like that."

He spoke as evenly as ever, without rancor. I remembered how I had almost mistaken this calmness for indifference when I had first gone with him on his rounds in the slums outside the Cité Universitaire in Paris. Indeed, a stranger might still have wondered whether it was merely resignation before a tedious job that had to be done, or whether Lucien instinctively found it the best way of giving himself to work in which he intensely believed.

As he walked near the window and came fully into the light, I saw his face better; I observed that his features were drawn and his eyes rather red. I suddenly remembered the telephone ringing just as I was going off to sleep.

"Here, Lucien," I said, "you were called out last night instead of me, weren't you?"

"Yes, for a delivery. You might have found it rather troublesome, and I must say it wasn't too easy. If you like, Jean, we'll go back there and see the mother together."

"That's very good of you." I knew he was embarrassed by expressions of gratitude, but I was as touched as ever both by his help, and by the unobtrusive way in which it had been

41

given. He would evidently have said nothing about it if I had not asked him. "When did you get back?" I asked.

"About four o'clock. I lost a good hour on the return journey because of the storm. The snow kept freezing on the windshield and the wiper was quite useless," he answered in the same placid voice as he crossed the hall.

I was going to thank him again, but he had already opened the front door and said: "Well, come on, Jean, let's get going." I remembered how four years ago he used to call me in exactly the same tone of voice: "Come on, Jean, time for some work."

His car was outside, a dilapidated sedan, which I mentally compared with Henri Philippon's smart yellow sports car. Lucien removed a blanket from the hood and began cranking the engine. Meanwhile I settled in the front seat, glancing at the back seat as I did so. On the floor beside Lucien's big medical bag, an electric torch and a candle, there was a shovel and a towrope which made us look rather like a repair truck starting off.

"As you've nothing on this morning," said Lucien, "I'll show you the countryside a bit."

He started off, amidst much clattering of chains. Directly outside Peyrac the road went winding down into the valley. At first Lucien drove down the icy incline in his usual sedate manner; but he started driving a bit faster at the bottom of the hill, when the road sloped round a hill rather more gently. It was a magnificent winter day, of a sharp bright frostiness. The corner of the glass in one window was broken, and through it came an icy jet of air. I turned up my coat collar, and Lucien, rummaging with one hand at the back of the seat, produced a piece of rag and handed it to me. "If you're cold, stick that in the hole. I'm used to it myself—in fact the first two winters I did my rounds on a motorcycle."

I was slightly puzzled at the route we were taking, but he explained to me that Peyrac is built on a kind of ridge where four valleys meet. "In the summer you can take the car direct from one valley into the next. But in the winter the roads are covered with snow and you have to keep between posts specially planted all along the ditches. So it's always wiser to go through Peyrac again. It makes seven or eight miles extra each time, but it's better than sinking up to your axles in snow, specially at night, and having to walk to the nearest farm to ask for a pair of oxen to pull you out."

Under a sky that was a purplish green, the narrow valley was brilliantly white, shining with a translucent purity. There seemed no limits in time to the glacial peace all about us. Lucien, watching the road carefully, drove in silence, and out of shyness I refrained from expressing my exhilaration at the beauty of the scene. Lucien after all was used to it, and he hardly spared a glance for the scenery as such. From time to time, however, as we went through some hamlet, he would throw out a name: "La Terrade...Chaudagaire...Combes-Chabre ... Veilleresse ... Plamonteil. ..."

These hamlets all looked exactly alike to me: snow-covered huddles of stone buildings looking down on squalid courtyards enclosed by low walls; the ends of a few dark alleys, a few narrow streets between the higgledy-piggledy houses; sheds, barns and outhouses, with icicles hanging from jutting roofs.

Eventually we went up a tortuous little lane between two stone walls, where the wheels only just made their way through the snow. I began to understand better the need for chains, but I could find no reason for the road being so narrow and wind-ing, when apparently it might just as easily have been wide and straight.

"It's really a cart-track," said Lucien, when I asked about this point. "It dates from an age when these parts were over-populated and good land was rare, bitterly disputed, and parceled up into little lots which were jealously defended. The lanes had to be made so that they didn't cut into anyone's fields and encroached on good land as little as possible."

We were coming to a farm set a little back from the lane: a long squat shack of a building with hardly any windows. One end of it backed onto a high bank of earth which came level with the roof. This roof itself was so unexpectedly high and sloped so steeply that it seemed to crush the house completely beneath it. From a wide door, evidently that of the stables, ran a thick stream of black manure, crossing diagonally the slush in the yard, amidst a disorder of harrows, manure carts, and wheelbarrows, before joining another stream flowing down from a small fountain into the virgin snow of the ditch.

"Look, there's my patient," said Lucien.

43

Near the fountain, face to the wind and with her feet in the mud, I saw a big woman filling a bucket with water. She had a black shawl over her shoulders and another over her head, enveloped as if she were in purdah. At the noise of the car she turned. The shawl over her head was tightly crossed in front of her face, allowing only one eye to appear. "Has she got toothache?" I asked.

"No," said Lucien, "she's got pneumonia."

I looked at him dumbfounded, thinking he must be joking, but he repeated the word without apparent emotion.

"You let her go out in cold like this? Is she living by herself?"

"No, she has a husband. And I can assure you that going out in this wind did not form part of the treatment I ordered."

"You'll have to tell her husband he mustn't let her go to the fountain in that condition."

"He would merely ask who else was going to do it. You see how isolated they are, without any neighbors, and you might as well learn right now that an Auvergnat farmer would die of thirst rather than go and fill a pitcher himself. No man of the mountains would lower himself to that, or to touching a broom. That's woman's work."

"I didn't realize your mountain folk were so like the Arabs in their treatment of women."

I was distinctly shocked, but Lucien calmed me with a soothing gesture: "Don't get worked up, Jean. I once went to Touraine as locum, and one of the farmers there, even when his wife had pneumonia, blankly refused to milk the cow. Woman's work again. That's how things are, and I doubt if you or I can change them."

While we were getting out of the car, the woman had finished filling her bucket and ran back into the house. Still muffled up, the poor creature waited shivering behind the half-open door on the cracked stone lintel. We hurried in, and she shut the door carefully behind us and began to take the coverings off her face. It was not one shawl but four, and there were also four petticoats which she had prudently put on in order to go out. Having relieved herself of these garments she took out her handkerchief to wipe her face; her eyes were feverishly bright, she had a flush over the cheekbones and breathed painfully.

44

Before lying down again she put a few logs on the fire, pushed a coffee pot towards it, set out on the table cups, sugar, a bottle of brandy and some liqueur glasses. Then she half opened a little door in the partition leading to the back of the house and called out: "Victor, Dr. Clément's come."

After this, conscious of duty done, she went back to bed in a dark corner of the kitchen, and with obvious satisfaction slipped beneath a huge eiderdown, still half dressed.

This single room doubtless contained all the poor furniture in the house. Like the walls and the low ceiling it was blackened with a hundred years of dirt and smoke. The room smelt strongly of livestock; it was a hot stifling smell, which almost choked me at first.

The door at the back opened, and the husband came in, dragging manure on his clogs. Having wiped his right hand on his earth-colored breeches, he held it out to us in greeting. He seemed to bring in with him a potent added stench. The door pierced through the partition opened directly into the stable, and through the simple row of boards you could hear the dull clumping of the animals against the swinging bail.

The man seemed pleased to see us. His first words were the common greeting of peasant hospitality: "What will you have?"

We were offered coffee or brandy. Lucien chose the former, but I let myself be tempted by the spirits. There is something very attractive about a good local brandy on a frosty morning; but this one was different. I swallowed it unsuspectingly, and as soon as I had done so, I felt it taking off the skin of my tongue, burning my throat, and going all the way down my windpipe in a trail of fire.

Lucien drank his coffee in small gulps, chatting the while to the husband in a harsh dialect which I found almost incomprehensible. The man seemed worried. In order to scratch his head pensively, he several times removed a battered and shapeless black felt hat, shiny with accumulated dust and years of sweat.

Eventually Lucien and the man got up—I thought to go to the corner of the room where the patient lay. But instead they passed by her bed, and went through the little stable door. Intrigued, I followed them out among the animals in the oppressively hot stable. Even without a fire the kitchen would never be cold with this source of heat so near. In the dusty ceiling, which I nearly touched with my head, there was a trap-door. Through this I saw the loft and understood better the strange concentration of stifling heat. Above the ceiling of the kitchen and stable, the immense sloping roof formed a single loft filled with hay. It was the heady odor of acres of mown grass which came in pungently through each crack in the ceiling—so pungently that the air at nose level was hardly to be breathed.

When I rejoined Lucien he was squatting in the dung with the man, near a post plastered with dried manure, and was examining a wound on the leg of a big dappled horse. It was a long examination, followed by an animated discussion; but when we came back into the kitchen, the man had ceased to scratch his head. His hat was pushed hard back onto his neck, and his face was beaming.

At last the moment seemed to have come to deal with the human patient. Her many layers of underwear left only small openings through which her chest could be auscultated, but Lucien managed as best he could, slipping his stethoscope through the openings from above and below. I had time, meanwhile, to inspect the corner which served as bedroom, to note the shelf across the bed (from which the chamber pot could be reached), and to marvel at the accumulation of quilts and pillows and mattresses—whose softness beneath the fingers told me that they were filled with feathers. When Lucien raised the sheet to begin his examination, a hot reek of concentrated sweat rose from the bed.

His examination completed, Lucien reassured the woman. Before leaving, we were apparently required to drink again, and this time I followed Lucien's choice. The coffee proved to be mainly a horrible chicory, bitter and like tar, but I hoped it might drown slightly the conflagration lit inside me by the alcohol. This had long reached the depths of my stomach, but from time to time the whole mixture would blaze up again forcing me to belch. As soon as we were back in the car, I cried ruefully:

"For God's sake tell me, Lucien, what the hell is in that vitriol?"

"It's plum brandy illegally distilled at the farm. Connoisseurs

46

sometimes refine the torture by leaving black currants or quince pulp to soak in it without sugar."

"It's first-class poison, if you ask me."

"Just tell them that. When I try they answer: 'You must be joking, Doctor. It's real good stuff, we make it here ourselves. Can't do any harm to anybody, a little nip of that. Does you good, in fact.' Luckily I can usually get out of poisoning myself with their home-brew by choosing the chicory instead."

"Why not simply refuse to have anything?"

"You couldn't possibly do that. In their monotonous life the doctor's round is after all an event. If you refuse to drink, even on the excuse of illness, they'll think you're stuck up and be offended."

"But every call takes you twice as long with all this cere-monial. It's positively Chinese."

"So what? All work is done slowly here, nobody bothers about the exact time. Do you realize, Jean, that in the summer these people work eighteen hours a day? That gives them the right to stop for a quarter of an hour when there's a visitor. And they'd take you for a madman if you spent your days dashing off from one place to the next."

He seemed to have inexhaustible supplies of indulgence for his patients, but this time I wondered if he was not also un-consciously trying to excuse his own leisurely manner. I had never felt him so profoundly rustic as in that farm, seeing him squatting in the dung quite undisgustedly, between the horse's legs, and talking the local dialect and patois. No, these people would certainly never have taken him for a townsman; they must accept him as a man of their own stock, with their coarse manners and their slow speech dating from centuries back.

"Yes, I see the point," I said, still rather irritated. "I know you can't make oxen gallop. I suppose I'll have to learn to take my time with them. Still," I added, thinking I might at least score off him here, "was it also a professional necessity to examine the animal so thoroughly before you got round to the human being?"

"Oh yes, it was," answered Lucien very simply. "That's all part of a doctor's job, you see, in the country."

He drove for a few seconds in silence before continuing: "In my early days I was called out to a farm where one of the

47

hands was sick. The farmer looked desperate, and told me that his splendid prize bull had urethritis. Quite at random he asked my advice, without any belief in it, perhaps just as a joke. Anyhow I had the good luck to cure that beast, and the way this cure was retailed from farm to farm, I became better known all through the district than if I'd discovered a cure for cancer."

We were coming to a tiny hamlet where a few dilapidated buildings were moldering amidst four wretched-looking farms. "This is where I delivered the baby last night," said Lucien. "When they phoned Dr. Delpuech, you'd been called out elsewhere, I told them, and I'd come in your place because it was an emergency. Their first child. A difficult forceps case. Then violent hemorrhage and a manual removal of the afterbirth. I had quite a bit of trouble."

"All alone?" I asked.

"One is always all alone in the country. The midwife you're going to see is worse than useless. She isn't a qualified nurse, but for thirty or more years she's been presiding by tradition over all the confinements in the district, and in that time she can take some very fine disasters to her credit."

"How about hospital?"

"Impossible. First of all, they don't call the doctor in till right at the end, when something goes really wrong, the midwife loses her head and the mother is quite unfit for the journey. And then you'll never get an Auvergnat farmer to admit that his wife could have a child anywhere except in their own matrimonial bed."

We were arriving. Heads moved behind the blue window panes. Lucien stopped his car before a door, knocked, and then brought me with him into a dark and dirty kitchen, much like the one we had recently left. We found there an assembly of old women. The coffee pot was on the table and also the brandy bottle. Abandoning her cup and brandy glass, the midwife rushed up to us, a huge woman with a pimply nose, a hairy chin and greasy hair in a bun. With a show of haste she dusted two chairs with the back of her hand, and offered them to us. All the gossiping women fell silent. Lucien's arrival with an unknown new doctor had evidently impressed them. At once, and before even accepting the cup of coffee she was offering us, Lucien questioned the midwife on the mother's

48

condition. Her sleeves rolled up on a dirty forearm, she half raised an obviously perjured hand to swear she had never left the neighboring room for a single instant, and that mother and child had slept peacefully. This reply set in motion among the other old women a murmur of enthusiasm: "Isn't he a lovely little boy then, a fine strong lad, already so good, a grand little fellow, isn't he," and so on. The midwife took advantage of the general emotion to fill the coffee cups again and also pour out a round of plum brandy. By the color of her nose and cheeks, by the smell of her breath between her stumps of teeth, you could guess that she was not taking her first glass of the morning and that this practice was not new to her.

While still drinking his cup of coffee, Lucien asked if the sterile water was the right temperature for washing the mother. The handy-woman pointed to a copper pot near the fire, the sides of which were black with soot and old grease. She went towards the fireplace, bent over the cauldron, dipped her dirty fingers into the water and stirred it around. After which she declared: "Yes, it's just right now."

Rising with a satisfied air she dusted the top of the pot with her skirt. I half expected Lucien to leap in the air with horror, but he remained impassive, even when she took a big tin saucepan out of a sort of pantry smelling of congealed old milk, and plunged the saucepan directly in the copper. When the saucepan was full, she kept it in her hand, to show she was ready to act as his assistant in the subsequent operations. Lucien rose and went into the next room; she followed him, and I went in after them.

By the side of the big bed of brown wood with its scarlet quilt the curtains above the cradle made a patch of brightness. When Lucien had had the shutters opened the young mother, who was dozing, woke up and turned her head painfully. Bending towards her, Lucien took her wrist, but before feeling her pulse he asked her gently: "Not too tired?"

"Oh yes I am, Doctor. It didn't go too easily, did it? But still Dr. Delpuech told us it would be a daughter, and I'm so happy that it's a son. Of course I'd have loved a little girl too, but our Daddy's so proud of his son!"

She spoke in a low voice, and the pale lips were rounded

with difficulty into a tired smile. Suddenly a little blood came to her cheeks, and she began to grow excited:

"He will live, though, won't he, the little fellow? He will live all right, Doctor Clément, after all you had to do to me last night? He'll grow up strong like the others?" There was a desperate pleading in her voice.

Lucien answered her in his usual even voice. For anyone else but the mother, tense with her passionate love for the new-born, what he said would have sounded like mere commonplaces of reassurance, vague promises whose precise scope could not have been very deeply analyzed. But for the young mother, through some mysterious vibration passing between the two of them, these promises and commonplaces evidently seemed charged with comforting certainty and hope.

Lucien opened his bag on a corner of the chest of drawers. He poured an antiseptic into the saucepan of allegedly sterile water, prepared some cotton wool, and asked for towels. When he lifted the quilt, I withdrew slightly from delicacy; but in the low-ceilinged room, despite the thick smell from the wood fire and the stable, I recognized the stale reek of antiseptic, coagulated blood, and hot entrails. It was the same compound of smells I had known four years ago when visiting the slums with Lucien—a compound supplemented in Paris by the stench of those slum hovels.

Lucien had always liked this painful work of midwifery. One night when we were returning to the Cité, exhausted after an extremely long and difficult delivery, I asked him about this, and he admitted: "Yes, I do find it very satisfying. I can't quite explain my feelings, but these young lives seem to depend on your skill, and you feel you're helping people who really need help. If I had to practise in a big town, I should certainly become an obstetrician."

However barbarious the slums were, civilization and the telephone were after all only two or three hundred yards away. Ambulances could come to the borders of the first huts, and the stretcher could reach the grim blood-soaked bed where the pregnant woman was waiting. A hospital was not far off, and there, less than a quarter of an hour later, in an immaculate theatre all ready for such occasions, two white-gowned men round an operating table would be struggling to save her.

Here, in the heart of these Cantal mountains, on this miser-able farm, I found almost as much poverty and filth as I had seen in the slum shanties. It took no great effort to call to mind in the brown-ceilinged room the dark recesses as they had been in the night, and the inadequate oil lamp which the midwife would have held with uncertain hand above the groaning mother. In my imagination deliveries performed four years ago and the one performed last night became confused in a single terrifying drama of the flesh: the blood, the darkness, the smell, the scarlet linen, the pale face. Lucien, bent tense and sweating over the bed, groping with his big hand plunged into the womb, while the woman, dazed and gasping with her pains, would suddenly recover enough strength to let out a long and terrify-ing scream, like one being murdered.

But in this mountain farm, at the end of a cart track in the snow, Lucien was far from all outside help, far from a surgeon, far from the white wards of the clinic, far from the simple routine of a birth at hospital. He knew he was alone. "In the country," as he said, "one is always alone."

I looked at him. He was finishing his treatment of the young mother. During this time the husband, the parents-in-law and grandfather, being informed that Lucien was there, had gathered at the door; they were waiting to thank him once more. To judge by the ecstatic note in the father-in-law's voice, it was the baby's sex which made the principal theme in this collective gratitude. "Oh yes," he almost crooned, "we're mighty pleased Dr. Delpuech was wrong and you've brought us a little boy after all."

They all reverted in turn to the sex of the baby, going into further ecstasies of appreciative delight, as if Lucien's obstetri-cal skill were the sole cause of its being male, and as if this were the only thing in the whole drama which really mattered. They had not a word to say about the long and terrible night throughout which Lucien had struggled desperately and un-aided before their eyes. What a wealth of intelligence, calmness, skill, devotion and initiative had been required to produce this happy result—a young mother "doing well," smiling near the white cradle where her baby was lying! How little of all this could these rustics genuinely appreciate! Looking at them and at Lucien, I felt as never before the singular grandeur of the

51

struggle—here in this forlorn mountain farm far from civilization. Perhaps it would always be like this for a country doctor: always struggling on behalf of people who never understood how much he was doing for them.

I should like to have said this to Lucien when he had started up the car and we were driving away, but I knew he would merely shrug his shoulders, so instead I asked: "Why did Dr. Delpuech tell them it would be a girl?"

"It's a good precaution," answered Lucien. "Families always want you to prophesy the sex eight months in advance. Tell them it'll be a girl, and if it happens to be one, your honor is preserved. If not, as you've just seen, all the relatives are so happy to see a boy that it wipes out your mistake straight away. The midwife uses the same little trick. It's about the only technique we both use."

"That woman," I cried. "What a marvelous creature! I specially liked her method of putting her finger right into the sterile water. But she must run into a few post-natal complications, doesn't she?"

"Well, no. Funnily enough, everything usually goes off very well. I've even had to use an old piece of washing soap for swabbing and antiseptic when I hadn't got my bag with me and there wasn't any iodine after I had been fiddling around right up the woman's uterus. I suppose it would have been disastrous in Paris, but here nothing out of the ordinary happened, not even a small rise in her temperature the day afterwards."

"And how about the babies? Have you ever lost any?"

"Up till now I've been pretty lucky. Only one so far, and I couldn't feel very sorry about that one."

"A forceps delivery?"

"No, a version, not a pleasant business at all. I was trying to get hold of the fetus by the foot to draw it out of the uterus. I touched a small limb and felt it right down to the bottom, hoping to find there the foot I was looking for. I found nothing, the limb ended in a point without feet or hands, just like a stick of candy. I searched again, and found another barley sugar limb. At last I managed to get hold of a foot, a real foot this time, and with that I was able to make the extraction; when the buttocks were out, I wasn't surprised to find a *spina bifida*. The little freak had no hands, and the tumor was in the neck, so that it was almost blue with asphyxia, a very nasty sight, but alive. I would rather it had been stillborn, but since it was living, I had to try and revive it of course. I was doing this when the mother suddenly had a pretty severe hemorrhage. Without any hesitation, naturally, I rolled the baby up in a blanket and put it on the bed, and after that I only bothered about the mother. When I was eventually able to return to the little freak, it was quite dead this time. I'll admit I was almost glad it ended like that."

"Do you remember that little club-foot in the Slum?" I asked. "The one the mother refused to breast-feed? You were afraid its grandmother would kill it or else hire it out to a beggar. You did everything to save it—yet that would have had a worse fate, Lucien, wouldn't it?"

"No, not worse, just different. On a farm people would have felt they were wasting their time looking after a little cripple which wasn't growing normally, and later on wouldn't be able to take care of itself. In the country they almost make a god out of good health and strong muscles. They'd have been ashamed of that little freak, and without exactly doing it deliberately, they'd have gradually let it die. So you see, it's a bit different from the city, isn't it? In the country there's no begging—a child without hands can't be turned to profit."

We were well on the homeward road and were going down the valley towards Peyrac. Lucien was silent, and then reluctantly, as if afraid of conjuring up old ghosts to no purpose, he asked: "How about the Slum? Is it just the same as ever?"

"It has disappeared," I told him. "In its place there is a magnificent playground."

In the middle of the valley through which we were passing, dazzling in a radiance of clear white snow, it was a strange contrast to evoke for Lucien's benefit that slum outside the Cité Universitaire and the workmen and trucks that had come to tear down and burn the shanties and grade the black soil into a park. Beneath our wheels the snow crackled, while I recalled the greasy mud in which I had floundered when trying to follow Lucien into the Slum for the first time. How very remote all that seemed to me now. It was almost a different life, and one which I avoided thinking about very much. He asked after some of our former friends at the Cité, and I gave him what news I had of them.

I was curious to know what sort of memory Lucien retained from those student years. "I sometimes think about them," he answered, "but then you see, Jean, I'm a man of the soil. Even at that period I knew I was only passing through town, as you might say, and that my real life was back here, with people who haven't much use for talk, people I know inside out from a single word or just a look."

"And you had no regrets at leaving?" I had turned towards him, but he continued to watch the road attentively, and I thought he hesitated a little before replying:

"Frankly, no. I know how hard you worked, Jean, and I know that in their fashion the rest did some work. But your way of life scared me. Too much time wasted, too many cinemas and theatres, too much extraneous reading and discussion and the like. I found it all rather silly and worthless, even wrong in a funny sort of way. I can't explain it to you properly but I suppose it's partly that for centuries back my ancestors have been working themselves to death under a hot sun, just about scratched a bare living from the soil. They can't ever have enjoyed much leisure or comfort. Somehow I felt their disapproval when I was in Paris. Come and help with the harvest one summer, only just for an hour or two, and you'll understand better the tremendous satisfaction of stopping work and stretching out for a moment in the shade of an oak tree at the bottom of a field. By comparison your amusements seemed a very useless, dilettante sort of pleasure. But then, of course, everything is all very well as it is. I should feel awfully sorry for any of you if you had to come and live here all your life instead of me. When *I* left Paris, I had nothing to regret or forget, I was born to live here, that's all. Between my job and the mountains, I'm quite happy."

We were traveling very slowly because of the continual hairpin bends. After a long pause he cleared his throat, and I thought he was going to speak; I turned my head towards him. He looked fixedly at the road, and still remained silent. Despite the cold he apparently scorned the use of gloves, and I saw his big bare hands clenching over the steering wheel. We came to a stretch of straight road, and suddenly Lucien put his foot down hard on the accelerator, so that the car seemed to jump forwards and a howling gale came in through the hole in the window. I was astonished at this abrupt burst of speed, so different from Lucien's normal method of driving, very even and careful. I almost called out: "Not so fast, *please*, Lucien." The roar of the engine rose to a frantic shriek, and perhaps in the isolation provided by this noise Lucien found it easier to say what he wanted. In a muffled voice, which I could hardly catch because of the wind, he asked, after this inexplicable hesitation, a very natural question: "And Marianne?"

I had no time to fathom the mystery, nor to answer. How much did he know of what had passed between Marianne and me before we had parted in Paris? Was he afraid of being tactless, and embarrassing me or hurting my feelings? Of course he would think it was my fault we had broken up, and I should either have to lie or else try to explain, to excuse myself. I did not feel at all like doing either.

We had finished climbing the Peyrac hill and Lucien stopped the car in the main square in front of the post office.

"I'm off to La Besse-Haute now," said Lucien. "Are you coming?"

I did not want to go at all. There was still his question between us, which till now I had been able to leave unanswered. I said hastily: "Thanks all the same, Lucien, but I think I'll go back to Dr. Delpuech's. Don't worry about me though. I'll walk."

Evidently Lucien was just as loath as I was to continue the conversation. As soon as I was out of the car he drove off.

"You've come just at the right time," said Félicie, as she opened the door. "You're wanted at Plamonteil and at Combes-Chabre."

"How stupid!" I exclaimed. "We've just come from there. Why on earth didn't they ask for me before?"

"They're all the same," said Félicie. "They wait to call the doctor till he's left on his rounds. Three times, four times in the same day they used to get Dr. Delpuech coming back to the same village right at the other end of the district. Twenty-five or thirty miles they could have spared him every day, and if they had, the poor man wouldn't be in the state he is today. But you'll never make them understand. People think only of themselves and their own convenience. There was no one like Dr. Delpuech for always putting himself out for others."

Then she took me into a former stable, which had become the garage. The old doctor's car was waiting for me there, a rather old-fashioned model but probably quite powerful still I judged. The bonnet faced the former manger, where an old worn-out tire was lying.

Before touching the car I thought I had better find out a few mechanical details from Dr. Delpuech, and I went up to his room. So gloomy yesterday evening, the whole room was now bathed in a serene white light. The old doctor welcomed me from his bed with a smile; he looked more rested.

He told me the car was all ready for the road. The tank was full of fuel, the anti-freeze in the radiator was proof against the worst temperatures the region could provide. As I was leaving the room he told me with a laugh: "And don't forget your prescription book!"

I started. How did Dr. Delpuech know my secret? I felt myself blushing, but already the old doctor was telling a different tale:

"It's something that happened to my father once at a small mountain farm where he could find neither paper nor ink nor pencil to write his prescription. He saw a whitewashed door and wrote his prescription on that with a piece of coal from the fireplace. Then he said to the farmer: 'Yoke your oxen, take the door off and bring it to M. Mandaroux. As quick as you can because your wife needs it badly.' Mandaroux Senior seeing this prescription arrive, never got over it; and sixty years later his son talks of it still. Times have changed, but all the same don't forget your prescription book."

When I reached Plamonteil, I deliberately ignored his advice. I put down the prescription book on the back seat beside my pocket pharmacopoeia. The strategy consisted in leaving the car, thus equipped with prescription book and textbook, a short distance away from the patient's house, preferably in the shelter of a bush or around a corner. When the time came to write out a difficult prescription, you authoritatively unscrewed the top of your fountain pen, and then felt in your pockets ostensibly in search of the good old prescription book—in vain, needless to say. Apologizing to the family for your carelessness, you were then obliged to go and fetch the pad from the car—where the precious pocket notebook could easily be consulted. The only snag was that you had to be very quick about it, photographing the right page in your memory. Nevertheless it was a good deal better than nothing.

Three tall elms on the edge of the road, Félicie told me, would locate the farm where I was expected. I had no difficulty in finding it; it seemed well-kept and prosperous. Set some way back from the road, the house was a two-storied building in fine white stone, which looked almost dark in comparison with the snow on the roof and all round it. On the right there was a big barn full of wagons and tools, very tidily disposed; on the left the hay loft and stable bounded a very large yard on three sides. As I came up to the house a dog barked fiercely, so that I did not have to knock. Recognizing the car, a youngish woman in blue overalls, holding a vigorous baby in her arms, opened the door and brought me into a large clean kitchen-livingroom. A log fire was blazing in the fireplace, and two middle-aged farmers were smoking as they warmed themselves in front of it, near a fine enamel range. They seemed to be awaiting my arrival, and I gathered that one was the woman's brother-in-law and the other a first cousin. The brother-in-law at once pronounced the ritual phrase of welcome: "What'll you have, Doctor?" Without even waiting for my reply, the young woman put the child down on the ground and brought cups and small glasses.

The room was really pleasant. The whitewashed floors brought out well the dark red cherry wood of the huge table, the bulky sideboard, the pendulum clock, and a radio—carefully placed on a stand to avoid anyone bumping into it. An electric light hung from the ceiling at the end of its cord, with a pink paper shade. The young woman had put curtains on both the windows. Despite the mud outside, and although scratched here and there by the nails of clogs, the floor was clean. As I looked round me I thought I had at last met country-folk who could claim to be civilized, and a house which did not look like a mere extension of the stable. After all the others

57

I had seen this morning it was a comforting thought. We chatted about the weather and Dr. Delpuech's health, and being anxious not to appear in too much of a hurry, I accepted a second cup of coffee, which I drank without displeasure. When I had finished it, I asked, more from curiosity about the case which awaited me than from impatience or boredom: "Well, and what's the trouble here?"

"It's my husband," replied the woman; "the lungs, you know. He caught it two years ago, and he has his ups and downs. This is the fourth time now, and we'd like to know what you think about it." She went into the next room with me by herself.

Covered by a huge eiderdown, a man watched us come in. He was plainly dying. There could not be any doubt of this, merely from seeing his face, half propped up by pillows. Seeing me, he wanted to speak; but first he had a fit of painful coughing, which brought perspiration to his pale brow and sunken temples, and a flush to his cheeks, from which the bones were already protruding. Then he gasped, turning his eyes anxiously towards me. Instinctively, as soon as I was near his bed, he took one of my hands and pressed it in his own bloodless hands, scored with blue veins—as if this mere touch might help to relieve him. His palms were clammy, his finger-nails long and claw-like. When at last he succeeded in speaking, all he could say was: "I'm not too well, Doctor, am I?"

It was difficult to give an encouraging reply to this, but I did my best, and asked him to be patient while I made my examination. I then bent over a pitifully moist chest; a sticky acrid tuberculous sweat was dripping from the arm-pits. The patient breathed very carefully as if he were staking his last chance of recovery on this examination. I had no need to sound his chest or auscultate it long. There could be no more hope for him.

Worn out by the effort, he let us leave without saying anything. The two men were sitting at the table in the kitchen, waiting for us. As soon as I had come through the door his brother, without even lowering his voice, asked: "He's a goner this time, isn't he, Doctor?"

The question was asked quite placidly, as if it concerned a stranger. I was astounded; but then, thinking he might not have noticed how far his voice would carry, I closed the door quietly behind me before answering: "I'm afraid he can't recover this time."

"Well then, we ought to fetch the solicitor?" asked the woman immediately. In this sort of tone she might have asked whether it would now be wise to call the priest.

I found the question cynical, but the door was closed on the patient; his wife had the right to ask such a question, and as a doctor it was my duty to try to answer it with precision. I did so, but could not keep out of my voice a note of scornful coldness.

"Your husband," I said, "may live for several weeks yet, but considering the condition in which I find him a sudden fatality is always possible."

There was a moment of heavy calculating silence which I found shameful so near the dying man. The man's wife and his brother looked at each other. The cousin finished his small glass and then spat thoughtfully into the fire.

"We'll get him to come at once, it'll be safer," decided the wife. Then turning to her brother-in-law she added: "Can you go and fetch M. Albessard this afternoon?"

After this sentence everything necessary seemed to have been said; they had only called me in to have an exact prognosis. Disgusted, I rose. There was nothing more for me to do in this house with its deceitfully attractive atmosphere. It had given me quite a false impression about its occupants, and if I were to stay longer, I felt I should have become an accomplice of these three rustics, better washed than the rest but no less heartless and greedy.

The brother rose at the same time as I did, and went to the door. As he went out, quite normally and almost affectionately he called out to the dying man, who could be heard gasping in his bed, this terrible sentence: "I say, Léon, from what the doctor tells us, we'd best call the solicitor at once!"

The next farm where I had to go, about a mile away, was really only a tenant's small house. I knocked, and as there was no answer I pushed the door, and walked in. It was a dark smoky room serving all domestic uses, with a board in the window instead of panes. A baby wrapped in dirty diapers was kicking about and crying in an old baby carriage. Another child, slightly older, was crawling on the floor, its bottom bare.

59

Nobody was looking after them. The elder child had an old teething ring in its mouth; when he saw me he hid under a table. From there, sniveling anxiously, he watched me without moving.

Below a piece of matting attached to the ceiling joists, from which cheeses were draining, I saw a door in the wall. I opened it onto what seemed like a black hole; the rancid smell told me that it was the pantry. The brick partition was broken a little further by another door, and this led into the stable. The smell which greeted me there was scarcely less fetid and ammoniacal than the smell in the kitchen round the baby. The man and woman, both young, were busy changing the straw in the stalls and had not heard me come in. They started on seeing me, and I told them who I was. The man had a low forehead, and his face looked dull and rather stupid; the woman, however, stared at me with shrewd calculating eyes. They left their forks stuck in sods of dung dripping with wet manure, and came back with me into the kitchen. The baby was still screaming. The mother picked it up in the pram, brought one of her breasts out of her black overalls and put it in the baby's mouth. Silence ensued, and the man explained that he had called me in to see his father.

The kitchen possessed two dark alcoves, which I assumed were used for sleeping accommodation. They took me to the darker of the two, where perhaps, I thought, the patient was asleep. But on bending forward I was able to distinguish an old man with a dazed look in his glassy eyes; the eyelids were turned up and bleeding. He mumbled a few words in patois and then relapsed into apathy. I came nearer and obtained a clearer view of the face. There was a growth of gray beard several days old, and his brow was lined with the small brownish scabs of "old man's cancer." His lips caved in round a toothless mouth.

A dewdrop was dripping from his nose; he wiped it mechanically with his sleeve. So that he should not be too cold, they had left him a woollen waistcoat shiny with wear and dirt.

His son was about to speak, but the woman started first. "There you are, Doctor, he broke his hip a year ago, and since then he's stayed in bed. Last winter he went and got pneumonia, but Dr. Delpuech succeeded in curing him. It looks as if the pneumonia must have started again about a fortnight ago. We waited, seeing Dr. Delpuech was ill, and he looks after us free. The Mayor refused to have him put on relief, and as for the old people's home, there's no end to the papers you need for that."

While she was talking, to begin my examination, I had taken off an old blanket. The top sheet must have been changed in my honor, for it was clean. The bottom sheet because of its filthiness and the traces of vermin looked as if it had been cut out of brown oilcloth. With disgust I unbuttoned the waistcoat, which under my fingers had the consistency of old greasy felt, and the shirt which I pulled open was equally repugnant. The only thing which seemed more or less human on this poor old wretch was the white hair in thin tufts over his chest.

His daughter-in-law was right. On auscultation I found the bottom of both lungs affected; but the heart was fairly sound. A little digitaline and he would survive. "Does he drink all right?" I asked.

The daughter-in-law showed me a cracked bowl on a board fixed to the wall by the bed. I picked it up. It contained a whitish liquid with a pungent smell; the old man was fed on some of the whey usually given to the pigs. For once, however, avarice had produced a favorable result; by its diuretic action this whey must be helping the work of the kidneys and heart.

"Well, Doctor?" asked the son, when he felt I had had time to reach a conclusion.

"His heart is sound," I replied. "With a little care he'll recover again this time too."

"Good God! Will we never get rid of the old fool?"

His wife tried to stop him, but he was too furious to heed her. "Look at the expenses we've had," he cried, "and this has been going on a good year now. Of course Dr. Delpuech never charges us for coming to see him, but there are the drugs and the food and the washing; the dirty old pig does everything in the bed just to annoy us. Even before the fracture he wasn't much good for anything, except perhaps looking after the cows. Now he just makes work for us. With two children to look after, and the house and the stock, my wife doesn't need to have a lot of extra work for nothing."

He had expressed his views so frankly that his wife evidently

61

felt she must come to his rescue by softening the clumsy words. But in fact she went a good deal further, sniveling slightly for the sake of appearances.

"The poor old man," she said. "It would certainly be far better for him and everyone else that he should go quickly. He's finished now, and it's no kindness to keep him alive in that condition."

Sitting at the table, I wrote out my prescription as if I had not heard a word they had said. While I wrote I wondered if this couple in their miserable shack were more or less disgusting than the three others on their prosperous farm. I made my prescription and instructions very detailed and explicit. When I had finished, I rose. The man and his wife, finding me silent, did not dare say anything. Of the two she seemed the more dangerous; he was probably given to doing what she said. I remembered the way Lucien years ago had spoken to the grandmother of the club-footed baby in the Paris slum, and did my best to imitate his manner and words. I looked the young woman full in the eyes, and as I handed her the prescription, I added, stressing each word carefully: "You will do exactly what is written here. Your father-in-law *must* recover. You understand that! He must recover. In any case I shall come and see him every day."

The woman nodded obediently, but as I reached the door, I saw her turn a look of hatred towards the corner where the helpless old man was lying in his filth.

I was glad that this ended my rounds. On my way back to Peyrac my head was aching furiously, whether from annoyance and disgust, or from hunger, or perhaps from the excessive dazzle of the snowy landscape, which was very wearing for the eyes.

It did me good straight away to come into the warm darkness of the hall. Félicie told me she was going to make a nice cheese soufflé for me, it wouldn't take her more than a quarter of an hour. Meanwhile she suggested I should go up and have a chat with Dr. Delpuech.

I was too overexcited not to tell him all about the end of the morning's work. On the way back I had been thinking, and decided that it could not be an accident that I had been called out for two such unpleasant cases, one after the other. In both of these farms they must have known I was new, and they must all have said to themselves that they would perhaps have more luck with a locum than with their usual doctor. I asked Dr. Delpuech whether he thought this was so.

"No," he said, "they'd have behaved just the same with me. Finding out when it's vital to fetch the solicitor—that's absolutely typical when the head of a farming family is very ill. And I've seen worse before now than people merely wishing the death of a helpless old man. I've been asked, as something quite normal, whether there weren't some sort of injections to help finish off old men a bit quicker."

"Normal!" I cried. "These people find that sort of thing normal?"

"There you are again," said Dr. Delpuech with a smile. "Our young town doctors try to grasp peasant psychology and the whole business of medicine in the country before they've been here a couple of days."

"Sorry," I said, "I find both subjects fairly baffling."

"Well certainly," he went on after a short silence, "medicine in the country is almost entirely conditioned by peasant psychology. Take the case of the man dying of T.B. They told you this was his fourth relapse. Three times I've treated him, and put him back on his feet. Four times he started working again too soon. Doubtless he won't be able to do that again. I suppose you'll think the three others forced him back to work."

"I might have thought so," I admitted.

"Then you'd be wrong. They've even gone to the length of locking him up in the barn to stop him coming to help them with the harvest. Last August I went to see him without being expected, and I found the old fellow looking very sheepish, wedged by the waist in a window of the barn, having lost his foothold when trying to escape. At each relapse the three others told me, 'We can't very well tie him up'—and it was true. Besides, his case isn't unique. All my T.B. cases are prepared to rest in the winter, but from May onwards, because of all the work to be done, no more resting. They insist on returning to their fields and only stop when they start coughing blood again."

"Meanness or stupidity?" I asked.

"Meanness—yes, I suppose you'd call it that. But money is

hard to earn for the man who gets up before dawn, and who at ten o'clock at night, not having extra hands to help him, may well not have finished looking after his animals. Two hands less is a tragedy for him: no money coming in, drawing on his savings, and perhaps gradually having to sell his land—which for any farmer, however small, is the tragedy of tragedies. So I suppose you might call it meanness. Not stupidity, but the feeling that stopping work for illness is a kind of disgrace, something shameful which must be avoided at all costs."

"Yes," I said, "that does make things easier to understand. But how about shouting that you're fetching the solicitor, as the man did at that farm, without any consideration for the fact that your brother is dying in the next room and overhears you?"

"You can be sure the dying man understood better than you did what his brother meant. Although he's dying himself, if the solicitor comes he knows all the necessary precautions are being taken to see *his land* remains intact. That's one of the main preoccupations of a farmer's life in these parts, to avoid having his land parceled out and lost. Suppose you failed to tell them clearly when death was likely to occur, and because of that the will didn't get drawn up properly, and cousins in Paris could make them sell their property by auction—that would be far worse for your reputation round here than if you had deliberately allowed a woman to die in labor. In his brother's place your patient would have said exactly the same thing with equal bluntness. Compared with his single-minded passion for the land, the farmer treats everything else as unimportant, even including respect for the dead and dying. To be fair, you must recognize that this passion, even in its excess, is not without a certain grandeur."

"In a way," I admitted reluctantly; "but I still can't honestly admire a passion which makes people express frank desires for their parents' death, nor do I find anything admirable about the way that bed-ridden old man was treated by his own children."

"Oh well," replied Dr. Delpuech, "children in towns can get rid of their old parents quite easily, sending them to workhouses and so on if the parents go on living inconveniently long. But I can quite see, Jean, how terrible all this must seem to you. I only want to help you to understand. And one thing you have to understand is that an old farmer, who has all his life obeyed the demands of the land, the rhythms of the seasons, knows in advance that he must resign himself to the inevitable. People in towns haven't got their cemeteries constantly under their eyes, and they forget about death. But here the cemetery is almost in the middle of the village, and at each moment of the day the facts of death are thrust upon you. On a farm, everything old, everything no longer productive, is condemned: all his life your old man of this morning has got rid of his old dogs and old livestock. You can be sure that in his heart he passed sentence on himself and accepted his own disappearance the first day that he hadn't the strength to drive his oxen any more."

Another idea seemed to occur to him all of a sudden, and he stopped to ask: "Did you prescribe a bottle of digitaline for your old patient?"

"Yes, I did," I said, feeling somewhat uneasy. "Was it wrong?"

"No. You were quite right to give something to strengthen his heart. Only, as you hadn't too much confidence in his family, it might perhaps have been more prudent not to leave a whole bottle in the hands of his daughter-in-law. The poor wretch could easily be *too* well looked after in that way, and swallow an overdose. It's too tempting. The next time I should have the digitaline put in a mixture to last for a day or two, to be renewed only with a prescription. That would slightly reduce the chances of his being poisoned."

In the middle of lunch, Félicie, who must have put down a dish to go and open the front door, announced on her return: "You'll have a lot of people today. There are already seven waiting, and there may be more coming till two o'clock at least. There, another one's ringing now."

As soon as I had swallowed the last mouthful, I dashed into the office. The hall clock read half past one.

It was not until nearly five o'clock that I showed to the front door my fourteenth and last patient. Returning to the office I opened the windows wide, in an attempt to clear the atmosphere of its frowstiness from fourteen armpits and groins and dirty feet, mingling with the heat of the stove and the reek

65

of dung and sour milk. A trail of dry mud and spittle ran from the office to the waiting-room, and the former, except that it lacked the fumes of broom for the fire and the smell of hay, smelled otherwise just as strong as the farms I had visited in the morning.

I was very glad to have finished the day's consultations. Fourteen patients in three hours and a half, that made fifteen minutes per patient. Only a quarter of an hour to find out if a "fallen stomach" was really a complaint of the heart, the lungs, the intestines, or even (as once turned out to be the case) a genuine complaint of the stomach. For the second day in practice it was not too bad, and I felt fairly pleased with myself.

In examining the first patients without X-rays or laboratory checks, I was haunted by the fear of missing an early cancer from an ill-localized pain, or of failing to recognize the beginning of a Pott's disease in a vague back complaint. I was fairly soon reassured: the patients lying in hospital wards are mostly quite seriously ill. They have been drained off for the specialized care obtainable in a hospital from among all the thousands of ill people to be found in a big town. The patients here did not seem at all like that. Compared with the sort of case I was afraid of, most of this afternoon's cases seemed to be very mild, and my formulas, copied out with authority, seemed to work wonders for them. "Give medicines, and by the ladleful, rather than little pills. You'll find that impresses rustics more," Paul had recommended, on handing me over his notes. So today I had prescribed plenty of medicines, with doses in quantity.

My fourteen patients, together with the four from the day before, gave me preliminary statistics on the prevalent diseases in the Cantal. I found that each sex and age seemed to have its particular morbid tendencies. The men complained most of "blood pressure," while the women more often had "fallen stomach" or "pain in the back." As to the children, they seemed all to suffer from worms.

I had listened patiently, and for three hours and a half had nodded my head politely, indicating that I had been listening, but also, I hoped, that I approved of what they were saying. I learned in passing that impetigo is a good thing, since it is the bad blood coming out, and that plenty of lice on a child is a sign of strength, since it needs a strong body to be able to keep the lice fed.

I lost my composure with two patients only. The first had a hernia, and when I made him cough, his groin bulged like an orange. I started to advise an operation, but the patient had got it into his head that his hernia would go away with the aid of a good tonic. For the sake of peace and quiet, I compromised on a bandage, and the man went away content.

After that I had another discussion with the first patient who came to complain of blood pressure. In his newspaper he had unfortunately read a detailed advertisement for a drug to reduce blood pressure; and in this advertisement he had recognized all the symptoms which had been tormenting him ever since. Alas, taking the drug had altered nothing in the ear-buzzings and various other troubles due to his blood pressure. In return for my fee, the man demanded of me a really effective cure.

I had spent six months as dresser on a ward for cardiac cases and had picked up some precise ideas about questions of blood pressure. Repeating the lectures of my Parisian specialists, I tried to explain to this patient that it was often preferable to keep blood pressure high if the organism was used to it and was well adapted to it, rather than try to bring it down too violently. Unfortunately the advertisement in the paper asserted exactly the opposite, and my high blood pressure case flatly refused to hear any contradiction of that particular part of his gospel. Certain for once of my knowledge, and piqued in my pride as one who had studied at Paris, I pressed my point. I developed all my arguments, and even went into details, but after a quarter of an hour in which the patient continued to shake his head obtusely, I felt my conviction diminishing and then disappearing.

Since my arrival at Peyrac I had seen and heard too many startling things. Three hundred miles away from Parisian hospitals, what I had learned suddenly seemed a very uncertain and changeable art, dealing mainly in abstruse and hair-splitting differences of professorial opinion in pure theory, in various academic schools of thought without practical value, all more or less contradicted by the facts. Might not this obstinate old countryman be right against the professors of

67

cardiology? Perhaps he was seeking the drug which would save him, as cats go straight to the plant which purges them, guided by a sure instinct. A discreet glance at my cards suggested to me a formula and diet particularly good for reducing blood pressure. The two together might, as well as reducing that, bring the man to his knees; but after all I had warned him. Without venturing on new discussions with the succeeding high blood-pressure cases, I used the same prescription and diet four times during that afternoon.

I also had children brought to see me. I found their cases fairly simple to deal with, for the mothers informed me at once that their complaints were produced by worms—one had a cough from worms, and the other a diarrhea. I was therefore not rash enough to diagnose an ordinary bronchitis in the one case, and a common enteritis in the other. It was almost automatic now to find out, by a discreet glance at my precious cards, the right doses of respectable antidotes with which I at once sprinkled my prescriptions—otherwise these consisted mainly of the traditional mixture which they expected.

But the toughest ordeal came from the undressings and dressings, both of which in themselves threatened to last longer than the quarter of an hour's examination. To gain time, I first tried to continue questioning the patient while he was undressing. The result was worse still. Suddenly arrested in some delicate unbuttoning process, the patient stopped all activity immediately, repeated the question several times in a startled way, and only returned at last to his buttons some time after he had finished giving an answer. So I set myself to wait patiently and in silence.

The re-dressing ceremonies were equally long, but it was with the women that their slowness became most excruciating. There was always some vest or bodice which, in the emotion of the time and place, had not been put on again in the predetermined and immutable order; and they had to begin everything again from the beginning. I was startled to see that afternoon several bizarre forms of hernia harness which were a mixture of bandages, corsets and belts, attached with elastic, straps, laces or buttons, both with and without padding. While the good woman was straining to don once more, in their correct places, these complex creations of imaginative orthopedists, I could open my pocket textbook without any risk and peacefully copy out my prescription from it. Indeed, I could easily have copied out three whole prescriptions.

Fourteen patients had come expressly to see me on my second day as a locum—it was an excellent beginning, I thought. I went up the stairs to chat for a short while with Dr. Delpuech. I thought he would be quite pleased with me, and I was looking forward to providing this pleasure.

I saw no light under his door, and thought he was perhaps sleeping. I knocked very quietly, and he called out at once: "Come in."

The room was lit only by reflections from the half-dead fire, and I heard rather than saw the old doctor groping in the darkness for the knob of his bedside lamp. This he at last succeeded in finding, and when the lamp was on, being dazzled by the sudden light, I at first found him almost unrecognizable. The face thrown back on the pillows had ceased to be Dr. Delpuech's face; it belonged to a stranger. It was ravaged with pain, and his whole body lay worn out and passive, as if forcibly stuck down to the bed. My first idea was that he was having a heart attack, and I made a movement as if to try to help him. I noticed with dismay, moreover, that I was instinctively lowering my voice to speak to him, as if in the presence of a dying man. He must have guessed at my fears, for he forced himself to smile at me as he answered: "No, it's nothing. It'll pass...thank you all the same."

His half-closed eyes, sunken features and pinched lips made him look so exhausted that I almost retired at once; but he made a movement of his hand to keep me there, and began to say: "I was waiting for you." After this he stopped, and then painfully spoke again: "You see, I was wrong in my forecast... you've had lots of people today, and tomorrow, market day, when the people up from the country know you're here you'll have them all."

His voice sounded bitter to me, and I said hastily, as if my protest must soothe him at once: "But they're all asking for you, Dr. Delpuech, they're all hoping to see you again soon."

The old doctor shrugged his shoulders, and I insisted: "Honestly they are. Just by the way they ask for news of you I can feel how attached they are to you."

"Not to me," he said in a dull, almost plaintive voice. "They're attached to having treatment, which is quite a different thing."

He stopped, and then began again after a new effort: "I was wrong yesterday afternoon to tell you that Lucien had brought you here for nothing important, even then I should have told you that you would have all my patients. I could even have told you in advance which ones would be your first. It's always the same with every new doctor coming to the district. Only we always refuse to believe things will go the same way with us as they have with others."

He hesitated before going on, and the silence was only broken by the whistling of a three-quarters-burnt log breaking in the fire.

"First of all," he said, in a voice so low that I could only just catch what he was saying, "first of all you'll have the incurables. They'll rush to you full of despairing hopes in the power of any new doctor. The whole collection of miserable chronics, rheumatics, paralytics, people with cancer and neuralgia, all those Lucien Clément and I have been able to do nothing for. A new broom sweeps clean—and merely from seeing you they'll feel better at once. You'll do them good at first even if you put down bread crumbs or pure water on your prescriptions with a Latin name. At first, I say, for afterwards, of course, it'll be a different story...."

"Yes, of course they'll soon find out I can't do anything for them either. But I can't really help their coming to me just because I'm new, can I?" I felt he was blaming me quite unfairly. But he was not to be deflected, even though it was evidently a great struggle for him to talk so much:

"You'll also have all those who hope to watch a nice little battle between rival doctors with no holds barred. They'll be thrilled to go and cheer first one side and then the other, getting hold of plenty of insinuations and sly gossip as they go. They must have been very disappointed when Lucien and I didn't play, but they'll be eagerly hoping that you'll start up this agreeable sport again. Then, in this land of feuds, of hereditary family quarrels and grudges, you'll sometimes find yourself called in simply to avoid bringing in the enemy family's doctor. But all that would be as nothing, and you

70

might well not see many people in your surgery, if you hadn't, besides all those, the crowds of casuals who, in due course, for no very clear reason, just get tired of their own doctor, and want to see a different face. Remember how the fellow in ancient Athens voted for someone else because he was fed up with hearing Aristides called the Just. After all, they're quite entitled to have a bit of a change now and then. I'm not even mentioning the patients for whom any doctor they haven't yet been to see seems sure to be the best...!"

He sank back on the pillows, exhausted. The smile he gave was meant to be detached, but only a pitiful grimace came through. I did not know what to say, beyond expressing a vague hope that he would soon be feeling better; and I got up to go. As I opened the door he said sadly: "You mark my words, Jean, you'll have them all, you'll have them all."

I left on my rounds. My first patient was a grocer. His wife led me through a rather evil-smelling shop and up a very narrow staircase to a room just above. A little square hole pierced in the floor allowed anyone who got down on his knees to look down all over the shop, and to absorb right in his nose the smells of kerosene, dried herring and old dust which came up through the hole. The woman having had to leave us to answer a customer, I began an examination interrupted, every time a new customer came in, by the endless irritating jangle of an aged shopdoor bell.

The husband complained of sciatica. To allow me to examine it, he withdrew his right leg from a thick layer of sheep's wool. A sickening farmyard smell rose from this strange wrapping, for the wool, apparently freshly sheared, had been neither washed nor carded, and under my fingers I could feel it still sticky with grease.

The diagnosis of sciatica seemed to me indisputable, and as the man complained of terrible pain from it, I thought of bringing spectacular relief through an injection. I wrote the name of the drug on my prescription pad, and then, as directed by the husband, I dropped the paper through the trap-door. The grocer's wife, leaving the shop temporarily in the charge of her customers, ran to the pharmacy, which was quite near, and returned almost at once with a box containing ampules of the

71

drug. I had already taken a syringe, cotton wool and iodine, and put the patient in a good position on the bed. Instead of going downstairs again at once, the wife, very excited and still out of breath from running, watched me cut through the top of the ampule, fill the syringe, and check carefully the right place for the injection. When I thrust the long needle sharply down near the nerve, she gave a little cry of horror, pressing both hands to her breast. To make doubly sure, I prescribed also some anti-neuralgic pills, promising the patient that as a result of this energetic treatment he would have a much better night.

"Do I put my leg back in the wool, Doctor?" he asked.

"If you like," I answered, shrugging my shoulders.

"And the leeches, should we put them on him all the same?" asked the woman.

This time I was completely taken aback. I had never seen leeches used at the hospital. "Why do you want to apply leeches?" I exclaimed. "They've never yet cured a case of sciatica, that I know of."

"Ah!" breathed the woman eagerly, glancing at her husband, "every time he has one of his attacks, Dr. Delpuech makes us put on twenty-four leeches, and the sheep's wool is also part of the treatment he recommended. But they're very old-fashioned cures, of course, not nearly as effective as a good injection. But when we ask him for injections, Dr. Delpuech says he's not very keen on them."

"I think the pain's started going away already," announced the man.

I tried hastily to redeem my clumsiness concerning Dr. Delpuech by explaining that every doctor has his own methods, and that with sciatica you sometimes use injections and sometimes leeches but hardly ever both together. Till now, I went on, it must have been the right sort of case for leeches, whereas to-day it looked as if it had turned more into a case for injections. The man and his wife listened to me politely, but continued to exchange knowing looks. From now on both of them had fixed opinions on the use of leeches for sciatica and on old Dr. Delpuech's outmoded practices.

The wife came down with me. As soon as we appeared in the shop, there was a silence among the collection of gossiping customers; I nodded vaguely to right and left as I went towards the door. The grocer's wife walked behind me, looking very important and obviously bursting with her sensational news. Almost before I had released the outside handle of the shop door, through the window I could see all the customers dashing round her like flies onto a pot of honey. My expression of opinion on leeches was certainly having its effect.

After that I went to look at the child with tonsillitis, where the day before I had had such difficulty in finding the house in its dark alley. This time I had provided myself with a torch, which for the rest of my round eliminated the only difficulty my visits could have presented. None of the cases I saw proved at all serious, and there were no complications.

To return to Dr. Delpuech's house, I had to cross the main square. Mandaroux's shop was still lighted, and the red and green globes in the window made me want to go in there and find out the effect produced by my prescriptions. I was perhaps not uninfluenced by a desire for the little pharmacist's praise; and if so, I was not disappointed. At the sound of the doorbell he came out of the shop at once. On seeing me he raised his short arms heavenwards with every appearance of sincere delight, and exclaimed:

"Marvelous, my dear Doctor, marvelous! And you came here yesterday to ask me to check your prescriptions. You're really too modest or else you're pulling my leg. For all your youth you could show a thing or two to plenty of experienced practitioners."

He stopped abruptly, as if these last words had reminded him of something; and glanced towards the back shop, turning towards it with an agility unexpected in so stout a man. He coughed uneasily before announcing in a voice whose cheerfulness seemed somewhat forced: "This is really very lucky, you know. It so happens that Dr. Legros from Mazerol is here. He's come to collect the results of a test for a diphtheria epidemic; and by the way I forgot to tell you yesterday that to avoid sending everything to Aurillac, I do some laboratory analyses. Chiefly emergency cases, of course, but I'm always at your disposition. May I present you to your colleague?"

Mandaroux pushed me into the back room. Beyond a central

73

counter littered with bottles, mortars and pipettes, one corner of the room had been turned into an office.

Dr. Legros was seated between the table and a big stove. He seemed to be slumped in his armchair, his hands placed on his lap as if he had been taking a nap while waiting for us. Beside him on another chair he had deposited a bowler hat, and because of the heat in the room he had unbuttoned a huge brown fur-lined coat with an astrakan collar. Above this garment, making a rather painful impression, you could see a ravaged face, with features deeply hollowed in a pale unhealthy swelling. The big nose, purplish and aquiline, was striated with small veins. When the man raised his eyes heavily to look at me coming in, I saw big quivering pouches beneath yellow bloodshot eyeballs.

Mandaroux bustled between us, performing the introductions. My colleague held out to me indifferently a soft fleshy hand, and said good evening rather sullenly. His voice was rasping, and almost inaudible.

I must have looked somewhat disconcerted by this greeting, for the little pharmacist exerted himself with even greater volubility to break the silence. He explained to Dr. Legros that I was at Peyrac as locum to his colleague, Dr. Delpuech. Legros looked drugged, and I felt he had hardly heard what had been said. I observed with painful curiosity the dismally bovine quality of this sullen face. Mandaroux had pushed a chair for me opposite Legros. I sat down, and not daring to look at him straight in the eye, I gazed successively at the frayed edges of his fur coat, the untidy waistcoat, the worn-out shirt front and the stained yellow flies on his trousers. I wondered if thirty years earlier he could really have been a clear-eyed student with a healthy complexion and gay laugh, then a young doctor full of courage and enthusiastic enterprise, full of happy optimism for the future. I could see he drank, but surely there must have been some subtler poison than alcohol to bring him as low as this and make him gradually used to living in so pitiful a state without self-disgust.

While talking, Mandaroux had taken three glasses and put them down on the desk. Then he went to find the precious bottle of aperitif in his cupboard. Dr. Legros greeted these preparations with a grumbling: "Still your terrible medicine-mixture for old maids with sluggish stomachs?"

74

Mandaroux was evidently used to this scorn for his hygienic aperitif, for he received it with an indulgent smile. But the bell rang, showing there was a customer in the shop, so he had to leave the two of us together. With the bustling Mandaroux gone, the room seemed empty.

Legros continued to say nothing. There was a moment of embarrassing silence, then, not knowing how to start a conversation, I feigned an interest in the contents of the back room. On the central counter a double saucepan was simmering gently over a spirit stove. At my side the slow filtering of a reddish liquid was beginning, and time seemed to be slowed up a little further by the drip-drip of the liquid as it went through the funnel into a big carboy going right down to the ground.

Moving heavily, Legros made his armchair creak, and I turned to look at him once more. I was most embarrassed to see that he seemed to be observing me attentively. I was about to turn my head away when he asked me, to my considerable surprise: "Are you from these parts?"

He had made an effort to be polite; this time the harsh voice was almost distinct. "No," I answered, "I'm from Toulouse, but I did my medicine at Paris. I'm just finishing and have my thesis still to do."

"And afterwards you're going to set up in practice in the country?"

I hesitated as to what I had best say to please this old doctor, and not feeling sure, answered evasively: "I don't know exactly. I've not yet decided."

"Well now, if you don't know yet, let me give you a piece of advice."

He laughed bitterly, and with the laugh the soft pouches under his eyes wobbled. It gave a touch of hardness to his expression.

"If your parents weren't countryfolk," he began, "and if you didn't spend all your boyhood on a farm or in a village, do not at any price set up in the country. Do anything else you like, go anywhere else you can think of. Go to the Lapps or Bantus or Kaffirs. That'll be far better for you. At least when you go there you know exactly the risks you're running, and if you get frost-bite or your liver is rotting away, perhaps someone will be

75

sorry for you. They may even send you home. But here, when you first set out, nobody gives you any warnings and you're left to wallow in your mudhole right to the end. Naturally they wouldn't be so stupid as to warn you. Doctors are needed in country practices."

"I haven't had very much experience of the country," I said nervously, "but you hear a lot of talk about going back to the land and all that."

"Yes, I know, that's the worst of it. It's always the same people sitting nice and warm in their city offices who talk so lyrically about the beauties of rural life, the fine upstanding character of the noble peasant—a pinch of Theocritus and Vergil can be thrown in here; and a splendid peroration about the nation's best stock and the living strength to be drawn from the soil. There isn't a university professor, with his buttocks firmly wedged in his professorial chair, who doesn't, in front of his students, develop a little sob-stuff along these lines."

I nodded tentative agreement. Some university lecturers did make rather a point of their bucolic propaganda.

"It's just like cannon fodder for wars, isn't it? To arms, young men, the nation needs you. In my time I was hooked by so many ardent appeals that although I'd never set foot outside a town I accepted a country practice because it was free and I hadn't enough money to set up elsewhere. Delpuech is a good chap, but if he offers you his practice free, refuse it. Refuse it even if he throws in his house as well. You're young, with something to give the world. If you stay here, you'll see how much this part of the world will stifle you and rot you away. Talk about the peace of the mountains, the serenity of nature, the quiet of the vegetative life—and all that glorious tripe. To keep the brain alive, you do need something more occasionally than a continuous vacuum. To remain a human being you need some more or less human contacts every now and then. Personally all I've found here is a bunch of stubborn, sly, lecherous gorillas. I suppose it isn't their fault they're like that; nor is it mine. I've been enduring them now for about thirty years, and the more I see them, the less I know what goes on in their so-called minds. I tried to understand them at first, but it was quite hopeless. Now I think of them as little as possible. I ended up by finding my little consolation...."

76

He stopped and looked at me sharply. I felt extremely embarrassed and must have showed it plainly. He shrugged his shoulders, and returned to his outburst. "Everyone will tell you about it, but of course you'll have seen it for yourself if you've got anything of a doctor in you at all. Poor old Legros is done for, they say, he's damn well had it. Only poor old Legros is long past worrying what they think. However, seeing him in this state may at least be a useful lesson to you."

He was still looking hard at me with his yellow and bloodshot eyes, but his voice became thicker as he added with a disagreeable chuckle: "You listen to my advice, my young city slicker. Do not at any price lose yourself in the country. Here, to be appreciated by your patients, your medical practice will have to depend on all sorts of medieval quackery and witchcraft. You'll be forced to descend to the level of stupidity all round you. But if you really do mean to make your career at Peyrac and don't want to go mad with loneliness, think a lot about your wife—always supposing you find one simple or heroic enough to follow you here and stay waiting for you through the long lonely day to put your slippers on in the evening. Give her children to keep her amused; eventually that'll make both of you feel sad when they're old enough for boarding school and you have to say goodbye to them. But if you reject family felicities, then try and invent some nice little vice for yourself as I've done. Above all, if you want to keep going at all, don't rely too much on the joys of your job."

Mandaroux had just come back, looking as busy as ever, and Legros shut up at once. The little pharmacist looked at each of us in turn. Seeing that I looked somewhat uncomfortable, he discreetly gave me a reassuring wink. Then he asked Legros: "Do you want me to write a separate report on the germs found in each of your samples?"

Legros lurched up, answering crossly: "It's diphtheria all through, isn't it? Then why the hell do you think I want to bother with all your rigmarole?"

Mandaroux looked a little offended by this, and remarked: "I thought you might want them for the families."

Legros was now near the door. He turned and looked at me to demonstrate that what he was going to say was chiefly for my benefit. What he said was: "To hell with the families."

77

After which he explained: "By the end of the summer I already had a small diphtheria epidemic, which luckily wasn't too serious. As the children didn't go to school, it was limited to a few hamlets. But I thought what an epidemic would be like coming in midwinter, and I wanted to inoculate all the children in the whole area. I organized free inoculations—and didn't even get three little brats. So now at Mazerol alone I've already five serious cases and others starting up in the mountains all over the place. So as to the families, you see, they can go to Hell for all I care."

He shrugged his shoulders disgustedly. "Good night, Mandaroux," he added, as he buttoned up his coat.

He had opened the door into the street. All the wind swirling round the main square seemed to want to flood into the shop, and Mandaroux retreated hurriedly with a frightened shiver. I hastened to take my leave of him at the same time so that he could shut the door behind him as quickly as possible.

Dr. Legros was already trying to get his car going. Succeeding after he had cranked three times, he got into the car. As he did so, he held his hand vaguely out to me, but instead of saying a formal goodbye, remarked: "If they weren't children, I'd stay at home tonight."

It was late when I got back to dinner. Lucien had already looked in to see me. He had gone up to see Dr. Delpuech and been extremely worried by his condition. He asked Félicie to tell me he had given the old doctor an injection to make him sleep, but unfortunately had not had time to wait for me.

"It's market day tomorrow morning," Félicie reminded me. "People will come here very early. You'd best start consultations about eight o'clock and meanwhile go to bed at once. If you're called out in the night, you'll at least have had that much sleep."

I went up to my room. On the landing I looked, but saw no light under Dr. Delpuech's door, so Lucien's injection must be working; I went by without knocking.

Chapter Four

March 2nd

OF THE market itself I saw nothing. Félicie came in
to call me about seven o'clock. To push back the shutters she
opened the windows—only for a few seconds, but it was enough
to let in from the street a vast confused hubbub and at the
same time such an icy blast of air that I did not dare brave it
again till I was up and fully dressed.

Then I leaned out of the window to see the main street already bursting its bounds. It was swarming with a procession of
vehicles of every sort and kind, oxcarts and barrows and brakes,
gigs and carriages from a past era—as well as vans and even
sedans. They were carrying piles of sacks and baskets and bird-
traps, which reduced any pretensions they might have had to
urban respectability.

All down the pavements the itinerant street-traders were
setting up their trestles, planting stakes to hold up the awning
of their booths, and spreading out their wares. One man was
selling cheap earthenware pottery with a mere square of rope
for enclosure. I saw him pulling crockery out of great straw-
filled crates and heaping up his stock on the ground, apparently
regardless of how it would be affected by mud and rain and
the full force of the wind.

A tightly knit crowd of farmers in smocks, and women wearing black shawls over their heads, were crushed hard against
each other. When the crowd moved forward, it was a laborious
and difficult movement; but they filled any empty spaces there
might be, and streamed slowly between vehicles, stalls, and
shop-fronts, overflowing into the alleys leading off the main
street. Geese were cackling in fury, piglets gave piercing squeals,
and calves lowed piteously to the skies. These animal noises
mingled with the shuffling of feet, the shouts and abuse and
haggling; and the resultant uproar, raucous and ceaseless, was a

79

little like the long inarticulate throat-clearing noise men make when driving oxen. I shut the window again on this rustic hurly-burly and its accompanying smell: the urban touch provided by the auto fumes was all mixed up with the odors of straw, hay, oats, of stable and poultry yard.

When I passed by the waiting room on my way to breakfast, it was already more like the waiting room of a small country railway station just before one of the only trains of the day arrives. Sitting all round the room I could see a wide circle of patients, with several more standing near the door. Some of them had taken white napkins containing their "eats" out of wickerwork baskets; they unrolled the napkins on their knees and began silently munching the contents. They were all plainly prepared for a long wait, and seemed resigned to it, almost indifferent. Many of them had baskets or sacks between their legs, in which chickens and ducks—to be sold later in the day—incessantly struggled. Some disposed of their clogs on the tiled floor of the hall, so that they were sitting or standing in slippers. Near them they deposited fowls tied in pairs, and these came out of their inertia from time to time with an abrupt rustling of wings, making further vain attempts at a sudden escape.

During the morning, each time I began to recover some hope after clearing the waiting room of six or seven patients, a batch of new arrivals flooded in to wipe out my efforts. Félicie would explain briefly: "That's the end of the cattle market ... now that's the poultry market finished ..." and so on, with each successive wave of additional patients.

About a quarter to twelve all those still waiting opened their provision baskets, and the house, already full of farmyard smells, now began to reek disgustingly of greasy sausages and cheap wine. While my waiting patients were thus reviving their strength, Félicie insisted I should stop for half an hour and tried to make me eat some lunch. But I found it hard to swallow even a few mouthfuls, and spent most of this short respite in an armchair by the dining room fire, almost worn out, with a severe headache just starting up. But I felt a good deal stronger after two cups of strong coffee.

The second half of the day's consultations was awful. The patients, till then placid and resigned, all of a sudden started fidgeting restlessly, like cows on a hot summer day when they are suddenly attacked by horse-flies.

"The first buses going back," explained Félicie once more. "They're scared of missing them. Every week it's the same at this time."

She had by now abandoned the front door to defend the entrance to the office; for every time I showed myself, a dozen patients dashed forward together in an attempt to get in. Back in the office I heard them arguing behind the door, and unconsciously thumping against it in their excitement; they sounded rather like beasts in the stable clumping against the swinging bails.

About three o'clock calm was achieved, and then silence. I had just dealt with a patient who thought he had become deaf, and was departing thrilled with his new powers of hearing. I had extracted a huge plug of wax from one of his shaggy ears. When I showed him out, I found the waiting room and hall at last empty. All that was left was a straggling assortment of greasy paper, fruit skins, droppings from the poultry, amidst small heaps of mud left in front of every chair, and countless splashes of spittle now drying all over the floor and walls. Félicie, sleeves rolled back, was already attacking the filth of the hall with a basin of hot water and a mop.

"You're quite pale," she said. "I should get a little rest if I were you. And after that there'll be some calls to make—there's one at Lespinats. It's a good way off, near Montagut, and not too easy to find. Better start with that one if you're going to be back from your round before nightfall."

I had not seen Dr. Delpuech yet today, and asked Félicie if I could go up to him for a few minutes. "I think he usually has a sleep just now," she replied.

To sluice the dirty water out into the road, Félicie had opened the front door; the cold air awakened me. I felt dazed, half drunk, drained of all my energy; and I could confidently expect my racking headache to continue for the rest of the evening, as an extra effect of this day with its thirty-nine patients. The quantity of patients was easy enough to fix, for I had arranged in numerical order every one I had seen; and the man with wax in his ear was the thirty-ninth.

After eight hours spent in the stagnant humidity of the

office, I fancied the fresh air would do me good, and decided to start on my round straight away. By now the tumult of the morning had subsided. The merchants had already almost finished folding up their stalls. The last vehicles were departing, and the middle of the street was becoming empty once more, leaving only the crushed straw mixed in mud and dung and old paper. Only the cafés remained full, and the rise and fall of voices reached me on my road, blending with the echoes from many accordions.

When I had driven out of the town, I had at first to run very slowly while passing the straggling lines of assorted vehicles. At last the road was clear, and I was able to put my foot down harder. Traveling fast in this frosty air had an extremely bracing effect. I was skimming sweetly along, almost on wings, leaving all cares behind me, leaving far behind me the milling mass of rustics who had hemmed me in all day. This journey was indeed an escape.

Fourteen patients yesterday and thirty-nine today—it was real slave labor. Eight hours of harassing consultations of no great medical interest, with no possibility of stopping, and always the same procedure: first you listened to the patient's own garrulous discourse; then, after two or three minutes, you would have to stop the flow and ask a few questions so as to come somewhere near the organ affected. You made him or her undress as little as possible—just to the region apparently involved (so as not to waste too much time); then you made your rapid examination, intended more to reduce the risk of real "howlers" than to touch up your first highly impressionistic diagnosis. Finally you hastily ordered treatment and wrote out a prescription, wondering how much of it, if any, the patient could possibly understand, short of providing a detailed commentary on each part. All the time the hands of the clock were turning, and the whole thing was crammed into a breathless quarter of an hour; then quickly on to the next patient. So this was Medicine in the country!

Stupid, finicky, back-breaking work, as stupid as these rustics who all mysteriously fell ill at the same time, on fixed dates, whenever there was a market or a fair. But some of the patients produced old prescriptions from Dr. Delpuech, and judging his diagnoses from these, I had to admit in all fairness that this work had been well done. Yet it was not easy to do well, lacking the specialized assistance provided by microscope, X-ray and laboratory. This was work requiring sensitive intuition and real clinical flair, worthy of the great physicians of a past age, of Dr. Delpuech's distant youth. It was no wonder that after forty years of this job he still set store by old-fashioned remedies like sheep's wool, blistering and leeches.

Félicie had told me: "Carry straight on over the Pierrefiche plateau till you come to the cross-roads at the Croix Saint-Géraud. You'll be quite near then, and I should ask your way from there on."

At a meeting of four roads a battered signpost, minus its blue-painted iron plate, stood at the edge of a snow-heaped ditch. Near it was a granite cross, the position of which seemed intended to mark the center of a huge solitary steppe, devastatingly white, with hardly a single undulation or landmark. Near the horizon in either direction you could just pick out the hump of some stone hut, its outlines softened by the snow, some emaciated copse which still looked storm-shattered despite the evening's frosty calm.

Two or three miles further there was an abrupt break in the plateau and on the edge of it the road went down to the valley. I noted the first cart-track, then the second, which was a long time in coming; so I accelerated to reach the third more quickly. I saw it too late, about a hundred yards ahead, directly after a bend which masked its entrance. Not having expected to find it so near, I swerved, in an attempt to turn, and felt the car skidding; then, before I realized what was happening, it heeled over and came gently to a standstill in the ditch, in deep snow.

The whole of one side was half blocked by the bank, so I climbed out by the other door. A preliminary inspection showed me that the car had suffered no serious damage, and I even thought I should be able to get it back on the road again without too much difficulty. When I tried to do so the wheel in the ditch began turning madly in the snow, while the other wheel did not get a firm enough grip on the icy verge. I pulled a shovel out of the trunk, and looked for some gravel to put under the wheels; but it would have needed an axe to produce sufficient gravel, for the earth was hard as stone. The only

83

thing to do now, as far as I could see, was to find a good strong pair of oxen at the next farm.

I was just shutting the trunk when I heard the welcome whirr of an engine in the distance; there was a car coming down the hill. In a few seconds it was at the corner and I waved as it came round. A powerful sedan, one of the latest Citroens, I decided. It shot past me and then stopped sharply some twenty yards further on. Having carefully parked his car on the lower bank, the driver got out. He was tall and broad-shouldered, warmly wrapped in a roomy traveling coat, with thick woollen stockings showing beneath it. He was also wearing a good stout pair of boots, with which he carefully tested the icy road before setting firm foot on it. On closer inspection of this prosperous-looking figure, I saw bright alert eyes, a big jaw, and a wide cheerful mouth. Altogether it was a clean-cut healthy face, and the man was certainly both well groomed and well fed.

"I'm not mistaken, am I?" he said with a smile, holding out his hand to me. "It *is* the chariot of Hippocrates which I find in distress. You're Dr. Delpuech's locum, aren't you? I recognized his car straight away. I am your colleague, Dr. Bonnafy of Passou."

I explained the mishap I had suffered through trying to find the cart-track leading to the Lespinats farm. "Aha!" my new friend interrupted. "Do you realize that you are right in my territory there? Dr. Delpuech never trespasses on it, and the people at Lespinats are customers of mine. I ought really to leave you where you are just to teach you a lesson."

I was not unduly worried by this, for he continued to smile, and went on immediately: "This being your first offense, however, I'll be a benevolent monarch and let the good doctor have his straying locum back in good shape and order. Besides, I don't mind telling you that they've only called you out to Lespinats because they owe me already for quite a few calls."

I apologized at once for my unwitting breach of professional etiquette.

"Think no more of it," said Dr. Bonnafy. "It's my fault anyhow, I was wrong to allow them credit. We'll soon see how to settle the affair, but it can't be anything very serious they've called you for. Otherwise," he explained, looking rather self-satisfied, "they would certainly have asked for me."

I felt slightly mortified by this remark, but my colleague was already examining the car situation with an expert eye, so I remained silent. "Nothing serious," he summed up. "I'll give you a tow, and you can let in the clutch gently as soon as you feel the wheels gripping. It'll come out of its own accord."

A few minutes later the car was once more firmly fixed on all four wheels, on the edge of the road. Bonnafy was already disconnecting the tow-rope and putting it away in his boot. He came back to me directly he had done this, saying:

"Look, it's bitter cold here, isn't it? In more civilized parts I would have suggested that we go and have a little drink. It isn't every day you meet on the road a colleague who's not really a rival. As there's nowhere round here we can get a drink, how about leaving our cars and my walking with you as far as Lespinats? That would be the most sensible method of travel in any case, considering prevailing conditions. We shall be able to chat on the way, and you can dispose of whatever it is they want you for, while I may be able to manage a spot of debt-collecting."

We had already walked a few yards down the cart-track between two low stone walls. On each side of the lane the country looked so much like a desolate bare steppe covered with snow that I wondered what on earth could grow there during the summer. Presumably that would be the major reason for the poverty which had made the Lespinats farmer omit to pay his wealthy doctor. When I put forward this suggestion to Bonnafy, he answered in some heat.

"Poor—a cattle country! It *was* poor once, a hundred years ago, when it was so over-populated that every family had to work a small unfertile patch of land to the utmost limits in order to avoid starvation with a harvest of rye. But since stock breeding has become a paying concern, the folks in these parts have seen which way the wind is blowing. They've stopped scratching a living from arable farming, that is, and given everything over to grazing, which has brought them in a pretty fair profit. On the plain during the summer, you'll hear nothing but the sound of cattle bells: thousands of tons of first-quality meat fattening up for the market, not to mention the cheese and the whey-fed pigs. You certainly wouldn't lose if you exchanged your purse with the clodhopper we're going to see now—even now that his purse has just been somewhat lightened by his daughter's wedding. The old rascal doesn't pay his doctor's bills, but a fortnight ago he paid for a reception with fifty guests at the inn in Montagut, plus dance and band."

"What a queer habit they have of getting married in midwinter," I remarked, thinking of the wedding at the Café Albignac.

Bonnafy gave a sly chuckle, half to himself, and then interpreted. "In summer they'd be far too unhappy at the thought of missing a day or two's work. One must admit that they're as fond of their work as they are of their money—and God knows how fond they are of *that*. To extract it from them is quite a business on its own. I had a deal of trouble at first persuading them that I hadn't come here on a purely philanthropic basis. My predecessor had spoilt them."

"You look as if you *had* persuaded them, anyhow," I commented, observing his prosperous appearance.

"Yes, I can't complain, I'm doing reasonably well. I'm even obliged to have two cars. Vehicles get worn out very quickly in country like this, and I'm often glad to have a second on hand when one of them's in repairs. Of course that means money tied up and almost double the running expenses."

He looked only a little older than I was, twenty-eight perhaps. "You've been practising long?" I asked.

"Three years, and I've got five years yet in this stinking country. After that I'll be pulling out before I'm completely besotted. I'm giving myself eight years in all to make my pile, sell the practice, and have enough money to set up anywhere I like. First of all I thought I'd make it in five years, but that would have been pretty fast work. Of course I found everything splendid at first, you realize..."

"Barring the money question," I interrupted. "And you said your predecessor had spoiled them."

"Yes, that's quite true, but in other ways he hadn't spoiled them at all. He was an old physician of the old school, you see, and he practically never operated. I found an exceptional opportunity there; in fact that's partly what tempted me. Imagine a district where all the appendices, tonsils, and growths are intact."

"I don't suppose you left them intact long," I remarked.

86

"I did not," he replied, smiling wistfully at the memory. "The first year it was marvelous. I took out everything which seemed to me at all doubtful, in record time. Alas, it couldn't go on at that pace, in fact Providence is very unfair to doctors, don't you think? Once you've taken an organ out, it doesn't grow again—pity. That's what stopped me keeping to my original schedule. Ah well, can't be helped. In our profession one mustn't expect too much. I'll need three years more, that's all."

"And have you a special line now?" I asked, drawing him out—not that he needed urging.

"I have indeed," he answered happily. "A line that is almost as profitable as my surgical activities. I now puncture their purses with injections galore. At the beginning they didn't much care for this new method of treatment, but now they love having needles stuck into them, they think they're really getting something done—which has increased my prestige still further. I've also bought a small X-ray apparatus. They're crazy about it; in fact they'd feel a bit slighted if I didn't give them an X-ray each time I examined them. Apart from that I've got myself a lamp for ultraviolet-ray treatment. Yes, I'm building up quite a nice little business, I admit."

I thought of Dr. Delpuech and Lucien so devoted to their patients, who understood their devotion so little. Bonnafy was certainly a complete contrast, but I could not help finding his frankness rather engaging. He had already on one occasion referred to his patients as "customers"; it was a joke, but perhaps also significant of his whole attitude. He gave treatment for money, and money was all he expected from his patients in return. Two days earlier I might perhaps have been shocked by the cynicism with which he told me about his medical methods before he even knew me. But forty-eight hours of Medicine in the country made me feel considerably more indulgent.

The north wind, bringing heavy mists in its train, beat down on us in the narrow sunken lane. When I turned up my coat collar, Bonnafy remarked: "You're not used to it, are you? Personally I don't mind the cold, in fact anywhere else but here, in some winter sports place for instance, I'd quite enjoy the energetic life. But my objective, in five years, is Paris."

He stopped talking, and lifted his head slightly, as if measuring up to the full height of his ambition. A few yards further on he announced: "We're nearly there now. You see the little pine wood a quarter of a mile or so ahead? The farmhouse is just behind it."

It was a wild and dismal site for a house. Bonnafy glanced up at the lowering sky and then looked round him with a disgusted sigh, as if he had never before observed so clearly the desolate misery of the whole scene: "What a godforsaken spot!" he finally exclaimed; and then, in a tone of almost childish desire, murmured: "Oh Paris!"

"You come from Paris?" I asked.

"Oh no. My father's a postmaster at Limoges, so for reasons of economy I naturally did my Medicine at the university there. But for my last year I was able to go to Paris; and that's the year that opened my eyes. If it hadn't been for my stay there, I'd have gone and set up in any old dump I could find, like my Limoges friends, and then spent all my life till the day of retirement going round and round the same old six or seven miles of roads and lanes, like a squirrel in a cage and just as unambitious."

He paused as if to take in properly the awful fate he had almost accepted; and then continued: "I came up to Paris with just enough money to live on, and not a sou extra on which to enjoy myself. I found a very reasonable little hotel near the Latin Quarter, and in the evening when I felt I'd worked enough, I used to go up the Boulevard Raspail to Montparnasse. Oh, those pretty girls, those lights and cars and bars and night-clubs, all that luxury! I was like a penniless kid standing in front of a toyshop with his tongue hanging out. You were in Paris, weren't you?"

"The whole district seems to know that," I said. "Yes, I was—and there's certainly something about Montparnasse at night. I come from Toulouse, and I was pretty thrilled with Paris myself when I first went up there."

"Well anyhow," said Bonnafy, "you can imagine, can't you, what Montparnasse meant to me—the symbol of a life where money offers freedom and pleasure and power. At the same time I felt that for complete enjoyment this money must be earned and spent in Paris itself. It would be quite intolerable to go and spend just a fortnight a year in Paris, while vegetating the rest of the time in some hole in the country. But don't think I looked at the Montparnasse scene with a jaundiced eye, like a prig. No, I felt I was cut out for this sort of life, including all the intrigues and brawls it involved. I vowed I'd come back permanently one day, and set up there in practice. I felt I had the right formula for success. The folks in Limoges are practical and cool-headed, and have never been afraid of work, and hard work is still the best way to get on—given a fair amount of common sense, too, that goes without saying. I worked myself to death that last year, and I've gone on working like a nigger since I've been here."

"You have?" I asked rudely; the note of sarcasm came out more clearly than I had intended.

"Oh certainly," he answered. "I play the game according to the rules, you know, and I go to a lot of trouble about it. They can call me anywhere and at any time; I see I get paid for the call, but I always go. And they can't find fault with me professionally either—I've never had a patient die through my negligence—and I know my job pretty well. It's always simple enough to botch a job and bluff afterwards to get out of it, to make a mess of a confinement case through sheer incompetence and then explain to the family that the child was still-born; or to call the slightest bronchitis pneumonia and each headache meningitis, just to add to one's prestige. If the bluff is successful, the victims are too ignorant to notice what's happening straight away, and it may take quite a long time before they get wise."

"I shouldn't think they could get away with it for years," I remarked, thinking of some of my less scrupulous contemporaries.

"No, that's the point," said Bonnafy; "they can't. In the long run there's an unfortunate case here, another there, and a bad impression is created. People start talking and wondering and checking up on the accidents. Specially here in the country, where people are so suspicious and never trust anyone. On the other hand, their confidence, once acquired, is firm."

"And I may assume you have acquired their confidence?" I asked with a smile.

"You may. Mentally they've written me down quite definitely as a hard man to deal with but one who knows his job—capable, therefore, of giving them useful service. It's true enough. They obey me now with their eyes closed. I can tell them to have an operation without their hesitating at all, even when it may be a bit less than essential. But my predecessor, when he had a case of acute appendicitis and wanted to operate before the child died of peritonitis, used to have to call the parents murderers and threaten them with the police. Just think of it, poor old boy—he was like your old Delpuech—looked after them for almost nothing. They were very polite to him when he was there, but behind his back they just laughed at him. The proverb says pay your debts and you'll be respected. I've altered it, though, after my experience with the people here, to—get paid, and you'll be respected. I'm quite convinced that it's my toughness, modeled on their own, that reassures them. If I started being meek and mild with them, they'd suspect a trap. We're both tough, and they understand me."

He was walking with long vigorous strides, and I found myself liking the man a good deal. However sleek and well-fed his appearance, however frankly commercial his attitude, he was clearly cast in a different mold from Henri Philippon, for instance. For all his superficial cynicism and eye on the main chance, I suspected Bonnafy knew his job and did it conscientiously. After Dr. Legros's warning, and from my own limited experience, I could well appreciate that the rigors of a practice in these mountains did not provide much unselfish satisfaction to a doctor, either on the human or on the professional level.

Just as we reached the little pine wood he stumbled in a rut congealed by the ice, which rang like cement against the nails of his boots. He almost fell, and as he grasped my shoulder for support he said once more, with unusual emphasis, "Yes, a godforsaken spot!"

"How did you come down here in the first place?" I asked.

"Just by luck. In spite of my self-confidence, I wasn't fool enough to try practice in Paris right away, with no capital or experience. I was on the lookout for a practice which wouldn't be too expensive in a district which hadn't had too much medical exploitation already, where I'd have a fair amount of elbow-room. I landed up here as a locum; the old doctor I've told you about—actually he was only fifty-eight—was just dying of uremia, prematurely worn out by looking after patients for practically nothing and not looking after himself at all. Nervous uremia—it was terrible—convulsions, delirium, coma, the whole box of tricks. Right to the end he went on screaming with pain despite all the morphia I could pump into him; I couldn't give him too much anyhow because of his kidneys. In his delirium he always thought people were coming to call him out for an emergency case. The whole district turned out for his funeral; it was winter, and they had nothing better to do. In summer, with work going on in the fields, I'm sure I'd have been the only one to follow him to the grave—not counting the priest and the choirboys of course. By the way, Delpuech is in pretty bad shape, isn't he, from what I've heard?"

"Yes, I'm afraid he is. Angina pectoris. And two months ago he had a coronary."

"The hell he did—bad, that. Just one more doctor killed by his patients, I suppose. I tell you, Nérac, if I'm going to die of angina pectoris or uremia just because I look after my customers too well, it's not going to happen free or with any special discounts to patients."

We had passed the wood by now, and reached the farm, a collection of gray buildings huddled together against the edge of the wood, so as to give them protection from the wind. The muddy yard was cluttered with an untidy mess of old tools, faggots and tree stumps. In front of the stable there were large puddles of liquid manure, and the hens were scratching at the fresh dung, at the foot of the big manure pile covered already by the snow. I found the house's interior and its occupants almost equally unattractive.

We did not have to stay long. One of the children had a bronchitis without complications. Dr. Bonnafy's entrance appeared to cause some consternation, but he sat down by the fire quite normally, accepted the cup of coffee and glass of brandy which were offered, and talked about the weather and the prices at the last agricultural show as if he had just dropped in on an ordinary social call. Then I went to examine the child, and Bonnafy remained alone with the farmer. When I returned, my fee had already been counted out and placed on the table. My colleague was just putting his wallet back in his coat with a satisfied air.

As soon as we were a short distance away from the farm he

explained to me in a further burst of confidences, no doubt stimulated by the success of his strategy: "You're not all that keen, I take it, to come back to this out of the way spot?"

I shook my head, and he went on: "Well, I've pointed out to my dear patient that he was behaving like a lunatic and against his own best interests. 'Even if I never come back here,' I told him, 'you don't suppose I'll make you a present of the calls I've already made, do you? So instead of bringing a doctor all the way out from the next district at a cost of two francs a mile for his journey, you'd far better pay *me*, seeing that I live quite near and there's practically no charge for traveling.' This reasoning convinced him almost at once and he paid up with fairly good grace."

I had to admit that it was good peasant psychology.

"Anyhow," added Bonnafy, "this kind of thing doesn't happen very often nowadays. The main thing, old boy, is not to let them take you for a sucker when you start—though they'll try hard enough, as you can well imagine. Like one of my first patients in the office who, when it came to paying, asked me: 'How much will that be, Doctor?' He knew very well that it was five francs; my old predecessor had never dared get up to ten francs, which is really the minimum fee by medical association rules. Anyhow I answered: 'Five francs, as usual.' 'Oh no,' he told me; 'you're only the locum, so it's only worth half that.' To look for his two and a half francs, he put down the prescription on a corner of my desk. I picked it up, tore it neatly in half and gave him back one of the pieces, saying: 'Now, we're even, aren't we?' He saw my point, and paid up his five francs. Needless to say, as soon as I took the practice in my own hands, I brought the minimum fee up to ten francs."

"They took it quietly?"

"They certainly did not. The word must have been passed round quickly, for at first they all arrived with their five franc pieces and otherwise not a single centime on them, so they declared. As a precautionary measure I used to take the money, but would tell them that by next day they would have to let me have the other five francs. I laid low for a week, and on the eighth day I was still waiting for my first additional payment. So without hesitation I gave the whole list of my debtors to a collection agency. The firm's manager wrote to me quite dumbfounded. I was going to spend twenty francs in order to recover five. That's what happened, and that time I lost fifteen francs per head. But all my faithful patients realized they'd found someone as tough as they were, and since then they've paid me what I ask on the nail."

He broke off at this happy conclusion, and stopped walking for a moment. Suddenly he leaned over and picked up some snow on the side of the road, made it into a ball and hurled it at a big crow standing out as a black mark in the middle of a field. The bird took off in a hurry, easily avoiding the direct hit. Bonnafy watched it flying away, and observed: "I didn't stand much chance of getting it. There's one of the typical fauna of this plateau, with as many tricks as an old monkey."

"Thinking of your patients or yourself?" I asked with a laugh.

Bonnafy laughed too, and replied tolerantly: "Let's say a bit of both. Only my patients were like that before, and when I first came, I found they could teach me plenty. Look, when I was getting them to have all those operations they used to leave for the clinic dressed like paupers, almost in rags. They made themselves into regular church mice just to get the fees reduced. When you've no experience of country life, it's very hard to judge how well off people are. Talk about the struggle to keep up appearances—the people here are so mean they do just the opposite. Keeping down appearances, would you call it? Look at the Lespinats, for instance, they had electricity put in two years ago; for a farm of that size they might have needed at least five or six outlets. Actually the farmer put two in the stable and kept kerosene lamps in the house. After that, what hope can you have of judging by outward appearances?"

"How about counting the number of head of cattle and so on?" I suggested.

"Quite right, my friend. But how would you set about finding out the exact number? I used to ask my surgeon to question the patients when they were just coming round and were still a bit dopey from the anesthetic—but he always forgot."

"Wouldn't the neighbors tell you? From what I've heard, everyone knows everything about everyone else in these parts, and they're only too willing to pass it on."

"Quite right again, with the single exception of money. That's a sacred subject, and you'll get a complete conspiracy of silence, as far as money matters are concerned. The only thing I could do was to ask to look at the farm. I used to go round very thoroughly, counting the number of pigs, the number of cows and horses and so on, for my personal card index. By now I really know more about all their economic situations than the tax-collector. Anyhow, since my surgical work's been on the decline, I've doubled my medical charges, without losing a single patient—quite the contrary."

"Naturally. Who else would they go to? You're the only doctor here."

This again was unnecessarily rude, and I regretted making the remark almost before I had said it. Bonnafy had been talking to me from the start without irritating affectations or boasting, in fact with obvious sincerity. Luckily he did not seem to take offense easily, and replied without heat: "I suppose you think I'm practising on an island, and that my community is the only one in the whole of France not surrounded by other communities, all provided with rival doctors. I'd have thought your presence here was the best evidence against such a curious idea. It's true that I've no complaints about Peyrac; it's a godsend having neighbors like Delpuech and Clément—never a patient lured away, never a frontier incident. On the contrary I might one day gain a few extra patients from that quarter. People find them almost too kind, which means soft; and from there it's only a small step to thinking them fools. Sometimes I'm half inclined to share that opinion."

I was on the point of saying that several times in three days the same idea had occurred to me; but then, from a sense of loyalty, I protested: "Clément's an old pal of mine from Paris, you know, and I assure you he's no fool by any means—nor is Dr. Delpuech."

"Sorry," said Bonnafy, shrugging his shoulders; "didn't really mean it, my friend. After all, you can take it as a compliment. They're natives, and it's entirely their business, their own funeral you might say, if they want to be led up the garden path and die of overwork for the sake of their fellow-countrymen. Didn't you ever hear the old rhyme:

"Tender-hearted, stroke a nettle, and it stings you for
your pains.
Grasp it like a man of mettle, and it soft as silk remains.

I prefer the second method, and the funny thing is that everyone around here seems very pleased I do."

We had still some way to go before we reached our cars, and
I thought Bonnafy would provide me with some valuable information about the other doctors in the neighborhood. In
particular I thought it was a good chance to find out what he
thought about the drunken Legros. I told him of my encounter
in Mandaroux's shop.

"Ah, you've seen Legros, have you? A remarkable phenom-
enon, isn't he? I'll never forget the call I made on him when
I first got here. I wanted to have some idea who I'd have to
deal with in the vicinity. After one visit to him I lost all my
fears about rivals. He lives in a big derelict house with a one-
eyed old girl to look after him. I found the old man in the same
neglected condition you saw him in yesterday. He was flopped
in front of a desk which you could hardly see for papers,
magazines, drugs, and dirty syringes, the whole thing sprinkled
with an accumulation of several years of dust. He had a quart
of wine by him. He asked me about my family background, as
he did with you, and when he found out I'd been brought up
in Limoges, he advised me to go back there at once."

"He might have been trying to discourage a young rival."

"Yes, I had that idea myself at the time. But he was sincere
enough, just the same as he was yesterday with you. After I left,
I found out all about him—really a very sad story. He set up
here twenty-five years ago because he didn't have enough money
to try his luck in a town. He was a young married man when
he arrived, and the first two years he worked like an ox from
morning till night. He wanted to make a success of it. Moreover
he was an excellent doctor—as he still is on the very rare occasions when he's sober."

"But then he started drinking?"

"Not without due cause. After two years of this rustic life,
his wife had had more than enough of it. I can see her point
of view—try and imagine what it must be like for a young
woman who's always lived in a town. Now she has to live all

95

by herself, shut up between four walls, without any comforts, her only distraction being the sound of the doorbell or the telephone—while her husband dashes off on calls into the mountains day and night. However that may be, at the end of the second year Legros's wife went on a little journey to her family—and never came back. He wrote tearful letters and threatening letters and imploring letters—all to no avail. Mandaroux, who discreetly told me the whole story one day, says they were even afraid at the time he might kill himself. Well, he chose a rather slower means of doing so; but as you've seen, he's working towards that end."

"But once he'd got over the immediate crisis," I remarked, "I can't quite see why he'd go on being such a complete drunk."

"Can't you really?" Bonnafy guffawed. "Don't you know that every country doctor is a likely candidate for professional alcoholism? It might be called an occupational hazard—he's only got to let go for a short while. In every house you've been to, haven't they tried to get you to swallow some poisonous concoction?"

I admitted this freely, remembering the fearful plum and quince brandy at the farm I had visited with Lucien.

"Well then," said Bonnafy, "if you had accepted each time, try and work out the number of glasses of brandy you'd have had by the end of the day. Let us suppose that Legros, sober up till then, after his matrimonial disappointment allowed himself to be tempted, and then developed quite a taste for his little consolation. In practice, in both senses of the word, he's been drunk for years now, two days out of every three. The last time I met him he was on a delivery. He had forgotten his doctor's coat, but had borrowed a woman's gown from the cupboard, one of those very long old-fashioned gowns with a high collar. He'd put it over his suit. That day the wine he'd been drinking must have been a very tonic brand, for he was sitting by the bed and humming the *Tannhäuser* overture while he waited. Except for the woman who happened to be giving birth everybody else was drinking steadily. They also had a great game filling up his glass so as to get him really blind."

"What!" I was really incredulous this time. "Wasn't the family afraid of the consequences?"

"Oh no, not at all. The people round here are quite content

with the treatment they get from him. First of all, they find alcoholism a very minor vice, rather an endearing one. They even think old Legros is specially inspired when drunk— *in vino veritas*, you know, and all that. But I fancy the chief reason why they don't mind seeing him drunk is because on days when he's drunk he always forgets to make a note of how many patients he's seen."

He walked a few yards in silence before summing up: "Just one more doctor who has paid dearly for coming and setting up in the country."

"You think it's better to keep away from it unless you have family roots in the land?"

"For most townsmen," said Bonnafy, "I certainly do. We've got a good example not far away from here, in the youngster who came to Montagut six months ago. Montagut is a horrible dump on the other edge of the plateau. The village ran an advertisement in the medical papers to the effect that they required a doctor. This chap answered it, came along and opened an office with a small dispensary in the back room. His wife looks after that, she was a medical student herself. They're expecting their first child, and meanwhile they've been polite and self-effacing and elaborately conscientious—all the things one should avoid appearing before peasants who are only too ready to take advantage of it. In fact they're already playing every kind of dirty trick on him."

"What's his name?" I inquired.

"Ricaud, Antoine Ricaud. The natives, most of whom haven't much use for religion, consider him a bit queer because he goes regularly to mass, and he actually still believes in medicine as a sacred mission. Apparently the life they've been leading him hasn't yet discouraged him. He's only got a bicycle, but in every sort of weather he goes pedaling round the countryside, with a wool helmet on his head, knitted by his wife, and cardboard shields fitted over the handlebars to give him a little protection from the cold. I felt terribly sorry for him, and tried to give him some commonsense advice, even to help him. But I suppose he must have thought me a cynical swine, and I've never seen him since then. In any case he's not likely to become at all dangerous to me. My guess is that with the life they're leading him, he can't be far from a nervous breakdown. And then the

97

poor wretch has even got Chassagnon against him as well. *He* certainly won't give Ricaud any peace until he's forced him to get out of the district altogether."

"Who's Chassagnon?" I asked.

"Our colleague at Farlat, Mayor and County Councilor, the great political boss of the whole area. He's feared the length and breadth of the Auvergne. He mixes politics and medicine with extreme cunning. In fact that's the only thing about him which really worries me personally: he makes his electioneering propaganda by giving out quantities of forms guaranteeing free medical assistance. I've nothing against that when it's Chassagnon the patients will see. But sometimes when I've been six miles to see people with two pigs in their sty and six oxen in their stables, instead of my fee I get a nice piece of paper informing me that the local authorities will very generously pay me three and a half francs at the end of two years."

We were nearly up to the main road where we had left the cars. Night was beginning to fall, and an icy fog was coming up. Bonnafy looked at his watch. "Hm," he remarked, "I'm afraid I've been talking a lot. I'd urge you to get back pretty quickly, but don't take your corners too fast again. An accident on the plateau isn't specially funny after nightfall. When you feel like it, please give me a ring—perhaps you'd come to dinner with me one evening, and I'll show you my set-up. I've got a damn good cook and not a bad cellar, and I'll take the receiver off the telephone so we shan't be disturbed. I'll count on you to set a date—do come, I'd enjoy it so much."

We reached Dr. Delpuech's car. I took the blanket off the bonnet and climbed in. Bonnafy stayed by the door and said again: "I'll be waiting for your call. We'll have a pleasant evening together, and in return, five years from now you can give me a few good phone numbers in Montparnasse."

Standing near his car on the edge of the road, he remained motionless for several seconds, watching me drive off as if I were on the way to arrange this date for him five years later.

When I was back again on the plateau, night had already spread over it like a thick dark smoke, but a few miles further on I ran into a genuine fog. I had to drive very slowly, and was terrified of getting off the thin black path which was my

98

guide and running into the treacherous snow of the ditches. At one point the darkness in front of the windshield became so extreme that I had to lower the window and lean out in order to make sure where the edge of the road was.

As I neared Peyrac, I at last came out of the fog, feeling soaked and furious and chilled to the bone. Accelerating again so as to make up slightly for lost time, I decided I was a complete idiot to be shivering in this ancient car on a winter's evening, on this mountain road far from the civilized world.

Bonnafy was dreaming only of going to live in Paris, while I had been fool enough to come and lose myself in this dump. Why had I not listened to Henri Philippon's advice, when he knew from his experience of the region just what sort of an idiotic adventure I was landing myself in? Bonnafy was right, and even Legros: it was strictly their own business if Dr. Delpuech and Lucien wanted to sacrifice themselves for their fellow-countrymen. But I had no possible motive for wasting my time with these dirty, mean, brutish countrymen, mostly half-witted, typical peasants à la Zola. I felt no single point of real contact with them, and I was quite ready to include Lucien too in the same rather scornful irritation—Lucien with his typically rustic placidity, his apparent absence of emotion, which made him accept anything people of his stock might do.

Thinking it all over, I found even Dr. Delpuech irritating, with his explanations and perpetual excuses on behalf of the least defensible social anomalies. Senile and sentimental, I decided. Underneath he certainly could not agree with these things. But he must in earlier days have tried to fight them and evidently had failed, so now he covered up defeat with the modest if somewhat hypocritical veil of a weary tolerance. I saw no reason to show the same tolerance, to carry on with his out-of-date treatments based on blistering and leeches, or, in fact, to waste any more of my time amidst this population of yokels.

This evening I felt too many aches and pains, too much headache and heaviness, to accept the idea of starting another such stultifying market day, a similar uninteresting procession of pains in the back, "fallen stomachs," incurable rheumatics, high blood-pressure cases and worm-infested children. While I was driving painfully along on this dismal country road, Henri was probably holding some pretty girl in his arms, in a warm dance hall with soft lights and sweet music, and I could have had another such girl near me. Even Vicky, from whom I had felt the need to escape, suddenly seemed to me infinitely attractive and desirable. I must get back to her as soon as possible. But how could I leave now, when I had hardly arrived, without hurting the feelings of Dr. Delpuech and Lucien? I decided to write to Henri or perhaps to Paul Chavasse the following morning, asking them to wire me to come back, with the reasonable pretext of an exam. My present experience was conclusive: not a week's goodwill, not a month's steady determination, would offer the key to peasant psychology. Drunken old Legros admitted he had not found the key in a whole lifetime. No, I would willingly yield the Auvergne to the tender care of Lucien and Dr. Delpuech and those like them.

Fresh from these reflections and this decision, I was not looking forward to an evening's gloomy tête-à-tête with Dr. Delpuech as a conclusion to this wearing day. Luckily he had a visitor, his godson, a priest from La Besse-Haute. After a substantial dinner, which revived me considerably, I went up to join the young priest, whose name was Dieuzaide, by his godfather's bedside.

I remembered La Besse-Haute as one of the most miserable-looking villages I had passed during my rounds, and I did not imagine its inhabitants could offer much encouragement to a new priest fresh from a theological college, as this Dieuzaide plainly was. My conjecture on this point proved all too well justified: the poor priest seemed decidedly downhearted at the lack of response he was getting from his parishioners. So I judged from the conversation between him and Dr. Delpuech, in which I—feeling very tired and a little somnolent—took little part, though I fancied that some of the doctor's remarks were directed partly at me. He might be guessing at my state of mind with an intuitive shrewdness for which I had scarcely given him credit. Certainly the arguments he used with the young priest contradicted completely my idea of senile sentimentality.

Dieuzaide was a countryman himself, born in this region, as he protested bitterly at one point, and this should have given him a certain advantage in dealing with country people. But

Dr. Delpuech reminded him that he had been away since he was eleven years old, and would have to learn about peasant psychology all over again from the beginning—"almost as much as Dr. Nérac here, who was actually born in a town."

"People who work on and live on the land, Maurice, my son"—after a glance in my direction he turned back to the priest—"are likely to be earthbound for most of their lives. That's only to be expected. Occasionally, to one's great joy, one meets nobility of character, even momentary flashes of unselfishness and kindness, sometimes where one least expects them. But for the most part men are what they are. Notice I say men, not just people in the Auvergne or even countrymen generally—and their natures inevitably include a good deal of envy, hatred, malice, and uncharitableness."

The priest looked doubtful, but found nothing to say to this. Dr. Delpuech, though there was a look of affection in his eyes, went on rather ruthlessly, as I thought at first: "I shouldn't let myself be too discouraged by all this. I remember one of my anatomy professors saying to us at the end of a dissecting session: 'If the dead were as dirty as the living, I'd never have been able to do anatomy.' At the time this remark surprised me; but later on I came to see that it was the witticism of a man of pure science, not a doctor who deals with human beings. For a body which works long and hard in dung and dust is bound to be dirty, and the soul which lives with this mean body is probably going to be mean and dirty as well. But when you really think about the people here, is it their fault that they're such materialists? Doesn't it follow naturally from the soil, the sky, and the climate? Naturally they have a squalid down-to-earth mentality which cuts out spiritual yearnings, and makes them seem almost as determined as their own animals. They've been branded by so many factors of heredity, education (or lack of it), surroundings and environment generally, that there isn't a doctor who would declare them free in any real sense."

Maurice Dieuzaide raised his head abruptly, turning quite pale all of a sudden, as if faced by an unexpected blasphemy. In his excitement he stammered out rather than said: "But what about their salvation? Could they be saved if they weren't free?"

"Now you know quite well, my boy," answered Dr. Delpuech

gently, "that I'm no materialist and that I'm not trying to shock you. All the same, any doctor who knows a little physiology can't believe in complete freewill. If I inject a certain dose of thyroxine into a man, I know that I can deliberately give him a tendency to savage tempers. Suppose, instead of my injecting the drug, it's the thyroid in his own body which secretes an excess of thyroxine, will that man be responsible for his rages? Is the alcoholic free to stop drinking when the attempt to wean him from alcohol can bring him to hallucinations and delirium? You know as well as I do the terrible ravages caused by alcoholism in country districts these last fifty years. For the young drunkard, just starting on his vice, the need he wishes to gratify is less his own than the imperious call he has received through his heredity. He is already imbued with it, saturated with it right to his marrow. Only a drop of alcohol is required and the whole thing blazes up at once. If you have a religious procession passing, and he stands hiccoughing on the bank and relieves himself right in front of the procession, is this sacrilegious act born of complete freewill?"

He paused for a moment, then shook his head as if to remove all objections in his own mind before resuming his train of thought: "Forty years of Medicine have shown me hereditary effects and fatalities almost as unavoidable as physical laws. A determinism of glandular fluids and secretions binds men down from their birth till the day of their death."

To realize that Dr. Delpuech was right, I had only to go over all the evidence offered me during only three days of surgery and rounds: goiter in father, goiter in son, diabetics who were sons of diabetics, same with gout and epilepsy—as if some accident had struck down certain families and villages all at once; cardiac cases dying suddenly at the same age as their parents had; families with T.B. and families with cancer. There was even the family about which Félicie thought it best to warn me before I called. According to popular rumor the father in each generation violated his eldest daughter when she reached fifteen, as though observing some horrible traditional rite.

How could Dr. Delpuech have failed to believe in an inexorable hereditary fate, when besides the forty years of his own practice he had been able to meet and compare in each family the observations of three generations of doctors?

But I felt he had been strangely successful in opening my eyes too to this form of determinism. I could not recall having ever thought about the subject before with such realism and clarity. I could now visualize the whole thing with almost the precision of a model in anatomical pathology: Peyrac on its rock, and all the villages and hamlets of the mountain, enduring heat and then cold and then heat—in an infinite succession of seasons. They were grilled by the sun, then washed by the rain, whipped by the winds, smothered by the snow. For too many years, under the same harsh sky, the same cold earth had afforded just enough nourishment for the living, and then had taken back the dead beneath its soil. If I really saw and understood all this, I could see how inevitable it was that the race should become rough and wild like their land. I must give up some of my city-made ideas, and try to judge them as a real doctor. Quite definitely, these countrymen seemed to me less responsible now for the hardness of their hearts.

"Yes, my son," said Dr. Delpuech, "in forty years I've really had a close view of the full ugliness of human beings; but I repeat that I've seen some unexpected beauty as well, and you mustn't think of me as a sour old misanthropist. No genuine doctor can be. To continue bending over them in their sickness, all I've needed is to know they were in pain and despair, that they were appealing to me because they had no one else to help them in their distress."

"You admit, at least, that we can do something then, both doctors and priests, to help them?" exclaimed the priest. He seized on the word "help" with such avidity and insatiable hope that Dr. Delpuech's voice became gentler still.

"Yes, of course we can do something, with the help of sympathy and care, of patience and understanding. Only, it's a very tough assignment. You and I belong to a race where the flesh weighs on us more heavily than the soul—we must use all the props we can, neglect nothing, let nothing be wasted. The smallest progress achieved is an immense victory in itself, for it makes the second small advance less difficult—the first steps on the way to a cure have been taken. It's wise to choose fairly limited objectives at first, where you can at least be hopeful of victory. Nothing's so bad as a defeat in the early days."

Small advances, limited objectives—perhaps there was something in it after all, something to be given a trial. When I went to bed that night, my decision to write to Henri and have myself hastily summoned back to Paris became far less firm. As always, I began to waver and curse my weakmindedness, and when I eventually went to sleep the conflict was still far from completely resolved. But perhaps I felt somehow instinctively that after all I should be wise to wait a few more days before writing so defeatist a letter.

Chapter Five

March 10–11

ABOUT A WEEK later I again had occasion to cross the vast snowy fogbound plateau that brought me to the Lespinats farm. But this time I had worked out my route on the map, and was able without hesitation to take the left-hand road on reaching the crossroads of Saint-Géraud. At the edge of the plateau, the road plunged down into a narrow bleak-looking valley. I passed a few anonymous hamlets with smoke coming from two or three houses and some roofless ruined shacks slowly crumbling between dark holly and scrub.

I must be somewhere near my destination. An urchin in galoshes, walking on the lower side of the road where it was least slippery, directed me to a lane which would bring me out at the farm I was seeking.

Since setting off, I had been impatient to discover the reason for my being called out to such a distant spot. Félicie had tried to argue on the telephone, in an attempt to spare me the journey, but the voice had insisted. They must have the new doctor from Paris who was acting as locum for Dr. Delpuech, to see a lad who was very ill in the hamlet of Louradou, near

Montagut. In a way I found this insistence flattering—my fame had evidently spread well beyond the confines of Peyrac.

I found the farm, drank some coffee, exchanged a few polite remarks with the family, and then asked to see the patient. They had not exaggerated on the telephone. I found a youth of seventeen in an alarming condition.

When I expressed surprise that they had not called me in before, the parents looked vague and assumed that expression of abrupt vacancy typical of the countryman who is not going to give anything away: they didn't know, they never imagined it was so serious. Not relying on securing any further help from the family, I started questioning the boy himself. What he told me sounded rather like a pleurisy in the lower left lung: pain, breathlessness, and all the usual symptoms. I made a complete examination, and decided with a certain satisfaction that it was not pleurisy after all, but a rheumatoid pericarditis. With this particular patient it was a difficult diagnosis to make, but certainly I was having great luck with my serious cases. While I was dresser in a cardiac ward, my interne was preparing a thesis on pericarditis of a pseudo-pleuritic form, so I had had exceptional opportunities for auscultating and examining several such cases.

Bursting with the joy of discovery, I was about to give the family my diagnosis—how disappointing, I thought, that they could not appreciate its merits to the full—when I noticed a bottle of medicine in the bottom of the drawer of the table by the bed as I was putting back the thermometer there. Ordinary cough mixture would not have struck me specially, but the bottle contained calcium chloride, too unusual a drug to have been bought directly at the chemist's. There must have been a doctor there before me to have prescribed it; and from the geographical position of the farm I decided that this doctor, whose visit and prescription had been hidden from me, could only be Bonnafy.

The excitement I got from my fine diagnosis was instantly increased threefold, for several reasons. First, in view of professional etiquette I could ask them to call in Bonnafy with me, thereby gaining a witness fully competent to appreciate my discovery. Secondly, I had not forgotten Bonnafy's mortifying little comment which suggested that the people at Lespinats would not have wanted to see me instead of him, unless the case was obviously not serious. Thirdly, his having prescribed calcium chloride indicated that my colleague had probably diagnosed pleurisy rather than pericarditis. If it had not been for my interne's thesis I might well have made the same mistake, but I felt no obligation to confess this to Bonnafy.

I closed the drawer containing the informative bottle, and said firmly, showing I did not mean to be taken in, "You've had a doctor here before me."

The parents tried to look more vacant than ever.

"Yes, we have," the father admitted in the end. "But we didn't have any confidence in him, you see. It was quite obvious he'd never pull our Marcel out of this. So we were worried, you see, and we saw you at the Café Albignac. We were at the Rouquerolle wedding, you see. We're cousins of theirs."

"You ought to have told me beforehand. Professional rules do not allow me to see a patient who is already being treated by another doctor."

"Oh, of course," said the man at once, hoping to stifle my scruples. "We'll give you all you ask if you can cure our Marcel. Just look at our position: he's already doing a man's work, you see, and he's as good as an extra farm hand for me."

Turning towards his wife, he added: "I told you so, didn't I? It's no use trying to get him treated cheap."

Treated cheap—that certainly did not sound like Bonnafy. Very much surprised, I asked: "Well, who's seen your son till now, then?"

"Ricaud," said the man with a note of scorn in his voice. I noticed that he did not even say "Doctor Ricaud." "Yes, of course," he went on, "I'd have done better to speak to you at once, but then, you see, he's quite near us, he is, and with his bicycle he doesn't have to be paid traveling expenses."

I had completely forgotten the existence of Ricaud, mentioned by Bonnafy during our conversation coming back from the Lespinats farm. I had a sudden mental picture of him, as described by Bonnafy, pedaling along on the cycle, with the helmet over his head and the cardboard shield protecting his hands. I was glad to have said nothing which could do any harm to this poor creature. I even felt called, in elementary charity, to rescue him from the worst consequences of this affair.

I asked to see his prescriptions. The mother took two of them out of a drawer in the cupboard. They were certainly appropriate to a case of pleurisy. The parents were watching me eagerly; I pretended to examine carefully the make-up of the prescriptions before declaring: "Good, just what I'd have prescribed myself. Briefly, it's a serious case, but there's been no time wasted so far. However, I cannot accept your son as a patient till I have spoken to Dr. Ricaud, who has already been treating the illness. It is quite essential that we should see him together."

My tone was such as to indicate that I was not leaving them any choice in the matter. The parents looked at each other. They dared not talk in front of me, but I could almost see them mentally engaged on the same calculations: on the one hand they would have their son well looked after and soon cured, and he could again do a man's work and save them the expense of an extra hand, but they might have two doctors to pay instead of one. They must have thought simultaneously at this point that Ricaud after all would not cost them very much money—and as I looked at my watch, they came to a decision. "Since you say it's got to be like that," said the father, looking resigned, "well, that's how it's got to be."

Perhaps Ricaud would be at home now, I thought. I suggested going to see him, and bringing him back with me right away if he happened to be free. "Free," said the man, "of course you'll find him there *and* free; precious few patients *he's* got to take him out. With your car it won't take you a quarter of an hour to get to Montagut."

Behind the blue sign with its big white letters half worn away by rust, which indicated that we were entering Montagut, the road made some attempt to become a proper street, starting from a few abandoned shells of houses with broken doors and boarded-up windows. Further on, a building with a projecting gable roof narrowed the street by a good third. Then the houses spread out to form a small square, around which in doleful alignment stood the usual local centers: the inn, the general store, the post office—tobacconist, the village school, and the church. A few yards beyond, muddy roads opened up on both sides, bounded by crumbling walls and brambles; they soon lost themselves in snow-covered tracks through shivering fields. Montagut was really only a big village, hardly even that. Adding to it the deserted plateau, the almost ruined hamlets and the few little farms I had seen on my way, I found myself wondering where the doctor who had chosen this forlorn corner to practise could expect to find a sufficiency of patients to make a living.

I drove slowly, inspecting the house fronts. The street was deserted, the doors closed. Outside the houses all life seemed to be petrified by the cold. I found nobody from whom I could ask my way, but I felt I was probably being watched from behind a good many curtains.

I was nearly coming out of the village when I saw a plate which looked like a doctor's on the door of a house, poor and mean in appearance like all the others. On a small black board some local hack painter had done his best with a brush full of white paint (it probably served him for funeral inscriptions as well), and I read: *Dr. Antoine Ricaud, Office Hours 1-3 p.m.*

I rang. A very young woman in a gray linen overall, obviously the doctor's wife, came to open the door. Since coming to Peyrac, I had scarcely looked at a woman as such. I could not help observing my colleague's wife with some curiosity. I found her rather insignificant, one of those women you do not really notice or anyhow forget immediately afterwards. She had mousey hair parted in the middle, modestly tied in a bun at the back of her neck. Her eyes were blue, and she had thin frail shoulders which contrasted with the thickness of her waist—for she was obviously in an advanced stage of pregnancy. The overalls were too tight for her, and underneath them I could see a severe black dress of coarse wool. When she opened the door to me, she seemed embarrassed to be caught in her working clothes. I told her who I was and asked to see Dr. Ricaud. She gave me an anxious look, hesitated for a few seconds, and then, faced by this unexpected call, replied in a formal and colorless voice, as if she were only the maid: "Will you please come into the waiting room? Dr. Ricaud has just returned from his rounds. He will be able to see you almost at once."

She kept a hand on the door as she spoke; it was a small hand, but red and chapped and scored with black lines. She was clenching it, I noticed, so as to hide her trembling.

I went in. On the way down the tiled corridor, bare and gloomy, I noticed the cycle with the shields on its handlebars; near it was a small coat-rack in imitation bamboo, where a windbreaker was hanging, and also the home-knitted helmet.

The room where the young woman took me was icy. I looked round the row of odd chairs against the wall, the plaster on which had been deeply marked by the backs of the chairs. In the center of the room there was a hideous pedestal table of the Louis-Philippe period. In a corner was a wooden fireplace, which some zealous artisan, perhaps the man who had done the lettering on the doctor's plate, had tried to paint in a crude imitation of marble.

To try to give the room a look of comparative prosperity, some new curtains of a cheap material had been put on the room's only window. On the pedestal table there was also a cheap lace cloth, and all the furniture shone with much polishing. It was perhaps the need to keep up appearances, to make things look nice with as little expense as possible, which made the total effect of poverty seem even more pathetic.

The door opened, and Dr. Ricaud came towards me holding out his hand. He was a thin-faced young man of medium height, whose anxiety to appear at ease was immediately obvious, and unconvincing. "It's really awfully lucky that I'm here," he said as we shook hands: "I was only just stopping in before continuing my round. Please come into my office, won't you?"

Thanks to a small cast-iron stove, the office was at least warm. But to furnish it, my colleague had certainly been rummaging in the same second-hand dealer's, or family attic, as when he had furnished his waiting room. The desk-table, the armchairs, the bookcase, were in several different styles, and the only thing they all had in common, apart from the perfect polish with which they all shone, was ugliness. A little glass cupboard, imitation Henri II, had been white-enameled to serve as an instrument cupboard. On the walls were some amateurish *passepartout* pictures sent out by a firm making pharmaceutical products. In front of the window was a table,

also white-enameled, with a microscope on it and some med[i]-
cine bottles. Together with the glass cupboard, it barely suc[-]
ceeded in giving this motley collection something of the re[-]
assuring appearance of a doctor's office.

Walking round to his armchair, Ricaud offered me the chai[r]
where his patients, I guessed, would normally sit. When h[e]
was seated, I had a better view of his face. His cheeks wer[e]
thin, and his complexion was sallow. He looked extremel[y]
young; a big crack in his plump lips accentuated their slightl[y]
childish appearance, but at each corner of the mouth ther[e]
were sharp vertical lines which made this face, otherwise s[o]
boyish, seem disconcertingly serious and even bitter. His eye[s]
had a suggestion of deep sadness and also, I fancied, of anxiet[y]

He had taken up a reflex hammer which was lying on hi[s]
desk, and he now began fiddling nervously with it. He gave [a]
little cough, as if about to speak, but said nothing. He wa[s]
plainly afraid of betraying too much uneasiness by asking th[e]
reason for my call.

A common custom among doctors is to arrange the lamp[-]
shade in his office so that it only lights up the place where th[e]
patient is sitting; he can thus observe the patient better, whil[e]
remaining himself in the half-darkness. Ricaud, however, in[-]
stead of following this useful precaution, had clumsily place[d]
himself right under the light—so that I could not help observ[-]
ing his face even more closely than before. It was just a[s]
Bonnafy had described it, sensitive, delicate, shy. I could wel[l]
imagine how guileless and helpless he would look to these hard[-]
bitten farmers; no wonder they laughed at him and tormente[d]
him.

I myself, like Bonnafy, felt full of pity for this youth, for hi[s]
transparent act of being the overworked doctor. I cast around
in vain for some way of explaining my visit which would no[t]
be too humiliating. The silence seemed likely to extend itsel[f]
indefinitely, which would clearly be painful and embarrassing
for us both. To break the ice I finally said, "I've been called
to the Chanuts at Louradou to see the son. I went there withou[t]
knowing you were looking after him. I've come to apologize."

Ricaud started uncontrollably, and then affected extreme
unconcern. "Doesn't matter," he declared with a shrug, as if

he loss of one patient, in the course of a busy day like this, were really of very little importance.

Probably guessing, however, that his face would betray him, he bent over the desk and began doodling on the blotting paper. I could only see his narrow shoulders and the thin wrists emerging from threadbare sleeves. He seemed to have suddenly slumped forward in the chair.

Eventually he raised his head, and asked, still trying to sound indifferent: "How is the boy today?"

I started on a different tack, answering his question with another: "When did you last see him?"

He pretended to think hard, as if he were swamped with calls. "Let's see, it must have been ... yes, I think it was the day before yesterday, in the morning. He was just starting a pleurisy at the base of the left lung. I don't like looking as if I'm making too many calls. These farmers are so damned suspicious, you never know the best way to deal with them. I asked them to call me at once if anything went wrong. But I was meaning to drop in there this evening," he added hastily.

He could not maintain any longer the pretense of casualness. After a moment's further hesitation, without trying now to keep the anxiety out of his voice, he finally asked: "Was there some change in his condition since then?"

This time I had no escape channel.

"From your prescriptions," I answered, "I realize that you thought it was pleurisy of the left lung; and I'm sure that's what it must have looked like two days ago. But in the last two days the picture has changed somewhat. It's not pleurisy at all, it's quite certainly rheumatoid pericarditis."

Ricaud first of all looked at me as if he had not really grasped what I said. Then he repeated in a stupefied voice: "Pericarditis? Are you sure?"

He pulled a handkerchief mechanically from his pocket, and wiped his brow, then his hands. He was pale as a ghost, and stared at me vacantly as if unable to focus.

I hastened to reassure him: "Oh yes, I was damned lucky with that diagnosis. I did six months as dresser in a ward for cardiac cases, and if my interne hadn't been writing his thesis on certain forms of pericarditis which look like pleurisy, I'd have overlooked that possibility just as you did. Naturally, as

111

soon as I knew you'd already seen the patient, I made it quite clear to the family that we should now have to cooperate in our treatment—and in fact I've come to fetch you now, if you're agreeable."

He looked so utterly disheartened that I felt like going over and slapping him on the back, saying: "Come on, old man, don't take it so hard." It was the sort of thing I might have said to one of my friends at the university who had failed some minor exam. But when I saw the distress in Antoine Ricaud's eyes, I dared not treat things so lightly, and could find nothing to say. I guessed obscurely that he felt this whole affair not as a minor lapse but as an element in some stark tragedy involving his whole life. I was relieved when he at last rose and said: "All right, let's go now, if you think we should."

A ring on the front-door bell made him pause. He glanced in the mirror and must have noticed how disheveled he looked, the untidiness of his hair and tie. He passed his hands through the hair as if to brush it, straightened his tie, and tried to assume a mask of professional composure once more. With the air of one swamped with work, he declared: "Never a moment's peace. I only hope it's not an emergency case."

His wife could be heard opening the front door and talking to whoever was outside it. An indistinct female voice answered, then the door was closed and a pair of clogs could be heard clumping down the corridor.

"Ah," said Ricaud, "only for the dispensary luckily. There aren't any druggists nearer than Farlat, so I've opened a little dispensary here to help the villagers. As soon as the customer's gone, I'll let my wife know that we're just going out."

Almost at once the sound of the clogs could be heard going back up the corridor, and then on the pavement. Ricaud at once opened the door and called out "Marie!"

"Yes, Antoine." Mme. Ricaud came in, wearing the black woollen dress which I had seen under her overalls—these she had now taken off. Ricaud took her hand with a gentle, affectionate gesture and brought her over to me.

"So sorry, darling. I ought to have called you at once, but we got talking somehow and I forgot. Dr. Nérac happened to see young Chanut, and we're going off there to examine him, apparently the parents would like it."

112

He was again talking casually, as if about some very ordinary visit. I could see that his intention, achieved by a stern self-control, was to avoid alarming his wife. His face, so puckered up and unhappy a few minutes before, lit up suddenly in a smile of wonderful contentment. It suddenly made his light-heartedness seem more than a gallant "act"; this was a sincere and rather touching expression of the love he felt for his wife.

"All right, Antoine dear," said Mme. Ricaud, and then shook hands with me, saying she was pleased to have met me, hoped I would come again one day, not on business. She looked back at her husband, and her look was so charged with tenderness, so receptive and sensitive to all that concerned this poor husband of hers, that despite his efforts I felt fairly sure she would never be entirely taken in by his act, nor was so now.

Ricaud put on his cycling clothes. In this rig I found him even more ludicrous than he had seemed in Bonnafy's description. The thick woollen balaclava helmet, the huge wind-breaker, the big lined gauntlets, all gave him a stiff, loutish look; but underneath he wore tight breeches and stockings on those skinny thighs and calves. A big bear from the waist up-wards—and below the thin legs of a bird.

It was dark when we left. The main road, still deserted and icy, was lighted up by three pitiful street lamps, one at each end of the village and the third towards the middle, in front of the little square. Mme. Ricaud came outside to see us off, but her husband made her go in again straight away because of the cold.

I let the engine run a bit to warm it up. Sitting by my side, Ricaud kept silent. He had dug his hands hard into the pockets of his wind-cheater and was listening to the friendly whir of the engine turning over. The car started up smoothly and si-ently, and he murmured, almost to himself: "It's a lot better than my bicycle."

Going through the village I kept my lights dimmed; but when I reached the last houses, after the third street lamp, I wanted to put the headlights full on. As I was not fully ac-customed to the car's rather old-fashioned electrical system I made a mistake, pulled the wrong knob, and put all the lights right out. Suddenly we could not see a yard ahead of us. There was nothing ahead but a darkness so complete and palpable

that it felt like a vast black wall that we were about to bum
into—like blind men without a guide. I had to stop the ca
You could hear the wind whistling against the windows, ar
I imagined other pitch-black nights when Ricaud, called o
to a patient's home, having passed the third street lamp mu
have hesitated on the brink before riding onwards into th
night. Suddenly I saw him in quite a different perspective, th
absurd puppet-like figure huddled in balaclava and win
breaker, bent over the handlebars, his eyes bloodshot wi
the wind, peering anxiously ahead in the glimmer of the po
little bicycle lamp, seeking for some forlorn farm among th
dark woods and icy streams.

Then the road, picked out once more by the headlight
emerged as a thin black track amidst a moon-white expanse
snow. We set off again, smoothly and easily, as if gliding dow
some endless gentle slope.

Chanut and his wife had not even a word of polite greetir
to spare for Ricaud. I might just as well have brought alor
with me some third-class hospital orderly without any qualific
tions or skill whatever.

Ricaud went straight up to the patient's bed. Since his la
visit there was obviously such a marked deterioration in th
boy's condition that I could guess Ricaud was finding it har
to hide his alarm. The parents watched him with hostile look

Seeing him in his present state, I was afraid he might ever
in an excess of honesty, be clumsy enough to admit his mistal
in diagnosis. The Chanuts were so obviously prejudiced again
him that they would never think of trying to understand c
excuse him. To prevent this happening, I began the examin
tion at once, making a point of continually and obtrusive
asking his views, "Don't you think so, Doctor? You agree, Do
tor?" and so on. I also questioned him about the previor
treatment he had given, and nodded approvingly when I hear
what it was. Gradually the Chanuts' scowling faces began t
relax. When we had completed our joint examination, in orde
to observe professional ceremony to the letter, I asked with a
due solemnity if there was anywhere private where we coul
consult together on the future treatment to be followed.

Mme. Chanut took us into the room reserved for importar
visitors, and brought in a kerosene lamp. Then she left us o

r own, by a best bed covered with a fine lace quilt, and in
ont of a round table with an equally elaborate tablecloth.
ter looking at the mantelpiece with its profusion of multi-
lored glass and cups and plaster statues, probably won from
eepstakes or stalls in the local fairs, I turned back, to observe
at Ricaud had dropped wearily into a chair.

"Keep your chin up," I said, "you can see the family are
eling happier already."

"Oh to hell with the family," he muttered; and then in a
ghtly louder voice went on, "That's the state I'm in at the
oment. It's only the patient I'm thinking about. I really don't
ow what it's best to do. I don't like coming without being
lled; they're incredible misers, they'd almost throw me out.
hen I feel a case may get worse if I don't call often enough,
l be quite ready to come without charge—but I daren't even
ggest it, they'd never understand my motives. For instance,
u know my wife started studying Medicine?"

I nodded.

"Well, with her I tried to start a sort of pre-natal clinic, free,
r nursing mothers; nobody came. They're so suspicious they
ust certainly have thought I was trying to swindle them in
me way or other."

"Possibly," I suggested, "people in these parts don't see
ow there can really be much value in anything that's given
vay free."

"I dare say you're right," he admitted. "Anyhow that's the
rrible thing about this pericarditis. I ought to have had the
urage to face the father instead of waiting. I could perhaps
ive corrected my diagnosis, and the boy would have been on
licylate two days ago. If there are complications now, it will
e my fault, and I'll never be able to forgive myself. I don't
now what I'll do, honestly I think I'll give up Medicine al-
gether. There must be jobs where you can wait for someone
ask for your services without becoming a criminal."

"Don't be silly," I said, "you can't know everything, and
ery doctor makes mistakes sometimes." But he was not to be
mforted, and abruptly raising his head he asked me with
eat seriousness: "Does it ever happen to you too, when you're
sponsible for a serious case, that you go several nights without
eep or else you keep waking up with a start and thinking

115

you've overlooked something or made some fatal mistak
Sometimes I have to get out of bed straight away and che
up in my textbooks. It's awful to feel yourself so alone, throv
so completely on your own resources, when six months befo
you were still a student and there was always somebody clc
at hand in the hospital to be asked for help or advice. A
suddenly everything changes. It's a different sort of Medici
altogether—the signs and symptoms are all erratic, the strugg
is always in the dark, and most of the results are bitterly d
couraging. I feel I really don't know anything any more,
don't understand a single thing of what goes on in all the
bodies. I suppose you never feel anything like that?"

He looked at me with a pathetic appeal for reassurance, ar
I answered: "Of course I do, old man. I often feel just tha
It did not seem worth telling him at this stage that I was (
my first job as locum, that most of the patients I had seen sin
my arrival were very ordinary cases, and that in consequen
I had so far had little opportunity to commit blunders.

I had taken out my fountain pen and prescription pad. C
the top sheet I wrote down the ritual opening: "Recommenc
tions from Drs. Nérac and Ricaud." Then I stopped to as
"Well, Antoine, what are we going to give him?"

It was on a sudden impulse that I called him Antoine.
remembered from my first weeks at the university how mu
I had valued any sign of friendship, as when someone like Pa
Chavasse, so popular with everyone, had first called me Jea
My extremely brief acquaintance with Ricaud scarcely justifi
such familiarity, but I had found him so lonely and unsu
that I hoped this use of his Christian name might help to bre
down his discouragement. The effect was even more than
had expected. Instead of answering my question, he sai
"Thank you for that ... Jean, isn't it?" he added shyly.

He continued: "I must seem pretty pathetic to you goir
on like this. But if only you knew how dreadful it can be to I
always alone, without a single friend, or even a neutral,
listen to you every now and then. You can't imagine how goc
it is to hear you calling me by my Christian name all of a su
den, just like that. It takes me right back to medical scho
when I could talk frankly to people who spoke the same la
guage, who had the same sort of ideas and interests and hop(

116

ist eight months ago—and I never realized then what a marvelous privilege it was, being able to do just that."

"And here you're on your own," I put in gently, almost embarrassed by the success of my "treatment."

"Completely. Utter loneliness, enough to drive one mad, or worse than the isolation of a missionary among savages in the jungle. At least he knows what to expect when he goes out there. But I, just because I don't come from the mountains, because I happen to have lived most of my life in a town—they treat me round here not only as a foreigner but practically as an enemy as well. Yet I swear to you that I give them the best care I'm capable of, that I'm damned keen on my job. But I have to hold myself in and keep my mouth tight shut so as not to show how humiliated and angry I'm feeling. I can't even confide in my wife, I so much want to spare her all I can. I try not to let her see just how miserable these damned clodhoppers make me."

As he was speaking, he became quite excited, and I made a sign to him not to talk so loud—the Chanuts might well be listening at the door. He stopped abruptly, and then said, in a much evener tone: "How much salicylate should I give him, do you think?"

We discussed doses. To fortify his prestige, we kept the calcium chloride and some other parts of his treatment which would still prove useful. When we had both signed the prescription I called in the parents. I explained that we had arrived jointly at the necessary decisions, but that I was leaving their application to my colleague. I myself would only call again (I told them) if Dr. Ricaud should deem it necessary, but I felt sure, of course, that everything would be quite satisfactory.

In the car Ricaud stayed silent for some while, watching the road flash by. Then he turned to me, and said gravely: "You've been very kind about this business, Jean."

I decided to ignore the solemnity behind this commonplace remark. "Nonsense," I said, "anyone else would have done just the same."

"No they would not. You don't know my so-called colleagues."

"No, Antoine; but I do at least know Bonnafy, and he spoke very nicely about you. I'm quite sure he'd have helped you out too."

"Possibly. Or at least he'd have stayed neutral, which wou[ld] have been something. He hasn't much competition to fe[ar] from me, apart from fees; and he knows that almost the on[ly] patients I have pay me very little and very irregularly, or el[se] don't pay at all. I went to see him when I first got here, and [I] felt then that he was anxious to help me. On that day he ga[ve] me quite a lot of good advice about the psychology of count[ry] people—which I'd have done well to follow."

"I suppose like me you'd hardly ever set foot in the count[ry] before? Perhaps I ought to tell you now that I've only ju[st] come here, and that this locum job is the first I've ever don[e]. Old Dr. Delpuech, for whom I'm working while he's ill, h[as] already told me how important it is to study country psycholog[y] and what a life's work it is. All of which makes it pretty diffic[ult] for a doctor who's only just qualified and isn't very sure [of] himself anyhow."

"Bonnafy might have been able to help me," he went on; [I] could feel that he was rather sorry for me. Only, besides t[he] advice he suggested my sending him patients for X-ray or ultr[a] violet treatment, so as to keep his apparatus in use, and [to] call him in over difficult cases. I was to get my cut, of cours[e]. He explained this form of collaboration to me quite calm[ly] as something completely natural. I suppose I'm very naive, b[ut] I could hardly believe my ears, and I came away from him rea[lly] shocked. As I didn't study medicine just to become a procur[er] of patients for others, I've made no efforts to see him again."

This side of the story Bonnafy, of course, had not mention[ed] to me. But I remembered something else he had told me abo[ut] Ricaud, and asked, to satisfy my curiosity: "How about t[he] Farlat doctor, what happened there? I gathered from Bonna[fy] you aren't on too good terms with him."

Ricaud burst out at once, almost painfully grateful to find [a] sympathetic listener: "Not on good terms, Jean—that's [an] understatement. That bastard Chassagnon is the main reas[on] why I got off on the wrong foot when I first came here. But [to] explain that, I'd better give you a few more details about [my] background, if you don't mind hearing them."

I said I didn't.

"Well then," he began, "my father was killed in the war, a[nd] mother didn't find it easy to pay for me at the university."

"Same with me," I put in, to show understanding.

"I got married in my fourth year, having met Marie, my
fe, at the Medical School—she was a year behind me. . . ."

"Just like me and Marianne," I felt like saying, but pulled
yself up in time, while Ricaud went on with his story:

"My father-in-law died almost immediately after the wedding
d as Marie was the eldest of four children and wanted to be
le to help her mother, I was anxious to get qualified as quickly
possible and find a good country practice directly. I'd done
y military service."

"Why not a city practice," I asked, "seeing you were used to
y life?"

"Much too risky, takes years before you start to make a bare
ing. Remember, I had practically no capital to start me off.
followed the vacancies advertised in the medical journals,
t they were mostly practices to be bought, always far too
pensive for me. One day I saw a very tempting ad: 'Village
the Cantal, at present without medical practitioner, offers
tractive position to energetic young doctor, accommodation
ovided, possibilities for dispensary.' I got in touch with the
ayor who promised me a fine house and that the village would
y for all necessary repairs. He assured me I'd be the only
octor within a radius of ten miles, and complained how iso-
ed his villagers were from the point of view of health."

"Quite an attractive prospect," I admitted, "for an energetic
ung doctor."

"Took me in all right," said Ricaud with a sad nod of his
ad. "I imagined a fine active life, full of interesting useful
ork, while Marie would be kept busy looking after the dis-
nsary, which we could open because there was no qualified
armacist at all near. She was already pregnant, and when
r baby was born it would be nearly spring. I thought how
od the mountain air would be for the baby. It wouldn't grow
a sickly stunted specimen from the city like its father. . . .
," he concluded, doubtless weighing up once more all the
sasters born of that decision, "I accepted the post."

"And when you'd started here?"

"Oh, I understood right away why the village got me to
me. Very simple really. Farlat, in the valley, where Chas-
gnon is the big political boss, is mainly socialist in politics,

119

while Montagut and the mountain villages usually vote co
munist. But Dr. C. curries favor very successfully and give
lot of free medical attention to prospective voters, so t
Mayor of Montagut was beginning to find him rather dang
ous. By settling me here he hoped to remove part of Dr. C
medico-political influence. Of course the good doctor sm
out this maneuver immediately. In all innocence I paid him
courtesy call when I arrived. He felt out my political leanin
quite unobtrusively you know, and when I told him I had
any, which was the exact truth, he thought I was trying to p
off the Mayor of Montagut against him. Our private w
started at once—I can assure you he left no dirty stone u
turned."

"But surely," I commented, "you had at least gotten t
parish council on your side, and all the local radicals?"

"I can see," remarked Ricaud with a wry smile, "that y
haven't yet got the feel of parish-pump politics. Of course
ought to have had the radicals for me. Only they made a de
with Dr. C. behind my back. It's true that I can't really co
plain, seeing I gave them the chance myself."

"How do you mean?" I asked.

"Oh, very simple again. Because of an old man who di
of a strangulated hernia. Have you by any chance been call
out yet to an old man's bedside?"

"Oh yes," I grimaced. "The second day I got here. I was ask
if I could expedite slightly his departure for the cemeter

"Well then, you know the difference made by the famil
between a patient who's some use on the farm and a patie
who'd be no loss. Perhaps I'll get used to it in time, but at pr
ent I'm plain shocked and disgusted at the idea of letting
invalid or an old man die without any care at all, just becau
he's no longer useful. At first I must have been lucky, the c
people I saw were the type who just snuff quietly out, like
lamp which has run out of oil. You know, tired heart, nothi
much to be done, and above all nothing expensive in the w
of medicine. That's the main thing in the eyes of the fami
who are really only calling in a doctor at all to show the neig
bors they know what's proper. Because of my modest fees,
was much appreciated as medical attendant for these last rite
till the day I came on an old man dying not of mere senility b

of a strangulated hernia. I had to watch an actual murder, and was powerless to do anything. He was a strong old man, and his heart was still solid, so it only needed the classical operation, not at all dangerous, and a week afterwards he'd have been on his feet again—but his wife and daughter refused point blank to let it be done."

"Didn't the old man himself have anything to say?" I asked, thinking of the helpless old man I had seen so recently. "Did he make no attempt to look after his own interests?"

"Well apparently what *he* was looking after was the family's financial interests. From his bed he lay in, you might say, on all our discussions, listened to all my tempers and threats without saying anything but: 'That'll cost a lot of money, that will!'"

"I suppose he knew they'd refuse, and decided it wasn't worth putting up a fight."

"That was almost the worst thing about it, seeing him with that pathetic air of complete resignation. I threatened the two women with the police, I told them their neighbors would despise them forever and they'd be smitten with terrible remorse in their own consciences. They told me in reply, with quite placid cynicism, that neither the police nor their neighbors would pay the hospital charges in their place, and they had no remorse at all because nobody in these parts had ever heard of an old man like that having an operation. In his bed the old man himself went on muttering even in his delirium: 'That'll cost a lot of money.' I watched peritonitis setting in, and then hiccoughs and green vomit, then blackish vomit—which no one even bothered to wipe away. If I'd had a car, I really believe I'd have knocked the two women down and taken the old man off myself. The first few days I tried to reduce the hernia by hand. I used all the old medical methods, quite in vain."

"How long did he take to die?"

"Five days, and most of that time I felt I was almost going crazy. At the end I was so hopping mad I wanted at any price to create a scandal, to stir up the feeling of the village, to get an inquest held and at least frighten those two heartless bitches. I refused to sign the death certificate. After that I waited for the police."

"Who did not appear?"

"Quite right; I'm still waiting for them. The Mayor o
Montagut was most annoyed, and the only thing he could thin
of to get the certificate signed was to go and find Dr. C. a
Farlat. That gentleman received him very cordially, pointing
out to him how dangerous it was to stir up unnecessary compe
tition for respected local inhabitants by bringing in dangerou
young agitators from other parts of the country. To help hi
fellow-countryman the mayor (even when politics seemed t
separate them, a real understanding could always be established
though) Dr. C. signed the death certificate. After that the
talked quite a lot, and in exchange for his most considerat
action, the old fox obtained substantial support for the nex
election, plus a formal promise that the parish of Montagu
would no longer give me work."

"But if people were satisfied with you, what could they do?

"Oh, they had plenty of allies. I suppose they are always to b
found in such cases. First of all the two Farlat pharmacists wer
losing customers because of my little dispensary. I know the
sneer with pitying contempt whenever they hear my nam
mentioned, as if I were likely to sell rat-poison for bicarbonat
of soda. Besides them, Dr. C. got the postman as his agent fo
hostile propaganda. The postman, you see, no longer got hi
tips for drugs he brought from Farlat to the people here—s
he went from farm to farm telling them how I couldn't eve
bring a cow to calf, which after all is quite true. The postma
also spread around that I was a shark who wanted to stop ol
men dying in their ancestral beds after a long laborious life
He said I wanted them operated on, quite unnecessarily, a
great expense. He had no trouble in getting a hearing."

We were nearing Montagut again by now. In an icy solitud
that might have been the end of the world, the headlights li
up a road eaten into on both sides by the fresh snow of th
ditches. In the ascent before we came to the village, the power
ful car scarcely slowed down at all, but Antoine Ricaud mus
have been thinking of other occasions when he had come bac
by night to his house.

"It might have saved my face a bit," he said, perhaps guessing
my thoughts, "if I'd only had a little car instead of my bike
All my enthusiasm wouldn't have ended up in chilblains and
lumbago. But a doctor on a bicycle in this weather, a docto

lmost weeping with cold when he arrives—it doesn't make a ood impression. My patients are right to distrust me, seeing ne dismount from the bicycle, frozen and sniveling, with hick fingers and a blue nose, and my brain pretty well paralyzed t the same time. Only my legs are still warm enough to function properly. But even that's a handicap, for everyone sees I aven't exactly the style of a champion cyclist. When I come to . hill that's at all steep—even if the local urchins climb it easily n old wrecks of machines—I usually have to get off half way up. No, I haven't even got legs which can pedal properly. That eally finished me in their estimations."

The first street lamp of Montagut now loomed up about two undred yards away, and Antoine asked me to put him down here without going any further. I guessed that he would not vant the noise of the car to make his return known to the vhole village.

I saw him hurrying along, hunching his back beneath the ussault of the bitter wind. When he reached the lamp, he urned and gave me a friendly wave of his arm, before disuppearing into the shadows beyond. I could imagine him now entering a village that might have been hermetically sealed o the world. I could picture him like a felon shunning any faint gleams of light that might fall from the dirty frosted-over vindows; each window, framed in its hostile wall, would recall to him the malice of human beings. Traveling the long nomeward road, worn down by his vain efforts and endless .etbacks, how he must long to reach his resting place safely, ike some hunted animal dragging itself to its lair after the orments of the day. Pretending to his wife that he had urgent vork to do, he would no doubt shut himself up in his office, .here to brood bitterly on the long series of defeats which had .hattered his hopes of the early days, transforming them inexorably within a few months into the immense and abject ailure of the present.

At Montagut, with poor Antoine, I could perhaps afford to olay the great specialist; but after having left him at the enrance to his village, I had to stop at a certain farm on the oad back to Peyrac, to see a ten-year-old boy with broncho-

pneumonia. I still felt distinctly worried and puzzled when
left him.

Dr. Delpuech being ill, it was Lucien who had been called
in to see the boy at the height of his fever twelve days ago
When I arrived at Peyrac, Lucien had handed over this patien
practically out of danger. But since then something must hav
gone wrong, for the boy was still exhausted and feverish. Thi
particular evening there was a development which I found
even more puzzling and disturbing: an eruption of thousand
of small white spots, like so many pinheads, had suddenly ap
peared all over his body.

As soon as I got back, I went to Dr. Delpuech's library and
went through the volumes on pediatry. What I found there di
not remove my perplexity. Not wishing to tire the old doctor
I decided to ring up Lucien, who after all had already seen th
boy, and secure the benefit of his wider experience.

He had only just come back, and was finishing eating ;
hurried meal; after this he had to go out again immediately t
another case. I told him about the boy, and he listened to m
without interrupting. When I had finished, he declared in hi
usual placid voice: "Your patient has a purulent pleurisy.

"Is it possible?" I protested. "And how exactly do you mak
that out?"

But Lucien replied calmly, ignoring my irony: "That erup
tion on the twelfth day is a sure sign. Stick a needle betweer
his ribs, and you'll see!" He hesitated a moment, and then added
before hanging up: "I've got to be round that way myself to
morrow morning. If you like, Jean, I'll come in to look at the
boy with you."

Next morning we set off in his car, and for most of the way
talked shop about other patients. When we were almost at the
house with my ten-year-old boy, I ventured to ask Lucien:
"By the way, how about your sure sign of purulent pleurisy.
You may be right, but I can't think where you got it from.]
went through all the relevant authorities last night after I'd
spoken to you, and I couldn't find anything at all about it."

"I'm not surprised," he answered with complete assurance.
"You'll not find a written description of it anywhere. It's a
symptom Dr. Delpuech taught me."

"Oh well, in *that* case," I said with mock conviction, "there's

othing to worry about, all I've got to do is stick the needle in
t once."

Lucien turned his head towards me for a moment, with a
look which made me feel slightly ashamed of my sarcasm. I
thought he was going to say something, but he returned his eyes
to the road, and I found we had reached the house. The boy's
mother must have been on the lookout for my coming, for she
was waiting on the doorstep with a shawl over her shoulders.
We got out of the car, and Lucien muttered to me under his
breath: "No need to ask what sort of night the boy had. Look
t her face."

She opened the door for us, and I explained, to save my dignity: "Something's wrong with my car, so Dr. Clément was
kind enough to drive me here, and then, of course, he saw
your little boy earlier. How is he this morning?"

"Still just the same," answered the woman, her voice tired
and anxious. "A bad fever, he sweats all the time, and finds it
hard to breathe. He's been having a lot of pain in the same
place. I heard him groaning all night."

"Well, we'll see what we can do. In any case, just to relieve
him, I'm going to give him a little injection where the pain is."

The boy was lying in an iron bed, and he raised a flushed
little face, full of freckles, to watch us coming towards him.
"Well, young Dédé," said Lucien, "which would you like better
this morning, a fig or an orange?"

"An orange," answered the boy without hesitation.

While his mother was opening up a big cupboard to find me
a towel, Lucien explained to me that this also was a trick
taught him by Dr. Delpuech. "In the days when thermometers
were a rarity, you could tell just by the child's choice—if he
chose an orange, he certainly had a fever."

The temperature chart told a most disturbing story, as did
the boy's pale, sweating face, swollen eyelids and quivering
nostrils. He allowed me to sound his chest and auscultate him,
he obediently repeated "ninety-nine" without ceasing to watch
me closely in everything I did. I could sense that his mother
too was watching me tensely. When I asked her to light the
spirit lamp in order to get the syringe boiled up, she ruined
everything by announcing to the boy: "The doctor's going to
give you just a tiny injection, Dédé, to help you get better."

Immediately the child began screaming and clinging desperately to the iron bars of the bed. The mother, wiping his eyes, mingled her own lamentations with her son's cries. I tried to calm him by a caress, but only produced redoubled shrieks and trembling. I decided he could hardly be stopped except by main force.

Now Lucien approached the little bed. Bending over toward the boy, he at first did not touch him, but began to talk to him in patois; then he placed his hand lightly on the boy's forehead. The boy shrank away, pulled his chin back and hid his head in the pillow. It was only after stroking his cheek gently for quite a while that Lucien was able to lift up the small face. He still talked in a low voice, and as if a magic current of confidence were built up between them by the light touch of Lucien's fingers, the boy obediently stopped screaming. Although his eyelashes were still wet with tears, he finally relaxed and even smiled. "You're not scared any more now?" said Lucien. "You're a real man now, aren't you?"

The boy nodded his head; but as soon as he saw me draw the syringe out of the saucepan where it was boiling, he started screaming once more. Although repeating "Don't be frightened, Dédé, the doctor won't hurt you," his mother started sniveling too, thereby increasing the boy's terror so that he shrieked all the louder. Between two sobs he could suddenly be heard screaming: "Not him, not him, I want Dr. Clément."

There seemed no reason why this ludicrous situation should ever end, so I handed the syringe to Lucien, feeling much mortified. This action seemed to relieve the mother instantly and as if her recovery of confidence had somehow been transmitted to the boy, he too began gradually to grow calmer.

Eventually, bending over the little bed once more, Lucien told the boy: "Mummy's going to take you on her knee, Dédé, and hold you tight in her arms, just as tight as when she loves you. So this time you really won't be frightened any more, will you, and you'll stay nice and still."

The boy's heart must have been beating furiously beneath those thin ribs, but his mother seemed reassured and was almost smiling. She took him and half wrapped him in a blanket, then folded the little body in her arms. "Let's see if we find any fluid," said Lucien.

I had time to feel surprised at the doubtful way he put it, considering his former confident assertions to me; then he tuck the needle sharply into the thorax. The shock seemed to throw mother and boy even more tightly against each other, and brought a simultaneous cry from both; then they were both silent. I was jealous of the way Lucien had secured this silence so simply, almost without effort, restoring the distracted mother's balance with a couple of sentences. But I envied even more his treatment of the boy. Sometimes you would have thought Lucien was only happy when handling diseased organs and sick flesh, yet besides knowing their bodies he had this wonderful power of winning children's confidence through some mysterious quality in his voice or manner. So he had now mysteriously penetrated to the intangible secrets of a small boy's heart. Come to think of it, I had sometimes envied Henri, after some specially rapid conquest he had made, for possessing the same sort of indefinable charm with women.

I was not expecting any further surprises, but when Lucien, drawing on the plunger, drew off from the pleura a full syringe of green pus, the mother, laughing hysterically in relief and joy, filled with a confidence I could never hope to have communicated to her, kept repeating: "My darling Dédé, you're going to get better, you're going to get better."

Back in the car, hoping to score at least one small point for my wounded pride, I asked: "You said, 'Let's see if we find any fluid.' Now confess, Lucien: you weren't as sure as all that you were going to find any pus."

"I *was* sure," he replied unemotionally; "but I was following another piece of advice Dr. Delpuech once gave me. Every time you stick a needle in any part of the body, whether it's a pleura or a vein or a vertebral column, even if you're absolutely sure of finding fluid, never be positive about it to the patient and family, only say: 'Let's see if we find any.' If there doesn't happen to be any, or in case you make a bad shot and don't bring any out, that will save your being taken for a bungler or a fool by the people who are going to be watching you intently."

"You win, Lucien," I said ruefully, "that makes pretty good sense."

"Dr. Delpuech has taught me a good deal more," he went on,

"all sorts of things you never learn at hospital or in any Medical School lectures. I expect you'll have seen a good many of his old prescriptions. He writes them on very solid paper so that they can be used for a long time. In fact I've seen some of them dating back fifteen years, continually renewed to the patient's satisfaction. That's really good Medicine for you."

"He certainly can't be reproached for changing his methods too often or being over-eager to follow the latest fashion," said with a laugh.

"You find his methods too simple and old-fashioned, naturally. Don't think I wasn't just the same at first. After six years of hospitals, and lectures from famous specialists, I found Dr. Delpuech a bit behind the times. I know now that his patients often get better more quickly and easily than mine do. And a good many leading lights of our profession, who write learned articles in all the medical papers, have made fewer discoveries for all their laboratories, troops of assistants and other paraphernalia, than Dr. Delpuech, working all alone in the depths of the country, through sheer intuition, observation and common sense."

"Discoveries too?" I asked unwarily.

"Certainly," said Lucien. "Ever heard of Swineherds' Disease*?"

"No," I admitted, "or at least not under that name."

"Well, Dr. Delpuech was the first to identify and describe it in 1919, only nobody realized he had done so. Since then Swiss and Italian professors have produced a regular barrage of publications on it. They never mentioned Dr. Delpuech, of course."

"I suppose it's a very rare disease?"

"Since I've been here I've seen three cases of it. Of course, the first time, nobody had ever told me anything about it, so I didn't understand it at all. A young fellow up on the mountain got it, and he looked first as if he had typhoid, then an acute form of meningitis. I was at my wit's end, didn't know what on earth to do for him. Despite all my efforts, my patient seemed to be a goner, and it was my first month in practice. Dr. Delpuech was really wonderfully kind to me then—if he'd

* "Swineherds' Disease" was discovered in 1919 by Dr. H. Bouchet in a little village in Haute-Savoie, and was identified in the Auvergne for the first time by Dr. Cayla.

een that sort of man, he could so easily have shown up my complete inexperience and ignorance."

"Instead of which?"

"Instead of which he suggested coming to see the patient with me. It was in a hut in the heart of the mountains, without any sort of road suitable for vehicles. We went up there on foot, in the August heat. So as not to make me lose too much time on the way, he wanted to take steep short cuts, and I could see he found it hard going. Actually that was the first time I heard him complain of his heart. When we got up there, he confirmed his diagnosis and reassured the patient, telling him that if the illness followed its normal course, he'd be cured in a fortnight. But when he told the patient that, Dr. Delpuech spoke as if we had made the diagnosis together. You can see now why I'd do anything for that fine old man."

"Yes," I said, "perhaps I can."

"When we got back to Peyrac that day," went on Lucien after a short pause, "he took me into his surgery and opened a drawer at the bottom of a cupboard, from which he produced a monograph printed at his own expense in Aurillac in 1920. All the symptoms I had observed in my patient had been exactly described fifteen years earlier, but of course no medical journal at that time had taken the trouble to mention it. Naturally, oh very naturally, they'd be skeptical about the value of anything written by a totally unknown provincial doctor. It would never occur to a well-bred Parisian—no offense, Jean, you at least *have* come out here—that a humble country practitioner (that's how Koch and Zimmerman and several others started off, by the way) might one day discover something really useful. We're all utter fools in their eyes. You should see the Parisians who come here on holiday during the summer. They quake with fear at the very idea that some accident or illness might put their precious lives in the hands of some rustic quack."

This was an unexpected outburst from the usually imperturbable Lucien, and I decided it must be chiefly the injustice to a man he greatly admired that ruffled his normal calm.

Chapter Six

"OH DOCTOR, you've hit on the trouble right away!" exclaimed the patient I had just examined.

The diagnosis had not been as difficult as all that. First of all, I had seen the good woman removing in succession a powerfully whaleboned corset, a truss of double thickness and finally an ancient bandage which must have been handed down in the family from the days of some ruptured ancestor. This my patient had doubtless put cn as additional protection, as one might try to stop up the holes in a boat which was already shipping water everywhere. I made her lie on her back on the divan, and for a short time stayed bent over an abdomen flabby as flannel. Seven pregnancies had evidently not stopped the woman working up till the last moment, but each had left its own distension and weals. The present disastrous results had been completed by her rising prematurely seven times, in addition to hard work in the house, with the animals, and in the fields—unceasing work for back and limbs, from dawn to dusk, and without ever taking an hour of rest.

When I palpated this abdomen, I could not find a single organ in its usual place. Everything must have gradually collapsed beneath a wall of muscles with overtired fibers.

After this examination I was not taking any great risk in telling my patient authoritatively straight away that her stomach seemed to have "fallen." She was evidently pleased that I had understood her complaint so well and so quickly, but I was embarrassed once more by the same unspoken hope in her eyes which I had already heard expressed in words by other female patients: "Oh Doctor, if only you could stop my feeling so tired all the time, and getting such pains after meals, and my back always hurting. Oh Doctor, you can help me, can't you?"

While I returned to my desk to write out a prescription, she took a small air bulb out of her shopping basket, then stretched out again on the divan to "pull up" her stomach (as the bandage-maker must presumably have advised her), before reinflating the rubber of her truss.

All countrywomen, it seemed to me, were condemned to endless thankless toil in the house—beds to be made, pots and pans to be filled, muddy floors to try and keep clean, dirty crockery, huge copper kettles for the laundry, clothes full of holes to mend, with the younger children always hanging round and getting in the way. When the man finished his day in the fields, he would come and sit down at table, placidly roll a cigarette and enjoy a drink. But often if I reached a farm very early or very late, I would find the woman, always first to rise and last to go to bed, busy churning the butter, baking the bread, plucking the geese, or helping her youngest child at table. I knew too that for the hardest work in summer she would be off to the fields. She was the servant of all alike, beasts, children, men, and the land.

As the woman was finishing adjusting her corset, the telephone rang in the hall. I heard Félicie talking, then she came and knocked on the surgery door. I opened it slightly and put my head round, to be informed: "That's Dr. Ricaud, he'd like to speak to you."

I went to the phone. At the other end, sounding very faint amidst much crackling, I heard Antoine's voice: "Sorry to call you so late, I was afraid of interrupting you during your office hours. I've seen young Chanut today, and he's not doing well at all. The salicylate doesn't seem to have had any effect." He paused and hesitated, then went on: "Er, would there be a chance . . . would you mind awfully . . . going back there with me?"

It was easy to picture his anxious face at the other end of the line. "Of course not," I said, "I wouldn't mind at all. When would you like me to come?"

"Tonight, if that wouldn't put you out too much," said the voice, after a further pause. "I can wait in for you here as long as you like."

"Right," I said, "I'm just finishing with my last patient, and then I'll be on my way." After which I returned to the surgery, feeling somewhat baffled. So young Chanut was not doing well.

My patient with the "fallen stomach" was meanwhile waiting for me patiently. As soon as she had departed, with her very ordinary prescription preciously folded in four inside her purse, I went to Dr. Delpuech's library. Before going off to the Chanuts, I felt it would be wise to reflect on what I was going to recommend in front of Antoine and the family. But apart from the salicylate already prescribed, I could find no really decisive treatment in any of the authorities. Could I increase the doses of salicylate still further? I was doubtful if the patient's kidneys would support much more. How could one be sure with a patient one hardly knew, with no possibility of laboratory examinations and all the rest of it? Because of the parents, I should certainly be obliged to prescribe something; but what to choose among the different drugs suggested as potential supplementary aids? I felt all my self-confidence ebbing away, and almost rang up Lucien. But then I looked at my watch and decided it was too late, he would already have left on his round. So I should have to ask Dr. Delpuech. Before going up to his room, I skimmed through the thick tomes one last time. It would be better to seem hesitant through knowing too many alternatives rather than too few.

"All that! You want to give him all that!" cried Dr. Delpuech with a smile when I had put before him my newly won knowledge.

I smiled uneasily, and stammered something about thinking it might be useful, but not knowing which would be the best.

"You bellicose young doctors," he went on with a broad grin. "You dash out into the countryside like a daring general advancing into battle, ready for an all-out attack on the local diseases, giving every drug you can think of, pushing needles into all available buttocks, removing any sort of organ which happens to be sticking out. Luckily the local physique is pretty strong and able to stand up to such treatment. But hasn't anyone ever quoted to you Magendie's sensible advice: why not try doing nothing at all for a change?"

"Doing nothing at all?" I echoed, feeling, and no doubt looking, somewhat startled.

"Not always of course, and that's the great difficulty, probably even the only difficulty in medicine: to know the cases where it's best to let Nature do her own healing work, with only a very little help from you. There are other cases where you must vigorously oppose Nature without any hesitation. Between the doctor and his patient there is always this third, invisible actor, who sometimes lets things happen and is silent, but at other times makes her voice heard quite loudly. On those occasions we doctors have a very passive role. A doctor often has to watch his carefully considered prognoses completely turned upside down at the last moment, his most scientific treatments prove completely unavailing, and then suddenly some very unimportant device apparently brings a cure. As he grows older, he has so many experiences like this that he is forced in the long run to shed some of the vanity of his early days."

I had a sudden suspicion he was trying to tell me it had been a mistake giving salicylate to young Chanut. I asked him.

"No, that was quite right, of course," he replied, to my relief. "But at the same time try what I saw done some forty-two or three years ago when I was a young student at the Hotel-Dieu, where dear old Bucquoy was our Chief. One of the internes on his wards had an acute pericarditis, and like your patient today was in pretty bad condition despite the salicylate. They put him in a small private ward, and I can still see old Bucquoy in his apron and frock coat (they hadn't yet got white coats in those days) asking the sister for leeches and applying them himself, twenty-four of them, just round the heart. As he left, he gave these instructions: 'A big poultice, Sister, and let it bleed a good hour.' Next day the interne, slightly pale, thanked our old Chief effusively, feeling a good deal better after a night's sleep. Since then I've always used the little beasts, and they've never let me down."

"So you suggest I use leeches for my patient?"

Despite myself, I must have sounded rather disappointed, and the old doctor quickly went on to justify his advice.

"Yes, I do. Why not? With these full-blooded rustics, heavy drinkers, big eaters of pork and other greasy food, with their rheumatism and asthma and high blood pressure and hardened arteries, I don't know what I should do for the best without those useful little creatures, not to mention cauteries and blisterings and German brandy and aloes. It's a real art to be able to purge and bleed—Medicine's two keywords—unless Nature is kind enough to open the safety valve herself by sending your patients hemorrhoids or eczema or some other such disagreeable liberatory devices."

So the man with eczema from my first day had given me Dr. Delpuech's opinion correctly on the advantages of eczema; I remembered doubting at the time whether the old doctor had really said that. I must still have looked unconvinced, for he remarked: "I suppose you find my ideas rather absurd."

"They're just rather surprising," I hastened to say. "I don't find them absurd, of course."

"Yes you do," he persisted, half chaffing me. "Oh, I know that quite well. I know too that you laughed at my treatment for poor Cordier."

"Which is Cordier?" I inquired; the name was certainly familiar.

"The grocer with lumbago. You remember, I had ordered leeches and had his leg wrapped up in sheep's wool."

I remembered only too well. Damn the way things got round in this place, however hard you tried to cover them up. But there was worse to come. "I had a quiet smile that evening," went on Dr. Delpuech, "about your injection. Of course thanks to its anesthetic action you remained a great man for a good half of the night. But by dawn you had suffered something of a defeat, for our patient, finding the pain starting once more, put back my sheep's wool and leeches."

I flushed with embarrassment and annoyance, it was really not my fault that I had fallen into this trap.

"So you will excuse me, Jean," concluded the old doctor, "if I don't put too much faith in all your newfangled methods. In forty years of practice I've seen the birth and death of too many fashionable treatments and drugs and diseases. The only thing left now of most of them is their discoverer's name at the bottom of some obscure hospital corridor, and some thick tomes for doctors' children to sit on, to bring them to table-height at meal times. My experience of life has made me not so much skeptical as rather cautious; but I know that in the eyes of an impetuous young enthusiast, an old practitioner like me may easily come to seem an old idiot."

"Honestly, sir, I don't think anything like that, but...." My voice petered out and I felt myself blushing once more.

"Go on with you," he said with an engaging smile. "You

must think what you like, and you must get back to your patients. Only remember that to make a good doctor one grain of good sense is often worth more than a ton of erudite knowledge."

Half an hour later I was ringing at the Ricauds' door. It was Antoine who came to open it for me. He was in slippers, without tie or collar, for which he apologized: "My wife has a slight temperature, so I made her stay in bed. I'm doing the housework today."

From the kitchen came a sizzling of boiling grease, and the whole corridor gave off a succulent smell of roast rabbit. Antoine pushed me at once into his office, and asked me eagerly: "You've thought about young Chanut?"

"Yes, of course," I said. "I must confess that I hadn't really much idea what to do for him now, and I talked to Dr. Delpuech about the case. Giving him salicylate was right, he told me. But besides that he advises applying leeches on the heart and bleeding him freely."

Antoine looked even more surprised and disillusioned than I had been, but did not venture to pass any comments.

"We can always try," I persisted. "While continuing the salicylate, of course, as we haven't anything better to suggest. Only, let's have a different brand of salicylate, so we don't look too foolish, specially if we're only adding the leeches to the treatment we ordered yesterday."

Antoine got out his bag, then went out of the room. He returned almost at once with a new tin of salicylate and another small package already made up. "You wouldn't mind going a little out of our way, would you, to deliver this package of drugs?"

"All right," I said; but he must have still felt embarrassed to be asking me this favor, for he apologized once more: "I'm sorry, Jean, but it would be a great help. It's been ordered for a farm, through a neighbor. They hadn't given him any money, so I said I was waiting for a particular product as an excuse for not giving it to him. If I deliver it myself, perhaps they'll settle the bill."

"Sounds a good idea. Maybe they will."

He turned his head towards me: "You must think me very

sordid. But honestly I'm almost ashamed when I'm compelled to ask them for money. This money business between patient and doctor spoils everything for me, it makes Medicine seem so commercial."

He was taking a syringe out of the sterilizer as he said this. I looked at his back; his jacket was shiny at the shoulders, and both elbows had a patch on. "I hope all the same you make sure you're paid," I said, recalling Bonnafy's remarks. "Despite appearances, all these farmers are certainly a good deal richer than you are."

"Well, I've tried," said Antoine ruefully, "in fact that's what finally did for me, because according to local tradition the doctor is only paid once a year, in the week following Saint-Géraud's day. This is celebrated on October 13th, and in former times, I gather, it was connected with the traditional return of herdsmen hired out on the mountains during the summer months. They would just have been paid their wages for the whole period, you see. They don't hire out any more of course, but an annual payment for the doctor seems a very attractive custom to preserve."

"And when did you first come here?" I asked.

"I can tell you that exactly. It was the fifteenth of September. When we had paid for our move in and our stock of drugs, I hadn't any further capital at all. None of my patients paid me, either on my rounds or in the surgery, so we had to keep going the first month with sales in the dispensary and the gifts in kind brought back from the farms—the most venerable chickens in the backyard and last week's eggs rediscovered in the fireplace."

"It sounds as if you had plenty of work at first despite Chassagnon and Company."

"Yes, it wasn't too bad, I admit. I suppose people wanted to see what I looked like. Anyhow we waited with frantic eagerness for Saint-Géraud's day; that was the difficult point to get by, after which we expected to sail smoothly ahead as good as millionaires. But October 13th went by and so did October 31st, without bringing in a single centime. By that time I was absolutely broke."

"What did you do next? Sent statements to all your patients, I hope."

"Yes, I dared to ask for what was due to me, or at least what I thought was due. But I did it so bashfully they took me for a beggar and a lot of them slammed the door in my face. Imagine my audacity. I had only been here a month, hardly as much as that, and just because it was Saint-Géraud's day, here was I asking for my money. That was definitely cheating: tradition allows a year of credit, not a month. They must have felt I was an absolute crook, naturally." The scathing sarcasm with which he stressed this last word was redeemed by a wry smile, which I felt showed a slightly happier mood than I had seen him in before. "Perhaps they'd have forgiven me all the rest, but to ask for my fees after only a month, that was just too much."

"Our friend Bonnafy," I said, "told me his own difficulties in making people pay, but he got there in the end, even made them pay more than his predecessor had."

"Yes," agreed Antoine, "I remember his advising me to do the same with mine. Well, I tried that"—he shrugged his shoulders—"result nil. Then I lowered my charges, and they said 'He can't be much of a doctor,' and called in other doctors instead. My God, somebody would do me a real favor by explaining to me exactly what has to be done to satisfy one's patients, seeing them too often or not often enough, sending in bills or not sending them, incurring jealousy for your opulence or contempt for your poverty. I just don't know any more...."

The door of the office had remained ajar, and through it came a smell of something burning. Antoine dashed towards the kitchen, only to return almost at once: "Too late—This evening we'll have to eat eggs for dinner. And really I'm not sorry. Three rabbits a week for six months is going a bit too far."

I looked at him in some surprise: "Are rabbits your staple diet?"

"It's the cheapest sort of meat," he explained. "We have to save our face in front of the neighbors, when the butcher comes by and we don't buy beef. So I am officially supposed to have an insatiable, morbid passion for rabbit. People must think it was only on coming here that I discovered just what an ideal food this splendid animal made. My wife has tried every possible way of cooking it, just as one tries to disguise

137

the taste of castor oil when giving it to small children. Alas, they are still sick sometimes after castor oil, and we are just about sick of rabbit. But the saddest thing of all is that this will disappoint our grateful patient."

Once more I was pleased to hear in his voice a note of saving humor. It was something if he could laugh at himself, as now, with a little less bitterness than usual. "Ah," I said with a smile, "so there is anyhow one grateful patient."

"Yes, just one. Like Sodom and Gomorrha, you know, with only one righteous family. She's an old woman who ekes out a fairly miserable living through her goats and a small rabbit farm. She had choking fits, she could hardly move about any more: old people's emphysema. A little iodine and she got relief."

"Not even one of your more difficult cases," I commented.

"No, that's the interesting point. For six months I've worn myself out and given myself endless trouble trying to help people who, once cured, haven't even said thank you. But this poor old girl, whose case as you say wasn't at all difficult, is still immensely grateful to me, and wanted to pay me all she possibly could. I accepted a rabbit on condition that afterwards I should *buy* rabbits from her. Since then she has been coming down three times a week from the mountains—it's nearly eight miles—although she's seventy-five years old, simply to deliver to me at my residence my regular four-franc order for rabbits. Just for fun her neighbors have tried several times to tempt her on the way, offering her twenty sous more, but she always refuses. 'I've promised it to Dr. Ricaud,' she says, 'and he must have it.'"

During this conversation we had gradually moved into the corridor. As he took down his jacket from the coatrack, Antoine noticed his own pale thin face in the mirror. He shrugged his shoulders at the sight, commenting: "They don't think I look very strong. It's true enough, and unfortunately that's the worst of crimes round here. If you could have seen me in the early days, the first time I went into some farm, and the way they looked me up and down, all over and through me, weighing me up like a calf at the market. Because I looked so sickly, they immediately doubted my medical capabilities. In the end the husband or wife would say grudgingly: 'I suppose we may as well try.' The mere way they say it is enough to make anything you order or prescribe pretty well worthless in advance. Even digitaline for a heart case doesn't work when you meet that sort of attitude."

To go to the Chanuts' farm we of course took my car. As we drove out of the village, a dog suddenly jumped up against the window, barking furiously. Antoine started back in his seat, and seemed strangely unnerved.

"Sorry, Jean," he said, "I was bitten by a dog when I was a small boy, and since then I've always been scared of dogs. You should see me arrive at a farmyard when the dog is loose. You'd almost think the animal guessed my terror, the way it bares its teeth and dashes at me as if I were a tramp; while I beat a pitiful retreat, trying to use my cycle as protection. I suppose they're all slapping their thighs with joy behind the windows. Anyhow, despite the noise, they always wait a little while before coming to my rescue and calling off their hound. They can get a few moments of free amusement that way before my visit has even started."

Antoine had asked me to leave the main road on coming out of the village, so as to deliver his package of drugs. We were traveling along a deserted lane through some woods. The headlights shone on snow piling up to the lowest branches of the pines, here and there burying entire bushes so that they looked like mere shapeless flotsam.

"Do you think the people round here are always so bad?" I asked, mentally comparing his opinion of the natives with that of Bonnafy and Legros, as against Lucien's and Dr. Delpuech's—but after all *they* were natives themselves.

"Well, I try hard to be fair," said Antoine, "and I wouldn't like to accuse them of being permanently, chronically wicked, in the old-fashioned sense of that word. In fact, in the summer they're not, when they're completely engrossed in their work and they come back to their farms dead to the world with hardly enough energy left, after sixteen hours in the fields, to eat or even sit down to table. They haven't the strength."

"Well, that's very charitable of you, Antoine," I said, "but usually you feel they manage to think a good deal of evil all the same."

"Oh yes," he answered; "because in my opinion what makes them really vicious is sheer boredom. I sometimes wonder if one shouldn't try to cure them of that before anything else. You've seen what it's like inside these farms, when it's raining outside and the wind bites at your ears, and the snow blows in, and they have to stay at home idle most of the time, prowling from barn to stable, or sitting somnolent and completely vacant by the fire, simply waiting for dusk. I can imagine then how all the worst tendencies get control. In an utter mental vacuum like that every minor emotion is magnified, everyone spies on everyone else, becomes calculating and suspicious and soured. The smallest grudge turns into a bitter hatred, and the smallest grievance can have tragic results. In those circumstances to torment some poor unfortunate may well seem a refinement of pleasure, a wonderful distraction from utter tedium."

As we came out of the wood, Antoine asked me to stop in front of a farm. It was a very cloudy night, but the headlights revealed a gate with a pile of dung behind it, a cart with its shafts tilted skywards, and a house right at the back, with a light shining in the window. A dog on a chain was almost strangling itself with barking and pulling at the chain; a cock, deceived by the light, began crowing in the henhouse.

A door opened in the front of the house, and a man's figure appeared on the doorstep. I saw Antoine going in with his package. He came back to the car at once, with empty hands, and the whole household, evidently intrigued, stood on the doorstep despite the cold watching us drive off.

Antoine, his neck withdrawn into his windbreaker, stayed silent now all the way to the Chanut farm; and I did not venture to ask him if he had been paid for the drugs.

My prestige with the Chanuts had gone down distinctly. When we came in, the mother was making the boy drink water, the father was smoking by the fire, and two other children were busy with homework at one corner of the table. They all turned and looked at us without saying anything. Then the mother came to meet us, and the father, after spitting in the embers, got up too with a bad grace. It was the first time since my arrival in Peyrac that I had felt around me, when visiting a patient, that oppressive atmosphere of embarrassment and defiance, almost antagonism. More than anything he had told me, this uncomfortable moment helped me to apppreciate fully the torments which the nervous and sensitive Antoine must have endured at each visit during these six months. But I felt the eyes of all the Chanuts fixed keenly on me, and soon pulled myself together.

In any case these people had good reason to be dissatisfied. As Dr. Delpuech had explained to me when I arrived, his countrymen always expected miracles of any newcomer; and the Chanuts would not have brought me all the way from Peyrac at great expense, without expecting another "miracle" like the one I had been lucky, or unlucky, enough to perform at the Café Albignac. Moreover, I had been so elated by my skillful diagnosis that instead of keeping prudently to moderate promises, full of reservations and escape clauses, I had been bold enough to affirm positively that the boy would get better. In consequence I had doubly betrayed their hopes in me.

Antoine and I ceremonially began our examination of the patient once more. They left us alone in the guestroom as before, and there I hesitated a long moment before writing down on the prescription sheet: *24 leeches*. It still sounded extraordinary to me, but I could see nothing else for it.

The bulletin I gave to the parents this time was cautious and even rather gloomy. I told them how very serious cases of pericarditis usually were, but that since their son's organism was young and strong, it would be wrong to despair. I laid stress on the new form of salicylate we were going to try, and hardly dared mention the leeches, as a vague accessory treatment. But to my great surprise the use of leeches seemed to impress the parents most favorably. "Ah now," exclaimed the mother, "there's a good thing, as long as they take properly."

Back in the car we neither of us said anything for a good while. In my judgment the patient was not going to recover. It was my first really serious case since I had come, and the parents had called me in full of hope. In front of them and of Antoine I had played at being the great specialist, yet I was not even capable of stopping this youth from dying. I felt I had everything to learn, that I knew nothing at all—not even, it suddenly occurred to me, the way to apply the leeches I had prescribed. Very amusing, I thought sardonically.

While we had been seeing young Chanut, a little snow had fallen. Through the windshield I watched the pallid road flashing by in the midst of a bleakly hopeless landscape which seemed given over completely to desolation and death. It was certainly the right road back after a visit like this.

Antoine must have had the same thought almost simultaneously, for he asked: "Not a great deal of hope, do you think?"

I made an evasive gesture with one hand, and he went on: "I so much wanted you to succeed in saving him. A mere boy like that, I thought we might manage it. I'm hardly ever called in these days except for old people. My office is almost always empty now, and as I wait there alone, I go through hell. When I see my hands idle and useless, I long to be able to tell them all that I'd be willing to treat them free if only they'll call me in."

I could not refrain here from protesting: "No, Antoine, really. That would be too damn silly. You give them conscientious, devoted treatment, and they throw you over for other doctors who exploit them, like Chassagnon. If you're not going to be paid anyway, at least stay nice and peacefully at home with your wife and keep your feet warm."

He shook his head. "You can't possibly understand," he said, "you've as many patients as you can see. You don't know what it is to wait for them after having worked passionately for years to make yourself ready for them."

After this final outburst he was silent all the way back to Montagut. When we reached the first street lamp, I asked if I should drop him down there. "No," he answered, "if it won't delay you too much, would you mind taking me right home? I'm afraid my wife may be anxious."

The main road was absolutely deserted, and there were very few lights still to be seen in the houses. "At this time of day," Antoine commented, "they're all looking after the animals, so they'll be in their stables at the back."

As I stopped at his door, the telephone began ringing. Immediately he leapt like a madman out of the car, and rushed into the house, crying: "I don't want Marie to get out of bed. Do excuse me, please—or come in yourself for a moment."

By the time I reached the hall, Antoine was already bending over the receiver, making note of an address: "What did you say? Sorry, this is a bad connection, would you mind repeating it? Oh yes, I got it that time . . . yes, I know where that is . . . her pains began yesterday . . . and what's going wrong . . . . ? Oh, I

142

see, you're in a phone booth. It's urgent, yes, I quite understand.... Right, tell them I'll be there almost immediately, I've only just got back ... yes, just a few minutes ... good-bye."

He hung up, and turned to me, his face suddenly radiant.

"A confinement," he announced. "There I'm sure of myself. I knew it was something mighty important for a country doctor, and before I started in practice I spent all my nights for three months at the Maternity Hospital."

He looked at the pad on which he had written down the address: "That rings a bell. I must have been to that family before." He took a card index from the desk in his office and ran through several cards. "There we are. Hurrah for case records. Borderie, Victorine, thirty-seven, married, five children."

He read through the details on the card attentively. "Ah, now I've got it, I remember her quite well. It was one of my first examinations, and I did it very thoroughly with much loving care. I found a large fibroma and also a four months' pregnancy."

He reflected a moment. "There's one thing I don't understand, though. Because of the fibroma I was afraid of complications when she had the baby, and I gave her very definite instructions to go to the hospital at Aurillac to have this child. Borderie, the husband you know, looked as if he had gotten the point, and he nodded when I said 'hospital.' I'm not surprised the woman's still there. But I do find it a bit abnormal that her pregnancy should last ten months instead of nine. Unless I made some mistake in my reckoning—or the fibroma delayed the labor till yesterday.... Oh, well, I'll soon see."

While talking, he had opened the glass cupboard, and taken his delivery bag out of the lower shelf. He opened the bag on his desk, checked the whole contents at a glance, and then went over all the boxes of ampules one by one.

"No time to be leaving with an empty box," he threw out at me, "specially since it would certainly be just the box I'd need when I got down there. So I'm taking the whole thing. The woman on the phone was very firm about it being serious, which actually I could have guessed for myself. Before they incur a doctor's fees, the delivery must really be going badly. You don't know Mère Poulotte, the local midwife. She must

143

be really scared. Though naturally," he added, quite without his usual bitterness, "should the situation miraculously return to normal before I get there, they'd send a messenger to meet me on the way and cancel my visit."

His eyes shone, his face was animated, all his movements had a new life in them, a brisk cheerfulness which I had never seen in him before. As he closed the bag, he said to me with deep conviction: "No, Jean, you can't imagine what this call means for me. People who've dropped me for six months now all at once ask for me again. And for a confinement—It must be at least three or four months since anyone's wanted me for a confinement."

Poor Antoine was so very accident-prone, I thought, that something fairly disastrous must have happened in this sphere of his medical activities as well. "It's rather strange, isn't it," I murmured. "I'd have thought there at least they'd always be glad of your services."

"Yes, I often used to wonder why myself," he answered. "I never had anything go badly wrong, even in very tough cases. I only learned the reason quite recently, when I happened to ask the old lady who sells the rabbits. I'm accused, it seems, of behaving improperly with mothers in labor."

"My dear Antoine," I laughed, "what a fantastic suggestion."

"All I did was to make it my business to shave the pubis of my mothers in labor, as in hospital before any operation. It made it much easier afterwards to clean up thoroughly with sterile water."

"So that was your indecent practice: you shaved women?"

"Right again. I had been imprudent enough to criticize the walnut oil, the injections with unsterile instruments, and all the other unhygienic habits the midwife indulges in. So in return she went from door to door, telling everybody what I did. To put an end to such scandalous indecency, they stopped calling me in for confinements. You see?" he concluded, almost triumphantly.

In the corridor he fixed the bag to the rear-rack of his bicycle, then with a brief apology, dashed up to see his wife. He came down again almost at once, put on his balaclava helmet, windbreaker, and gloves, wheeled the cycle into the road, returned to the door and pulled it shut behind me.

"Many thanks again for your help, Jean," he called out to me, as he mounted the cycle; and then with sudden boyishness, breathing in a long satisfied draught of icy air, "Gee, but I feel better now!" And as he came under the light of the street lamp, his face framed in the dark balaclava, I saw his eyes wide with an immense hopefulness. Then he rode off, his head down, into such dense darkness that it swallowed him up in a few seconds.

Watching him go off in this mood, I realized clearly for the first time how infinitely sad it must be to feel full of devotion, compassion, and enthusiasm, humbly to offer these qualities to people who need them, and to find hardly a soul willing to accept them.

After dinner I went up to see the old man. I meant only to tell him about the afternoon's cases, but without intending to, found myself talking about Antoine Ricaud and his professional misfortunes. "I can picture him very well," said Dr. Delpuech; "not much muscle, narrow shoulders, but a good heart. Is that right, eh?" He had put down his book on the sheet when I came in, and was now smiling at me genially.

I admitted that the description fitted Antoine well, and he repeated, "Oh yes, I can just see him: the perfect newly-qualified medical student diving straight into his first practice, without bothering to find out whether he may not hit his head on some wretched stone right at the bottom. But it's very excusable. For a warm-hearted young man it's certainly a pretty exciting adventure, which may well turn his head a bit."

"It seems to be proving a pretty disappointing adventure for him," I said.

"Why, of course. But then the young are always the same. They think they've only to show themselves in order to solve the problems of a whole region and alter habits a couple of centuries old. Your friend is only inexperienced and over-zealous. Unfortunately these are faults which aren't forgiven easily in the country."

I had felt this about Antoine since first meeting him—splendid intentions, but no natural tact in handling people or things. I felt irritated, however, by Dr. Delpuech's patronizing tone and attitude, and felt impelled to speak up in defense of my new friend.

"What is there to reproach him with, really," I exclaimed, "compared with the good he's trying to do?"

"Nothing to reproach him with, of course," answered Dr. Delpuech. "Except perhaps," he added with a twinkle, "wanting to do all that good all at once. We don't welcome sudden changes in the country. They'll come about in good time, people think, and it's no use expecting it before that, any more than you'd expect to get figs when figs aren't in season. Young doctors must learn to be more reasonable in their hopes and plans, and realize, for instance, that a country district will never be as clean as a hospital ward."

"But there ought to be a bit of give and take," I protested. "Granted he may have been impatient, but they seem to have led him a dog's life ever since he came here, at the village's request too, remember."

"Yes, I know your friend feels persecuted, but actually he's only being watched. After all, he's a stranger, and before accepting him the folk here like to observe him, weigh him up. It's like a farmer at a fair: you want to sell him your ox, so he thinks there must be something wrong with it. He'll talk about something else for a bit while he tries to find out what's wrong."

"And what did they find wrong?" I asked. "Simply that he tried to do too much too fast. But at least he showed he was extremely keen to help them. That at least should have encouraged them to give him a chance."

"On the contrary, that's probably what made them most suspicious of all. They wonder why a young doctor they don't know should be so tremendously interested in their welfare, and what's behind it. So to give themselves time to find out, they've played a few jokes on him. Rather cruel jokes, perhaps— but then around Montagut one of the chief amusements for the youths of rival villages consists in bashing each other's heads in after a dance. In a year or two Ricaud will be the first to laugh at his early troubles, or else he'll have completely forgotten them."

"For the moment," I remarked, "he looks to me more like weeping at them than laughing. Personally that's where I find him particularly naive. Instead of practising indifference, he actually told me that he often sits at a window watching other

146

doctors go by, and feeling sad because his former patients no longer have his loving care."

The old doctor suddenly dropped his head back on the pillow. The feeble gleam of the lamp threw little light on the high curving forehead, and in the shadow of his ill-shaven cheeks the half-open mouth looked like a dark wound. Yet the mouth was smiling with a strangely unwavering smile which I found infinitely mysterious and sad. Then finally, almost in a whisper, he said very slowly: "No, he is not naive. He is a doctor, a true doctor."

For a few seconds he remained silent; abruptly I saw him half sit up. The effort seemed to give new color to his face, and with a vehemence alarming in so sick a man, he bent towards me and almost shouted: "It's the same with me, you realize. I too have felt sad since you started looking after my patients."

He let himself drop heavily back, and his face became contorted with pain. On the flushed brow, beneath the thin skin of the temples, big veins swelled out, thick and blue. I saw the arteries pulsing furiously on either side of his thin neck. He was breathing with difficulty. He groped for his handkerchief under the bolster, and not finding it, eventually wiped his brow with a corner of the sheet. I watched him in consternation. For a moment I thought a new and acute stage of his illness had just begun in which, for a few seconds of sudden delirium, he had discharged onto my person all the jealousy of a sick old man. His face was once more pallid when he turned it again towards me; but when he did so, the bitterness in his eyes was terribly clear.

To spare his breathing, the old doctor usually kept his voice very low, but after this outburst it became even fainter than usual. He might have been talking to himself, and in shame at what he was saying; but his eyes never wavered from my face as he went on: "Since you came to this house, I know with absolute certainty that I don't count any more for my patients."

The quaver in his voice as he said this was unbearably sad. "I assure you, sir," I said hastily, "they quite realize I'm only here temporarily. They're all looking forward to your return."

He shook his head and declared in a firmer voice: "I wanted to believe that your first day. The next day you already had fifteen patients to see you, and the day after that thirty-nine.

How do I know? Because I counted the times the bell rang, imagining you sitting in my place in my office, and I tried to guess which of *my* patients were now coming to see *you*."

I felt it was utterly unfair that I should have incurred such jealousy. Was I not here in the first place simply to do this old man a favor? "But surely," I remarked, "since you were confined to your bed, if they hadn't come to see me they'd have gone to Lucien, which would have been exactly the same thing?"

"Not for me," said Dr. Delpuech firmly. "I'm used to Lucien's being here. I've always had too much work, and I looked on him as a junior colleague rather than a rival. He was always full of respect and loyalty, and even the patients were faithful in their fashion: most of the younger ones went to him, while the old ones stayed with me."

The bedroom windows opened onto snow-covered roofs and gardens below. When he stopped talking the room was in complete silence, as if the noises of the town had all been muffled, stifled, submerged under the thick snow outside. In this absolute calm, under the dim light of the little bedside lamp, the unexpected conversation took on a strange relief.

"Of course," he went on, "among my old patients there were a few deserters whose going made me sad. You'll see yourself one day how hard it is to stay serene and fair-minded when a patient throws you over, specially when people take such sadistic pleasure in letting you know about it. And the worst of it is that the fault may always be yours. Perhaps he has left you because you did not understand him properly, or did not do enough to keep his confidence."

I still said nothing, and after a further silence he continued more calmly: "You see, Jean, since I've been in bed like this, I've had plenty of time for reflection, and one of the things I've thought about is why we doctors are always supposed to hate each other's guts. I believe that's the expression. Well, we certainly carry our mutual jealousy pretty far at times, but it isn't only a matter of fees, as some laymen like to make out. No, the trouble is that we all believe we alone know how to treat our patients properly. In fact the real doctor will almost feel a sense of destiny with some of his cases, as if all his previous

148

experience had been leading up to this new and unique encounter. You see what I'm getting at?"

"I think so," I answered. "You mean that when a doctor loses a patient, he isn't only losing a fee-payer, he feels his special skill and knowledge are being spurned and wasted."

"That's right. Like your friend at Montagut who worked fanatically hard for five years, I expect, to make himself ready for these very patients, and now he sees them going to other doctors. No wonder he feels sad and rebels against his lot."

The positions seemed to be reversed now; he was taking Antoine's side against me. I was about to comment on this, when he said abruptly in a stifled voice which was almost a groan: "Yes, I too have suffered from that sort of jealousy, though I sometimes wouldn't admit it even to myself, when old patients of mine secretly went over to Lucien Clément. But it was a thousand times less strong than what I've felt towards you."

"I . . . I'm terribly sorry," I stammered, horrified. "I never dreamt you felt like that. . . ."

"Oh, I'm not saying that to hurt you, nor to blame you," he told me. "But Lucien Clément is a native, he speaks their patois and is of the same race as they, and they've had two years now to form a judgment about him. But you—a foreigner from Paris, a complete stranger to everyone, how could you possibly hope to understand them?"

"But it's not my fault," I found myself saying, struck with the unfairness of it all.

"I tell you I'm not blaming you." Then the voice stopped and I wondered what more there was to say. After the pause it was as if the old doctor had decided to go through with it: "I'm not blaming *you*, but showing how far jealousy has been able to drive *me*. When I saw them, usually so suspicious, all running towards you simply because you were coming with the prestige of Paris, for some days I felt a kind of sarcastic joy because you despised them all and didn't understand the way country people think and feel. I saw clearly enough that their primitive qualities shocked you, so you were sometimes all too detached about the treatment you gave them—like a competent vet with sick animals. I felt that was my revenge. They had betrayed me so shamelessly to the first comer, after I'd always looked after them with so much love."

He let his head slump back on the pillow again with a further grimace of pain. I saw him take a small pill from a box on the bed table; he crunched it up in his mouth, then stayed motionless, with his eyes closed, as if he were going to sleep. Only a queer tugging of the lips gave a moment's life to the tired face, and then all his features relaxed. When he opened his eyes it looked as if he were reluctantly coming out of a beautiful dream. "For forty years," he murmured at last, with a deep sigh, "I thought myself irreplaceable, and loved."

These few nostalgic words made it easy to guess the beautiful dream he had just left, the afterglow of forty years when he had been the family doctor anxiously awaited on so many doorsteps, whose mere arrival seemed to chase away half the malady. But all that was in the past, and he must take up again the heavy inexorable burden of the present.

"The second evening," he said to me sadly, "after that afternoon which confirmed your success, when you knocked at my door you found me in the dark and thought I was ill. Yes, I was indeed in pain. Each ring of the front door bell all afternoon was like a stab in the heart. When night fell, and one by one in villages and farms lights were going up in all the windows, I left my lamp unlit, so that I could watch my ancient domains gradually lighting up."

He bent over towards the lamp, and said: "Look!"

Suddenly the room was in darkness. Immediately between the big curtains and through the open windows the sky and its constellations and all the glimmering lights on the mountain seemed to be rushing into the room. Eagerly I watched it coming to life beneath the ice and snow, across the starry night—the whole vast landscape, which till then I had always found inanimate and dead. From the roofs just below the house to the ridges on the distant horizon, this landscape really lived for the old man with an intense life of its own.

"Yes," said the dim voice coming from the darkness, "for one last time I felt I still possessed my domain. I could attach a name to each light. I knew the way to each fireside. I was a member of each family without their knowing it. I could see them and hear them and be with them in their lives, just as if I had once more entered their doors."

"Yes, I see," I said softly, and I really did see.

"From each house," the voice went on, "there seemed to be a light shining for me like a friendly torch, and I thought how many secrets I knew about each family, tragic or shameful or noble. On that evening all my patients stood before me almost as if naked. They did not need to explain to me their illnesses or worries or poverty or their ages. I had known it all for years, ever since they first called me in, full of confidence, sure that I would hear them at any time of day or night, would help them if it was in my power, and if not, would at least console and pity them. Yes, I have looked after them as if they were all my own children."

"Your own children," I echoed, deeply moved. I felt I too could now see them coming up out of the dark night, these foster-children of his, rising from each gleam of light, reappearing out of the past. I could see all the children the old doctor had brought into the world, the strength and love he had given them throughout their lives, trying to protect them against a thousand terrors, nursing them and consoling them in their sorrows, and helping to bring them a truce of relief and happiness. No, I should never again think him naive for believing himself bound to his vast "adopted family" by indissoluble ties of love.

But the voice in the darkness had not finished yet. "That evening," it went on, more sadly than ever, "I began my first sleepless night. For these people would no longer call to me in their distress, in their eyes I had already ceased to exist. Of course I knew them so intimately that for a while I could still follow them through their lives, the fundamentally unchanging lives of all countrymen. But their new everyday secrets, once my strongest bond with them, would now escape me. A little later, in their careless ingratitude, they would be telling you all these secrets with the same hope and confidence, having forgotten their former doctor altogether."

Dr. Delpuech hesitated for a few seconds as if nerving himself for an admission which was to him most shameful of all. When he next spoke his voice was heartrending to me.

"What I felt then," he said, "was an impotent fury at the

151

uselessness of my whole life. I had nothing left now but utter loneliness. Consoler of so many, I had not one real friend to console me in the bitterness of that night; instead there were only doubts and despair. A countryman who had stayed too long in the country, I cursed my wretched, stupid, stick-in-the-mud flock, doubting the value of all I had done. For forty years I had discussed things patiently with them, but had I even changed any of their most foolish habits? I even doubted the effectiveness of Medicine, remembering how all too often I had gone on groping forward in the dark, only to find a cure coming eventually from some cause I could not even have predicted. For forty years I had struggled alone with never any rest or peace, and perhaps with never a true victory. That evening I felt at the end of my tether, and sincerely wished I could be done with it all. In my weariness and disillusion I should have found it easy to die."

The voice stopped on the word die with a note of utter discouragement, filling the big silent room with the whole barren bitterness of disconsolate old age. "It was just then you knocked," he went on. "When you came into the room, I had to light my lamp, and I did my best, probably not a very good best, to chat with you. Then you went away again on your rounds, and I began to wait for you. I realized that my cast-off heart would not lie quietly on the scrapheap. Hopelessly and in vain, from sheer habit, it would go on beating for my patients, my former family, till there was no more life in it. So I waited eagerly for your return, hoping to question you and hear what you could tell me because you were my last link with these patients. Then when you did come back, I was ashamed of my childishness and did not relight the lamp. You passed by on the landing without daring to come in. That night I knew I should have many another night of unendurable loneliness which I must learn to accept and endure."

A log broke up on the edge of the fire, and a few fragments burst into flame, dimly lighting up the room for a moment with their reflection. Outside a clock struck. "And now I'm keeping you from going to bed," said Dr. Delpuech. The flame flared out and darkness returned. I stirred in my chair as if coming out of a spell. I sensed that the long sad confession was over, that it had served its purpose, as in another sort of confessional,

y relieving its maker. I of all people could not give this old
an absolution, but he had somehow found it for himself. I
eard the switch of the lamp knocking two or three times
gainst the head of the bed—he must have been fumbling with
e cord. Then there was a click, and the light went on again.
ying calm and still, the old doctor looked at me and said
gain: "I'm keeping you from going to bed."

"Good night, sir," I said almost under my breath, getting
p stiffly from my chair.

"Good night, Jean," he said, smiling at me with what I felt
a new kindness, "and I hope you'll soon introduce me to
ur friend Ricaud. But meanwhile please tell him from me not
 despair. He is young and even though at your age life seems
metimes a series of lucky or unlucky chances, yet nothing
ally happens in vain."

As I was opening the door he seemed to be following out
is train of thought, for I heard him murmur: "Yes, our work
 always our destiny." Then he turned his eyes towards the
indows as if hoping, despite the light in the room, still to
e out there beyond them. But behind the reflection in the
anes you could now see only impenetrable darkness. Perhaps
om now on, I thought compassionately, this darkness was all
e would ever see—till Death came to abolish all despair and
tterness, to end at last the long nights of silence, the slow
sipid succession of days bereft of patients to love and work
r and heal.

Chapter Seven

March 14th

ON READING over our prescription for young Chanut,
ntoine realized he did not have any leeches in his dispensary.
o ask the rival chemists at Farlat was out of the question, so
promised I would get them from Mandaroux and bring them
ith me to Montagut at the beginning of my round next day.

When I went into his shop the following morning, Mandar[oux] was busy trying to convince an old crone of the virtue[s of] burdock as a depurative. "Of course it'll do your husband go[od,]" he was saying, and then, seeing me, with a smile of welcom[e on] his face: "Isn't it true, Doctor, that burdock has been used [for] centuries and is one of the most potent blood-cleansers th[ere] are?"

I expressed agreement, but the old lady remained dub[ious] and regarded with regret the bottle Mandaroux had replace[d on] a shelf; this had an impressive multi-colored label on w[hich] I could see the name of a much-advertised "depurative." [But] Mandaroux was already filling up from a small demijoh[n a] humbler and less pretentious bottle with a mixture of his [own] fabrication.

"And in the spring," he continued persuasively, "you w[on't] even need to come here, Mme. Ducroix. All you'll have to [do] is tear up a few plants, cut the roots into round slices and [soak] them in water till they're reduced to about half. No boil[can] resist that treatment."

With his pudgy but agile little fingers he corked the bo[ttle,] put a hood of green paper over the cork, wrapped the bo[ttle] up and handed it to the old woman. "That'll be one fra[nc,]" he said, "and don't trust all the concoctions you see adverti[sed.] Seeing that there are beneficial plants on our mountains [and] even in our gardens, which the good Lord has put there [for] us free, it's more sensible to use them, now isn't it?"

When she had departed, still only half convinced, M[an]daroux commented to me with a shrug of his shoulders: ["I] can't take money off these poor old women for the expen[sive] drugs they plug nowadays on the radio and in the papers. [In] fact I just can't get used to all that extra publicity for pa[tent] medicines; I feel as if I were keeping a grocery or a stall [at a] bazaar. But then I'm one of the old school, you know, like g[ood] old Delpuech."

Coming to the purpose of my visit, I asked him if he [had] any leeches. "Leeches," he exclaimed, "why of course I ha[ve,] and best quality too. I've been supplied by the same man [for] thirty-five years now."

In a big pickle jar three-quarters full of water with a pi[ece] of gauze over the top, Mandaroux's stock of leeches clung to [the]

154

walls of the glass, and until required therapeutically, led a sheltered existence in which they dreamed perhaps of marshes, reeds, and water-lilies. The little chemist took out thirty of them, and transferred them to a jam pot. Having fixed a flat cork on this, he seemed unwilling to let me go, and held me lightly by the sleeve.

"How I admire you, Doctor," he exclaimed, "for keeping up with the solid traditions of the past as well as the latest discoveries of modern science. Most young people, I find, have their minds quite closed to the value of anything in common use by previous generations. Fanatics spend all their time inventing new drugs to clutter up our memories and our shops, and we're forced to use them while they're still fashionable, and as long as they cure anybody. Meanwhile we have to discard completely many splendid old remedies which have done their work well for centuries. It doesn't make sense, does it, Doctor?"

"I suppose not," I muttered, a little anxious to get on to Montagut.

Mandaroux hardly waited for my answer. "But the wheel keeps on turning, Doctor, and who knows?" He flung out his free arm in a triumphant gesture. "Perhaps in 2000 A.D. some poor invalid who has tried in vain all the marvelous inventions of nuclear chemistry will be paddling in the river one day and will feel a tiny insect sticking to his calves—and to his utter amazement he will find this insect has brought him relief. After which all the most learned doctors of the age will go down on their knees at the water's edge, and cry 'Miracle' at the sight of the humble leech."

He seemed very pleased with this flight of prophetic fancy; his face became a little more cherubic, his well-shaven double chin curved round, smooth and shining, like an Easter egg with pink icing. As I sketched a step towards the door he tightened imperceptibly his grip on my sleeve. Any attempt at escape would have been an offense against friendship. Luckily the arrival of a customer delivered me.

It was once more Antoine who came to open the door for me. His face was drawn, his eyelids were swollen and his eyes were red with insomnia. "What on earth's the matter?" I asked, but instead of answering he pushed me into his office, shut the door carefully behind him, and then said: "I'd rather there were no chance of my wife hearing."

Then he went over to the desk and slumped into his chair. "What on earth has happened?" I repeated, and now he answered slowly with a frightening calm: "Last night's child died." Then, unable to keep up any longer this impassive tone, he groaned heavily: "Why in God's name must it always happen to me? Always to me—my God, why, why?"

Then abruptly, as if his shoulders could no longer bear the weight of so many responsibilities and misfortunes, he sank forward, put his head between his arms, and started crying like a child. I looked at him helplessly. Putting down the pot of leeches, I went over and put my arms round his shoulders. I could think of nothing to say which might relieve this frenzy of despair.

Eventually he looked up at me, his cheeks still streaming with tears, and half sobbed, with a pathetic effort at recovery: "I'm so sorry, Jean. I never thought, when I asked you to come here this morning I'd be exposing you to a scene like this."

"It's all right, Antoine," I said soothingly, as if to an unhappy schoolboy. "It'll do you good to tell me about it. What happened?"

He took out a handkerchief, blew his nose loudly and wiped his eyes. "Oh, God," he said, "you remember how happy I was yesterday when I got that phone call. Somewhere I was needed, so all was not lost. I could still be of use, and what's more, old patients of mine were calling me in once more. Ten minutes earlier, as you'll remember, I'd been in the deepest gloom, but one ring of the phone made my heart race. Just one phone call, and I fell into the trap again!" He gave a bitter little laugh. "Go on," I told him.

"Half an hour after I left you," he said, "I arrived in the courtyard of the farm. I'd been cycling so hard I was completely out of breath, and my heart was beating fit to burst. This time they evidently didn't feel like having fun by unleashing the dog. I was able to get in without mishap. Mme. Borderie had plenty of company in her labor, not only her husband but a whole collection of gossiping women, all busy sipping their coffee, plus my special enemy, of course, the inevitable mid- wife, Mère Poulotte. They were all a bit embarrassed when came in, but that old witch seemed most uncomfortable of all. I expect she was wondering how I'd treat her."

"And how did you treat her?"

"Oh, she needn't have worried, I had no time to bother about her. I merely asked her briefly what the situation was, and she told me the pains had started the evening before without any result. Then I examined Mme. Borderie."

"If you were right about the ten months," I said, "she must have been pretty big by then."

While telling his story Antoine seemed able to master himself more, and by now was talking quite calmly. "She was huge," he said with emphasis, "a real freak. Her stomach pointed upwards like a tower, and bulged over both sides of the mattress. It was obvious she must be almost at the end of her strength. I only had to look at her sweating, exhausted face, with the nostrils pinched and rolling. I took her pulse, incredibly faint. Between two pains I listened for the child's heart: couldn't hear a thing. Baby dead, I summed up to myself, mother exhausted and too ill to be moved. The only chance was a forceps. It pointed pretty clearly to that, don't you think?"

He looked at me anxiously, really wanting an answer. "Of course," I said.

"For a moment," he went on, almost without a pause, "I thought I'd give her a little chloroform myself and then give the bottle and pad to the Poulotte woman to continue. But then I was afraid of a syncope with a woman in a state of such extreme feebleness. One clumsy draught while I was busy drawing on the forceps could have killed her. While I was getting the forceps in position, Mme. Borderie found enough strength to cry out, and then, when I began drawing, to shriek horribly. I should have liked to work fast, for I had a good grip, but instead I had to draw slowly in an attempt to spare her. With tremendous difficulty I managed to bring out the head. Her stomach was so big I knew I'd find a big child, but not that grotesque gigantic football of a head, all sticky with blood. Its mere size was terrifying, as big as a baby of at least six months. After that I just couldn't get the shoulders out, they were too wide. If I'd tried to draw them out I'd have completely ripped open the mother. I had a really horrible moment then. The baby was dead, and to save the mother I'd have to finish off

157

as quick as possible with whatever means were at hand; I couldn't possibly have done anything else, could I?"

Once more he looked at me anxiously, and once more, as soon as I had agreed that he couldn't, he went on with the grim tale.

"I'd made the five children go into the next room before I started, and I could hear them in there screaming with fear. Behind me I could feel the husband and all the neighbors watching in stunned silence. Mère Poulotte held up a kerosene lamp for me, and every time she moved, the lampshade threw fantastic reflections on the wall. I can still see it now as vividly as if I'd been looking only at that all night. Nor am I likely to forget in a hurry the groaning woman lying on the bed all red with blood."

"It must have been ghastly," I muttered.

"So as to get the body out without tearing the mother, I knew I would have to reduce the size of the shoulders. So I got out my dissecting instrument and started trying to cut up the child's collarbones, one after the other. Under the appalled eyes of the family, I had to rummage in the blood round the little freak's podgy neck, in order to see where I was, then to reach the shoulder and guide the instrument there. It kept on slipping on the oily skin covered with the traditional walnut oil the midwife had rubbed there. If you've never done it, I can assure you that it's not at all easy to cut a collarbone off by feel alone, through greasy skin which makes the handle of the instrument slippery—all without damaging the mother. I started slashing at random right into the flesh, removing anything of the collarbone I could find resisting under the skin, and probably a few ribs at the same time—till I eventually felt the shoulder soften up and flatten out."

He was reliving the horror of the night so intensely that he had to pass his hand over his brow to wipe away the sweat. "And then you had to do the other side the same way?" I prompted him.

"Yes," he said with a shudder. "I had to do the other side the same way. Once both collarbones were divided, I was able to knead the shoulders a little with the tips of my fingers, so that I could squeeze them in and reduce them. Then I drew on the head again—the child would certainly never have come out on its own. I brought up a staggering greasy mass, an incredible eighteen-pound Buddha. But I'd hardly had time to cut the cord and pass the corpse with the two holes in its chest over to the midwife, when the mother suddenly had a syncope."

"That must have been a bad moment," I said. "But you brought her round all right?"

"Yes, when I left, at about eleven o'clock, I made Mère Poulotte swear she wouldn't leave the mother for a single minute and would warn me at once if there was any change."

"I hope she kept her word," I said a little doubtfully—and regretted it at once, for Antoine immediately sighed. "Yes, I know. Already on the way home I started wishing I hadn't left her; but surely even such a midwife must see how serious it is. And then I was afraid my wife would be terribly worried if I didn't come home at all. I knew she'd be staying awake all night until I did. I was so exhausted and at the end of my tether that when I got here, I couldn't even bring myself to eat anything. I just heated up some coffee and drank that, and then went straight to bed. Of course I toned it all down a good deal when I was telling Marie what had happened, but after that I couldn't sleep. I dared not move or she'd have been awake, so I just lay there in the dark with my eyes open, and plenty of time to brood over this latest disaster."

"But why on earth?" I asked. "It wasn't your fault."

"Good God," Antoine exclaimed, "in all fairness, has anything been really my fault, right from the beginning?"

"Well no," I admitted, "but...."

"And yet," he interrupted, "it's always gone wrong and been turned against me. Do you imagine Mère Poulotte and Borderie himself will admit having ignored my advice and made her have the baby at home instead of sending her to Aurillac? And do you imagine my revered colleague, Dr. Chassagnon, will admit to having contradicted my diagnosis, which happened to be correct?"

"Oh Lord," I exclaimed. "You don't mean to tell me Chassagnon's in the thing as well?"

"Certainly, he's in the thing, very much so in fact. Mme. Borderie didn't forget my advice, and she wanted to go into hospital a month ago. But Borderie wouldn't have it, and of course he had plenty of moral support from Mère Poulotte, who would be losing a customer, and the neighbors, who would be losing the chance of a few cups of coffee and a little excitement. Mme. Borderie was very upset about this, and insisted on at least getting a second opinion from Dr. C. Naturally, as soon as he'd heard mine he said it was quite all right for her to have it at home, partly for the satisfaction of contradicting me and partly to get away quickly. It takes less time to explain to a dull-witted farmer that everything is quite all right, than to tell him there *may* be complications. Only what I foresaw six months ago did in fact happen. The fibroma delayed the beginning of her labor."

"So you were right," I said. "I remember your wondering about the ten month pregnancy, and thinking that might be the reason."

"Yes, I was right," he said, "for all the good it did me. And of course all the extra time made the child grow to that phenomenal size."

"What was Chassagnon doing about all this?"

"I don't suppose he even thought about it, he was much too busy getting himself re-elected as a County Councilor. But yesterday, when Mère Poulotte started getting worried and had him called, he could smell disaster in the air. He wasn't at all anxious to be involved in such an unpleasant affair. I suppose he found some plausible excuse to get out of coming, and advised them to call in his good friend Dr. Ricaud, who therefore gets the blame for a dead baby."

"You're not to blame," I protested, but he took no notice.

"Oh well," he sighed, rising wearily to his feet, "I suppose I'd better get back there now to see how the mother's getting on. As you hinted, one can't feel safe when Mère Poulotte has anything to do with it."

When he stood up he looked so pale and ill that I felt he could not be allowed to cycle in this condition, so I suggested taking him to the Borderie farm in my car. He must have dreaded being alone again, for this time he accepted gratefully, without any of the hesitation he had shown before at such an offer.

As we got into the car he gave me directions, and I drove off along the main road to Farlat. Once we were moving

Antoine said nothing more for a few hundred yards, but then he murmured: "This is the road I came here by, just six months ago." I said nothing.

"Just six months," he repeated, looking dreamily in front of him. "That first day how enthusiastic we were! I can look back on it as if it were yesterday. There was only one disappointment to disturb our optimism."

"What was that?"

"Instead of the fine house, newly decorated, which the mayor had promised us, we found that old wreck, with the floors rotted, the laths hanging from the ceiling, and the garden choked with weeds and nettles."

"Didn't you complain about it?"

"Oh, of course. We went to the mayor right away."

"What was his reaction?"

"Oh, he scratched his head and apologized. It was because of the drought and the cattle disease, and a lot of other agricultural arguments, the relevance of which I failed to appreciate."

He looked again at the deserted road. One of those sudden penetrating damp fogs had just come up, and on either side of us beyond the ditches only a few yards of snowy field could be seen.

"Ever been here in summer or autumn?" he asked abruptly.

"No," I said, "this is the first time I've been in the Auvergne at all."

"Then you can't possibly imagine how beautiful it is," he told me, with a note of touching tenderness in his voice. "That afternoon when we arrived was so wonderfully tranquil and serene. We came with the van which was bringing our furniture. Sitting by the driver we felt like slum children on holiday in the country, ready to be amused by everything we saw or heard. We smiled at the farmers' wives in their Sunday clothes cycling along with baskets on the handlebars and geese looking out. We smiled at the cows standing in the middle of the road, terrified of the oncoming car and worried by the dog snapping at their haunches. Then we got up to mountain level, driving through great forests where the trees were already turning gold and fiery red. It was very still, and the whole landscape seemed terribly lonely, but we did not find the

161

silence and the loneliness oppressive. My wife moved close to me and said nothing. I knew she was thinking, as I was thinking, of the serenity and peace and simple happiness we were going to find, in this remote spot far from the noise and dirt of urban life."

He stopped abruptly, and then muttered, with an anxious glance in my direction: "I'm telling you all this as if it could possibly interest you. I must be boring you stiff."

"Not at all," I protested politely. "I can promise it interests me a good deal." And the better to convince him, I added: "It could all so easily have happened to me."

Antoine glanced dubiously at my smart overcoat, my fur gloves, and tartan scarf.

"It's quite true," I said. "As I've already told you, my father was killed in the war, just like yours, and my mother had to keep working so as to pay for my medical studies. In fact I almost married a medical student myself, two or three years ago."

"Did you really?" he asked me, and then went on with his own story, apparently convinced of what I had said. So I had no chance to explain how sudden had been the change in my circumstances. While he talked I drove thoughtfully on, realizing just how many points of resemblance there were between my life and his. Marianne's family had little money, and my mother might have died leaving me with equally little. So if I had married Marianne, I too might have had to take a small country practice just as soon as I was qualified.

It required no great effort of the imagination to transpose the characters in the story Antoine was now telling. I could easily see myself as the newly-qualified doctor chugging up on a van to some unknown Montagut, one hot September afternoon, with a young wife sitting at my side. Then the van would depart leaving us on our own in a dismal cottage, alone with our meager luggage and the motley furniture we had managed to rake together. Faced by this depressing scene, Marianne would have smiled bravely and would have clapped her hands with delight when I suggested going along to the inn this first evening for a honeymoon dinner.

Alone in a corner of the room, we should have eaten cabbage soup with a good appetite while the villagers came in, sat down at the long table, ordered their red wine and stared curiously at us as they drank it down in silence. I should have looked at all those faces, ready to find them open, intelligent, sympathetic, because among them were my future patients. I should doubt- less have observed several listless unintelligent faces with oafish expressions and sagging jaws, typical of goiter or cirrhosis. I might have remarked on the heavy incidence of impetigo and even rickets among the children playing around between the tables. But I should have explained away and excused all this, as Antoine had done, by reminding myself indulgently how hard and stultifying was the labor which the soil demands. Seeing them, thinking of that unremitting and thankless labor, I should have sworn to devote myself to their welfare with equal persistence. I might have pictured myself, with Mari- anne's help, gradually restoring to health and happiness this whole little population delivered to my care.

"You can see," Antoine was saying, "how enthusiastic I was that first night—look out," he broke off to say, "here's where we turn left. And look out for the ice underneath. Last night I almost went into the ditch."

I turned left on an exceedingly bumpy road, and through the mist I could just see an isolated farm next to a clump of queer-shaped old pines. Antoine stretched his neck to get a better view. "Look," he exclaimed, "I wonder what that means. The shutters of the parlor are closed."

"Perhaps so as not to wake up the mother," I suggested.

"I very much doubt that. Healthy people here don't usually take such precautions for the benefit of the sick." All of a sudden he looked extremely worried as he added: "Closing the shutters in a sick person's room is usually a sign of death."

He said nothing more till we reached the farm. As I drew up in front of the drive, the front door opened slightly, and a girl of twelve or thirteen peered round it curiously. "She's the eldest of the five children," Antoine told me.

As soon as I had stopped the car, he leapt out and rushed towards the house. I followed him almost as quickly. In the disorder of the gloomy kitchen there was only the little girl with a broom in her hand. Antoine caught her by the arm, almost shaking her in his anxiety to hear what had happened. "Where's Mme. Poulotte?" he demanded.

"She's gone to Madurant. She took my brothers to Aunt Jeanne's," replied the girl in a tearful voice.

"And what about your mother?" asked Antoine, instinctively turning his eyes towards the closed door of the bedroom. "Mummy's dead," sniveled the girl, lowering her head. Directly after saying this, she abruptly shook free the arm which a stunned Antoine was still holding, bolted outside like a frightened animal, and vanished.

A hunted look now appeared on Antoine's face, and he murmured grimly: "Now I *have* done it. Both at one go—double murder."

Looking utterly resigned, with the face of a condemned criminal, he walked to the door of the bedroom, put his hand on the dirt-blackened latch, pushed the door open, and went in. The room was silent and almost in darkness, the only light coming from a candle on the bedside table near the dead woman. Antoine went straight towards her, and this movement of air made the candle flame flicker. For a moment the shadows flitting over the dead face restored to it a vague illusion of life; and in the dark room still full of animal odors and warm blood, the flickering little light threw on the whitewashed walls the same fantastic shadows as during the night. For a moment I felt that nightmarish operation round the head of the freak baby was going to start all over again—that haphazard carving of an amateur murderer or apprentice butcher, smeared with blood, stinking of rancid oil, mingled with entreaties, groans, and screams.

But as Antoine stood in silence looking at the dead woman, the slender flame burnt straight upwards once more; and on the bed, freshly made with clean sheets, there was now nothing more, after the terrible night, but a pallid young woman, her hands joined together, wonderfully calm and quiet for ever.

Now that I was used to the near-darkness, I noticed that there was a broad dark patch on the floor underneath the bed. The dead woman's blood had saturated the mattress and started dripping through it; the patch was where the floor had been newly washed down.

Outside, someone was approaching with an even step, and the sound of clogs could be heard on the doorstep, then on the floor of the kitchen—presumably the girl had told her ather, who was now returning. Antoine swung round and marched towards the door as if he would try to put a bold face on things despite all that had happened. As I was going to follow him, I noticed near the entrance a dog which had slipped into the bedroom. It hesitated because I was there, then went up to the bed and began sniffing avidly at the blood. I drove it away and then closed the door behind me.

When we came out of the gloomy kitchen a few minutes later, the fog was beginning to lift, and a dim scattered sunshine made the whiteness outside seem almost dazzling. On the doorstep Antoine blinked before the light, as if in a grimace of pain. He walked several yards almost reeling, and I felt this serene splendor of snow as an extra and gratuitous piece of mockery when the heart of the man at my side was bleeding in such black despair.

We went down the drive towards the car, paralleling a stream of liquid manure. I could not help regarding the wide brown trail with savage pleasure. In all that deceptive purity of snow here at least was something in the exact image of these people. For we knew now what had happened during the night. Pale with fury, Antoine had dragged the details, word by word, from the dazed husband.

After Antoine's departure, he and the midwife and the neighbors had continued to drink; then the neighbors had gone home. Borderie and Mère Poulotte had gone to sleep more or less drunk, and had slept so soundly that neither of them heard the groans and appeals of poor Mme. Borderie, whose blood was ebbing away drop by drop. When they woke up towards morning, they found her dead, already cold. She had quite simply bled to death.

As I was removing the blanket I had put over the bonnet of the car, I turned round. Borderie, on the threshold, had watched us go down the drive. Then he drew the door to, and walked down the three steps towards the cowshed where he was busy milking when we arrived. He had not removed the one-legged milking stool strapped to the seat of his trousers. The man shuffled along in his clogs with his head bent, while the leg of the stool, as if soldered to his bottom, waggled abruptly to and fro with each step like a queer sort of tail.

From avarice, stupidity, neglect, he had let his wife die—an unpardonable crime in itself. But while the corpse was still stretched out in the bedroom, he was stolidly going back to work as he did every morning, without apparent remorse. A few days earlier this attitude would have made me furiously indignant; but by now, after all that I had seen, I felt far less certain he was wrong. Perhaps this insensitive rustic was really suffering, was trying to console himself by repeating all his everyday actions at the same slow pace as usual, following the unchanging rhythm of the soil.

But the only words of true pity which I heard spoken over the dead woman came from Antoine, forgetful of his own tragedy; he spoke them when I stopped outside his door after driving back in complete silence: "A woman of thirty—and five little children. Think what dies with a mother!" And faced by this disaster, although he had done his duty and was in no way to blame for it, he added: "I shouldn't have left her. I ought to have stayed with her the whole night."

His face was ashen and I could feel that he was utterly disheartened. I was about to tell him how stupid it was to despair like this; for all his most devoted and unremitting efforts he could never stop his patients dying at the appointed hour if it was their destiny to die. He must accept this brute fact, sad certainly, but inevitable. He must make an effort to see events in perspective, and realize that in his future life as a doctor he would have the chance of saving many other mothers, to help him forget the death of this one.

As I went into his house these thoughts were in my mind, and this last argument I almost uttered out loud; but at the last moment I refrained. I was afraid of seeing him raise his tormented eyes towards me to say: "Yes, I suppose I'll save many others; but how about those five children? There's no saving *their* mother now."

He began pacing up and down his office like an animal caught in a cage and talked almost to himself without looking at me: "We all find out the truth about ourselves sooner or later; it's bound to come out in the end. Since goodwill and a conscience are not enough in our profession I now know that I have none of the qualities which make a good doctor."

"Don't be silly," I began weakly; it was exactly what I had

166

thought an hour before, but I felt impelled to say something in protest. Antoine had come to an abrupt standstill in front of the window and now stood looking out of it so that I could only see his back. But before I could go any further, he swung round sharply and broke in: "What do I know about Medicine? The names of drugs and symptoms and diseases, but how about men? I know nothing whatever about men, and the people here realized that straight away. They saw easily that I was inexperienced, clumsy, naive, and immediately they lost confidence. They were right, I'm not cut out for this sort of job. Now I have no more patients, and it's my own fault. I've failed to impose my personality on them. They sense that I'm unsure of myself and hesitant. People see *you've* got confidence in yourself, merely from the way you walk and come into a room and look as if you're at ease."

"But that's quite a different matter," I said gently, as if I were trying to reason with a headstrong child without hurting him. "My position at Peyrac is much easier. I can have confidence in myself because the Peyrac folk know and like Dr. Delpuech and my friend Lucien Clément, and that works in my favor. As for you, you know your job technically, and psychologically it would need very little for everything to change, only a little optimism and cunning. Men are like those dogs on the farm that worry you so much: you must avoid showing them your back if you don't want them to jump at you. A pal of mine called Paul Chavasse—I hope you'll meet him one day, I'm sure you'd like him—is never tired of repeating that it's hard to kick anybody's bottom if he happens to be facing you. When your patients get to know you better, they'll like you."

"No, it's too late, the battle is lost; they'll always despise me. So the only course open to me is to go elsewhere and try my luck from scratch all over again. But where? If I were alone it would be easy. I'd go anywhere, abroad or the colonies. But what about my wife? And the child which will soon be born."

He shivered and went towards the stove, thrusting his red chilblained fingers near the pipe. I did not know what to answer. His case seemed almost as hopeless to me as it did to him, and I could think of nothing to say or do which would encourage him even slightly. Yet more than pity made me

167

yearn to help him. Since I had grasped how disagreeably similar my life might have been to his, I had discovered in myself a feeling of friendship and affection stronger and more complex than the normal liking of one young man for another. He was like a twin brother who had taken on all my share of misfortunes, who had humbly sacrificed himself so that I could enjoy my youth to the full. When I looked at the pathetic figure of Antoine Ricaud, I felt not only his need for help, but also my own gratitude—and remorse—for all he had saved me from going through.

He had come back to his desk. Glancing at the pot of leeches, he shrugged his shoulders with an air of complete disillusionment, and said: "Would you like to know just how near I am to giving up the struggle? I'd be glad to see young Chanut recover, and after that never look after a single patient again. I've had a little dream of paradise lately. I'll tell you what form it takes: to be a local health officer with a little stove and a clerk and a filing cabinet and in-baskets and out-baskets, plus hundreds of circulars about vaccinations and whooping cough epidemics and sewer inspections. I dream of abandoning medical practice altogether. Then my ignorance and clumsiness and diffidence wouldn't be dangerous. When I think of it, I almost believe I'd become young and cheerful again like anybody else."

He picked up a periodical lying open on his desk; "Here," he said, "look at this."

Where his finger was marking the place, I read among *Situations Vacant* the following: *Applications are invited for the post of junior Medical Officer for the Aurillac District of the Cantal. Candidates should have first-class experience and qualifications.*

"Is that what's interesting you?" I inquired.

"More precisely that's what has formed the subject of my daydreams these last two days. But—*'first-class experience and qualifications.'* You know my experience, and as for qualifications, I'm an ordinary M.D. plus one small Certificate in Bacteriology. The other candidates are bound to have far more than that, and then, of course, they'll have heaps of testimonials and recommendations from local bigwigs, while I know nobody

168

anywhere around here. You can tell in advance, can't you," he shrugged again, "that I wouldn't stand an earthly chance?"

On the spur of the moment, simply to wipe the misery off his face for a short while, I exclaimed: "You don't know anyone round here, eh? Well, I do, Antoine. I've not only got a string to pull but it's a pretty powerful string at that. I believe I could have you recommended by Dr. Serres, who is not only Minister of Agriculture but also Mayor of Aurillac. A great friend of mine knows his son who's also at the university. That might help a bit, mightn't it?" I concluded complacently.

Unable to realize immediately the full significance of the help offered, Antoine at first looked at me in a dazed way and murmured: "You'd really do that for me?" Then suddenly he leapt towards me like a madman and clasped my hands convulsively. His whole body was trembling, and his face was puckered up with joy. He brought it so near me that I could smell his bitter feverish breath as he finally gasped out: "Oh no, it couldn't happen...it'd be too wonderful."

A few minutes later, starting on the drive back to Peyrac, I must say I was feeling extremely pleased with myself. When I remembered the joyful transformation on Antoine's face after his previous utter discouragement, I felt that giving new hope to this poor unfortunate was almost like performing a miracle— like raising a man from the dead. A presumptuous thought, but still.... I smiled to myself thinking how it would sound: "Jean Nérac, qualified performer of miracles and private benefactor—good old Jean Nérac."

Chapter Eight

March 18th

I LOOKED at my watch with a yawn: five o'clock, and I thought it must already be dinnertime. As usual, I had begun my office hours at one o'clock, and this afternoon seemed particularly long and tedious. "Give myself five minutes for a cigarette," I thought, while closing the front door on my last patient; and instead of taking a new patient from the waiting room on my way back, I returned to the office alone. The atmosphere was damp and stuffy, as always at the end of the afternoon. To get a little fresh air I opened the window, still trickling with steam, and then went to the other end of the big room to keep warm by the stove.

I found these office hours more and more wearing: a succession of minor patients bringing me unconnected minor symptoms without any serious lesional basis. A simple diagnosis, a conventional treatment, and that was that. Sometimes I had all the difficulty in the world to listen to these confidences droning on without thinking about something else. From time to time, to add a little variety, I heard expressions of surprise from a sufferer from constipation whom I had informed of the albumen in his urine, or from someone with violent itching in his legs when I told him he had hardening of the liver through alcohol. It would take a long palaver to convince them, as it often needed an endless series of questions to find out in the first place roughly what it was that had brought them to see me. The list of complaints was always topped numerically by "pains in the back," "kidney trouble," "loose" or "falling" stomach, and "blood pressure," but besides these I had established a more than nodding acquaintance with "nerve pains," "blood turning to water," "feeling all blown up," "dizzy spells," and "rush of blood." I also guessed eventually the significance of the expression: "I have a good digestion," which I interpreted too long in its purely gastric sense, whereas to most patients it meant a capacity to clear out the bowels very thoroughly.

At other times, to succeed in finding out whether the pain was stabbing or throbbing or dull, I had to behave like a barrister cross-examining a witness. But the most delicate question of all was always: "How long have you had this pain?" "Oh, it must be quite a long time now, Doctor," my patient would first of all answer cautiously, as if I had asked him the age of a horse he was selling at the fair. If I pressed him further he would make frantic efforts of memory, frown furiously, and finally assert, delighted by his own precision: "It was three months before the big fair at Aubières," or "It must have been just about seedtime at Sainte-Croix." When I insisted on his

170

trying, for my benefit, to bring the precious information into line with the Gregorian calendar, he would look at me in the greatest surprise.

Dr. Delpuech had done well to warn me. For hours on end I had to deploy fantastic resources of patience and cunning, to avoid a merely mechanical reaction to the monotonous series of routine minor ailments. For sometimes, in the midst of it all, I would get a patient whose case was superficially like all the rest: a middle-aged farmer, say, a little pale and tired, who for some time had been suffering from indigestion. He was not really worried, he had no pain normally, he only asked for a good powder to help him digest more easily. Or it might be a young man who found himself coughing a good deal and got tired very quickly; or a woman who believed herself near the menopause because she had irregular periods. None of these cases would seem specially disturbing, yet beneath such commonplace symptoms one might smell out a cancer or a tubercular lesion, and would have to warn the patients without alarming them too much, and convince them of the need for an immediate visit to the specialist at Aurillac. After hours of colorless routine, I would have to wake up smartly to deal with these sudden plunges into drama.

The telephone rang in the hall. I heard Félicie taking off the receiver and answering: "Yes, Dr. Nérac is here, Doctor. He's still in his office, but I will go and fetch him. Please hold on a minute."

From the rather formal way in which she spoke, I did not think it could be Lucien; most probably Bonnafy, who had phoned me two days earlier, reminding me of my promise to come to dinner with him. We had arranged it for that evening. Possibly something had cropped up to make him put it off.

When I picked up the receiver, however, it was not Bonnafy's breezy tones that I heard, but Antoine's nervous voice with the slight stammer. "Excuse my bothering you once more," he said; "but I wanted to give you good news about young Chanut. He's very much better, in fact there's been a tremendous improvement in the last three days. His parents put it down to the leeches."

"All right, let's not be ungrateful," I said with a laugh. "Let's give all due credit to the leeches, only continue the salicylate as well, just in case."

"That's what I am doing." There was half a minute's silence, in which I could only hear a crackling on the line. "And you sent off the letter to your friend?" Antoine went on finally, as if he had been deliberately putting off asking a difficult question.

"Yes, of course I did. I put it in the post that evening, as promised. But that's only three days, and we must be a little patient. Don't worry, Antoine, I'll let you know as soon as there's an answer, and I'm sure it'll work out as we hope."

"Yes, of course it takes time. I'm awfully sorry to go on like this, but I've been so thoroughly on edge these days I've been on the point of phoning you about twenty times already."

While he was speaking, it suddenly occurred to me that I should go right past his door on my way to Passou to see Bonnafy. "Look here," I said, "short of being put off at the last moment, I'm eating with Bonnafy this evening. He helped me get my car out of a ditch a fortnight or so ago, and I couldn't very well refuse his invitation." I added this little white lie in case Antoine should think I was betraying our friendship by having social relations with the cynical Bonnafy. "So I'll be passing Montagut, and if you're at home, I'll drop in for a few minutes. We'll have another chat about our patient, and also about yourself. How's that?"

"Thanks very much," said the distant voice. "I'll be seeing you soon then."

I put down the receiver, and went to take the next patient from the waiting room. A young woman rose, in her best clothes like nearly everyone who came to see me in my office. I was struck by her face. Most of the stolid phlegmatic peasants I saw were robust Celts with round heads, square jaws and strong cheekbones. This young woman seemed to come from quite a different race, with her sallow, oval face, delicate nose, big dark eyes and jet black hair. She wore a badly cut coat which heightened the vulgarity of her imitation fur collar and cuffs, yet there was somehow a touch of breeding in the four brisk steps she took to come into my office. Probably, I decided, remembering something Dr. Delpuech had told me, she was the great-granddaughter of a "Spaniard"—one of those men of Cantal who went off to seek a fortune in Spain, accord-

172

ing to the tradition of the time, and returned to his native region with a Castilian wife.

I asked her to sit down, and while I went to my chair, I saw her sitting straight and tense, with her hands clasped on her knees. She looked at me with such an apprehensive expression in her dark eyes that I thought I saw at once what was coming: she was pregnant and hoped for an abortion. She remained silent, and I almost asked her bluntly if this was what she wanted, so as to give her a firm refusal straight away. But somehow I did not dare; I was curiously impressed by the imperious bearing of this beautiful young woman. I coughed slightly and then asked the ritual question: "Please tell me what the trouble is."

"There's nothing the matter with me," she brought out painfully, and then after a further long pause: "I'd like you to come and see my little boy."

"In that case," I said, amazed at her hesitation before making such an ordinary request, and also a little vexed to find I had guessed wrong, "in that case you needn't have waited. All you had to do was leave your name with the housekeeper. Now can I have your name please?"

"Jeanne Orceyre, Doctor."

"And where do you live?" I got out my diary, put down the name and waited for the address.

"There's something I must explain, Doctor...." She stopped, as if for some strange reason she was very reluctant to go on. At last a little air must have found its way into her constricted throat, and she went on with a rush: "It's near Montagut, just by the Chanut farm where you went to see their boy."

She bent her face slightly forward, and fixed her eyes anxiously on my face. If I accepted this new visit outside the district, I could see all sorts of difficulties arising; and supposing this were a serious case, it would mean prolonging my round every day by twelve extra miles, just for the sake of one sick child. I tried to get out of it.

"But Montagut is a long way from here," I told her, "and you have Dr. Ricaud quite near where you live, and a little further away my two colleagues of Farlat and Passou. Which is your usual doctor?"

"Oh, we're not often ill, you know. Before, we used to go to

173

Dr. Chassagnon. He's a very good doctor, of course, but he has too much to do with his politics, so he never has time to come at once. And it's urgent now."

This time her lips trembled while she was speaking, and her big eyes carried so poignant an entreaty that I had to make an effort not to ask what sort of illness it was that she considered so serious; as long as I did not know this, I felt I had no responsibility towards her. "And Dr. Ricaud?" I said, to avoid asking the other question.

"We've not needed a doctor while he's been at Montagut."

"Then who's looking after your little boy now?" I supposed that it could only be Bonnafy.

"You won't be angry, Doctor? It's not my fault, I swear it isn't...."

Her voice had suddenly become very feeble, almost like that of a child when ashamed of something. She gave a sob and then quickly mastered herself. Bravely restraining her tears, she still held back their explanation too. "It's my mother-in-law who trusts him," she said.

"Trusts who?" I asked, much intrigued.

"Lacan, the healer, the miller of Laubat. Please excuse us, Doctor, but my mother-in-law says that doctors don't know much about children's illnesses. Old people aren't very well educated round our parts, you know, and she's always telling us how, when my husband was a boy and had convulsions, it was the miller of Laubat, the father of this one, who cured him with herbs and passes. So she got the son Lacan to come for my little boy's accident." She was talking quite easily now, in a clear decisive voice.

"So now you've come to me?"

"Yes, Doctor. I can see poor little Marcel is very ill, and I'm sure Lacan can't save him. At the Chanuts too they had Lacan come in without telling Dr. Ricaud, but you were the one who saved young Chanut. Oh Doctor, please come too for *my* son. If you could *see* him ... I'm afraid ... I'm afraid."

Once more she gave me a look of intolerable entreaty. She believed in an absolute right to have her child saved, so that her request to me was almost a demand. But if the child was dying, as she seemed to be telling me, what could I do? Doctors may know quite well that for all their care their patients often

174

die, even children. But do mothers ever admit it? What would this mother say to me in a few days' time if I could not prevent her son from dying? I made a last effort to escape. "But why don't you call Dr. Ricaud or Dr. Bonnafy? They'll surely treat the little boy as well as I could."

The young woman rose abruptly, and appealed to me in accents of such despairing hope that few hearts, and certainly not mine, could have failed to be touched and flattered. "Oh Doctor, you're the only one I *trust*," she said.

This time I could not shake free.

When the young woman went away, ten minutes later, transfigured by my promise to come, I had already made up my mind about the case of which I had just taken charge. Mme. Orceyre had given me all the details of the illness very clearly, and I thought I should at least be able to give some effective help when I got to the boy. I had often been struck by discovering on the faces of the dullest country people a sort of intuition which could almost be called divination, where their sick children were concerned. I had always attributed this to maternal instinct; but what I found in this case was intelligent love.

Ten days earlier little Marcel Orceyre had fallen through a trap door while playing in the barn. He bruised his shoulder and injured his foot against one of the pickets in the stable. Old Mme. Orceyre, his grandmother, took him at once to the miller of Laubat, who "reset" the shoulder and then treated the injured foot with a plaster of his own fabrication. Next day the ankle was swollen, and after that the boy found it difficult to walk for several days. Then one evening, coming home from school, he complained of feeling very tired and having a bad headache. He had a bad night, and on waking refused to eat because his throat hurt. Old Mme. Orceyre, taking charge of the case, smothered him in several eiderdowns and gave him great bowls of herb tea to drink, so as to make him sweat. But in the afternoon the first alarming episode occurred: about three o'clock Marcel cried out for his mother, and she found him stiffened up in his bed, his head thrown back, with a kind of grimace on his lips, "like a dog that's just going to bite," Jeanne Orceyre described it. The attack lasted only a few seconds, but the following day Marcel continued to be in pain, and began to find it difficult to move his lower jaw. Soon he was unable to open his mouth, and shrieked with pain when they tried to part his teeth with a teaspoon to make him drink. They did not even dare touch him now, for every noise, every touch, gave him what his mother called convulsions.

Two days later old Mme. Orceyre had the healer called in, considering him the great local specialist in this very complaint. He came, made some passes over Marcel's stomach and head, recommended certain herbs, and declared the trouble would pass over. The following day, finding this optimistic prognosis contradicted by a worsening in her son's condition, Jeanne Orceyre became extremely worried and wanted to have a doctor called. Her mother-in-law furiously opposed this, and Orceyre merely bent his head, not daring to intervene. After two days had passed, Jeanne therefore came to me without saying anything to her family.

My diagnosis was already made. Dung getting into a wound, a dirty dressing, contraction of the jaws and body—without a shadow of doubt this was a tetanus which had shown itself several days ago. Those days must certainly have compromised the boy's chances considerably, but this I did not dare admit to his mother when she rested her eyes on me with gratitude, full of new confidence in his recovery.

An hour later, crossing the icy plateau, I had not stopped thinking with warm goodwill of this young woman who put her only hopes in me. I was ready to make this long journey several times a day. But if Marcel's condition now was such as I feared it to be, could I make the journey as often as would be needed? As I came to the lane which went towards the Orceyres' farm, an idea suddenly occurred to me and I drove straight on to Montagut.

I found Antoine reading while he waited for me. He seemed fairly relaxed. "You see, Jean," he said, showing me the medical revue open on the table, "I was taking my little dose of sedative for tonight. Since I phoned you, I've felt much better; but I needed it badly during those three days of waiting I couldn't keep still at all. I couldn't sleep."

I looked at the title of the article: *New Treatments for Malaria*. "You expect to find cases of malaria in the Cantal?" I inquired in surprise.

"No, of course not," he replied, "but since I've been here and above all since I've started having time on my hands, I've got into the habit of reading everything—catalogues, advertisements for medicines, medical revues, absolutely anything that's sent to me free. I almost watch for the postman's coming so that I can dash to the box as soon as he's filled it. And I assure you I read everything right through from beginning to end, however stale or extravagant, even articles about rare maladies which only occur in Manchuria or Zululand. It stops me feeling quite so isolated, you know, keeps me in touch with the rest of the world."

He paused and smiled at me placidly, but I did not get a chance to broach my idea, for now he went on with increasing animation: "They read a lot in prisons, don't they? I used to read as an escape from my prison here, but I go on reading now so as to forget for a little that I have a chance of release."

"Look, Antoine," I began, but he broke in at once:

"Oh, you couldn't hope to understand, you've only left Paris for a few weeks. One has to have lived here at least six months to appreciate the joy of living in a town."

I tried again. "Look, Antoine, I said I'd be dropping in for a chat, but I've really come now because I need your help."

"Anything I can do," he answered. "What's wanted?"

"Well, it's like this. This afternoon I promised a young mother to see and treat her little boy. They're the Orceyres, neighbors of the Chanuts. This time old Mme. Orceyre, the boy's grandmother, has called in a healer, and the case is serious. In fact it's probably tetanus."

"But they've asked *you*," said Antoine, "why do you want me to go?"

I explained the idea which had occurred to me on the way. "We'll see the boy together as we did with young Chanut. By myself, miles away in Peyrac, and with all my work there, I'll never manage it. If it *is* tetanus, the boy obviously ought to be treated several times a day."

Antoine looked at me attentively, and then said: "You've

asked me to do you a favor, but your delicacy does not take me in. You're trying to do *me* a favor by getting me some work so that I'll earn a little money. And in that case I thank you very much, but refuse."

"But why?" I asked.

"Because the Laubat healer is mixed up in this business."

"Well, we'll send him back to his mills. He can make as many passes there as he likes. Afraid he'll put a spell on you?" I asked with a smile, seeing Antoine's grave expression.

"I'm refusing because I can predict he'll beat you."

"Beat me!" I exclaimed incredulously. "How do you make that out?"

"Believe me," said Antoine, "that's another of the lessons I've learned in six months."

"Has he a large following round here, your miller?"

"I should say he *has*. He's supposed to have his gift of healing from God, handed down in the Lacan family from father to son. Long ago the founder of the line while tilling the soil one day found a broken crucifix in the earth and piously gathered up the pieces. In return for which Christ appeared to him during the night and gave him the power of setting injured limbs. This fracture specialist's descendants have extended this power to include all a general practitioner's other functions as well."

"Dear me," I commented, "an M.D. direct from God. Much better than merely submitting a thesis after five years of hospital and medical school. But why are you so impressed by his powers?"

"It's because I owe him my first death," replied Antoine grimly. "It was a boy with typhoid, who had naturally been put on a very strict diet. Then the healer came in and told the mother her son couldn't possibly get better if he were kept starving like this. The mother immediately gave the child some eggs in chicken soup. Result: lightning hemorrhage."

"I suppose you were too late to do anything?"

"Yes, he was dead when I arrived. It was a terrible blow for me, particularly for my morale. I never dreamt my diet had been discarded, and naturally they never mentioned this fact."

"When did you find out about the healer?"

"Oh, a few weeks later, from a boy who had an abscess on the forearm. This time, when an extremely worried family eventually called me in, they didn't try to hide that Lacan had been there. I found the patient delirious, in full septicemia, with a poultice of marsh herbs on the wound to 'draw out' the fluid."

"And what did the family say then? You obviously hadn't any responsibility for that?"

"The surgeon was obliged to amputate the poor lad's arm. I thought that would open the eyes of people round here to the value of proper scientific Medicine. But I underestimated their credulity. Lacan had no difficulty convincing them that it was entirely the boy's fault. Imagine it: in spite of Lacan's precise instructions about gathering his aquatic plants, the boy had let the full moon go by without doing so. After such an enormity the idiot deserved to lose his arm. Everybody in the district agreed, of course."

"Didn't any of them see how absurd it was?"

"A few, I suppose. But very few. I tried to take people singly, to explain to them, and argue, and tell them in very simple sentences about antiseptics and germs. At the third or fourth attempt I realized it was not worth it: the healer would beat me every time. For one thing he's of their race, he understands their mentality. He knows their primitive instincts and can play on them very skillfully. And then of course there are his magic powers and spells and exorcisms. Secretly they fear him, whereas they only laugh at our academic pretensions. For all our degrees we can't make a cow go lame simply by staring at it, or poison a well with a couple of words."

"Please come with me all the same," I said, putting my hand on his arm. "Tonight it's not your reputation nor mine which is at stake, nor even that of a crazy healer. What counts is a mother who believes in Medicine and a little boy whose life can perhaps be saved only by serum. You can't desert now."

But Antoine remained motionless. "No, it's quite useless," he muttered. "I couldn't do a thing to help you."

I pulled at his arm, and went on trying to persuade him: "At least this one evening come with me. If I have to stick a needle in the vertebral column to give him intrathecal serum, I'll need to have you with me. Afterwards you can stay home or not, as you wish. I don't want to make myself a nuisance."

At that he agreed to come with me.

The first person we saw on coming into the kitchen was the mother-in-law, an old peasant woman in a black coif, with hard eyes, a toothless mouth, and a hairy chin set in a thin brown shriveled face. She did not dare insult us directly, but turned her fury on her daughter-in-law. Orceyre himself, who was at the table eating, got up, turning embarrassed eyes towards wife and mother, and then fidgeted about from one leg to the other, without daring to come and greet us. Jeanne Orceyre gave me a look full of pathos, begging me to forgive this reception. I pretended to see no one except her.

Taking the kerosene lamp from the table, she went before me into the bedroom, where little Marcel was lying in an iron cot beside his parents' bed. In the bad light we could at first see only a small face peeping out above a brown counterpane. Flushed and sweating, his curls sticking to his forehead, the boy had his head thrown back and was sleeping fitfully. The sleep seemed to bring him no rest or relaxation, for there was still a mask of suffering over his face, on which each muscle stood out clearly beneath the skin. His brow was deeply lined, the alae of the nose were dilated, and his lips were so distended that they showed his teeth, clenched in the ghastly grimace of a dead animal.

Gently I removed the counterpane and blankets, but as soon as I touched the sheets, the boy opened his eyes, which were dark like his mother's, and turned an anguished look on Antoine and me. Only his eyes seemed to be still alive in that death-mask of a face. His nightshirt had worked its way right up his chest, and when I finished taking off the sheet, we could see his legs stiffened, his stomach muscles hollowed out, and his chest muscles sharply outlining the furrow of each intercostal space.

Suddenly the whole little body, motionless till then, was seized by a horrible kind of shaking. From neck to ankles it was twisting and writhing and madly arching itself. With wild eyes and grinding teeth, the boy began shrieking with pain.

Powerless to reduce his pain, I dared not look at his mother

180

and Antoine too stood near me saying nothing. But almost immediately after the first convulsions, the boy's respirations became gasping, with a sort of rattle every time his chest painfully swelled out. His face began to go blue, and suddenly the breathing stopped, while his eyes rolled madly and he tried desperately to suck in a little air. He gulped but seemed to catch nothing. This fruitless silent effort was so poignant that I felt as if I were choking, myself. In an unreflecting impulse to come to his rescue, I tried to open his mouth so as to seize his tongue and begin rhythmical traction. But I had forgotten the locking of the jaws. I could not get his lips apart at all.

His face had now gone completely black. The child was dying. "Quick, in the bag, a knife and a probe, a drain, anything you like," I cried to Antoine, and bending over the cot I watched for the slightest movement of the chest.

In a few seconds Antoine had taken out and handed me the instruments, and I had the sharp point of the knife poised over the boy's throat when suddenly he gave a faint gasp, after which all the body began relaxing a little, and very soon he was breathing more easily. The attack was over.

Only then did I have the courage to turn towards Jeanne Orceyre. She was ghastly pale. She must have been supporting herself against the big bed, but she had not ceased to hold the lamp over the boy to give me light, and it had not trembled. Like me, she had seen her son dead, and now that he was beginning to live again, a kind of hesitant uncertain joy gradually spread over her face. Despite the horror of the scene we had just witnessed, she responded to my look with a brave attempt at a smile.

I had brought the anti-tetanus syringe with me, and I was lucky enough to give the injection successfully without provoking a new attack.

Mme. Orceyre watched me give it in silence, but she followed all my actions with a passionate attention. While I pushed the plunger of the syringe, I could feel her still gazing at me imploringly, and I wanted to send her away. Her pathetic confidence in my powers made all the sorrows I had met in years, all the sinister procession of patients condemned to death without appeal, seem unimportant. What was important was to save this thin childish body. I felt a desperate will to action

181

sustaining me, giving me extra strength. Turning to the young mother in an almost physical desire to stop seeing that tormented expression on her face, I told her positively that little Marcel would get better. A look of wonderful appeasement spread over her face, and I felt I was really sure of succeeding.

Before leaving the room, I explained the treatment to be given between my visits, the need for darkness and silence in the room to avoid a return of the attacks, and I added that I meant to come in twice a day to see the boy.

When we went through the kitchen, old Mme. Orceyre pretended not to see us and turned towards the fire. Her son, looking stupid and undecided, hesitated so long on the attitude to adopt that we were already outside the door before he rose.

Despite the cold the young mother came out with us and accompanied us to the car. I got in, and before starting the car held out my hand to her. She seized it, and without giving me time to realize what she was doing, she humbly kissed it; then she ran back into the farm.

This exalted gesture of gratitude and the icy air outside the house brought me sharply back to my senses. I was mad to have made such a promise to the poor woman! It was all too probable that I had arrived too late on the scene; the serum should have been started the day the old woman called in the healer instead of the doctor.

Antoine must have had the same thought, for as we drove off he said doubtfully: "Do you really hope to save him, Jean?"

"At hospital, with a special nurse by the bed, I think it could be done. But in this remote spot, even with his mother's love and goodwill, he's at the mercy of every crisis of asphyxia like the one he had just then."

We were driving down a narrow bumpy lane, and I was silent for a while, avoiding the ruts. But when we were back on the main road I added: "To feed him, I'll try and slip a probe between his jaws next time, and I'll fix up a rectal drip to prevent dehydration. With that degree of asphyxia, I didn't dare give him even a little chloroform on the pad, but I can begin tomorrow morning, and while he's under I'll inject more serum."

Antoine still said nothing.

"In a hospital ward," I summed up, "it would all be so easy, if one were the interne on duty instead of out here where you

182

have to rush across country from patient to patient. Don't you agree?"

Antoine did not answer. Only when I stopped in front of his house, as he was getting out of the car, he asked quietly: "I have no patients to rush to. Would you let *me* be your special nurse, and keep watch by the boy's bed?"

Whereas Peyrac seemed to hang precariously at the top of its basalt hill, Passou in the hollow of its valley could afford to sprawl in comparative ease. I had no difficulty in finding Bonnafy's house, which was pointed out to me by a local inhabitant with as much pride as if I had asked him the way to one of the sights of the town. "You can't miss it, sir," he told me. "It's that new one on the Grand'rue. Look, you can see it right from here."

The new building was certainly striking enough, a block of bright-hued cement set amidst the normal collection of shabby and straggling old stone houses. When I got nearer I felt it looked like some ultra-modern sanatorium with its wide bay windows and wooden blinds, but all its lights were out.

Then I noticed lights in the windows of the next house, and also a brass plate on the front door. I decided that both houses must belong to Bonnafy, and looked curiously for a moment at the two façades next to each other, yet so symbolically dissimilar. One was very much like the doctor who must have built it a century or so earlier. I could imagine him in his wide-brimmed top hat, frock coat and stiff collar coming out of the house and mounting a sturdy cob to begin his rounds. Next door was the new hygienic building for the white-coated modern practitioner, sure of his science and his powers, armed against all possible microbes with his vaccines and serums and drugs. The rambling old house seemed even older than its years, standing next to the cement block, which had but one story yet was crushing in its arrogant self-confidence.

I rang the bell of the old house, and heard two doors opening inside at the same time. Then I heard the voice of Bonnafy: "I'll go Maria, that'll be Dr. Nérac. We can have dinner whenever you're ready."

"It'll be about ten minutes more," replied Maria. The thought of a good dinner, and the sound of Bonnafy's breezy confident tones were certainly most agreeable after the tense session at the Orceyres.

Bonnafy appeared at the door and shook hands heartily.

"Sorry I'm a bit late," I said. "Think no more of it," he answered. "Doctors' cooks know all about that. In fact they're so used to seeing us come in late, they're quite startled if we're ever punctual."

"Anyhow," he went on as he helped me off with my coat, "I've only just got here myself. I've been at a confinement, watching the hands of the clock for nearly four hours. We didn't seem to be getting anywhere so I thought I'd better shake up the old forceps box to expedite matters. Worked like a charm, of course. It always does, don't you find?"

"I'm afraid I don't quite see," I began, but he broke in with a laugh: "Don't you know that old trick? It's far simpler, and far safer for that matter, than a pituitary injection. You know what usually happens in these confinement cases. The husband arrives panting, desperate to find you, the child's just coming out, they can see it already. You dash off there like a madman and the labor pains stop at once. All you can do is take out a cigarette and wait."

"That's the usual story," I agreed.

"Well then, if you don't want to spend the whole night there, you begin preparing your forceps, clicking them loudly against each other. Immediately, as if by magic, the mother finds new strength, and in a few minutes the whole business is over."

"To the satisfaction of all parties," I said with a smile.

"Certainly," said Bonnafy. "When the labor drags on indefinitely, it's not too good for mother or child, is it? And as for the doctor, he can get back all the sooner to his rounds or his guests or his night's sleep. But don't let's stay freezing out here. We'll be eating soon—how about an aperitif?"

He opened the door and bustled me into his sitting room. The furniture was modernistic, in Brazilian rosewood. It had an impressive polish; the armchairs were of stamped velvet. All of it gleamed with extra brilliance under the light from a chromium chandelier. I found the general effect over-lavish and rather tasteless, but naturally did not say so. My host went to a sumptuous cabinet which looked more like a safe, opened it and extracted a bottle and two glasses, explaining complacently as he did so: "Radio underneath, drinks above—quite nice, don't you think?"

"Very convenient," I murmured politely.

"It used to be my predecessor's office in here," Bonnafy told me. "You can imagine what it was like. Old dusty black furniture, and plush curtains, and a lot of faded pictures on the walls. Last year I threw it all out as junk when I built next door. Now I keep my living and working quarters quite distinct; combining them is definitely a mistake."

"Must have cost you a lot," I commented.

Bonnafy gave me a sly wink, and stretched himself contentedly. "Oh, I worked it all out beforehand. Don't forget that in four or five years I'll be reselling the practice, and I ought to get my money back and a good deal besides. If a prospective buyer sees a good practical well-equipped office, and his wife finds a comfortable house for herself and the family, away from the patients with their messes and germs and muddy shoes, they'll pay for it. It's like selling a car really, I imagine. To attract the husband you fix the engine up, and to charm the wife you provide nice new upholstery—and you get double the price for the whole job."

"You've got something there," I agreed. "A friend of mine who sells quite a lot of cars works just like that."

"There you are then. And then I'll have it all for my own use for five years, more or less free. Don't think I'm particularly sensitive or fastidious, but I don't enjoy having patients turning up all the time in my own house."

"And spoiling the beautiful furniture, I dare say." I looked round the room once more, in a way which might be taken for admiration.

"Yes, if a country doctor is going to keep his head above water, he must have a comfortable place to work in, and his wife ought to have pleasant quarters to keep her happy."

"How about a bachelor like yourself?"

"For a bachelor like myself it's ideal. Why, my dear chap, once I lock up this office I could almost believe I was on vacation—apart from the phone, of course. Perhaps you'd like to have a glance at my little clinic before dinner's ready," he concluded, stressing the word "clinic" as if it were only half a joke.

He opened a communicating door, and with glass in han
led the way through to the adjoining building. Doubtless th
Passou farmers were as much impressed as I was when the
first went into the new office with its shining white walls, im
posing chromium-plated desk and magnificent armchair in dar
red leather. I had hardly had time to take it in, when Bonnaf
had pulled me into the next room, where he did dressings.

"Don't you think I've done it rather well?" he rattled on
like some enthusiastic guide in a famous church. "I've even go
a little electric sterilizer for my instruments. I just plug it i
here, and it comes on automatically. Neat, eh? In this cupboar
is my stock of cotton wool, gauze and bandages. I feel equippe
to tackle almost anything."

He opened the doors, and showed me two cubicles where th
patients could dress and undress. I expressed appreciation c
this, mentioning my own irritations about the waste of tim
usually involved. "Yes," he agreed, "it's painful, isn't it? Bu
when I've finished with my patients, I shut them in there
They can take as long as they want pulling up suspenders o
adjusting petticoats . . . here's the waiting room."

Like all the other rooms, it was paved with gray tiles, whic
here also covered the walls to a man's height. The only furnitur
consisted of some stout oak benches and a few sturdy chairs
it was furnished like a guardroom, in fact, or a cell in a mode
prison. "Pretty severe," I commented.

"Yes," said Bonnafy with a laugh, "no superfluous furniture
and nothing they can damage. You see that door? They even
have their own toilets where they can do what they like, spi
vomit, flood the lavatories, deposit their poultry—I don't care
After office hours I let in some fresh air, have it all sluiced ou
with lysol, and there we are. In the old days, every market day
for a week afterwards the whole house smelled of garlic an
cheap wine."

We turned, and he brought me into a room with wall
painted black, where I saw a gleaming new X-ray apparatu
standing, majestic as a guillotine, with the ultraviolet-ray lamp
of which he had already spoken, at its side.

"They find it exciting here in the dark," he said, "with thei
nostrils tickled by the smell of ozone, and the X-ray cracklin
and spluttering all over the place. When they see themselve

ing the color of a jack o' lantern under the ultraviolet, they
ll clamor for more. I give most of them a little of it, they're
o keen on it I don't like to disappoint them."

Bonnafy looked at his apparatus with the satisfaction of a
arnival manager demonstrating a new slot machine. Without
uite knowing why, perhaps because of the white sheet which
overed the narrow canopy over the lamp, I suddenly thought
f the thin writhing body of little Marcel Orceyre, stiffening
nder the mournful lamplight. Before going to the Orceyre
arm, I might have found it funny to give ultraviolet ray treat-
ent to small farmers who were in the fresh air and sunshine
ll the year round. But suddenly I did not feel like laughing
ny more, and I could not refrain from remarking drily: "The
ay you run it, I can see that it must be quite a good racket."

Bonnafy appeared surprised by my sarcasm. He looked at
e, and was about to reply, when his housekeeper, Maria, a
leasant-looking middle-aged woman, appeared at the door and
aid with dignity: "Dinner's been ready several minutes, but
ou evidently didn't hear me calling. I'm afraid your soup will
e quite cold by now."

The dining-room was as loudly and expensively furnished in
modern style as the sitting-room. If the X-ray and ultraviolet
id nothing else but supply money, I thought, they must cer-
ainly fulfill that function very successfully. We sat down op-
osite each other and drank our soup in silence. Maria then
rought in a dish of brook trout which smelled delicious, and
fter this was served and we had both helped ourselves to
egetables, Bonnafy filled our glasses and emptied his at a
ulp. He was evidently hungry, and continued to eat without
aying anything.

This concentration was entirely justified by the trout, which
asted even better than they smelled, and I followed his lead.
n any case I was not at all sure how to resume the conversation,
fter saying something so impolite to my host. When he had
inished eating, Bonnafy glanced at my glass, which I had
carcely touched, and then refilled his own and drank that down
oo. After these preliminaries he said quite placidly, showing
o trace of annoyance at my previous remark: "Listen, my
riend, I like to know where I stand with people."

I had not eaten as fast as Bonnafy, and was still enjoying th
trout. I lifted my head, wondering what was coming.

"Right," he said. "I'd like to explain my own position. Sinc
our meeting on the road I've talked to you quite freely as
friend. Partly because I'm like that, and partly because I don'
often have the chance in this miserable hole. I quite appreciat
I may have shocked you by my bluntness, and you probabl
look on me as a bit of a medical shark, getting rich quick o
poverty-stricken patients."

Somewhat embarrassed by his candor I was beginning, "
didn't mean . . ." when he cut me short: "Oh yes, you did, eve
if you wouldn't have said it quite in those words. Living nea
Delpuech and Clément, you could hardly be expected to thin
otherwise. Everything gets round very quickly in a small plac
like this, so you won't be surprised at my knowing all about you
seeing the Chanut boy with Ricaud. Well, Ricaud will certainl
have told you some of his tribulations since he came here. H
did, didn't he?"

"He did indeed. In fact, it's partly because of him—"

"Wait a moment," interrupted Bonnafy, "what I feel is this
If you aren't from these parts, there are only two alternatives
either you accept things, or you react sharply as I have. A purel
personal question, I know, but I myself have no inclination t
win the martyr's crown. I'm a professional doctor, not a profes
sional saint—Ricaud, for all I know, may get his reward i
heaven, but that's another story."

"That, as you say, is another story," I remarked, thinking o
Antoine's present plans. "I'm sorry if I said anything to offenc
you."

"That's all right. You were a bit unfair just now when yo
used the phrase 'quite a racket' in referring to my extra equip
ment. You're only here as locum, so you're not really in th
same boat as the permanent country doctor. I excuse you o
those grounds, but may I ask you a few questions?"

"Please," I said. I drank some of the wine, and that, in com
bination with the excellent food, made me feel decidedly mor
cheerful.

"First of all," said Bonnafy, "assuming Delpuech and Clémen
to be your prototypes of the model doctor, have they as goo
equipment as I have?"

"No," I admitted. "In fact they've almost nothing outside the instruments in everyday use."

"Right. Then my second question is this: haven't you sometimes found it very annoying in a difficult case not to be able to X-ray a lung—or a stomach—on the spot?"

"Yes, I admit that too."

"Consequently, by having a large and varied collection of equipment, I am rendering my patients a service."

"A potential service," I answered. I was not embarrassed any longer. Bonnafy was putting his points so objectively, it seemed to take the argument out of the field of personalities. "The actual service depends on how you make use of all that equipment."

"Granted. But before we come to that, have you ever wondered why neither Delpuech nor Clément has any?"

"One's an old man and probably not used to it. As for Clément, that sort of equipment is much too expensive for him."

"Well now, Nérac, surely you don't imagine I was made a present of it. I can assure you I paid for it all right away. There was no question of credit."

"All right if you've got the money," I commented.

"Yes, one has to have a bit of capital, but you'll admit anyhow that it's useful to have an X-ray apparatus in one's consulting rooms, and that many doctors haven't got one because it's too expensive to buy one, or rather because it wouldn't pay to buy one to use it only once in a while."

"Yes, that sounds logical," I said.

"Right then, once more we have two alternatives. Either I go without an X-ray apparatus and all the advantages in diagnosis it provides for my practice, and send my patients to Aurillac at their great expense and inconvenience. Or else I buy a rather expensive piece of apparatus, use it only in strictly necessary cases, i.e., two or three times a day. Then I'd lose money fast, and might as well sit by the fire and read detective stories. Either way it's bad. See anything wrong with the argument so far?"

He grinned at me, and I admitted: "If there is, I can't quite trace the fallacy."

"Well, if both alternatives are failures, one must find a third; and I believe my third alternative gives good value to all parties.

189

I bought an X-ray apparatus from a reputable firm. I worked it out, and decided I had to do about ten not strictly necessary X-ray examinations daily, so as to make my profit and pay for depreciation. With this system, my T.B. cases, my abdominal and gall-bladders and kidney cases, all gain because I can afford to examine them myself. Without having to send them off to distant specialists, I can give them all the benefits of modern medical science."

"And what do the other patients think about it who haven't quite such an urgent need to be X-rayed?"

"My dear chap, they're delighted, and proud. It's very much the thing, you know, at Passou—not being X-rayed by Dr Bonnafy is quite looked down upon. Oh, one other thing. These slightly superfluous examinations not only pay for wear and tear and give me a small profit, they often allow me to diagnose in good time lesions which can't be recognized clinically. So may I ask if you still find my racket so unworthy of our honorable profession?"

Under the influence of the wine he had already drunk Bonnafy had become distinctly excited, and conducted his own defense with skill and enthusiasm. He seemed sincere enough too, but several times while he was talking, I found myself again imagining Marcel Orceyre's pale little body under the ultra-violet ray. Each time I raised my eyes from my plate, I saw the expensive room with its garish over-polished furniture and decorations. I would have found it easier to accept the argument had Bonnafy used the word "profit" less proudly. "Well," he challenged me, "how about it?"

"Yes," I sighed, "I dare say your argument will hold for the X-ray, but surely your ultraviolet ray is a very expensive rival for ordinary sunshine. In a mountain area like this, sunshine can't cost your patients a great deal?"

I thought this might annoy Bonnafy, but instead he merely threw himself back on his chair and burst out laughing. "What's so funny?" I inquired in some irritation.

"My poor friend," he said, "when did they let you out? There are places near here where I have up to forty percent of rickets cases, genuine rickets. Of course the local population is still pretty robust, I grant you that, but all the same you must have noticed the amount of rheumatism and bad teeth and

190

pinal curvature and deformities there are about, not to mention he infected pelvises which give us such a lot of trouble in confinement cases. All those things are signs of rickets. Sit in at one of the medical examinations for the draft, and you'll find more are graded unfit here in the country than in the towns."

"Damn it, you're quite right," I said ruefully.

"Well, that's honest anyhow," remarked Bonnafy with a final chuckle. "And even if the ultraviolet-ray treatment was quite unnecessary, and I didn't have so many patients with rickets, at least it's without danger or consequence for their health. Poor old Nérac, stop worrying about my exploiting the population of Passou all the time. If you knew how many racketeers really exploit them, you'd call me a public benefactor. The worst of it is they almost seem to like being fleeced."

"For instance?" I inquired.

"For instance the swindlers we had here last summer who went round selling an elaborate apparatus which they claimed had radioactive properties, when inside there was just ordinary cotton wool and tin-plate. They'd organized a big meeting in the village hall the day before, and when they went round the neighborhood in their smart car they found plenty of buyers at a price for which I could have given a whole family ultraviolet treatments every day for three months. As I said, people seem to like being fleeced."

"Sounds harmless enough anyhow."

"Harmless! My God, Nérac, it wasn't harmless for three cancer cases who bought the apparatus instead of having operations, just as I'd about persuaded each of them that an operation was necessary. Result is that six months later two of them are dying, quite inoperable now, and the third died a fortnight ago of cancer of the rectum, spreading in these six months all through the anus—a nauseating death. But I won't spoil our meal by describing the dressings I had to do at the end. Now you can see why I don't find those swindlers so harmless. By the way, have some more trout."

"Thanks very much." I held out my plate, and he served me, then gave himself some more.

"I must say they're delicious," I said. "Félicie, Doctor Delpuech's housekeeper, you know, is a damned good cook too, but she's never given me trout."

We began on our second helping. A little later I remarked "Yes, I can see that type of racket can be extremely dangerous, but you don't get rogues like that very often, do you?"

"Only about once or twice a year," said Bonnafy. "But there are other things going on all the time which do just as much harm if not more. Some of our local quack-healers, for instance, really believe in their own powers, but I'd say they were responsible for more deaths in a year than the radium racketeers... sorry, Maria," he broke off. "We've been talking instead of eating, I'm afraid. But you can bring in the dessert, we'll be ready by then."

For a moment, knowing how quickly news traveled in the countryside, I thought Bonnafy must already know about my visit to the Orceyres and was skillfully turning the conversation to healers for my discomfiture. But he returned to his plate with such obvious zest that my fears were at once dispelled.

"Where did you get these delicious trout?" he asked Maria when she returned with the dessert. "Dr. Nérac seems to have enjoyed them."

"I certainly have," I told her.

"They're the first we've had," said Maria. "They came in very nicely today, as we had the doctor coming to dinner. Old Jules from Chantepie brought them in this morning. He said it was Yvette's birthday—his little girl you cured of pleurisy last year, and wouldn't take any payment for."

"Oh yes," said Bonnafy, and then explained for my benefit. "A poor devil who poaches a little and fishes, and hires himself out round the farms during the summer. But it doesn't bring him in much and he has seven children to feed."

I suddenly thought of Bonnafy arriving at the Lespinat farm with me like a process-server to collect his fees, and I remarked with a smile: "You look after that family for nothing. Isn't it a bad example for the others?"

"Not at all," he replied, returning my smile with a disarming grin. "All doctors have their deserving cases, it's the normal thing; and I've selected mine myself. I think it's only right to look after patients for nothing when they haven't the means to pay. But I know which people are really poor and which only pretend to be, and I don't allow any impostors. I keep my card-index in my head, and if they really have no money they get free treatment. If they've got some, then there are no reductions. In fact the better off they are, the more they ought to pay, to my way of thinking."

"A good old-fashiond idea, rob the rich to help the poor. Mind, I quite agree with you."

"If it's old-fashioned," said Bonnafy, "it's because I imagine things were like that in the old days when doctors knew how to look after themselves."

"Don't they now?" I said.

"Oh no, everyone snaps their fingers at us now, even the government."

"How do you mean?"

"Well, as one example, in a great impulse of generosity the government decrees that all disabled ex-service men can have free medical attention at state expense."

"Don't you agree?"

"Oh yes," agreed Bonnafy, "but when the government figured out the expense of this step, they said to themselves very shrewdly: 'This is all very well, but it's going to cost us a lot of money. Luckily doctors are kindhearted idiots, so we'll appeal to their sentiment.' Since then we've had to look after disabled ex-service men at a ridiculously low rate, for almost nothing. On the other hand the state, which is so generous with our labor and our fees, takes good care not to forget to tax us for them. Anyhow, if I'm going to look after some people for almost nothing, I like to choose the right ones. At least," he added with a smile, "it means I can sometimes enjoy these excellent trout. Have some cheese, old man?"

He took some himself, and once more started eating in silence. I thought I saw a chance of bringing the conversation back to quack-healers and the miller Lacan, but Bonnafy cut me short at once: "Oh to hell with all these lunatics and their private witch-doctors. You might think we were in darkest Africa, they're so backward here. Maybe we doctors often let our patients die, but I can assure you the miller of Laubat kills off *his* more or less certainly. To my mind it has the advantage of selecting the stupidest for non-survival. Anyhow don't let's talk any more about all that. I want you to tell me over coffee what's going on up in Montparnasse."

193

Chapter Nine

March 19–22

WHILE I was with Bonnafy, Antoine had been spending the night at the Orceyre farm. He had returned there directly after dinner, and gone straight to little Marcel's bedside. This I heard next day from young Jeanne Orceyre when I made my morning call. For the next four days I called twice a day, usually morning and late afternoon, and almost always I saw Antoine's bicycle leaning against the side of the house.

He had hurled himself into the struggle immediately with fanatical fervor. In an illness of this sort disaster might come at any moment, and Antoine evidently intended to stay there day and night, contesting patiently every foot of ground, only leaving the boy's room to eat or answer the very few other calls he still received. Directly afterwards he would return to his vigil, watching at the bed in shifts with Jeanne, who was also in the room most of the time. When she was keeping watch, Jeanne would sit by the bed with her hands clasped, gazing miserably with wide eyes at her son's tense and flushed little face. But she was ready on the instant to put on a soothing smile, as the first thing which should meet *his* eyes when he half opened them in pain.

Several sleepless nights made Antoine seem more strained and haggard every time I saw him. Yet I could feel that he was upheld and sustained by a singleminded devotion to this one concrete task which had fallen to him as a doctor—a doctor almost ready to despair of his power to follow his calling. At all costs he meant to save this life. Success here was the one thing which could restore his faith and self-confidence.

I was deeply moved by the continual presence at the bedside of these two watchers, the doctor and the mother. Although each movement in the house made little Marcel wince, even in his sleep, and seemed to send a shudder through every fiber in

194

his body, nobody else showed any special consideration. Ordinary life went on as usual, apparently impervious to pain and unhappiness, and from the bedroom you could hear all the time the dull clumping from the stables, the careless scraping of clogs on the floors, the pitiless chattering and gossip of the neighbors, and endless trivial noises in the kitchen which easily penetrated the thin wooden partition. Only Jeanne Orceyre and Antoine seemed capable of continuing the fight right to the last breath, to soften as much as possible the terror of Marcel's death. For I did not now feel there was much hope left of saving his life, though at times it seemed as if these two, through sheer persistence, love, and devotion, might still perform a miracle and rescue the forlorn little body from the black abyss.

Not once when we were there together did Antoine again mention his idea of leaving the district. He seemed to have forgotten it, as one might forget a wish to run away from everything, conceived in a moment of depression and weakness. I took great care not to refer to the idea again, especially as I had often regretted the promise I had made in an unreflecting impulse of pity. Carried away at the time by my enthusiasm for helping a lame dog over a particularly difficult stile, I had only remembered later on that in all probability my letter to Henri Philippon would prove quite fruitless. As Mayor of Aurillac, M. Serres would very likely have his own candidate to recommend, and there was only one vacancy.

Once Antoine did make an indirect allusion to his leaving. The second day I had no chance to return to Montagut till evening, and at half past seven I rang up Antoine, who had waited for me at the Orceyres and had only just returned home. I suggested seeing the boy myself without making him turn out again, but as he insisted on coming back with me I offered to pick him up.

When I reached Montagut, he was waiting for me in his office. His wife was sitting near him, knitting. He had the stove on in my honor, as it was freezing outside. I was very willing to drop into an armchair for a minute or two to warm up. When I was in the corridor there was an appetizing smell from the kitchen, and I suddenly felt very much at home in this peaceful family picture. Antoine was reading at his desk with a short student's pipe in his mouth, and Marie quietly knitting next to him.

Her eyes were on the needles, but sometimes she stopped, and with a heavy gentle movement let her hands rest on her stomach. Her slender neck was slightly bent towards her swollen body, as if she were listening to the little creature inside it, which she could feel moving and growing every minute. But when she raised her eyes and looked at her husband with her serene smile lighting up her thin, pale, rather insignificant face, I understood that Marie Ricaud would always be wife as well as mother. Antoine, wherever he went, would have near him a source of strength and comfort and happiness.

For a moment, contemplating the tender face turned towards him, I sincerely envied Antoine's good fortune and felt a surge of affection for them both. Then Marie turned to me with the same warming smile on her face. I wanted to tell them both how happy it made me to see them together, so much in love despite all their troubles. I could not quite manage to say this, though, and contented myself with returning Marie's smile.

Antoine looked at his watch and rose, saying: "Do you think we should go?" Marie asked if he would mind waiting just one minute. She was knitting a sweater for him, and wanted to measure it on him. "I began it five months ago," she told me, "but it was postponed because I had so many baby clothes to make." Antoine smiled indulgently, and let her take the necessary measurements. "It's going to be a polo sweater," she told him. "It'll go nicely with your windbreaker, and perhaps you'll be able to do without a scarf next year."

Antoine said: "That's fine, darling." Then he glanced at me, and I read in the glance that I was not to mention in front of her any of his plans for the following winter. He started getting ready to go. He had closed his emergency bag, then opened it again to check the contents, and went through his syringe case. I saw him raise his head with sudden impatience; his face was quite red. "Where's my ten-centicube syringe?" he asked sharply.

"Oh, I'm so sorry, dear," answered Marie immediately. "As the alcohol lamp was empty, I boiled the syringe on the kitchen stove, and I must have left it there. I'll go and fetch it at once."

"No, don't get up. But it's lucky I checked it. Otherwise I'd have gone without, and you realize what the consequences might have been." I had never seen him like this; he had spoken harshly, almost unkindly, and now he went out, slamming the door behind him.

"His nerves have gone to pieces, he's been working far too hard," said Marie. "I wish I hadn't annoyed him like that." She looked at me with warmth and affection, as one who knew her husband well too; almost at once Antoine returned. The few yards he had walked had been more than enough to allow his temper to subside. He said nothing, merely stood at the door and looked at his wife, telling her he was sorry without any words being used.

She rose, and just at this moment the bell rang. "This time I'll go," she said. She went out, closing the door behind her. As on the first occasion when I came to the Ricauds' house, I could hear her in conversation with another woman, and then the sound of clogs in the corridor.

Antoine strained his ears: "It's someone for the dispensary," he said, "not so much because they need medicine as because they're hoping to see *you*."

"See me?" I echoed in astonishment.

"Of course," he answered. "Since young Chanut's recovery, the whole place is talking of you with deep respect. You've become 'that young doctor from Paris.' You'll see how our present customer will take a tremendous while deciding between various different vermifuge mixtures, just to give Marie more time to talk about you. I can hear the questions just as if I were there myself. Thank God all that will soon be over. Some days I'd love to throw out all the gossiping old women in the whole village. When we first came here, they used to come in on the pretext of buying a franc's worth of this or that. Then they'd go on idly chattering while they sniffed all over to find out what we were having for dinner, glanced at our belongings to sum up how much we were worth, looked at the laundry hanging out to dry. All their questions were full of feigned benevolence, of course. They only wanted to help newcomers to the village."

"Marie must have felt very uncomfortable."

"She certainly did. The worst of it was that she didn't dare say nothing or give evasive answers. For one thing she was afraid of hurting their feelings, and she was anxious not to seem touchy or aloof, putting on airs. Then the early questions turned into sarcastic comments and mean insinuations."

As usual he had begun pacing up and down. Now he stopped in front of me, almost as if I were the culprit, and clenching his fists exclaimed: "What I'll never forgive these brutes for is not the harm they've done me, but not being able to make her life here better. They've even made me cowardly enough to let her suffer. I've allowed her to keep on smiling bravely, hiding all her own troubles, just so that she can try to keep me cheerful."

The clatter of clogs could be heard coming back down the corridor. When the front door closed, Antoine muttered hastily: "By the way, I've not told Marie anything about my plans, so please don't mention them to her. I don't want to worry her with all that in her condition. When I tell her about it, I want to have her believe I'm going away for purely selfish reasons, for the sake of my own happiness and not to try to save her. Otherwise she'd probably refuse to accept the sacrifice."

Chapter Ten

March 23rd

"He DIED two hours ago. Just what you were afraid of from the start—syncope after the nerve centers had been affected. I couldn't do a thing."

Antoine was sitting at the desk in his office, and he spoke in the dull, apathetic, lifeless voice of a man who is exhausted. You could feel that this death, after four days and nights of ceaseless struggle, had touched him to the very depths of his being. He sat hunched in the armchair, and his reddened eyes stared vacantly into the distance, as if he were still stunned by the shock. Everything else in the world was wiped out of his vision except that little face, flushed and sweating, with its ghastly grimace of a dead animal. He was a doctor, accustomed

198

to frequent defeat in this sort of struggle right from his first weeks in hospital, yet he had fought so hard and so hopefully for Marcel Orceyre that the death of this one patient seemed to shatter him as it might have shattered a layman.

I, on the other hand, as I observed with some shame, was impelled by scientific curiosity to want to hear further details about the actual death. Antoine still sat motionless, his face as blank as ever, and I told myself, as an excuse for questioning him, that making him talk was the only way to shake him out of his inertia. "You gave him chloroform?" I asked.

"I did not," he answered, turning his pallid face towards me. "And I'm glad I didn't. I was just going to begin. A few minutes more, and all my life I'd have felt as if I'd killed him myself."

"Why?" I said. "You know as well as I do how often the nerve centers are affected in tetanus. And these repeated anesthesias might have offered a chance of pulling him through."

"Oh yes—and the serum too was just as much of a chance as the chloroform, wasn't it?"

"Of course."

"Well, if you must know, when Marcel was having his final attack, the old grandma kept prowling round near him. She knew at once that he was dying. Suddenly she gave a terrible shriek, flung herself on the bed, and picked up the child. Next minute the stiffened little head fell gently backwards for the first time for days and days, rolling from one shoulder to the other. It was just like a ventriloquist's doll."

"Poor little boy," I murmured, remembering ruefully how I had promised his mother he would get better.

"The old woman put down the body, and simply went for me with her nails, ready to scratch my eyes out. She hurled threats and curses at me, she was pretty well crazy with grief and hatred. Orceyre managed to restrain her, but in the flood of her insults, half in French and half in patois, I realized that she was calling me a murderer, or rather calling both of us murderers. Still, I also realized that she'd been driven to it by the healer."

"The healer," I exclaimed. "My God, he's the real murderer."

Antoine shrugged his shoulders. "Naturally," he said. "But he used the same strategy as with the boy whose arm had to be

199

amputated—the best defense is attack, you know. He told them it was our serum, a poison made from the blood of dead horses, which killed little Marcel."

"And they believed him?"

"Utterly. All the farm hands and neighbors gathered in the room near the bed and formed a hostile circle round me. They started moving in and I heard them muttering threats. I felt like an innocent man who has been hunted down by a mob. They were about to fall upon me and lynch me."

"A very unpleasant situation," I said. "And did you try to defend yourself?"

"Oh yes, I tried to defend myself. Not for my own sake, but to get them to see the truth, so that other little children like Marcel Orceyre should not be murdered by stupidity and ignorance. I tried to ram into those thick-headed stubborn idiots that serum is not taken from dead horses but from well-cared-for living horses, and that it's carefully made in special laboratories by expert hands."

"Did any of them believe it?"

"Not a single one. I looked from one brutal face to another, and saw nothing in any of those eyes but hatred. I realized nothing I could say would ever stop them from believing the healer."

"What about young Madame Orceyre?" I said. "She saw you working day and night to save her child. Didn't she defend you?"

Antoine became ghastly pale. He had been talking in an increasingly bitter tone, but now his voice abruptly sank to little more than a whisper. I was half expecting him to begin crying again, and felt that perhaps it would help him.

"I thought she would," he answered miserably. "I turned and looked at her kneeling against the cot. She seemed almost rooted to the floor, and she was looking at the boy's dead body like a lunatic, her eyes wild but not crying. And then she turned her look on me. Of course, up to the last minute, she'd been too optimistic, expecting the miracle we promised."

"I promised."

"It doesn't matter who actually made the promise. I always tried to keep her courage up, and she was certainly expecting too much. Or perhaps at the end she may have been almost out of her mind with grief. I don't know which it was, but anyhow the scorn and hatred in her eyes when she looked at me were so terrible that I instinctively put my hands up to protect myself. If someone had taken down a gun off the mantelpiece and shot me, it couldn't have been more deadly. Since even the boy's mother condemned me, there was nothing more for me to do or say. I just left the house."

I could think of nothing to say, and Antoine raised a sweating contorted face towards me as he continued: "There you are. It's all over for me now. I've done my best, why should I go on battering my head against a brick wall? After all, people only get the doctors they deserve. If they're satisfied with a Bonnafy or a Chassagnon, or an old wreck like Legros, it's no damned use my having good intentions. I might just as well go away at once."

"Now look here, Antoine," I began.

"It's no use," he said, looking at me with pathetic determination in his eyes. "It's all decided, I'm giving up. We'll leave as soon as the baby is born."

I was now extremely worried by the responsibility I had taken in promising so light-heartedly to help him. There had been no reply from Henri about Antoine's candidature for the Aurillac post, and I had put off writing to him again or trying to telephone him because I hoped Antoine might change his mind. I remembered what Dr. Delpuech had said about Antoine, and made an effort to encourage him.

"Look, Antoine," I told him. "Dr. Delpuech knows the people round here and their mentality. He ought to—he's been here forty years. When I told him about you the other day, he asserted that people were only observing you, that you were still on approval, so to speak. 'If your friend can only be patient a little longer,' he said, 'the day will come quite soon when the whole district takes him to their heart.'"

Antoine shook his head gently.

"No," he answered, "I'd believe old Legros sooner than Delpuech. You can put everything you've got into it, you can learn the local patois, but you'll still never learn the right way to go up to a cow in a stable and touch a diseased udder without hurting the beast. So for people here you'll always remain a foreigner. To expect to adapt yourself to all that is a fairy tale.

Perhaps in the long run there might be something worth while in such a life—but after how many years and efforts!"

The more he talked, the less powers I felt of dissuading him from his new course. To realize I was speaking to no purpose, I only had to look at that exhausted face, the face of a man who had prematurely aged, and those shoulders sagging because they now seemed too weak to carry all these burdens. Lucien had said to me one day that Medicine in the country was "a war of attrition," and Antoine for all his courage was not cut out like Lucien for such grim battles.

I soon saw that he was so absorbed in his own troubles that he was hardly listening to anything I said; and eventually, in a very low voice, he muttered: "I'm finished, finished."

After this we both sat there in silence. I felt as if I were at the bedside of a dying man who knows he is dying. There is nothing which can give him real encouragement, and you wonder how soon you can decently leave, for surely to stay there any longer will only prolong his agony. I looked discreetly at my watch and saw it was half past eight. I took as much care not to make a noise getting up from my chair as if I had really been sitting with an invalid, and when I was on my feet I saw my figure in the mirror standing behind Antoine looking very embarrassed. It made me feel ashamed to be escaping like this. Antoine came with me to the car, not saying a word. I smiled at him half-heartedly, and when we shook hands I gave his an extra squeeze, trying to make up for the words of encouragement and comfort which would not come to my lips.

It was an icy night, but I deliberately wound the window down, and when I had started up the engine I breathed in a great draught of cold air to help clear my lungs. I felt strangely cheerful and light-hearted, as if I had been set free. In a way I had left behind at Montagut another Jean Nérac, who would never be anything but miserable and unlucky.

I got back to Peyrac about nine, and went straight in to a meal. I was glad to hear from Félicie that there had been no further calls for me, and as soon as I had finished dinner, I went up to see Dr. Delpuech.

Although he still could not get up, he was a great deal better and Lucien had allowed him to have a few more visitors. One of his regular visitors was an old school friend, Joseph Maury, who had come back to Peyrac on being retired from a minor civil service post at Paris.

At Peyrac Joseph Maury had continued to lead the same narrow empty existence as before. Having remained single, he was looked after by an old housekeeper, and he had built up an elaborate ritual for all his everyday activities, including his diet, which he observed with great rigidity and in minute detail. You would pass him in the street, always at the same time, wearing a bowler hat, but muffled up to his eyes with a huge scarf to avoid the drafts which might attack him at street corners. He was almost always sucking a lozenge, for he lived in terror of catching some infection.

When he came to see Dr. Delpuech he never hung up his overcoat in the hall, since he was afraid of contagion from the patients who had been in the office. In the old doctor's bedroom, however, knowing that his friend was suffering from an illness which was not contagious, Maury considered himself safe, and moreover took advantage of any advice which the doctor might provide on questions of health. When he was not expressing some mild platitude or dozing in his armchair, he would often be questioning his old friend on the possible significance of the gastric rumblings he had experienced that morning, or the four visits he had made to the bathroom that day instead of the customary two.

He was certainly harmless enough, and did not talk a great deal, so Félicie let him see Dr. Delpuech regularly. He came in nearly every afternoon at exactly a quarter past two, to drink a cup of coffee. Every time, Dr. Delpuech told me, he would ask anxiously as he raised his cup, as if it were a matter of ritual: "You're sure this isn't bad for the health?" After which the doctor would invariably reassure him with the same sentence: "Quite sure, as long as you take a small quantity regularly every day." Then Maury would relax in his armchair and take a nap, and Dr. Delpuech would laugh and say: "Ah, these habits—you must think you're back at the Ministry." At five o'clock Maury would leave immediately, as if he had an urgent call elsewhere; but he would reappear in the evening at exactly half past eight and stay until it was time to go to bed at twenty to ten. A few days seemed to have been sufficient to establish an almost unalterable timetable, and I was not at all surprised to find him this evening in Dr. Delpuech's room.

When I came in, Maury was saying to his friend in his usual rather crotchety tones: "I always think it's very queer, Daniel, the way you can't stop reading medical papers and medical books. I should have thought you'd have had enough of all that. And when it's not medicine you're reading about, it's science or philosophy or something deep like that."

"Yes, Joseph," replied the doctor, "it's my recipe for keeping young. First of all a doctor must remain a student right till the end, and I feel just as anxious to learn as when I was twenty. Secondly, a passion for science stops a man from growing old. Thinking, even when the thought is not original, sustains physical activity. Why don't you develop some such passion yourself, Joseph?" he concluded with a smile.

"Passion?" Maury recoiled, rolling startled eyes, as if his friend had said something obscene.

"Certainly," said Dr. Delpuech: "I assure you it's a serious piece of advice. Retirement is a very dangerous thing, a murderous invention thought up by administrators to get rid of their old and faithful servants without delay. Our organs don't know anything about retirement. In order to renovate one's hormones and maintain the balance of one's health, some little passion is essential. So if I were you, I should try to fish, garden, study botany, collect stones or stamps, gamble at cards or else on the stock exchange. If you can't think of anything else, go in for politics. Doesn't matter what you do, but you must do something."

"I don't know what you mean," said Maury, wriggling more and more uncomfortably in his armchair, and Dr. Delpuech added mockingly: "Oh well, if you want another way to revive your glands, why not take an interest in some of the village girls? Remember that Claudius Hermippus lived one hundred and fifty-five years and five days, according to his epitaph, due to the pleasure he took in beautiful maidens."

"Village girls!" snapped old Maury, going very red in the face. "I think your brain must be affected. Beautiful maidens indeed."

"What," exclaimed Delpuech, affecting to have misunderstood him. "Do you mean you'd rather follow the advice of

Cornaro, the celebrated Venetian centenarian who kept eleven handsome nephews near him? You'd rather have the village lads, would you?"

"Aren't you ashamed at your age to talk of such disgusting things like a young medical student? I don't care for this conversation at all, Daniel. I wish you good-night." Joseph Maury had suddenly noticed that it was a quarter to ten, so that he was already five minutes behind schedule. He rose hastily.

"Good-night, Joseph, don't take my remarks too seriously," Dr. Delpuech called out after him. We could hear the sound of his boots squeaking as he hurried down the stairs, and both the old doctor and I burst out laughing. "Do you think it's good for him to have his leg pulled like that?" I chuckled.

"Oh, I think so," said Dr. Delpuech, becoming more serious again. "And perhaps I only do it, you know, because I've often envied him."

"Envied M. Maury?" I exclaimed incredulously.

"Sometimes," nodded the old doctor. "When I've come back harassed and discouraged after a day's heavy work and a night without sleep when everything's gone wrong. I expect you're beginning to know that sort of night, and those disastrous days when your efforts to save a dying man have all been in vain."

"Yes, I'm beginning to know about that," I said, intending to work the conversation round to Antoine's vain effort to save Marcel Orceyre. But there was no immediate opportunity, for Dr. Delpuech returned to the subject of his old school friend.

"After one of those nights and days, I meet poor old Joseph, placid, rested, going out for his usual constitutional without a care in the world, and I've envied him."

"You could have retired yourself, sir," I put in, "if you'd really wanted to."

"Certainly I could, long ago. I'm on my own, with no dependents and simple tastes. In fact I'm much better off than many other old doctors I know who are absolutely compelled to go on in order to support their families. Anyhow, at these moments of discouragement, I've compared my lot to Joseph Maury's. We're exactly the same age, and he has always had a regular job with no excitements, worked fixed hours, with undisturbed nights, vacations, paid sick leave, no insecurity for the future, and a cushioned old age at the end of it."

"It's a bit different for you, isn't it?" I said with a smile.

"Quite different, Jean," he answered. "For forty years, as you know, I've been caught in a mesh of duties and cares and struggles, and a month ago I was working the same average of fifteen hours a day at sixty-two as I did at thirty."

"I was at Camejeanne yesterday," I said, "to see a patient who was farming on land owned by M. Maury. He quite envied such a landowner, I could see. For him M. Maury was a clever man who had 'got on in the world.'"

"Yes," replied Dr. Delpuech with deep conviction. "I'm sure people envy him more than they envy me; only he's never known the joy of being loved."

"Don't you think he's rather an extreme case?" I said.

"Possibly. But there are many nearly as bad, and you can't really blame them either. Working in a dusty office doesn't offer much scope to develop your libido—I think our friend Freud would call it. And of course I was quite serious now when I told him we need enthusiasms, and libido in that sense, to survive and keep healthy. If our legislators were doctors, they wouldn't try to lighten people's work by shortening working hours. They'd try to give each man a chance to really enjoy his work."

"That would be pretty hard to legislate for, though."

"Of course it would—it's the major problem of the modern world, as I see it, and perhaps the problem isn't soluble. But unless we solve it soon, unless every man and woman has the chance of a minimum of happiness, then the whole social machine may well go up in smoke."

"Well, at least doctors have real enthusiasm for their work, which helps to keep them going, wouldn't you say?"

"The real doctors—always," he said with a smile which seemed to be thanking providence for having called him to this work. "Our job will always be something more than a job. Every moment there's a new situation, a new responsibility, a battle which one feels compelled to fight with the whole of one's personality."

"And so one sticks to the job," I prompted him, "and is ready to begin the same old struggle over and over again."

I found his remarks both sad and inspiring, showing me once more how even the best medical men have to overcome moods of weariness and discouragement. It did not seem a good moment to broach Antoine's troubles, the decision of a young doctor to surrender after six months and not stick to his job. I could not find it in my heart to blame Antoine after all he had been through, but I did not think Dr. Delpuech would see matters in the same light.

"Yes, Jean," the old doctor in fact said: "he begins the same old struggle because there's something in him which tells him he must, that his work is worth while after all, that Medicine is a magnificent and ennobling profession in which the real practitioner will find no time to feel tired. He'll go on working till he drops, not heeding the wounds he may have sustained on the way. Medicine does not tire us, its servants, it wears us right out."

"Well, I mustn't wear you out any further, sir," I remarked after this peroration. "I think I'll go to bed now."

"Good-night, Jean," he replied. "Forgive my preaching at you again—I hope it's a sign I'm a good deal better. I'm not at all tired," he smiled, "even after lecturing both Joseph and you on the same night."

"Good-night," I said, and went along to my room. Conflicting emotions seethed once more in my brain.

Chapter Eleven

March 24th

DURING MY office hours today a man came into the hall who did not look like a patient. Nor, by the air of authority with which he strode up to me, did I think he could be one of the sellers of patent medicines who occasionally strayed as far as Peyrac. He was smartly dressed, his hair was well oiled, and he looked decidedly well fed; smooth was the word which automatically came into my head on seeing him, smooth in every sense of the word. I guessed he must be in his early forties.

He handed me a visiting card, announcing at the same time in hearty and incisive tones: "Gérard Cabouret at your service, chief representative in Central France of the well-known Bricard Agency, which has specialized since 1902 in the purchase and sale of medical practices. You are Dr. Jean Nérac, acting as locum for Dr. Daniel Delpuech?"

I nodded.

"Then, Doctor, I would be obliged if you could spare me a few minutes."

Directly I had shown him into my office he came to the point: "If it is not indiscreet, Doctor, may I ask if you are already discussing with Dr. Delpuech the purchase of his practice?"

He looked at me acutely, and I replied, in some surprise at the question: "Not at all. I'm only acting as locum for a few weeks. I have still to submit my thesis, and also to do my year of military service."

M. Gérard Cabouret was clearly delighted. He had, however, something else to find out. "Confidentially, of course, do you happen to know if anybody else is thinking of purchasing it?"

He was beginning to irritate me, and I said rather coldly: "Not that I know of. In fact I had not heard that it was for sale." I should have liked to stop there, but curiosity was too strong for me, and I could not resist asking: "How did you know there was a chance of its being for sale?"

Cabouret looked both amused and pleased with himself. "Just a little trick of the trade, Doctor. You only need to be in touch with someone working on the District Council. When a doctor of forty years' practice has never once asked the Council's permission to take on a locum, the day he makes up his mind to do so, especially during the month of February, you don't need to be a learned professor to work out that he is not intending to go away for a few weeks' winter sports. In this season one's first guess would be pneumonia or pulmonary congestion, and in this part of the world, with an elderly doctor who can't have looked after his own health very much, these illnesses take a pretty fair toll. Because of his age, one couldn't, of course, exclude the possibility of cancer or above all of a heart complaint. At the hotel I learned that it was in act the heart which had laid Dr. Delpuech low. Angina pectoris, isn't it? Too much muscular fatigue and excessive pressure on the nervous system? Yes, I thought so. Three quarters of the doctors I've been concerned with have died of that."

He glanced round the room, starting a kind of valuation. "Office and equipment rather old-fashioned," he commented, and then, going up to the glass cupboard: "Not many instruments. Certainly no electrical equipment." His frankly commercial tone made me think of Bonnafy at his least attractive, and when he looked at me inquiringly, I said tersely: "No, no electrical equipment."

"Too bad. Means a lot of expense, as it'll be quite essential for the successor to get some. And the practice generally? Must be quite good, I'm sure. Only two doctors for such a big district, and one of those very young. Yes, with the right man, it could even offer a living to a third doctor. And the annual turnover—have you any idea about that?"

While he was talking, he had continued his expert tour of inspection. He stopped in front of the photograph of Dr. Delpuech's wife and son on the mantelpiece. Perhaps more even than his blunt questions, I found myself revolted by the bailiff-like way he was surveying everything in the room, including this photograph.

"I've no idea at all," I said still more coldly. "Since I came here, I have not had any dealings with questions of fees. If the turnover interests you, however, I suggest you would do better to ask Dr. Delpuech himself."

Cabouret realized at once that his question might have been a little too direct, but it needed a stronger snub than this to abash him. He at once left the photograph, and hurried over to where I was standing, raising his hands in a soothing gesture.

"Oh, Doctor, please understand my motives. In the general interest I have to find out everything I can. It is such a delicate matter when one has to put all these questions directly to the doctor concerned. You never get a really frank answer. He may not tell you because he doesn't like admitting how few patients he has, or because he's too modest to admit that he lets most of them off without payment. When you ask them, almost all these doctors will work out their turnover from their daily record of patients seen, and they always forget to mention that a third of the patients pay very badly, and that about another third, say, get treatment free. Look, let's take an example. How many people have you seen at your office this afternoon?"

I nearly told him that was none of his business, but his last remarks had been made in such persuasive and conciliatory tones that against my better judgment I glanced at my notebook. "Fourteen," I told him.

"Nice gross figure. Let's see the details. First caller?"

"A good woman who came to ask me to visit her husband as if I just happened to be passing. I've already seen him—alcoholic enlargement of the liver. He still drinks, and I must put the fear of God into him without letting him know how I know about it or who told me."

"At least ten minutes wasted in explanations with the wife, isn't that so? Plenty of 'And you *will* tell him that...', and 'remember to say that....' She may well pay you for your call at her house, but certainly not for the ten minutes of your time she's wasted this afternoon."

This summed up the position very accurately, and when the suave M. Cabouret said: "Right, go on to the next," I was rather amused and looked up my second case docilely. It was an accident at work, and I had dressed the arm.

"In other words," said Cabouret, "a good quarter of an hour, which you will be paid for at the reduced rate for industrial accidents. Third caller, please."

This one was at least picturesque. He had happened to find in an old purse a former hospital card dating from 1916 which bore the diagnosis: *Furunculosis of the neck*. He had ingenuously come to ask me whether, thanks to this precious document, he wouldn't be entitled to a small pension "like everybody else." When I discouraged him in this idea, he looked terribly disappointed, and then wanted to know if his old hospital card, proof of his active participation in the World War, would not at least give him the right to have a free X-ray of his back at Aurillac, seeing that ever since the war he had had terrible backaches. To avoid disappointing this former warrior in *all* his hopes, I at least gave him a free examination.

A little later, on the other hand, I saw a genuine disabled ex-service man whose lungs had been affected by his being gassed in the war: this meant a reduced charge for examination and treatment. Next came an old woman on public assistance—more free medical attention—whose particular need was a prescription whereby she could obtain half a liter of codliver oil from the chemist's. Then there was a woman who wanted me to see her bedridden mother, and though I was not sure whether I was expected to perform a miracle and put the old lady on her feet again, I agreed to go and see her, chiefly so as to avoid further garrulity from the daughter.

"In fact," said Cabouret, when we had been through all fourteen patients, "five will pay at the normal rates, if they ever pay at all, three at reduced rates, and all the rest have automatic free treatment. Well, Doctor, can you rely on outward signs after that? If the tax-collector had been round here this afternoon do you think Dr. Delpuech would have been let off paying a high tax next year? But just calculate the receipts, actual and potential, and you can tell yourself that in all practices the number of reduced rates, free treatment and bad payers, not to mention the time wasters, is just about the same."

"Is that so?" I said politely, impressed with his reasoning, despite myself.

"Of course it is," he told me triumphantly, "and just imagine that instead of a tax-collector a young doctor with no experience in such matters were to keep watch outside the door before buying a practice, and work out the number of patients who ring the bell at ten francs apiece, wouldn't his reckoning be quite a bit out?"

"I suppose it would."

"So you see, my dear Doctor," he went on, with good-humored forbearance for my earlier brusqueness, "my question on the business turnover was basically quite a fair one. I should know better than anyone from seeing so many of your colleagues that Medicine is far more a sacred calling than a profession, but all the same one needs to talk about money from time to time. Even the priest," he concluded, with a refined smile, "is obliged to earn his bread and butter from the altar."

He stopped a moment to allow the force of his logic to sink in, then inquired: "Do you think Dr. Delpuech would be able to see me for a few minutes? Please don't have any fears, I realize that he is easily tired, and I will be both brief and on my best behavior. I'm used to these old veterans, you know."

Helplessly, I led the way to Dr. Delpuech's room.

The conversation, however, did not go exactly as the representative of the Bricard Agency had hoped.

Dr. Delpuech welcomed him politely as usual, waving him to an armchair in front of the bed. Cabouret did not allow himself to sink back against the cushion, but sat on the edge of the chair as if the better to dominate his audience. He began with a preamble in which he apologized politely for disturbing the doctor, but ventured to offer his services. After all, he said, a general practitioner certainly had the right to think of himself a little after having spent all his life thinking of others.

Here he gave an ingratiating little smile which contrived to be both familiar and respectful at the same time, and then stopped for a moment to give Dr. Delpuech time to raise any objections. But the latter still said nothing, which Cabouret evidently considered a good omen. He sank deeper into the chair, stretched out his legs and brought his guns up a little further: "In case you are intending to retire, the Bricard Agency can put you in touch with a high-class young doctor —the agency has been in existence since 1902, and only has high-class people on its books. We should choose some young physician of excellent family who would consider buying such a magnificent practice as you have, Doctor, at a very fair price."

He stopped again with a smile of obsequious cordiality, rubbing his hands as if already congratulating himself on a successful issue of these negotiations. Dr. Delpuech was as pale as during one of his most painful attacks, and his tense features told me clearly how far he was struggling to control himself. But he must have found Cabouret's last sentence intolerable, and after obvious hesitation, he finally boiled over and said irritably: "I understand the purpose of your remarks, my dear sir, but what makes you think there is a practice for sale here?"

Poor Cabouret looked at him in some perplexity. Abruptly he straightened up on the edge of the chair to resume his battle position, and began his new attack rather more indirectly: "I was speaking in general terms, my dear doctor, thinking of the future, of some time when you might be considering taking a well-earned rest. I had not of course any immediate interested motives, merely the interest I take professionally in every good practice."

"I have no practice to sell, sir," broke out Dr. Delpuech with sudden vehemence. "You have been talking to me as if I were a common tradesman. But one does not sell patients as they used to sell Negro slaves, or like livestock at a fair. As to your purchaser of excellent family, I know just what that means: some profiteering butcher's son who'll slip off to a town as soon as he's bled the rustics white, or else the son of some big farmer who wants to make a gentleman out of his boy. Those are often the worst of all, you'd think that they kept nothing of their country upbringing but the faults—greed, and selfishness..."

Dr. Delpuech stopped. Already, no doubt, he was regretting this show of temper so foreign to his usual character. This importunate visitor was only acting as intermediary—he had said so himself—and he used the technical terms of his profession without any malice. Therefore as Cabouret, a good loser, rose to his feet apologizing profusely for having stayed so long, Dr. Delpuech's kindly smile returned. "The Bricard Agency must forgive me," he said. "My patients not being for sale, I can unfortunately only give them away, and I am hoping to choose for myself my successor. But please believe, my dear sir, that on any other matter I shall be delighted to oblige you if it is within my power."

By the time we were going downstairs, Cabouret had already recovered his aplomb, and he now revealed to me his conclusions: "Curious," he began, "how difficult some of these old doctors find it to retire. It's a queer profession that gets under your skin to that extent. I hope *I* shan't have to be dashing around from place to place when *I* turn sixty."

He stopped on the landing, and turning to me, added: "But your Dr. Delpuech is a different case again. He has no wife or child, I believe, so he doesn't need to bother his head about financial problems. Probably he doesn't see how ill he is. I suppose he thinks he'll be able to start his rounds again in a few weeks' time. So he is very high and mighty about giving away, and not selling, something he hopes to keep himself for a good while longer."

"Not at all," I said, "he is quite aware of his own condition."

213

Cabouret appeared slightly disconcerted and started down the next flight of stairs.

"Well then, it must be something else. But anyhow these old quacks are terrible. They make my job very difficult. Now, if we only had to deal with their widows, we'd be in clover. Dr. Delpuech talked about tradesmen just now, but at least when a tradesman dies he leaves something definite to his heirs, a shop, the goodwill, and the stock which enable the widow to know more or less where she stands. But for a doctor's widow, from one day to the next it's just nothing at all, everything disappears along with her husband. Haven't I seen those wretched widows going through the books? The whole town has gone right to the cemetery with the poor woman behind her husband's hearse, but as soon as she begins to send out statements regarding unpaid bills, there's nobody to see her. One might almost think the town came to the funeral just to make sure that their doctor was thoroughly dead and that there was no further risk of having to pay their debts. I know cases where over ninety-five per cent of the debts have had to be written off completely."

We were near the front door now, and I listened to this discourse in embarrassed silence. Cabouret took a pair of comfortable fur-lined gloves out of his pocket, and put one on. He was about to put the glove on the other hand, but at the last minute plunged the hand beneath his beautiful overcoat, brought out a wallet and took from it a new visiting card:

"Here, Doctor," he said. "You might as well have my address. I shall be completely at your service should you one day be looking for a position. But to prove to you that the Bricard Agency can also be disinterested, here is a free piece of expert advice for you: unless you have a private income, don't start a practice down South—people south of the Loire don't pay."

A little later, before starting on my round, I went up to Dr. Delpuech's room again, meaning to apologize for having allowed him to be disturbed by such an unfortunate visit. But I did not have the chance, for as soon as I went in, the old doctor, instead of referring to Cabouret, said: "You know, I'd like to meet your friend Ricaud. Now I'm so much better, wouldn't you like to bring him round here some evening?"

I was greatly surprised, and did not for a moment reflect

as to the motives which had made Dr. Delpuech express such a desire on this particular evening.

"That's queer, sir. For several days now I've been meaning to talk about him."

"How is he getting on?"

"I left him last night absolutely desperate. The little boy with tetanus we were looking after together died yesterday, and the miller of Laubat accuses us of having poisoned the boy by the serum we used. I don't think Ricaud's got a chance any more round there."

"Please don't say that," protested Dr. Delpuech firmly. "A doctor with real enthusiasm and professional conscience always succeeds in the end. Your friend must stick to his guns without worrying too much about prejudices and suspicions, and gradually, eventually, he'll make the grade."

"Ricaud has decided to leave," I said.

Dr. Delpuech had suddenly gone very red. He broke in sharply. "Where does he mean to go?"

"For the moment," I said, "he doesn't know. He's hoping for a job as a local health officer at Aurillac."

"No, he must not go." The old doctor shouted out these words as if he had had a sudden spasm of acute pain. I looked at him in amazement. He was gasping, and had grown pale once more. When he had become a little calmer and was able to speak, he asked me, "Why did you not stop him?"

I was taken aback by the depth of emotion and reproach in his voice. As if a total confession could somehow help to make up for any harm I had done, I admitted that far from trying to restrain Antoine, it was I who out of pity had encouraged him in this idea, by promising him a contact with the Mayor of Aurillac.

"Out of pity?" the old doctor repeated thoughtfully. "Yes, I can see you thought you were doing him a good turn, and that you acted out of kind-heartedness. But your kind heart has misled you this time."

"But Antoine was so terribly discouraged," I protested. "I know M. Serres' son quite well, or rather I know a friend of his very well, and as it was this post as medical inspector which Antoine particularly wanted...."

"No," cried Dr. Delpuech with extreme vehemence, "that's just the point. It's *not* what he really wants."

"But...but he said," I stammered.

"He said!" exclaimed the old man. "Don't you know then that a lover who has been jilted and humiliated can renounce in words the woman he once adored, can long for her death, can even kill her in a fury of delirious jealousy—but afterwards he'll hurl himself on her body and implore you to save her, because he still loves her?"

"And you think it's like that with Ricaud?"

"It is just like that. Of course we need administrative doctors and health officials. They do useful work with their annual reports and statistics and files and circulars. But when your friend Ricaud, thanks to your intervention, has been shut up for a few weeks in his municipal office, instead of thanking you, he'll hate and curse you."

"I find that a little difficult to believe, judging by his present attitude."

"It wasn't to sit in an office that Ricaud did Medicine. Think how empty and purposeless, and joyless too, life must seem for one who is at heart a real doctor, never to have his own patients to see and try to heal. Your friend renounced his vocation, believing he meant it. But you should have shown him a more objective viewpoint, instead of naively allowing his temporary mood to deceive you, and actually encouraging him to follow it. There, I must say, you took a very heavy responsibility upon yourself."

"I didn't look at it like that. I couldn't just have done nothing, could I?"

"Forgive my religious language," said Dr. Delpuech slowly, "but I believe that no one here below is tempted beyond his strength. You have acted like a child in trying to turn your friend away from his appointed path. His real place, the only place where he will be able to find satisfaction and happiness, is by the bedsides of his patients."

I tried to think hard and clearly, and felt that perhaps what he said was just. "I expect you're right, sir," I said with a sigh. "It seemed the best thing to do at the time."

He seemed calmer now, and looked at me kindly. "Yes, Jean, but I think I am right, you know," he said. "For you see, my son, for us doctors the secret of happiness is very simple: it lies in the resolute performance of our daily work. Only a little time would have been needed to make your friend Ricaud understand this and find new heart. Perhaps it is not too late to put things right. I hope you'll be able to get him to come over here very soon."

I phoned Antoine immediately after this conversation and asked him to come over the following night. He accepted ungraciously, being softened only when I suggested it would be a break for his wife.

Chapter Twelve

March 25th

NEXT DAY Félicie had the door of the kitchen slightly jar, and most of the afternoon whenever I crossed the hall I would catch sight of her agile hands kneading dough, or moving about pots and pans on the stove amidst much clatter. She had promised me a magnificent meal for this dinner which was being given at Dr. Delpuech's special wish, and I thought to myself, knowing Antoine's upset and depressed state: she'll need to surpass herself for the atmosphere to be at all tolerable.

When I went to fetch the Ricauds from Montagut, I found Antoine in an even more alarming state than when I had last seen him. Usually his was a very expressive and highly sensitive face in which changes of mood were transparent, but on this evening he wore a stubborn dull frown and a fixed stare. All his features were so set in this mold they seemed almost unrecognizable.

We upset Félicie's culinary plans by arriving a little late. We immediately went up to Dr. Delpuech's room, and found Lucien there already chatting with him. I had only just finished making the introductions when Félicie, wearing the tragic face of a cook whose masterpieces will soon be ruined, came in and declared, as a polite excuse for dragging us out of the bedroom at once, "The young lady will surely be very hungry by this time, specially having to eat enough for two."

"You'll have plenty of time to talk after dinner," she told us as she shepherded us downstairs, "but a good meal is like a selfish woman, wants everyone to wait for her but doesn't like being kept waiting herself."

From the old mahogany sideboard Félicie had produced a fine tablecloth and a handsome dinner service. The crystal glasses and the silver shone brilliantly. The soup tureen was steaming on the table, and a big fire blazed in the fireplace. The whole dining-room with its good but unpretentious old furniture breathed a long tradition of honest provincial comfort.

As she came in, Marie Ricaud glanced round the room with the keen eyes of a natural housewife, taking in the scene with an admiring half-possessive look on her face. Félicie bustled about looking after her, helping her sit down, going out to fetch a stool to slide under Marie's feet. Marie smiled contentedly, letting the atmosphere of warmth and light seep through her, running her fingers lovingly over the heavy silver and the fine smooth linen. Her lips were half opened in her contentment, and she seemed eager to absorb fully all these domestic luxuries of which she had been deprived.

Reassured about her, I looked at her husband. In the car Antoine had hardly spoken the whole way. He shook hands politely enough on being introduced to Lucien and Dr. Delpuech, but while the latter was talking to Marie, Antoine stayed silent, with a frown of reserve on his face. By hurrying us to the table, Félicie luckily shortened the beginning of this meeting with Dr. Delpuech before it became too painful. Between the courses, which she brought triumphantly from the kitchen, she remained near Marie's chair like a zealous but poorly trained footman, keeping watch over her plate, passing remarks to her as one housekeeper to another, and suggesting recipes which Marie might care to try.

I blessed the loquacious Félicie for her continual flow of talk. She was unwittingly helping matters immensely, for you could not expect a great deal of support from Lucien should the conversation start to lag. Moreover Marie was evidently amused. She laughed, and answered, and started questioning Félicie herself, but at times she threw a quick glance, anxious

218

nd tender, in the direction of her husband. She might have
been half apologizing for her innocent joy, or else imploring
him to join in with it so that her pleasure should be complete.

But these glances were in vain, for Antoine did not seem to
be listening, and did not even take the trouble to feign an interest in what his wife was saying. He seemed not only indifferent but even hostile. Sitting straight and tense in his chair,
he looked vacantly at the agreeable scene before him. It might
have symbolized for him a successful medical career which he
would envy but feel forever out of his reach—the sort of comfort he had probably hoped for in his own house eight months
earlier.

He ate without a word, and emptied his glass, which I at
once refilled. At home I knew he drank only water, and for a
moment I hoped that Dr. Delpuech's wines would make him
a bit more sociable after dinner. But quite soon I was alarmed
to see that his cheeks were becoming very flushed and that a
quarrelsome gleam was appearing in his eyes, as if the wine
were liberating evil instincts inside him. After that I was more
cautious, and left his glass unfilled.

Dinner was nearly over. Before leaving the table and going
up to Dr. Delpuech, I made a last effort to draw Antoine out
of his shell, and could think of no better chance of interesting
him than by starting to talk medical "shop" with Lucien. On
my rounds that very afternoon I had treated three huge goiters
in a single village and these I immediately flung into the con-
versational arena; it seemed a reasonably safe subject. Only
Lucien took it up, however, declaring that since he had been
at Peyrac, he had seen a great many goiter cases, ranging from
the gland in front of the neck which you could scarcely feel,
to tumors the size of an orange, and beyond that to what the
local people called "Ox-neck." In some villages, he told us,
almost half the inhabitants had goiter.

I glanced towards Antoine. He was continuing to eat indifferently, but when I asked Lucien's opinion as to the cause
of all these goiters, I saw Antoine raise his head so as to listen
to the reply.

"What they eat certainly has something to do with it. Cabbage, potatoes, chestnuts, pork and ham, oil, which constitute
the basis of their diet in this part of the country, have been

recognized for a long time as causing goiter. The water too certainly plays an important part, for it's been observed that the villages most affected are those with a piped water supply while the least affected are those where they drink water from wells, tanks and springs. What exactly that means, however isn't altogether clear."

"I don't see the difficulty. It proves, of course, that the water from wells, tanks, and springs is less infected than water brought by pipes." This sudden utterance came from Antoine in aggressive tones, as if challenging anyone to disagree. But I was relieved to hear him talking at all, and Lucien answered placidly "Oh yes, I quite agree, but how does it come to be infected?"

Antoine's tongue now seemed to be well loosened, and he proceeded to tell us how, after carefully studying the geographical disposition of goiter cases in his area, he had wondered whether the water might not be infected when its course ran near the surface of the earth. I asked what started him on this idea.

"Elementary, Jean. I noticed that a stream used for water by several hamlets became harmful only after it had crossed grazing land. The people living down-stream from these fields were more liable to get goiter, those up-stream much less so. I began to make a map of the streams, their sources, and the grazing area, and also of the various villages and hamlets. My theory was confirmed in almost every case, and I was able to check on the spot that the catchment areas in summer were in fact always grazing areas. Also, the district engineer told me that almost all the pipes were in a very bad condition and not at all airtight, which would explain the contamination of the water for villages which have a piped supply."

I congratulated myself on my luck. Unwittingly I had launched Antoine on a subject in which he seemed to take a passionate interest. With the action of the wine, he became extremely animated, talking freely with flushed cheeks and vigorous gestures of his hands, replying fierily to occasional queries or objections from Lucien or myself. But his vehemence was much more normal, like the heat of an argument between friends, where one of them is utterly convinced of something and is dead keen to convince the others of it too. Marie's face lighted up with joy at this change in her husband's mood. She obviously guessed what efforts I had made to draw him out, and several times she threw me grateful glances.

I feared, however, that Antoine's animation might not last long. As soon as dinner was over, I hastened to help Marie up from the table, and offered her my arm at the bottom of the staircase. Antoine and Lucien followed us upstairs, comparing their results in treating goiter with iodine. I felt the evening was saved.

Dr. Delpuech was waiting for us, and Félicie had arranged the room in a way which made it look very cheerful. She had just put some logs on the fire, which flared and crackled as the bark caught. Between the bed and the fireplace the armchairs formed a companionable semicircle around a small table loaded with cups and liqueur glasses and a fine silver coffee pot.

In this large, well-heated, friendly room, while everyone was settling in comfortable chairs, there was a moment's silence, as if the final echoes of our conversation at dinner were still with us, submerging latent tensions. I was about to pour out the coffee, when Marie claimed this function for herself. "I'll be mother," she said with a smile at her body—and as she started pouring, even Antoine laughed half-heartedly and looked fondly at his wife. The business of handing round the cups, the noise of coffee spoons and china, the opening of liqueur bottles, all delayed the moment when a new conversation would have to be launched.

Lucien put his pipe and tobacco down by him on a stool, sank into his chair, stretched out his legs, and warmed his brandy glass between his hands. The night before, he had twice been called out into the country, and as at the Cité Universitaire in other days I was afraid he would doze off by the fire if the conversation did not prove stimulating. Marie went round handing us our liqueurs, and Dr. Delpuech followed her with his eyes. I knew his face too well now not to see that something was stirring him deeply when he watched her bulging waist and heavy walk, and the extra radiance of the face which expectant mothers so often have. Perhaps it made him think sadly of his dead wife and son, or perhaps the thought of that mysterious little life so visibly swelling within her brought out to him even more clearly his own age and decline.

When Marie had given us all our glasses, she lifted her head to meet the old man's gaze resting poignantly on her face. For a second she almost recoiled, but at once, in shame at this reflex of fear, she smiled. It was like a shy caress, that smile, and when he saw it, Dr. Delpuech's impassive face relaxed and the sadness there was transformed into something quite different.

She sat down again and we all drank our coffee in almost complete silence. Lucien's eyes began to droop, and his lips were half open. Antoine sipped his brandy and looked vaguely round the room. As for Dr. Delpuech, I could feel him silently urging me to start up a conversation.

I tried to resume our discussion of goiters, but this time there was no reaction from Antoine. Hoping to flatter him, I told Dr. Delpuech in detail about his theory of the contaminated water supply as one of the main causes of goiter in these parts.

"Very interesting," commented the old doctor with obvious sincerity, turning encouragingly towards Antoine. "It seems to me a very valuable piece of research. I dare say you'll meet a good many difficulties on the way, and it'll take you quite a long time to get the results you want. But it's certainly a most useful contribution to the problem."

"My dear sir," answered Antoine in an aggressively offhand manner, "if it is up to me to complete that piece of research, I'm afraid they'll have to struggle along with their goiters indefinitely. I imagine Nérac will have told you already—I'm leaving the district."

I did not want Dr. Delpuech to admit I had told him about Antoine's plans, or the latter might guess the main object of this dinner party. I made a sign to the old doctor to answer in the negative, and obediently, as if to win over a difficult child, he said: "No, I didn't know you were leaving so soon."

But Antoine must have seen my sign, unfortunately, for he went very red, and answered defiantly: "Yes, I've decided to leave the good folk of Montagut to their goiters. Anyhow they'll cling to them as they cling to their filth and lice and meanness and malice. Sometimes I think it would almost be better if the whole lot had ox-neck. If they were all more or less idiots, at least one couldn't hold them responsible for their actions."

"Antoine," I began, "I don't think you really mean what you're saying. You can't..."

"Don't I?" He turned and interrupted me at once. "I know just what I mean. Trying to improve their lot has cost me too dear already. There's one more dirty trick played by our kindly villagers that I don't happen to have told you about yet."

Then he looked again at Dr. Delpuech and went on with savage sarcasm: "I was a great Balzac fan, you know, and I thought I was doing the right thing by following Bénassis, paragon of country doctors. I ought to have had more sense, of course—successes like his only happen in novels."

He threw his head back to drain his brandy, and I wished now I had not encouraged him to drink so much wine at dinner. He finished the glass and banged it down on the table as he began declaiming mock-heroically: "*'Sir, when I came here first I found a dozen cretins in this hamlet. Its situation in a narrow valley, near a torrent whose water comes from melted snow, deprived of the benefits of the sun, which only shines on the top of the mountain—all this encourages the propagation throughout the hamlet of this terrible illness. Would it not be a great service to the whole district merely to stop this physical and intellectual contagion?'*"

Dr. Delpuech was sitting straight up in bed, listening keenly. I could not guess what he was thinking at this moment, but when Antoine stopped, he pointed to a bookshelf and said: "Jean, would you mind getting out my *Médecin de Campagne?*"

As I was getting the book, Antoine went on with renewed insolence: "All right, you'll find something like it there, though I confess I'm only quoting from memory. It was just to show you I knew my Balzac too. But a hundred years after Balzac, nearly halfway through the twentieth century, in our civilized modern France, it's quite amazing what you can find on reaching a country district. Not a mere trifle of twelve cretins, but in certain hamlets almost all the children from fourteen years on are afflicted with ox-neck, with huge flabby ballooning bellies, and umbilical hernias—poor kids who remain three-quarter idiots under the completely indifferent gaze of their parents."

"Aren't you exaggerating a little?" I put in.

"Not a bit. Of course I was dumbfounded myself at first, but then the role of a Bénassis quite inspired me, you know. You remember that he resolved the question by having the cretins expelled and deported, and that before becoming the local hero he was shot at by the population for this exploit, as cretins in that distant era were supposed to be bearers of good luck. Anyhow I thought I'd work on the goiter problem, discover its cause, and instead of being shot at by intellectual reactionaries in this century of universal education I should be encouraged, helped, congratulated."

He stopped to give a mirthless little laugh. "Go on then," said Dr. Delpuech, "get it off your chest. What went wrong?"

"Oh nothing at all serious. *Tout va très bien, Madame la Marquise*—nothing really wrong. When I was more or less sure my theory was right, I drew up a fine report, hoping to receive some help. Then, following the example of old Bénassis when he wanted to obtain authorization to deport his twelve cretins, I sent my report to the Aurillac district council, and waited. Bénassis at least received a verbal authorization from his council, whereas mine at Aurillac never officially replied at all. Unofficially but officiously, the egregious Dr. Chassagnon and the Mayor of Montagut learned that I was advocating cement ditches for dung and the replacement of all pipes which were not watertight. Their reaction was far more effective than a pistolshot at the corner of a wood. They got the postman to spread it about from door to door that I was putting germs in the water to infect people and force the village and all the big farmers to spend heaps of money on new piping and ditches. Calling it harmful, the good pure water sent by God, which men and animals had drunk without mishap since the beginning of the world. It was just such a crazy idea as one of these city doctors *would* have, who was cunning and obstinate enough to try to poison them. In fact some of them even announced that I was getting a percentage on the work from the contractors. From a Balzacian benefactor, I was becoming an Ibsen character, an enemy of the people."

He paused, but evidently felt he must end on a note of stronger defiance. "And you really think," he said, looking angrily at Dr. Delpuech, "I'd be fool enough to stay here and go on with my goiter research?"

The old doctor had opened the book I brought him, and I saw him marking a page. He now took the marker out and said gently: "Do you think wherever you go you won't find men being stupid and ungrateful and malicious? I too at your age knew whole pages of this book by heart, and I remember still a passage, which I have just turned up. I should like to read it to you, if I may."

"Oh go ahead," exclaimed Antoine aggressively. "We can all quote texts, can't we?"

"Listen," said Dr. Delpuech, reading from the book with quiet emphasis: "*'I dedicated myself like a missionary to the life of a country doctor, having no illusions about the character of the villagers or about the obstacles one must expect to meet if one tries to make men and things better. I have accepted the people unsentimentally for what they are, poor peasants, neither wholly good nor wholly evil. Their unremitting toil does not allow them scope or time for fine sentiments, and one can influence them in the first place only by considerations of interest and immediate benefits.'*"

The only effect of this quotation seemed to be to irritate Antoine further. "All that's just words," he shouted. "A doctor is not a saint, capable of putting up with any amount of injustice and misery. I have a wife, I shall one day have children, and it's my duty to give them some chances of happiness. In ten years our son is not going to have to go to a sordid little country school at Aurillac because I've decided like an idiot to vegetate here all my life. The young people round here aren't such fools either. They've seen the point, and given me my example. They go off to the towns and become porters or policemen or anything to get away from here. Look at the houses you see empty all over the place, the villages going under through sheer depopulation. And although the natives won't even stay here, you'd like me to be the only one simple enough to bury myself in this godforsaken spot."

His voice became increasingly scathing, the more excited he became. The torrent of words went from violence to violence. We were all silent. Lucien, shaken right out of his somnolence, looked in amazement at this ranting figure in whom so many demons had been so abruptly let loose. He must have wondered whether Antoine could really be talking of ordinary country people, cousins of the stolid rustics he had been dealing with morning and evening for the last two years. Faced by this frenzy, sometimes rising to hatred, he probably put it down as a form of persecution mania.

Marie evidently dared not intervene. Her hands were clenched on the arms of her chair, and she looked miserably at her husband, then turned in great anxiety towards Dr. Delpuech. Perhaps his expression reassured her a little, for he did not look angry or even surprised. Motionless in his bed, his body now slightly bent forwards, he regarded the young face convulsed by rage with keen attention and compassionate insight. And when Antoine paused to regain his breath, the old doctor's voice rang out with immense power and sympathy: "You are just a child. . . ."

Then still more paternally, as if he himself had once drunk the same cup of bitterness to its dregs, he went on: "All our lives are a battle, you know, and at your age life may sometimes seem a mere succession of lucky or unlucky chances. Yet nothing that happens to us happens in vain. I once told Jean here to give you that message, and I asked him to tell you too that the career we choose is always partly our destiny."

For a short while Antoine gazed at him in silence. The kindness in the old doctor's look and voice seemed to have made their impression, even more than the words. For a moment a shadow of troubled doubt flickered in Antoine's eyes, and then suddenly he seemed to take fright. He must have felt a panic urge to escape from this wise and kindly look, to lock the door against it and defy it. A blind rage took hold of him once more, insisting he should deny his calling at all costs.

So, in a voice of determined brutality, he exclaimed: "A child! I've come of age, you must know, and I know enough now to last me the rest of my life. It's easy enough to look as if you despise money and only make the rich pay when you've inherited a nice fat fortune from your father, like our old friend Dr. Bénassis. Oh yes, Dr. high-and-mighty Delpuech, I'm all for that sort of philanthropy. I might quite well have managed it too, if I'd started my practice by inheriting my father's patients so that I could let my family live in honest comfort. I could even preach resignation and patience to a young doctor starting from scratch. If it amuses you to look at the behinds of your local yokels for nothing, I leave them to you gladly. Over there at Montagut they're all yours for the

226

taking, and I'll even give you my bicycle as a bonus. As for me, I'm getting the hell out of here. I want to live, I want my family to be able to live, I've had enough of Dr. Bénassis and his selfless devotion to the Hippocratic oath, of being called out at night, of unpaid bills and dirty feet and all the rest of it. Do you hear me, I've had enough, I've—damn—well—had—enough!"

He brought his hand to his collar as if gasping for air, then rose abruptly with an utterly wild look on his face, crossed the room in three strides and went out slamming the door, leaving us all dumb with amazement. It was Marie Ricaud who was the first to rise. She was white with shame, and began crying. She ran up to Dr. Delpuech's bed and said between her tears: "Please, please forgive him, Doctor. He's been drinking."

Lucien meanwhile thrust me to my feet, muttering "Go after him. I'll come too." I opened the door hastily, and as I did so, I heard Dr. Delpuech giving Marie this answer: "Go to your husband, and don't upset yourself about me. I know just how he's feeling—you needn't apologize."

When I went downstairs, I found the hall almost in darkness. Antoine was fumbling with the coatrack by the staircase light. I put on the hall light, and he pulled his jacket off the rack and put it on without a word. His hands were trembling and he could not seem to button it. Marie, followed by Lucien, came downstairs almost at once after me. She too was silent, anxiously watching her husband. Her lower lip quivered pathetically.

The car was standing outside the door, but the starter refused to work. "Sounds as if your battery's flat from the cold," said Lucien. "Don't try any more, I'll use the crank." After he had cranked several times, the engine started turning over, and I was about to drive off when Lucien got in by my side (the Ricauds were both in the back), remarking, "I think I'd better come with you. It would be a nasty business if you had a breakdown at this hour and in this weather."

We left Peyrac. The Ricauds remained silent. It was dark, but I could imagine them both without difficulty: he sitting stiff and stubborn, with Marie motionless at his side, helpless, as if she were in an ambulance with a seriously injured man whose pain she could not relieve.

For a long while I drove on without anybody saying anything. But abruptly Antoine exclaimed with obvious bravado: "Anyhow I gave the old man something to think about, didn't I?"

I did not feel this piece of childishness called for any answer, but Lucien evidently did. I was surprised to hear him declare slowly and firmly: "I don't as a rule go in for long speeches, as Nérac will confirm, nor do I wish to interfere in your business. All the same I would like to tell you that what you said earlier to Dr. Delpuech was as unfair as what you said just now. It proves you don't know him very well, or rather that you don't know him at all."

Antoine made no comment, and for a minute or two Lucien said nothing more. I received the impression that he only went on after some hesitation because he felt it his duty to speak.

"You may not know that before Dr. Delpuech both his father and his grandfather were doctors at Peyrac, and when he chose a profession, naturally he wanted to take up Medicine as they had done. Of course his father was delighted, but he wanted his son to have a different life from that of a country doctor. You sound as if you found our country very uncivilized and isolated, and the life of a country doctor very unpleasant. But forty years ago it was far worse. Strangers hardly ever ventured as far as Peyrac in winter, and journeys even from here to Aurillac were hazardous, so that you could easily spend an entire day in the coach on the terrible roads they had in those days. Round Peyrac the country lanes remained impracticable from October to April. The only means of locomotion was the saddle horse, and you needed to be not only a good doctor but a damned good rider as well, able to slog thirty miles or so every day in any sort of weather. Very old people here will tell you that in the last fifty years the winters have been becoming much milder. In the old days it snowed so long and so hard that houses were often buried in the snow and one had to cut trenches and even tunnels so to be able to move from house to house or take the cattle to water. Sometimes in the mountains, the horse would have snow up to its girth, and the rider had to dismount and walk waist deep leading it. My mother often told me how the doctor, when called out for a very serious illness of my grandfather's, took five hours to walk the six miles separating Peyrac from the hamlet where my family was living."

Lucien paused again and Marie Ricaud, who I could guess

228

was listening enthralled, whispered under her breath: "Please go on, Dr. Clément."

"So," continued Lucien, "when the present Delpuech announced that he too wanted to be a doctor, his father wanted him to have a little easier life than his own and *his* father's. He decided to send young Daniel to study medicine at Paris. He had already been a brilliant pupil at Aurillac, and his father had ambitions for him to achieve a high hospital post. He dreamed of seeing his son a specialist in Paris, or else coming back to Aurillac surrounded by the prestige of his Paris training. So in Paris Dr. Delpuech went to lectures by the great men of those days, Charcot, Potain, Dieulafoy, and the rest of them."

"Didn't he specialize in bacteriology?" I inquired, remembering something the old doctor had once told me.

"That's right, Jean," replied Lucien. "He knew all about it even before he'd qualified. It was just at the height of Pasteur's discoveries when you only had to spit on a glass slide, so the humorists said, and look at it under the microscope, in order to discover a new microbe. Delpuech was an enthusiastic researcher in the laboratories of the Institut Pasteur. Roux, then at the peak of his glory for his discoveries about diphtheria and the anti-tetanus serum, became fond of young Delpuech, whom he soon had working for him. You'll find the name of Delpuech beside those of Roux, Metchnikoff, and Salimbeni in papers dated 1895 on the serum treatment of cholera. He was friendly with Yersin, Calmette, Charles Nicolle, all of whom were not much older than he was."

"All right, you've made your point," interrupted Antoine sullenly. "You don't need to go on with all that string of names."

"I won't," said Lucien. "I'm only mentioning them because the whole world knows them now, as it would certainly have known the name of Delpuech if his father hadn't died during the terrible winter of 1896."

"What did he die of?" I asked, and had a curious feeling of certainty even before Lucien answered: "Angina pectoris."

"The same illness," I said, and Lucien went on: "Yes, and I hope it won't be the same sort of death. His father died coming back from a confinement at Plamonteil. For some months he'd been complaining of his heart, and one evening a messenger from there came to fetch him after dinner. He wasn't feeling well, and it was a cold night, but he didn't want to refuse. The road had been more or less cleared, and his wife got him to take the carriage instead of riding the horse. It was a difficult confinement and lasted almost all the night. The people at Plamonteil saw the doctor was tired and tried to keep him there but as soon as he'd finished he insisted on leaving at once so his wife wouldn't worry. He died during the journey back on the seat of the carriage—the horse brought the carriage back to the stables all by himself. It was a little before dawn, and from farm to farm all down the valley the dogs howled at the passing of death, but no one was worried. They thought the dogs must have scented wolves."

Lucien stopped again, probably recalling the scene he had just described to us, and I could feel that even Antoine was stirred, for when he spoke this time it was in quite a different voice—restrained, almost shy. "Was the present Dr. Delpuech there at the time?" he asked.

"No," said Lucien, "he was in Paris. They wired to him, but he only got back to Peyrac two days later. They waited till he was there to have the funeral. The whole town filed piously in front of the mortuary bed, it was as if the late Dr. Delpuech were lying in state. When the coffin came out of the house, the bearers ignored the hearse and carried the coffin on their shoulders right to the cemetery. The whole population lined the streets with tears on their faces, and the lid of the coffin was left open so they could see for the last time their doctor's face."

"Did Dr. Delpuech mean to stay here?" asked Antoine, with a note of fierce eagerness in his voice.

"Not at all. He planned to be here for a few days only. But the day after his father was buried, the people of Peyrac with the complete confidence they felt for their beloved doctor, knowing that his son was there began to ring at the door which had never been closed to them. I don't know if our Dr. Delpuech still balanced the faith of Peyrac against the magnificent medical career opening up for him in Paris. I don't think he has told anyone, except his wife and son, what he thought about during the three months' compassionate leave he had asked for from the Institut Pasteur. But I do know that during his leave he took his father's leather-hooded carriage and his father's horse, and went on his rounds every day. And that at the end of the three months he sent his chief, the great Roux, a letter of resignation which decided the whole course of his life. That was exactly forty years ago."

Lucien said these last six words very slowly, and then stopped dead as if exhausted by the effort of telling such a long story. We had almost reached Montagut by now, and nobody said a word more till we came to the Ricauds' house. When they got out of the car I realized that Antoine was half asleep, but he managed to say good night reasonably enough, shaking hands rather sheepishly with Lucien and myself. "I'm sorry I made a fool of myself," he muttered. Marie thanked me for the dinner, and turning to shake Lucien's hand said firmly: "Good night, Dr. Clément. Thank you very much indeed for telling us that story."

As soon as Marie Ricaud had opened their front door and helped her somnolent husband inside, I drove off. For a few minutes the only sound was the noise of the chains on the icy road. But Lucien's thoughts seemed to be still at Montagut, for he eventually remarked: "He's got a fine wife who loves him. She'll help him to pull himself together. And then there'll soon be the child."

The car took several corners rather noisily, after which he added in a very low voice as if half to himself: "A wife, and soon a child. Whatever he may think about it, he's lucky."

I sensed in his voice so much gentleness and also so much wistfulness that I could not refrain from smiling, and remarking: "If you envy him, Lucien, the remedy's simple. A doctor and single, you must have had all the girls for miles around angling for you as a husband."

He did not answer, and I put it even more bluntly, as if I somehow failed to grasp my meaning: "Get married, Lucien. Get married."

"No," he answered, "I don't suppose I shall ever marry."

This time I caught a break in his voice and I was sorry that it was too dark in the car to see his face. He did not seem any longer the unemotional, imperturbable Lucien I was used to.

"Really?" I exclaimed. "You surely can't be looking for
ward to an old age like Dr. Delpuech's with an old housekeeper
as your only companion. Of course it's not *his* fault he's alone
now, he lost his family. But at least he had one. Why not you?"

"You've chosen a very bad example, Jean. His wife died, and
he has not remarried. He preferred to remain faithful to her
memory."

I was most disconcerted by the deadly seriousness in his
voice, and tried to hide my embarrassment by being facetious:
"Heavens, this is a surprise—Lucien in romantic mood. Am I
to believe you've already been caught in the toils of an unhappy
love affair?"

"Please don't joke about it, Jean," Lucien entreated in accents of such distress that I realized I must have opened up
some deep wound, and dared not ask any further questions.
In the half-darkness of the car I saw him pass a hand over his
brow. He shifted awkwardly on the seat, and began again very
slowly, as if still hesitant to speak: "Yes, I've got to tell you...
I've got to tell you," he repeated, articulating the words with
great difficulty, "since you ask me."

"Tell me what, Lucien?" I exclaimed in alarm, and then he
said, still more slowly, as if each word were burning his lips:
"After this I'd be ashamed to hide it from you. I shall never
marry because I love Marianne."

It was as though he had now drawn out the knife, and at
once torrents of blood began spurting from the wound. With
a fluency of speech which I had never known in him before, in
the solemn tones of an accused man defending his honor even
more than his life, he continued.

"Oh yes, you know, I've loved her hopelessly ever since the
first day you brought her into our little group at the Cité.
Before that I'd never thought much about love. I wasn't in
Paris to look at pretty girls or indulge in amorous adventures,
and at that particular period I was very busy with exams. But
that evening, when I happened to be out there in the long grass
behind the hostel, and often after that, I found it a sheer joy
just to look at her and listen to her, even though I could never
mean anything to her, and I felt more than ever I was a mere
country bumpkin she'd hardly look at."

"But Marianne admired you a lot," I broke in. "I used to

232

tell her what you did in the slums, and she'd have liked to come with us. I admit I wasn't very keen on the idea. Whenever you did see her for half an hour or so, she was always trying to draw you out, and I always wondered why you shut up like a clam. I tell you she thought the world of you."

"Did she really?" There was a note of astonished gladness in Lucien's voice.

"Certainly," I told him. Then the gladness faded out, and he continued with a sigh: "Even if that's true, it was obvious that you were the one she loved. And even without you, there was still François, not to mention all the others. I could see they were all trying to shine for her benefit, and each of them wanted to believe that she liked him more than the rest. I'm sure I had the least hope of all, and yet was the happiest. Whatever she thought of me—and I hope you're not just telling me that out of politeness—"

I shook my head.

"Anyhow she always spoke to me with the most wonderful kindness, and I can remember so well even now every remark she made to me. They are something I cherish and shall cherish all my life. It's something inherited, I dare say, but for me to love a woman and to make her my wife can only mean one and the same thing. And *she* has made all other women seem ordinary and insipid."

I noticed that right from the start he had continually avoided repeating Marianne's name. He stopped, then asked me miserably: "You're not angry with me for telling you the truth?"

But he did not leave me time to reply. He went on talking in the same accents of passionate emotion. "I was ashamed, I felt I was being dishonorable in daring to think of her in your presence. Your first morning here, when we were driving back to Peyrac together, you gave me news of all our pals in the hostel, and in the end, as you didn't say anything about her, I could not contain myself. You remember, I asked you in a voice which trembled in spite of me."

"Yes, I remember," I said gently. I recalled vividly, in fact, wondering what on earth could have made Lucien ask such a normal question so peculiarly.

He went on: "I expect I'm explaining myself very badly, but anyhow my love for her is something decent and pure, I swear to you. Only now that you know about it, I'm ashamed of it. I'd like you to feel a little sorry for me, and if you're sure of my loyalty, to forgive me."

Such heart-rending humility and self-abasement throbbed in this confession that I answered bluntly, as soon as he stopped speaking: "Lucien, I've nothing to forgive. I'm neither engaged nor married to Marianne. As a matter of fact, since I stopped living at the Cité, I've only seen her now and then, quite accidentally, at the Medical School."

I heard Lucien gasp in amazement, and realized that he had turned towards me and was trying to look at me in the darkness. "Jean," he exclaimed, as if still dazed by the shock, "what happened?" I did not reply at once, and he added with a terrible note of reproach in his voice: "Then all that time, when we were at the Cité together, you were lying to her?"

"No," I said simply, "at that time I was absolutely and utterly sincere in my love for her. But I'm not a very strong character, you know, and the summer vacation after your last term, when I was alone in Paris without Marianne, I happened to have a good many temptations to be unfaithful to her. I tried hard but in the end I failed to resist them. It'd take too long to explain in detail, but that's about what happened."

"I see," said Lucien noncommittally, plainly not seeing at all. How could I expect him to see? How could someone with Lucien's integrity, who was ready to cherish a pure and hopeless love till the end of his life, who had always marched straight towards his duty without illusions or compromise or weakness, like a farmer with his eye steadily on the furrow stretching ahead of him—how could he possibly understand the bitter conflicts I had suffered in that decisive summer and autumn three years earlier? He did not say another word the whole way back.

With Lucien sitting beside me in a silence which I could feel charged with reproach, I tried to chase out all the heavy thoughts his scathing question had brought up: they came from a past which for months and months had been pushed into the very back of my mind, which I hoped I was slowly forgetting. But as I drove on, despite my efforts, the attitude of other friends kept coming back to me.

Paul Chavasse, for instance, had hurled abuse at me the day

234

he found out that all was completely over between Marianne and me, and thereafter had cut me dead at school for the rest of the term. Then we met accidentally early the following term, and he had decided to make it up, remarking, "You *are* rather a bastard, you know. It's a pity but I suppose it can't be helped. If you'd only had a hook nose or a double chin, you might have been a nicer guy."

I gripped the steering wheel, and tried to concentrate only on the bumpy road and the way the wind was rising, on my work, on the Ricauds and Dr. Delpuech, even on Lucien's eligibility as a husband for one of the Peyrac girls. Damn—that brought up again his reasons for not marrying, and whatever train of thought I followed, it always led back to my buried past, and my treatment of Marianne. There seemed nothing for it but to face the facts squarely, to marshal them as in a criminal case. In the dock would be the young Jean Nérac, in the last few months before his twenty-first birthday.

Obviously the first witness to be called would be Henri Philippon, though I was not sure yet whether he would be a prosecution witness or whether the defense might use him to plead extenuating circumstances. Anyhow it had all started with his coming to live at the Cité Universitaire on the orders of his father, who threatened to cut off his allowance if he refused. His father apparently believed that the Cité would provide a healthy studious atmosphere, without distractions. Henri had insisted on coming to live in the room right opposite me, which happened to be free, and was soon using my room as his lounge, both while I was at the hospital in the morning, and also in the afternoons and evenings when I should have been working for the interne's exam two or three years later.

When the foreign students began arriving at the Cité at the end of July, and girls' voices and laughter were heard in our monastic corridors, Henri became more and more nervous and distracted. One afternoon he left my room abruptly, and returned that evening to ask an urgent favor. He had picked up two Austrian girls, one of whom he wanted for himself, so would I please come out with them and take the other one off his hands for this one evening? I had refused, been pressed, reluctantly accepted. Martha, my allotted partner, was a thin, rather frail-looking girl with ash-blonde hair and eyebrows, and at first I had been little attracted by her. During the evening, at Montparnasse and then in Montmartre under Henri's stage-management, with the aid of his fast sports car, I became very drunk, and it ended with Henri and me taking the two girls to our rooms in the hostel for the night. Henri told me they were only staying for six days, and I could see no harm in having a little fun when it could be ended so soon and so surely.

After six hectic days and nights Martha and the other girl had departed. The day afterwards I found a letter from Marianne, infinitely tender and loving as ever, but concealing beneath an elaborate casualness her obvious anxiety at not having heard from me in answer to her last letter. When I read this I felt sick with self-disgust.

Here the defense might seize its first chance. That afternoon and early evening I substituted for Jouvet, the interne on my ward at the Charité Hospital, who was on call for the rest of the day. For a good part of the afternoon, when not occupied in the ward, I was busy with a long letter to Marianne, humiliating myself, confessing my complete guilt, imploring her forgiveness for my abominable betrayal. That evening, on leaving the hospital, I tossed the letter through the letter-box at a nearby postoffice. Even after three years I could still hear the noise of the envelope slipping down the slot and the flap inside banging shut. After this I felt a new lightheartedness and peace, and when I returned to the hostel, I found that the cleaner had put my room in order again, so that all trace of Martha's presence there had been wiped out. For that night I felt saved from my weakness and passions, ready to start again in a new spirit of innocence and purity, loving Marianne in the letter and in the spirit. When I heard Henri's step in the corridor outside, humming the tune he always hummed when he was coming to fetch me to go out with him, I had a moment of panic. But the panic passed, and I knew my future lay with my work in the world of doctors—my work and Marianne. When Henri knocked, I had already opened my notebook and started to work; tonight he would have to go out alone.

That night he did—but only that night—and my gesture was robbed of much of its significance by Henri's refusal to take it seriously. He merely said I had still not gotten over my sadness at Martha's departure, which he found very normal and natural. I had not the courage to explain my vow of future fidelity to a girl I had never even mentioned to Henri.

My resistance was lowered again that night by the loneliness of my flesh, longing for the lost Martha. The more I tried to regain my sense of vocation and love for Marianne, the more a devil in my mind and flesh protested that surely I could go on having a little fun until I had actually received Marianne's pardon.

The opportunity occurred next morning at half past twelve. Henri came to the hospital in his car, and finding me just ready to leave the ward asked me very considerately, as if I were a convalescent patient, whether I was feeling better.

"A little better, thanks," I said ambiguously.

"That's right," he burst in, "I told you you'd be all right in a day or two. To complete the cure you need to be taken out of yourself a bit, and I've found just the right person to do that for you."

"How do you mean?" I asked, interested despite myself.

"Don't act dumber than you can help," said Henri with a laugh. "I've just discovered two Czech girls who arrived in Paris this very morning. They talk a little French, what's more, so you won't have any of the language difficulties you had with Martha. I've told them about you, of course, and I'm taking you to lunch to meet them. How about it?"

"It's very nice of you, but...."

"Never knew such a man for buts. Don't spoil the girls' fun. They're so thrilled to have found two kindly natives to show them around Paris. Just come to lunch and spend the afternoon with us, if that's all you want. That doesn't commit you, does it?"

"All right," I said, "just for lunch and the afternoon." But it *had* committed me, and by the end of the afternoon all my resolutions had gone overboard almost without trace. I was back where I had been before Marianne's letter arrived, and the third night after Martha's departure Anna, "my" Czech girl, spent the night in my room. Physically, she was quite satisfactory.

Each morning for the next week, still rather dulled by the night's prowess, before leaving for hospital I went to my pigeon hole in the porter's office to see if Marianne's answer to my letter had arrived. The first few days I waited for it with a feeling of guilt. When I was working on my ward at the Charité, every detail would remind me of Marianne, at each step I would picture that radiant figure, that lovely fair hair and clear complexion, and the charmingly forlorn expression she used to assume whenever we were to be separated for a moment. These first mornings, when I thought of all this, I felt deeply unhappy at having tarnished our relationship so badly. Yet about noon, as soon as Henri appeared at the door, beckoning me to hurry up, I would rush to the changing room to take off my apron and white coat, then dash out to the little car where he was waiting for me with the two girls—as if I were on a desert island, and in danger of being left behind by the rescue party.

For a few days suddenly in some bar or restaurant or night-club I would have moments of bitter self-reproach, and I would be ready to get up and go. Thinking of the Jean Nérac who had wanted to be so strong and pure, I despised this miserable weakling who followed the selfish Henri in every sordid step he decided to take. But then at a collusive smile from the girl at my side, a furtive pressure on my arm, a brief caress, I would be seized by a kind of sexual vanity, and relapse instantly into a compulsive enjoyment of the moment's pleasure. Naturally I stayed where I was, and the pangs of conscience were quietly and quickly submerged.

Very soon even these pangs became less frequent. I decided I had done my duty loyally by writing to confess everything. As long as I had not received Marianne's pardon in black and white, I was still free, I thought to myself.

Besides, I had not loved Martha. The adventure with her had been pleasant but unimportant—nothing of it would remain with me later on, beyond a refreshing memory amidst a sultry summer and a life too ascetic for a normal young man. With Anna it would be just the same, equally ephemeral. Compared to Marianne, Martha and Anna were "something quite different," and from this I eventually persuaded myself that they did not count at all.

Having thus resolved that until Marianne's answer arrived I should be doing nothing irreparable or really serious, I told myself that my last days of liberty were already numbered, and plunged eagerly into all the pleasures they could offer me. In my complete egoism I never dreamt for a moment that Marianne would refuse to forgive me: she loved me too much for that. Moreover, although I allowed myself the right to sleep with other women for the time being, since that was "quite different," I was sure she could never love another man. Not for a moment did her silence awaken in me any idea of jealousy.

After three or four days of waiting, receiving no answer, I decided that she must simply have gone away somewhere unexpectedly and that my letter was perhaps being forwarded. Then eventually, as this strange silence continued, I thought no more about it, except sometimes to congratulate myself on my reprieve.

On the morning of the ninth day, going into the porter's lodge, I saw an envelope in my pigeon hole from some way away; I had forgotten that it might still arrive. My mother had written the day before, and I felt sure this letter could only be from Marianne. It was.

On the boulevard I hesitated before opening it. Here was the letter which must bring to an end my holiday affairs, and I suddenly felt a certain rancor against these thin sheets of paper I held in my hand. It seemed terribly unfair. Why had Marianne come so soon into my life? Why had she imposed so heavy a duty upon me, while I was still so young and had had no proper time to enjoy the end of my adolescence in my own way? Why did others remain free, while I was in bondage to this tyranny of loving one woman only? Yet as I tore open the envelope I was firmly resolved, if my pardon were there, to fulfill the promise I had made to behave better.

I skimmed through the pages, meaning to absorb first of all their general tone: it was tender, anxious, and apologetic—I could not grasp what had happened at all. Then it dawned on me that the all-important letter had never reached her. She apologized for writing out of turn once more despite our agreement on this subject. Her previous letter had been written ten days ago, and even then she had expressed anxiety at my silence. For twenty days now she had been waiting eagerly for a reply with each post, and still she had heard nothing from me.

I read feverishly right to the last line. Under the signature there was not even a last-minute P.S. to say she had got my letter, and suddenly this was the one thing which stood out for me: Marianne knew nothing, so I was still free after all. Standing on the edge of the pavement I gave an immense sigh of relief. I was free, free for a day or a month, to follow all my fancy, to carry on with the life I was now leading. No convict released from prison could have felt more tipsy with exhilaration.

After this I read the letter through again more calmly. *For ten days now,* she wrote, *I've been in bed with pleurisy. The same evening I sent off my last letter, I went out for a swim in the Dordogne. After dinner I started shivering and had violent cramps. Two days later our local doctor found all the signs of a pleuritic effusion which has gone on increasing till now. It seems to be stationary at present, and the last two days I've been coughing less and having less pain. Please forgive this letter, darling—I've still got a high temperature and I keep on imagining the most awful things. Of course I quite see there might be all sorts of reasons why I've not heard from you, darling—probably the letters are going astray, or you may be too busy working, and then of course you must have some distractions. Do remember it's really a vacation, though, and don't work too hard, Jean dear. I'm so sad being so far away from you here. I look at all the furniture and things all round me—I've known them and loved them all through my childhood, but now I hardly recognize them. You see, dearest, love has changed me so much that I no longer recognize my own past any more. Isn't that silly? But perhaps I'm only really ill because you're not here too, seeing that my only real life is near you. . . ."*

All her long letter was like this, right to the last line, bursting with trust and belief in our future together. I felt incapable of walking. I stopped a taxi and on the way to the hospital I was genuinely horrified once more at my unfaithfulness. I must write my first letter over again, I could almost remember it now by heart. I must humiliate myself once more, implore her—otherwise all I had done in the last fortnight would degrade me forever.

When I reached the ward, before even starting my work, I asked the sister for a sheet of paper, and sat down in a corner

240

of her office. But as I was about to begin my letter, I suddenly realized that Marianne was seriously ill, with a high temperature, already imagining I might be dead or had had an accident. I could picture her lying in bed shivering feverishly, and when she found there was still no letter from me, I could almost see her face puckering up like that of a little girl just about to cry. Could I really break the silence by telling her all the wrong I had done her while away from her? It would be almost more of a shock to her than news of some physical accident.

If I thus destroyed all her unbounded hope and confidence in me, I should be indulging the most selfish cruelty, whereas with different words, without being hypocritical, I could preserve her happiness. For it was surely not hypocritical to tell her I loved her. I did love her, and after a year of perfect understanding like ours, our love could not founder forever simply because of a fortnight's wretched weakness on my part.

I did not hesitate further. My reply was one long lie, except that it was mixed with a passionate tenderness which at the time I sincerely felt. As I was about to lick the envelope flap I stopped. The public holidays of August 15th were quite near, and I was on the point of adding that I would try to get someone to take my place on the ward, so that I could come to her for these two days. Then I hesitated again. I was not really sure that I could find anyone willing to stand in for me those two days, and perhaps it was better for the moment not to give her any false hopes. I stuck down the envelope without mentioning the possibility; but decided to look round actively for a substitute, and not tell Marianne I was coming until I was sure of being able to get away.

All this put me behind in my work, and when as usual Henri came to look for me shortly after twelve, he found me busy cutting muslin bandages for a plaster cast. I told him I should not be ready for half an hour, hoping he would leave me alone. But part of Henri's technique with the women was to keep them waiting, so he did not mind sitting down comfortably in a corner of the ward watching me finish my work.

I was on the point of telling him I had decided to stop this existence of taking girls out and sleeping with them. But he smoked his cigarette so serenely, explaining the while our program for the afternoon—a *short* visit to the Château at Fontainebleau, followed by a *long* walk in the forest of Fontaine-bleau—that I could not summon up the courage to speak. He had seen me so much "on the loose" these last three weeks that in his eyes I had quite redeemed my excessive sobriety of the first weeks, and he plainly considered me now as a boon companion in crime. To try now to take a completely different line, I would really have needed superhuman forces.

To give myself an excuse for keeping my Czech girl at a distance, during the walk in the forest I pleaded a terrible head-ache, and after dinner suggested abandoning the three of them and going straight to bed myself. Henri, perhaps already begin-ning to tire a little of his partner, felt in a stay-at-home mood too, so in fact all four of us that evening returned early to the Cité; I slept alone. But this night of loneliness allowed me to measure the importance which sexual pleasure had taken on in my life. In twenty days I had become like a drunkard who almost loses his sanity when you suddenly take his drug away from him.

At hospital next morning, Jouvet the interne, after making his rounds, asked me if he could have a word with me in private. "Do you by any chance," he said when we were alone, "know a Mlle. Marianne Duriez?"

"Yes, of course," I said eagerly. "What's happened?"

Jouvet grinned. "Then if your Christian name is Jean"—I nodded—"I think this letter must be yours. It's been on the Commonroom board several days, I'm afraid, and no one claimed it. We don't happen to have many Jeans in the Commonroom at present. We were wondering who on earth it could be, and I suddenly remembered you'd stood in for me one afternoon. If I were you, my boy, I'd be a bit more careful in future when sending off your love letters."

He pulled out of his pocket an envelope marked: *Return to sender, Jean, Interne's Commonroom, Charité Hospital"* by the postoffice. "Don't worry," said Jouvet, as he gave it to me, "it's not been opened." I blushed furiously and just had suf-ficient presence of mind to thank him. When I took my en-velope out of the postoffice one all that was written on the former was: *Mlle. Marianne Duriez.*

In a flash I now realized what I had done—could almost see myself doing it. Perhaps I had been tricked by some unconscious

242

wish not to send off this letter, which contained so much that was unfavorable to my own vanity. I remembered starting to address the envelope, when the very act of writing Marianne's name made me feel I must re-read the letter for the third time, to see if I had been humble enough, if I had really earned Marianne's forgiveness. So I had added a postscript: *I need you, Marianne darling, I need you so badly.*

I refolded the letter, put it back in the envelope already stamped, sealed the envelope address side down, put it in my pocket, and without looking at it again I tossed it through the slot in the postoffice box.

I looked at the two envelopes wondering whether to tear them up. Some obscure instinct that they might one day serve as evidence made me keep them, and the letter. Later on I destroyed almost all Marianne's letters, only keeping those she had written up till then, and this ill-fated one of mine. I had these tied up in a small bundle among my papers even three years later.

But at the time, of course, I was even more relieved that Marianne had not received this one after all. There was no question of re-posting it now. So when Henri called for me at the usual time, my feeble and hastily planned excuses failed again—as usual—and I could not break loose from his influence. We spent another hectic afternoon and evening with the Czech girls, and that night I did not sleep alone.

My life thereafter became once more what it had been since my first night with Martha. In my rare lucid moments I realized that the burning cry of love I thought I was sending to Marianne in the returned letter was not sincere. It was only a vague cry of pity such as might be pulled from a selfish passer-by who sees an accident in the street. Yes, all I was capable of in return for the love she offered me, was a little pity. Of course the August 15th holidays passed by without my trying to find a replacement.

Two or three times a week I found a letter from Périgord to which I would reply on the same day, relieving my conscience by this act of charity. If Marianne had returned to Paris, I should never have succeeded in lying so calmly and coldbloodedly. When I was with her, I could never hide from her the slightest change of mood or feeling, and I knew that she would have guessed my treason straight away.

Every time I replied to one of her letters, I found myself more adroit in my lying. I managed without any difficulty to write her from hospital, telling her all about the patients on the ward and the progress of my work for the interne's exam, which I had actually not touched for weeks. I tried to believe that I only lied with such perfection to spare Marianne pain. My letter stuck down and posted, I felt my conscience at ease for the next two or three days.

I had realized that this existence of debauchery and disorder and lying could not go on indefinitely, and once more I put a firm date for its end: in the last week of September my own fortnight's holiday from the hospital was due. I would go home to Toulouse the first week of my holiday, and then either go to Marianne's house, or, if her health continued to improve, I would try to get her to come to Toulouse to meet my mother— who had already heard from me a great deal about Marianne. I thought this would make up to Marianne a little for my present treatment of her.

Soon after that the new term would begin, and Henri would leave the Cité and return to his room in the Latin Quarter, while Marianne and I would resume our sober habits and virtuous happiness of the previous year. For I felt that even while I deceived her I still loved Marianne. It was she who in relation to Martha and Anna was "something quite different," and something infinitely precious, unique, and absolutely necessary for my moral balance and happiness.

But then two things happened which made me feel that fate was taking a hand once more. The dresser who was to relieve me on the ward when I was on vacation had a motorcycle accident, and the hospital authorities asked if I could possibly postpone my holiday. I asked for a couple of days to think it over.

This offered all too good an excuse for staying in Paris and putting off still further the perhaps difficult meeting with Marianne. But that meeting was bound to come anyhow in a month or so's time, so I thought, when the new term began, so I resolved—quite courageously for me—to face it sooner rather than later. I was preparing to tell the hospital that

I could not be expected to alter my holiday plans at this late date when a letter from Marianne brought news which altered everything. Her doctor, it seemed, was adamant against her resuming the strenuous life of a medical student after such a serious illness. Instead she must rest for three or four months in the mountains.

Marianne seemed to accept this decision bravely, though it kept her from me still longer, and this letter, like all the others, overflowed with tenderness and courage. I, on the other hand, was deeply shocked by this news, and at the same time, once more, secretly relieved. Shocked because now not even the beginning of the new term would bring me Marianne to save me from my baser self. Relieved because if I stayed in Paris with the splendid excuse of the hospital's request, I could continue on the primrose path, undetected and unhindered, for many weeks more. Fate had first tricked me into failing to address a decisive letter, and had now thrown this double temptation in my way—surely I could not resist it.

Ah, said the prosecutor in myself three years later, but perhaps it was just thrown in your way to give you an opportunity to assert your willpower. Remember what Dr. Delpuech said about nobody being tempted beyond his strength. All very well, said counsel for the defense, but how could I possibly see that at the time? In any case the trial was academic: I am a weak character, as I had admitted to Lucien, and in fact I did not resist. I stayed in Paris and closed my eyes, drifting steadily downhill, without further efforts to restrain myself.

"Jean Nérac," declared the judge, my conscience, "you have been found guilty of inflicting immense suffering on the girl you loved, by unpardonable weakness and dishonesty. Your sentence is to lose that love with all that has been most worth while in your life so far." A heavy sentence indeed, I thought, as I drew up in front of Lucien's house.

I had been too busy with my thoughts to regret his silence during the rest of the drive back to Peyrac, but I could not help wondering in what manner he would leave me. "Well, good-night, Lucien," I said casually. "Many thanks for coming over to the Ricauds with me." He got out of the car without a word, and as he slammed the passenger's door, muttered good night

245

in a very low voice without stretching out his arm to shake hands. It was as if he were now saying goodbye to me at a great distance or across some invisible barrier.

I watched him with pity as he walked up to his front door. His broad shoulders were bent, and his back was hunched. It was not the icy wind which made him walk in this unnaturally downcast way, but a far heavier burden, the load of a single-minded and hopeless love that was likely to weigh him down till the end of his days.

Chapter Thirteen

March 26–27

IT WAS raining about half past two the next morning when Félicie shook me awake. I was extraordinarily tired, and must have been very deeply sunk in my first sleep not to hear the stubborn, harsh shrilling of the front doorbell vibrating throughout the house. For it was a well-established tradition that the messenger charged with summoning the doctor in haste should go on positively leaning against the bell-knob until Félicie appeared at the window in her petticoats and camisole.

Probably the man had also in his impatience thumped on the door with his other hand. This slumbering sealed-up doctor's house must have seemed to him like a great mass of petrified selfishness requiring to be stirred to life by any means possible. When a window lighted up in the front of the house, and Félicie leaned her face out of the window to give a first guardianly glance, only then would the house relapse into silence, for then the messenger, at last reassured, would consent to withdraw his thumb from the bell. Félicie was awake, Dr. Delpuech was awake, his locum was awake—so the machinery of Medicine was starting to operate.

The most curious thing to me was that for forty years now Dr. Delpuech had probably never refused to get up and come,

nd yet night after night the exasperating ritual of the bell
vas resumed, as if only this frantic noise were capable of
naking the doctor willing to appear. I had eventually decided
hat people could not stop reasoning from what they would
ave done themselves in similar circumstances. If it had been
hey, and not Dr. Delpuech, who had been asked to come out
n the middle of the night, especially a night thick with rain
r snow or ice, they might easily have listened right till the
norning to such a bell, without any idea at all of leaving the
varmth of their beds.

That night, despite the usual bell-ringing and door-thumping,
t was Félicie, as I have said, who had to come and shake me out
f my sleep. Sitting up in bed, I stayed for a few seconds rubbing
ny eyes, and made strenuous efforts amidst the shock of this
rusque awakening to find my bearings again in consciousness.
Then I looked at my watch. I had been asleep hardly two hours,
nd was quite disgusted to be awake again after this pitifully
hort sleep. Since first starting in Peyrac I had become used to a
ood many unpleasant things, but these repeated calls almost
very night, varying only in their number and the exact hours
t which they came, remained for me perhaps the most painful
rdeal of all.

Sometimes the sound of the front doorbell or telephone
vould come straight into my dreams, and I would unconsciously
lig my head into my pillows to ward off the harsh insistent
ummons. But as the shrill ringing gradually woke me, I had
o recognize it as the distorted echo of a distant appeal for help,
f a patient's groans and cries—and sooner or later I would
;et up.

Tonight's patient lived in Peyrac, luckily. The woman who
:ame to fetch me departed immediately in great haste to re-
urn to her son who, she told me, was spitting blood. It was
not worth taking the car for a call so nearby. Félicie showed
ne how to find the lane where my patient lived on the other
ide of the main square; and after equipping me with rubber
boots and a heavy raincoat of Dr. Delpuech's she accompanied
me to the door to test the strength of the storm.

It had not been raining two hours earlier when I drove the
Ricauds back to Montagut, nor even on the return journey
back, although the wind was rising a good deal. But I was

amazed there could be such cataracts of rain in so short a time. "They call it the *plouxal*," explained Félicie, "which means the rainwind. We need it to let the spring come, but I've often noticed it always makes people get ill more easily. You won't be out of work today, I'm thinking."

As the street was not lighted, and I mistrusted the pavements, which had water splashing on to them from the overflowing gutters, I squelched through the puddles in the middle of the road without too much trouble. But when I reached the square, the squall, which seemed to be waiting for me, choked me and froze me with a single gust. My coat collar turned up to protect me slightly from the stinging rain, I ran on, bent double, stumbling in the water which splashed about my feet, and did not stop for breath till I reached the shelter of the lane.

I identified immediately the house where they were waiting for me. On the dark fronts of all the houses in the lane, only two windows were lighted. Besides the patient, his mother and myself, there were probably not many awake in Peyrac at this time of the night.

As on each occasion when I was on my way to a patient who might be seriously ill, all my tiredness abruptly disappeared and my brain became completely clear. I wiped the rain off my face and tested with my foot the first step of a rickety wooden staircase, leading up from a narrow passage which smelt of mold and livestock. The mother must have been watching for me, since she hurried out on the landing with a lamp and in her anxiety came downstairs to meet me.

When I got up to their floor I found a young man sitting on the bed and regarding, with a startled, almost panicstricken stare, a basin swimming with sticky scarlet blood. Little bubbles floated on the surface.

There were also huge bloodstains on the pillow and sheets and towels. Since he had felt in his mouth the first mouthful of the warm salty bitter liquid, the young man had not yet grasped exactly what had happened to him, except no doubt that it was something serious. My first care was to reassure him.

When I left the house an hour later, the room no longer looked like "the scene of the crime." The mother had more or less restored order everywhere, scrubbing out the bloodstains washing the basin, bringing towels and clean sheets from the cupboard, while I had helped her to change the patient's pajamas without disturbing him too much. Now he was resting, half sitting up, supported by clean white pillows. The morphine I injected on my arrival was beginning to take effect, and he no longer looked so scared. Soon he would be asleep, and at the foot of the bed, his mother, hands clasped over her stomach, looked at me with gratitude and relief.

Outside the *plouxal* was still driving huge sooty clouds over the sky, but it had stopped raining. Walking through the puddles without any hurry now, I caught myself humming. I was happy, not only because the rain had stopped and water was no longer dripping down my neck. I was happy because I had been able to use my skill to treat and calm a patient. Once I had overcome my reluctance at having to wake up, I liked these night calls, even when, after an hour's drive on bad roads, they took me far from Peyrac to some hamlet lost in the mountains.

What should I find when I got there? Each time there was something stirring and solemn in this journey towards an unknown objective. The phone call was almost always vague, the messenger who came to fetch me and guide me to the patient's home could usually tell me nothing beyond the fact that the people who had sent him were worried and I must hurry. Until I was actually there, there was nothing definite to prepare for. Almost anything was possible.

When I arrived, alone with the patient and a scared family, I would have to see clearly and fight hard. I often felt overawed when I thought of the responsibility awaiting me compared with my own very slender powers. I knew that the whole family would be gathered in the kitchen, already watching anxiously for my headlights or the flashlight of my guide. Under their tense gaze I would have to take a vital decision without appearing to hesitate at all, before beginning a forceps delivery, ligaturing a bleeding artery, or performing a tracheotomy on a choking child. I was the man sustaining the patient's life and the family's hopes.

Sometimes at the moment of action, lighted by a dim kerosene lamp, with a clumsy yokel or sobbing old woman as my only assistant, I would doubt my capabilities: was this the right diagnosis, the right treatment? I ought to have known all this, and was ashamed to have missed so many lectures and practical demonstrations in Paris by bribing the laboratory attendant, according to Henri's methods, to mark me as having been present. I was ashamed of the exams only just passed after stuffing my memory in a few nights of cramming with what I ought to have learned in a whole term.

Only one thing saved me: the fact that I was a salaried "dresser" attached to a particular block of the hospital. I had to be on the ward every morning on pain of dismissal. For five years I had profited, almost in spite of myself, from the incomparable training offered by clinical instruction and practice. Very often I thanked my stars that I had acquired in the course of time enough knowledge and practical skill to prevent my falling down too seriously on the job—when, say, I found myself in the corner of a smoky kitchen, delivered over to my own resources, in the presence of a dying man.

I remembered an earlier call when I had been awakened a little before midnight by the bell in the hall, and found a man in a sheepskin coat stretching his chilled hands towards the fire. Melting icicles and snow were dripping off his coat. He wanted me to come and see his brother-in-law, who had had a fall and hit his head on a rock.

We left at once, and as soon as we were out of Peyrac we ran into a really thick blizzard. The raging wind had driven powdery snow into the hollows and ditches, leveling them out with the road, so that the whole surface was one vast flat plain. The only landmarks I could keep my eyes on in this nightmarish journey were the rows of telegraph poles. At times the whirling gale seized the snow angrily, lifted it and hurled it against the windshield in thick clouds like a fog, so that I had to come to a standstill as the road would be completely invisible for several minutes. "It's the *écir*," my companion informed me at the first squall, and now I understood how even Lucien, despite his knowledge of the district, had almost got lost, probably on just such a night.

About two miles from the farm, the road ceased to be passable for cars. We left my car sheltered under a barn, and went the rest of the way on foot. All trace of road had disappeared in this white desert. Without my companion, whose arm I held

nd who lighted me a little with a lantern, I should have been
ost after a few yards. Clinging to him with one hand while the
ther gripped my bag, I stumbled forward in the soft snow,
ent in two, choking and blinded by the gusts of wind, my skin
asped by the cold, smarting under a hail of snow-bullets.

On the way the man showed me where his brother-in-law,
leceived by the darkness, had slipped in a ravine. The family
vere worried not to see him home for dinner, and a little later
ny guide went out to search for him. Luckily, about a quarter
f a mile from the farm, he had noticed the bicycle still on the
oad and already half covered with snow. He discovered the
ody two yards further down against a rock, and with the help
f his sister managed to pull the man up to the road and then
oring him back on a sledge to the farm. After that he had come
lown to Peyrac to find me.

We went into the kitchen, where a big fire of pine logs was
olazing, and my companion pulled away the icicles which had
ormed on his moustache and took off his sheepskin coat. In a
noment of utter weakness I had to sit down without even taking
off my coat, and could only look on stupidly when the injured
nan, lying on a bed in the corner of the room, vomited onto
iis pillow. My overcoat, crackling with frozen snow, was beginning to drip round my chair and I eventually summoned up
he energy to rise and go over to the bed.

The man seemed very weak, and was almost unconscious.
He had a bandage of towels wrapped round his head, beneath
which his eyes looked out distractedly. He tried to speak, but
only succeeded in mumbling a few unintelligible syllables. In
the effort he made to move, a little cerebral matter, seeping
through between his cheek and the improvised bandage, flowed
down his face, mixed with blood. I undid the bandage gently,
and when I had separated the hair, all sticky with blood clots,
I found a wide wound going right to the bone at the level of
the temple. There had apparently been bleeding also from the
ear, so that the cheek, as well as the neck, was smeared with
blood.

I had to break off my examination almost at once while
the patient was sick again, and then had a convulsive fit. While
I was waiting for this to stop, extremely unpleasant thoughts
were turning over in my mind. Even without a closer examina-

tion the lesions seemed to me to be very serious: the convulsions and vomiting proved this, as did the traces of cerebral matter which began to flow from the wound whenever he tried to move. What could I do on the spot? Practically speaking, nothing at all. Should I have to decide on his being taken to Aurillac immediately? Standing near the patient, his wife and brother-in-law looked at me, awaiting my decision.

For a few seconds I imagined the fearful journey through the hurricane with the patient strapped on a sledge. The lesion was already seven or eight hours old. From my year of neuro-surgery under M. Legendre I had definite ideas on this sort of case, and was reasonably sure that in the patient's present condition, he would arrive at Aurillac too late for an operation to be of any use. I was not going to make a nearly dying man travel in this storm without the least hope of success. But at the moment of announcing this decision, I vaguely felt I was taking the line of least resistance, letting my brain be dulled by the heat of the house, finding good reasons not to face the wind and cold and black night again, but wait till morning.

To give at least an impression of competence, I began cleaning the wound, shaving the hair round it, cleaning up the ear (which I found after all had not been touched), and washing off the congealed blood and mush of brain matter. When I pulled apart the two lips of the wound, which were already partly dislodged from the skull, I could easily see the irregular orifice of the fracture. A large fragment of bone, blocked across the hole, was immobilizing a second fragment above it, which was pushing the brain back. With the aid of a forceps I tried to free the two fragments. After a few efforts the first came away with a sharp cracking noise; and after that the second piece, surrounded by smaller splinters, was easier to remove. But hardly had I cleared the orifice in this way when a pocket of half-coagulated blood started emptying in bursts at each beat of the heart, flooding the whole pillow. As soon as this pocket was emptied, I saw the white covering of the brain beating. It was all lacerated, and clots were dribbling through the lacerations. There was nothing for it but to plug the holes gently with a wad of sterile gauze and put on a large head bandage. For the moment I could do nothing more.

The woman had made some coffee for me. I took it and sat on

he bench against the side wall of the fireplace, very near the fire. Outside the wind was whining and shrieking, shaking doors and shutters, battering against the whole sturdy building furiously but in vain. I felt all too comfortable, and feared at any moment I might drop off to sleep. After a short while I shook myself hard, got up, and went back to the bed.

Since my treatment the man had had no further vomiting attacks or convulsions, and there was no more discharge coming from beneath my dressing. I took his pulse and examined his pupils, and was most surprised to find a distinct improvement. In my pleasure at this unexpected success, putting the whole prognosis in a different light, I said to the brother-in-law on impulse: "He's much better, and I think there's still a chance. We must get him down to Aurillac at once." I had to say this without giving myself time to reflect, for fear selfish instincts might have betrayed me if I started thinking about the *écir*.

The man went off immediately to fetch his sledge from a shed. He brought it into the stable, where he hung his lantern on a hook. The awakened animals were mooing softly in the darkness as I helped him prepare a mattress. Then we rolled the patient up in a blanket with big stones, warmed at the fire, to act as hot-water bottles. By the narrow door joining the kitchen to the stable we then carried him to the sledge, strapped him to it, and fixed a canvas hood above his body. When this whole operation was completed, the man took the lantern and opened the door.

An icy gale lashed out at us immediately, dispelling with one huge blast all the warmth of the stable. I was almost choking before we were properly out of the house. The cold had gripped me, and I was deafened by the shrill clamor of the wind. I had to stop, but the man was already harnessing himself to the rope strap, and bent in two from the effort, lowering my head so as to avoid getting the full force of the blizzard in my face, I started dragging the sledge at his side.

We went forward slowly without speaking, and in any case we could never have made ourselves understood through the bellowing of the storm. But occasionally the wind did drop, and then all we could hear in this hostile universe was the crackling of frozen snow under the runners and under our feet. Almost at once the dark hood, which vaguely outlined the prone form of the body beneath it, became completely white. We might, by the look of it, have been dragging a giant's body through the night in an immaculate shroud, for some fantastic funeral rites.

When we reached the barn where we had left the car, I was gasping and exhausted. My shoulder was hurting, sawed into by the strap; my eyes and nose and lips and cheeks were all burning; my fingers were all thick and numb. I should have loved to make a hole for myself in the soft snow, sink into it and lie still. But my companion, without wasting any time, started taking off the frozen hood, so I was obliged to go down on my knees by the injured man, pull off my gloves and try to revive my benumbed fingers sufficiently to make a rapid re-examination before we continued the journey.

The vomiting had recommenced and the pulse was once more alarmingly weak. Without a moment's pause it was vital to get the car ready, lay the patient as flat as the back seat allowed, scrape the windshield clear of the thick ice crystals which had formed over it, and start off again on the uncertain road. I stared feverishly into the blackness ahead, terrified lest at any moment the car might stick in some hole covered over with powdery snow. Every minute lost now would reduce the chances of saving the patient's life.

I was hoping to stop at Peyrac and put the injured man in the hands of the garage proprietor, who would then take him on to the Aurillac hospital in his own car, as he usually did with urgent cases. But when I reached the main square, the patient's condition had deteriorated still further, and there was obviously no question of wasting half an hour ringing at the garage man's house, dragging him out of bed, making him get out his car and transfer the dying man to it. I was afraid he was slipping fast. No, I had begun, and evidently I must carry on right to the end.

So we set off on a further thirty miles of slippery roads and icy winds, until at last we reached the plain, and the wind suddenly ceased its obsessive dirge. When my headlights finally picked out the smooth, safe, tarmac road with regular clear-cut ditches on either side, and a little further on the lights of Aurillac came in sight, then I felt that life was splendid.

The interne on duty gave a short whistle as he glanced at the patient. "Well," he said, "it was certainly high time...."

Compared with that harassing trip, the visit I had just made to the tubercular young man spitting blood was a mere country walk, and I was not likely to forget the *écir* because of the present *plouxal*. All the same, as I crossed the main square on the way back to Dr. Delpuech's house, I was surprised to find a further image of that other wakeful night coming back to me very vividly for no apparent reason.

When the injured man was stretched out on the operating table at Aurillac Hospital, the theatre sister spread a mass of sterile towels over him, covering almost the whole of his body. Despite his weak condition the man regained consciousness for a short while. Although he could not see anything, his face being covered with more towels, he could still hear the noises of the theatre, including the clink of instruments being prepared for the operation. The surgeon put on his gown, and while I was talking to him, I noticed outside the area of sterile towels the patient's hand. It was a big brawny farmer's hand and it was clenched over the edge of the table, quivering with fear. It was still trembling when the surgeon had regularized the hole in the head.

A man who has not been anesthetized and is still conscious may well be afraid when he hears the crack of a bone, even though he will in fact feel no pain. I knew that this was the case, and that his apprehension was therefore unnecessary, from having watched many neuro-surgical operations performed by Charles Legendre at the Charité. The skull-bone becomes more or less insensible as soon as you remove the sensitivity of the skin covering it; while as to the brain itself, the surgeon can cut away a whole lobe without even needing to have his patient anesthetized.

But why was I so busy recalling this scene, really so insignificant beside all the dangers my injured man had been in before? I fancied now that it was reminding me of another scene which I had forgotten a long time ago. As I crossed the square, I tried to think of it, and suddenly I remembered.

But immediately, like someone dropping a red-hot object he has picked up by mistake, I tried to drive away the memory—

too late. The image conjured up was there, as distinct and detailed as if four years had not slipped away in between. Hauberger's block at the Charité, a workman fallen from some scaffolding, and brought in to Casualties with a fracture of the skull. Legendre had him taken to the theatre immediately, and I dashed there too, thrilled to watch this operation being performed.

Marianne followed me. I could picture exactly Legendre and the interne in their white caps and gowns bent over the narrow operative field. At the moment when the brain could be seen through the round breach, beating in rhythm with the heartbeat, I turned towards Marianne. She was not following the operation. She had noticed the patient's hand, a thick leathery hand like that farmer's hand the other night, also trembling in agony at the edge of the table. Without saying anything, abandoning the engrossing spectacle of the operation, she gently rested her lovely fingers on the big brown hand, soothing it with her touch.

Because it reminded me too imperiously of Marianne, recalled too clearly the innocence and purity and sensitivity of her heart, I would now have liked to chase away this image with all my strength. Why should I be unhappy, even vaguely, because of this vanished past? Our two lives had separated, and we meant nothing more for each other. Our love was utterly dead, and it was Marianne herself who three years ago, in her courage and wisdom, had first guessed this, and deliberately released me. It is true that Pierre Prichard used all the means at his disposal to open her eyes.

The end of the vacation, and the beginning of the winter term, brought back most of the group in our hostel, but it did not bring back to the Cité the convalescent Marianne. If all went well, her stay in the mountains was to last nine or ten weeks, but her doctor in Savoie finding the young patient still too weak to face the tiring life of Paris and hospital, kept on postponing the time when she could return. After all the foreign students, including the female variety, had gone back to their own countries, Henri abandoned me for a few days and visited his "old man" at Vichy, to report in his own way on his vacation work and also to extract a little further pocket money. I found myself waiting impatiently for his return, feeling completely at a loss without his company. As soon as he did come back I resumed my place in the little yellow sports car.

In January I had the surprise of receiving the student scholarship offered by the Senegal Government. Although I was already seeing much less of my friends in the hostel, most of them were generous enough to congratulate me on this piece of unexpected good fortune. Only Pierre Prichard saw fit to comment grudgingly: "Some people have all the luck, don't they?" When he said this, I happened to be holding in my hand a letter from Marianne, whose handwriting he undoubtedly recognized. "Maybe," he added with one of his usual laughs which were three parts sneer, "they won't always be quite so lucky in love. You can't get away with everything all the time."

After this he departed, a depressing figure in his old overcoat flapping miserably round him like an old sack. A week or two later, when he met me again in the porter's office, and I happened to be reading another letter from Marianne, I was wearing an expensive new suit I had just bought, The unfairness of this must have seemed like the last straw to the envious Prichard. This time, with the corners of his lips turned bitterly down, he said sarcastically: "How beautifully turned out we're looking these days. I suppose that's the suit in which you'll be getting married to some wealthy heiress? To think there are poor little girls who aren't quite so well off and start building up false hopes—and no one has the kindness to warn them."

His sallow face was so twisted with jealousy and hatred that for some days I was really afraid he would send Marianne an anonymous letter. But I was soon reassured, for in the following weeks Marianne's letters kept their tone of unqualified love, without a break. It was very gradually that their passionate tone changed, turning to the light-hearted manner of good friends and nothing more. Almost unconsciously I began answering in the same tone, probably because it was easier to keep up, and in my selfishness I was even beginning to tire of writing still in the part of passionate lover.

It was a further reflection of Prichard's, however, which opened my eyes. In the same gradual way, Marianne was also spacing out her letters more and more, so that now I usually received only one a fortnight. One morning Prichard found me outside the lodge opening the fortnightly letter.

"Well, well," he remarked with malicious pleasure, "it looks as if Marianne isn't writing to you quite so often these days." And then he added, in his usual sly way of making elaborately casual generalizations: "What was it someone said about not fooling all the people all the time?"

His double chin shook with a dismal laugh, but his eyes sparkled so evilly that I could be in no further doubt: he *had* written to Marianne. I was so furious I was on the point of doing something melodramatic like trying to knock him down. He evidently read these feelings on my face, for he abruptly checked his sneer, and left me in a hurry. He knew I knew, and could congratulate himself on having done the most damage within his power.

I stood there alone on the boulevard in the very place where, a few months earlier, I had hesitated to open the envelope which should have contained my pardon. This letter would not be bringing me pardon, but more probably indifference. Marianne, disgusted by my conduct, had detached herself from me. It was she now who was only writing from pity. I had lost her.

At the thought that she was escaping from me, I felt I was suddenly dashing into a black fog, rising sheer and grim like a wall against me. I was so used to her, and to her loving me, that I found it quite unbearable to lose her. Then my vanity, incredible in retrospect, cleared away the fog and reassured me. I thought I understood the heroic act she was putting on in response to mine. Prichard's anonymous letter must have shown me to her as I really was, or had become: dishonest, cowardly, selfish, sensual, unfaithful—but that was not the real reason for her withdrawal. She was acting according to her code of honor in love.

One evening in the old days she had said to me: "I want the man I love to be free." To make herself less of a burden to me then she had generously tried to send me off with my former friends at the hospital. Once more, despite her inevitable pain and jealousy, she was refusing to violate her own principles by imploring me or scheming to get me back. She would not stoop to putting pressure on me, she would not dream of trying to excite *my* jealousy so that she could hold me despite myself. Instead, warned by Prichard that I had grown tired of her, she had decided quietly to sacrifice herself by moving further and further away from me, retiring to the very fringe of my life. I now suddenly noticed that she had stopped writing "we" in her letters. If I had let other women come between us, it meant to her that "we" was inappropriate, that *I* wanted to live in my own right.

Standing on the pavement I was again ashamed and truly unhappy. But it might still not be too late. I would write to her, as I had never written to her before. My heart swelled and I took a few enthusiastic strides down the boulevard. It was so easy! To make up for everything I would ask Marianne to marry me. But immediately something in me rebelled, and I pictured my present life with all its liberty and pleasures. At the idea of going back to that past life, tied to one woman for ever, I felt in the grip of an immense inertia: marriage was not the solution.

No, too many things, too many people, too much time had come between us, and at least for me all was over. There had been too much waiting and too long a separation, long weeks and months of irrevocable withdrawal and estrangement. I was not to blame if the past no longer tempted me. By this imperceptible process all the love had gradually withered in me.

Yet on the boulevard, when I started walking again towards the Porte d'Orléans, the same road we had so often taken together on our way to hospital, I had a bitter taste in my mouth, and I felt weighed down by an intolerable load. It was my own selfishness and calculated cruelty to Marianne which now and for many weeks more lay heavy on my heart.

Daytime saw me caught up immediately in the net of daily occupations, which possesses the priceless virtue of forcing one to forget one's troubles. A doctor has often little leisure for thinking of these things, as he is too busy trying to help others to carry the burdens of fear and unhappiness to be found at each house he visits. By the end of the long day he comes home almost worn out with the same weariness he has tried to allay in others.

At eight o'clock that morning I went along to see my patient of last night. Thanks to my injections, his mother told me radiantly, her son had had a good night and had not spat any more blood. This first satisfactory result of my efforts made me ready to go on with my usual round from farm to farm, from hamlet to hamlet without too much inward discomfort, despite the continuous rain which had not stopped since the early morning. During the night, mingling with the melted snow, the rain had transformed the cart tracks into a slushy morass.

About one o'clock I returned to the house soaked, filthy and irritable. My first patient of the afternoon was already waiting for me, and others kept on arriving all the time I was eating a hasty lunch. Félicie's statistics had been all too accurate: the *plouxal* seemed to have made everybody ill at once. But it was Antoine whose views on such outbreaks I now mentally acknowledged as particularly to the point: the malady working on them all was boredom. The people I had seen, imprisoned in their kitchens all day long by the torrential rain, with little to occupy them, often sent for me in order to provide them with a little distraction; while the hordes who invaded my office offered themselves this excuse to escape briefly from their gloomy homes.

I did not have the chance to go in to see Dr. Delpuech till it was almost dinnertime. "Father Pailhès has called," Félicie told me as I was going upstairs. "He's one of the doctor's oldest friends, you know. He's still up there now, but I'm sure they'd like you to go in."

Already on the landing the rugged booming voice of Peyrac's rural dean could be clearly heard through the door. It was a voice which exactly suited the figure I had often met on the roads or country lanes, slightly bent and corpulent, but still extremely vigorous.

Father Maurice Pailhès, I had been told, was not at all the ordinary type of priest. For years he held the post of diocesan missionary, dashing unceasingly through the countryside, tirelessly scattering the flames of his eloquence on all sides. Then when he found his physical stamina weakening, he asked for a more modest field of action where he could still spread the Gospel, and his bishop sent him to sow the good seed in the same part of the country where his parents had sown their wheat and barley. But he retained from his first apostolate a direct and fiery manner of preaching which put the fear of God into lukewarm parishioners, at least for one Sunday morning.

The whole district from church council down to choir-boys watched their step in front of the rural dean.

When I went in he was sitting by the fire and turned toward me a rugged lined face crowned by white hair. He was lying back comfortably in his armchair, his hands clasped beneath his ample black belt, his feet stretched towards the fire. His heavy shoes and the bottom of his cassock were steaming as they dried off. After a benevolent smile and a vigorous handshake he made a place for me in front of the fire.

"You haven't had too much trouble with this infernal rain?" Dr. Delpuech asked me. "If you'll excuse that word in this context, my dear Maurice," he added with a wink at the burly priest. "No offense," murmured the latter, evidently used to such chaff.

"Oh no," I said, "I was quite all right, thanks very much, what with your raincoat and those fine boots."

"They are almost priceless, I agree," said the old doctor. "In fact one of my friends insists that rubber boots and a pocket flashlight are more important in the life of a country practitioner than the discoveries of Pasteur. Father Pailhès and I have been talking about careers in the country, and although admittedly it's good to be able to keep your feet dry and to be sure of lighting up a lane or the bottom of a ditch in the middle of the night, if boots and flashlights are the only weapons we have we'll never tempt the best products of the medical and theological colleges to leave the towns and come out here. Look at my poor godson for instance—you remember him, Jean, don't you?"

I nodded, and the rural dean pricked up his ears.

"What do you think about him, Maurice?" He turned to Pailhès. "The last time I saw him I was very worried. He seemed terribly depressed about the effectiveness of his ministry and most dissatisfied with his parishioners at La Besse-Haute."

"He certainly is," said Pailhès. "I've done my best to cheer him up and give him new courage, and I pray constantly for him, which is really about all I can do to help him just now."

"Yes," said Dr. Delpuech. "I can well imagine how hard it must be for a young priest who's starting in, just about as hard as it is for a young doctor." He looked at me sadly, and I realized he was thinking of Antoine. The rural dean, however, also noticing his look, must have thought it was directed at me personally, for he immediately turned towards me with an expression of sympathetic inquiry on his face.

"No," said Dr. Delpuech, "I'm not thinking of Dr. Nérac. He's only here till I'm better, as a favor to me and his friend Dr. Clément. I doubt very much whether this period as a locum is giving him a strong desire to go into exile so far from urban civilization."

"I see," said Pailhès. "I thought that was why you looked at him just now. Were you thinking then of some particular young doctor?"

"Yes, I was," replied the doctor. "A friend of Jean's he brought over to dinner last night because I wanted to meet him. I'm afraid the dinner party didn't go quite as planned, did it, Jean?" He smiled ruefully. "This young doctor, whose name is Ricaud and who is practising at Montagut, was full of enthusiasm and a genuine desire to improve the health of the population. He went to them as wholeheartedly, with as much crusading spirit, as my godson did in his different sphere. Yet he only stuck it out a few months and now he's deciding to leave, demoralized and disgusted. It is discouraging when I think of all the good that a doctor really worthy of the name can do in a small community. I don't see what incentives I can suggest to keep him here, any more than I can for my godson."

"Yet your young doctor," said the rural dean, "is to some extent free to go and plant his tent elsewhere, whereas young Dieuzaide's future depends entirely on the Bishop's decision. He may be the parish priest at La Besse-Haute for ten years or twenty, you cannot tell. Please God he may not become too hopelessly discouraged by the ineffectiveness of his attempts to save souls. In four or five years he will see too many children whose spiritual education he has tended with loving care throwing over that education as soon as they're fifteen or sixteen. On my missionary journeys I used to meet so many of these ardent young priests, lost in a parish where there are almost no faithful left, without a living or any support, becoming vague clerical functionaries amidst a deserted church, their garden and their beehives."

He paused, and drawing a large handkerchief from his pocket, blew his nose. Each nostril was blown separately, and as he performed this action, he turned away his head, observing one of the fixed rules of rustic manners.

"It sounds a pretty miserable existence," I remarked. I remembered feeling very sorry for Dieuzaide, and hoped his superiors appreciated his plight. "Are you able to tell Father Dieuzaide frankly how you see the situation?"

"I wouldn't dare, my son," answered the dean, "and if I did he would find it far from reassuring. Almost every young man doing his military service finds the army, as at present organized, an incredible waste of time and energy, both physical and mental. But I can't very well explain to a young priest that the present organization of the rural ministry squanders still worse the strength and vitality at its disposal. For years now I've been going from one presbytery to another, so I've had a chance of viewing the problem at close quarters. I must say the initial enthusiasm of many priests goes for almost nothing, the isolation they're left in is so horribly depressing."

"Have you ever thought of a remedy?" asked Dr. Delpuech, and at the last word Father Pailhès sat up straight with an expression of extreme animation on his weatherbeaten countenance.

"I've thought about a remedy for years, Daniel," he answered, "every time in fact that I've seen one of these young priests in the depths of despair. And the fundamentals of the remedy are not far to seek, for they are in the Gospel. Why have we all gradually forgotten the experience of community living among the early Christians? You remember how the apostles used to go out in pairs. Well, to sustain the faith and strength of young priests, to make their labors fully effective and allow the Church to win back souls, I can see only one effective method, which comes to us from Christ himself: a sort of religious cooperative."

"A religious cooperative?" murmured Dr. Delpuech reflectively. "All living and working together, you mean? Yes, I like that idea a lot. In fact I've sometimes thought..."

"Living and working together, *and* praying together," broke in Pailhès, his face flushed with enthusiasm, his voice rising unconsciously, as I imagined it must at dramatic moments in his sermons. "Just imagine that communal life in a deanery,

263

which would be the center of a whole district's spiritual activity and would coordinate the efforts of each individual priest. They would all pool their experience and help each other in training and action. Not to be alone any more, what a joy it would be, what strength it would give! Even from a strictly practical viewpoint you can see what extra facilities this new communal life would provide for so many priests who can never find a servant, who haven't the resources to keep their libraries up to date or run any but the cheapest of cars, who can't even buy a little cinema apparatus for their church hall whereby they could bring progress into God's service."

"So that's your remedy?" said the doctor.

"Yes," said Pailhès, in a more normal voice, shaking his head a little sadly, as if he had been letting his hopes rise too high. "Yes, that's the remedy, and I'd willingly give the rest of my life in an attempt to apply it. But alas I shall never have enough preliminary capital, nor the sanction of my superiors."

"Have you mentioned the idea to them?" I asked.

"I told the Bishop about it." He gave a wry smile. "And he listened to me very kindly. But possibly an episcopal palace is not the best place from which to imagine what the life of a village priest can really be like."

From a pocket hidden by his belt he drew a huge silver turnip watch, and sighed regretfully as he replaced it: "Oh dear, I've a service to take at eight o'clock. The church is very cold and some of my parishioners, especially the old ladies, don't like being kept waiting."

"The whole countryside is scared stiff of you, Maurice," said Dr. Delpuech with a laugh, "and yet, if I understand you correctly, you're frightened of your troop of old maids."

"You should know that pious old maids are usually up to all the tricks," answered the rural dean. "If I'm late for my old dears, they'll clear their throats reproachfully when I arrive and keep up their coughing all the way through. Well, good night, Daniel," he ended, going up to the bed and shaking the old doctor's hand. "And may God return you to health very soon."

"There's not much hope now," said Delpuech, "of a complete return to health. So if you'll be kind enough to pray for me,

Maurice, please ask God to grant me patience, as the greatest gift He could now bestow on me."

He spoke so simply and firmly that the priest must have realized how useless would be any mere polite protest. "That," he said gravely, "is a prognosis which I shall not spread among your patients. They are all hoping you'll be really well again, and too many people would be sad if I told them any such thing. Really, Daniel, you've done wonders for the whole district."

A smile lit up the doctor's face. "Thank you for that, my old friend. At least I've looked after them to the best of my ability. But as Hippocrates said over two thousand years ago, life is short, art is long, and opportunity is fleeting. Medicine is a difficult career which satisfies nobody, not even the doctor himself. I don't know if I've succeeded in doing them any good, but at least I've tried not to do them any harm. Good night, Maurice, and thank you for your good wishes."

The rural dean said good night again, and I followed him downstairs. As soon as he had left, Félicie called me in to dinner.

After dinner I had to go back into town for two more calls. It was still raining, and when I returned I was very glad to sink for a few minutes into the armchair by the fire which the rural dean had occupied earlier in the evening. Before going to bed I wanted to ask Dr. Delpuech about a case which was puzzling me. A man of about fifty had had a temperature for five days, also diarrhea, and albumen in his urine. At first I believed it was a form of influenza and treated it accordingly. But when the fever and diarrhea continued I began to feel worried. The man had also shown me a round purplish mark on his left hand with a slight swelling. This, he told me, had developed out of a scratch from his cat about a fortnight earlier. He was trying to chase it off the table where the whole family was busy carving up a pig.

I looked in various textbooks but could find no definite connection between the scratch, the purple mark, and the fever. When I asked to see the cat I was shown a big tom, purring by the fire, which had no obvious disease and seemed a very pacific lover of pork.

When I had finished telling Dr. Delpuech about it, he said to me quietly: "You suspected the cat, which was reasonable.

But besides the cat you should have thought of the pig which the cat had already scratched with its paw. Your patient is suffering from swine-fever contracted through superficial abrasions made by the cat. If you doubt this, try having a bacteriological examination. If I were you, though, I should start the man tomorrow on special serum."

"Gosh, you have to know a lot to be a doctor round here," I said, stretching out my hands to the fire. "I find it rather discouraging sometimes, I feel as if most of the medicine I learned in Paris was quite irrelevant."

"I know how you feel," said Dr. Delpuech. "I know too, without your needing to tell me, that you're only staying here out of friendship to Lucien and sympathy for me. However, as tomorrow Lucien agrees that it'll be all right for me to get up for a few hours in the afternoon, I hope you'll soon be able to go back to Paris."

"Really, sir..." I began, but he broke into my protest at once. "I find it quite natural, you know. Snatched away from the rapid tempo of a big city, you must feel everything here is more or less dead. It's not the same for me, I've made this my life now for so long."

"Would you start here again, sir, if you had the chance?" I asked. "Lucien told us last night on the way to Montagut how you came to stay here instead of carrying on a promising career in Paris."

"Did he now? That was nice of him. So you'll know now that once it wasn't so easy for me either. Yes, Jean, I've adapted myself so thoroughly by now to my life near the soil, near realities, among people of my own race, that if I had to start my career again, knowing all I do, I'd choose to live it out here."

"I think even Antoine Ricaud was impressed by what Lucien told us," I said, angling a little for his further reflections on the Ricauds.

"I'm glad," said the old doctor. "Since yesterday evening I've thought about your friend a good deal. At times God allows some of His children to believe He has forsaken them, and Ricaud seems really to be one of them. Believe me, Jean, I do understand his discouragement. When an ordeal like that goes on and on, the inevitable result is disgust, stagnation, indifference, an inferiority complex, a disbelief in all good fortune—

like poor Legros, for instance—or else departure as with Ricaud. In any case there's one more member of what is virtually a rural elite disappearing. No," he gave a pale smile, "boots and flashlights aren't enough to attract talent to the country or keep it here once it's come."

"Surely," I protested, "there must be a good many new amenities since you started. Judging by what I heard last night anyhow."

"Oh yes, that one must admit. As an immense advance on making my rounds by horse or carriage, I remember the first asthmatic cars, open to the rain and the wind, with the pressure of the tires so high that they gave up the ghost at every piece of sharp flint, and acetylene headlights pointing their narrow beams towards the sky more often than on the road. And in those days surgeons and other such specialists were rare and far away, X-rays were nonexistent—you had to do everything on the spot, reduce fractures, remove tonsils, slit up strangulated hernias."

"That's what I mean," I said. "At least a lot of things have changed since then."

"Agreed. They have radiologists and surgeons even in the smallest districts, and it's years now since I've done a hernia myself. Cars break down less often, and the tires put up with more. We find electricity all over the place on our rounds these days, and at first sight, I agree, the life of a country doctor seems a good deal easier. But having known both periods I have to admit that at least in some of its fundamentals it has remained much the same."

"For instance?"

"In its isolation and overwork and weariness, Jean. The specialist is still usually a long way away, and the small farmer is still chary of costly journeys to reach that specialist. The summer is still extremely hot, and the winter can still be quite severe, as you have found yourself." He smiled.

"I have," I admitted, "and how I am enjoying this fire!"

"Women haven't stopped having babies, nor patients panicking because of a bellyache in the middle of the night. And it's always just when you have an urgent case on your hands that your tires happen to pick up a nail on some farm track. That nail may come from the shoes of a farm laborer who's very

267

little different in his muddy breeches from the farm laborer a thousand years ago, stolid as his own cows, unchanging as his own soil. Modern medical equipment becomes increasingly dear and fewer and fewer individual doctors can afford to buy it."

"Well," I said, "you've often told me that things take a long time to change in the country."

"Yes, but that doesn't mean the country need go right to sleep as it sometimes seems to in France, or that country doctors should resign themselves to going to sleep with it. It's really only natural, I suppose, that when a doctor with any ambitions takes a country practice and finds so few scientific amenities, so few personal or intellectual incentives, he very soon starts thinking when he can leave. Yet there is the countryside emptying and dying, and it's up to the doctor to do something about it."

For a few minutes he remained silent, looking dreamily at the fire. I said nothing, not wishing to interrupt his reverie, though I wondered whether it would lead him to any conclusions. To me the problem seemed more or less insoluble.

"There's the dilemma," he continued eventually, half to himself, "yes, there's the dilemma: either demoralizing isolation, sterile individualism and a second-rate sort of medicine, or..." he paused again.

"Or what?"

"Or perhaps an attempt at communal living and working, a sort of health center, which at least materially would be something like the religious center the dean dreams of for his priests."

"Did that give you the idea?" I asked.

"Perhaps, Jean, though there's been the germ of it running in my mind for a long time. It was your friend Ricaud who started my thinking of it seriously, and old Maurice's reflections made me want to formulate the same plan for doctors. Why not a single clinic where the two or three local doctors would practise together, pooling their extra equipment so that it would be a possible economic proposition? Without being too elaborate it would at least give them far better chances for sound diagnosis and effective treatment. Why not a nurse in common who would relieve them of an infinity of small chores and material details? In fact why not a sort of medical cooperative in an easier professional atmosphere, without bitter rivalries? Each doctor would still preserve his independence and his personality, of course, and the patients would have more satisfactory treatment in every way."

But the old doctor was not to develop his ideas any further that evening. Félicie had burst into the room while he was speaking, and she waited politely till he had finished a sentence. Then, while gusts of wind could be heard beating against the shutters, she exclaimed to her master: "You ought to be ashamed of yourself. Now you're a bit better yourself you want to kill off all the others. You know very well that calls never stop day or night when the *plouxal* is here, and poor Dr. Nérac must be simply dropping with sleep."

I was, it is true, feeling extremely tired, but I protested mildly. Félicie, however, began pushing me forcefully out of the door, so Dr. Delpuech and I said good night, and I then went obediently to my room, thinking with dread of some distant mountain farm where a child might be choking or a woman beginning her labors, and of the messenger hurrying into his heavy shoes and sheepskin coat so that in an hour or two he would be ringing away at this front door bell down below.

The following day, accompanying a patient to the door during office hours, I noticed M. Albessard, the Peyrac lawyer, arriving. I happened to have seen him professionally for his bronchitis, so I thought he was probably coming to see *me*. After greeting me politely, however, he crossed the hall, and went upstairs.

All the patients strained their heads towards the waiting room door, highly intrigued; and when M. Albessard left two hours later, I had to answer the question of one patient, obviously devoured with curiosity. "Dr. Delpuech got up today for the first time. The lawyer's merely paying him a friendly visit, I suppose," I said.

"Oh no," the woman who had asked me said very firmly. "For a friendly visit M. Albessard wouldn't have brought his brief case with him, or gone straight to his office when he left here. We all saw through the window where he went. It'll be for his will, it's plain as plain. The poor doctor thinks he ought to be settling his affairs. The whole town's wondering who'll inherit, you know. He hasn't any family, has he now? He'll be leaving a fair amount, won't he?" she added with a sigh.

There was certainly something there to cause excitement in the Auvergnat soul. The woman looked at me attentively, hoping I might drop some hint. In all good faith I shrugged my shoulders innocently, for it did not then occur to me to establish the slightest connection between M. Albessard's call, the dismissal of the representative from the Bricard Agency, the Ricauds coming to dinner, and Father Pailhès' apostolic cooperative.

Chapter Fourteen

March 28–April 5

As soon as word went round that Dr. Delpuech was better and that he had opened his doors a fraction, there was a general rush to get a toe in the chink. Félicie's protests were all in vain, and so were my own attempts to shut out the invaders. "They'll kill you," I told him.

"On the contrary," said the old doctor cheerfully, "they're bringing me to life again. A few weeks ago I thought I had become a permanent invalid, no use to anyone. I was sorry to go on living for a few extra months what couldn't honestly be called life. I'd much sooner have quietly faded out. But now, thanks to all these people who still need my services and come to me as they always used to, I'm enjoying my resurrection. So don't worry about me, Jean."

His visitors usually began to arrive from noon onwards and did not wish to be mixed up with my office customers in the waiting room, so they waited patiently in the hall, where a steady buzz of conversation could now always be heard. Félicie might try her hardest to discourage them, telling them that her master still tired very quickly, that he could not leave his room or his armchair. Nevertheless they insisted on talking to him "just for a few minutes." All gave the most pressing reasons for seeing him.

During my consultations I used to hear through the door these interminable palavers, Félicie's definite refusals, the visitors' stubborn and tireless pleading, their continual tramping up and down on the tiled floor of the hall, their whispering and nervous coughing. When I opened the door, most of these faces did not turn towards the office as they used to, and the first day this happened it was *my* turn to feel slightly jealous of Dr. Delpuech. What did they all expect of him? Were they hoping for a miracle by coming to beg for health at an old man's armchair?

Very soon, however, I realized that it was not solely for medical advice that everyone was queueing up to see the old doctor. For the whole district he was not only a doctor for the flesh, he was the guide, philosopher and friend for the spirit, whose opinion "strictly in confidence" they all required. What did he think about a marriage, say, or an investment, a mortgage or the education of a child? Sometimes, no doubt, their eventual conclusion would be exactly the opposite from what he had advised or suggested. But the point was that he had guided them all at each important stage in their lives, had reconciled feuding neighbors, preserved broken households, resolved quarrels, and now he knew all about them almost better than they did themselves. He seemed to be the father of an enormous family stretching over the whole of Peyrac and its confines.

But like Félicie I was very much afraid that Dr. Delpuech, in his willingness to listen to them all, might go far beyond his strength. To keep a watch on him, I used to go up to his room several times in the afternoon between office patients. Each time I was amazed at the new vitality in his eyes, shining with ingenuous eagerness, at the new color on his face, as if cheerfulness and enthusiasm had succeeded in renewing his blood as well. He would listen patiently and attentively to the most garrulous prattle, always finding simple, clear, decisive words with which to encourage, advise or console. I had never found his brain so lucid, his judgment so ready. I should probably have stopped worrying if I had not at times seen him slump a little further into his armchair, his brow suddenly pale and moist, and the whole of his body crumpling over to-

271

wards his left shoulder while he unconsciously brought up his hand to his heart.

Usually the visitor would go on talking, insatiably and imperturbably, without noticing anything, or perhaps pretending not to notice anything so as to keep more time for the discussion of his own business. Yet when they came into the room, those who were seeing him again for the first time since his illness could not always hide a start of shocked surprise at the ravaged face of their old doctor.

Every time I could I tried to shorten the interview, and to take the chatterbox with me when I went downstairs to my patients. I found it almost incredible when the same visitor, who had promised Félicie to be brief and had then been talking ruthlessly at Dr. Delpuech for three-quarters of an hour, remarked to me on the landing with an air of sadness which seemed completely sincere: "Poor old Dr. Delpuech, he doesn't look too well, does he! He's not the man he was. After a month's illness he looks twenty years older. He really ought to look after himself more carefully. Of course he should know how to keep his health, a good doctor like him."

Almost before he had left the house, the man would pass on these gloomy forebodings to a neighbor just making for the front door. So the procession of clients grew each afternoon, most of them so much better off in the priceless gift of health than their unfortunate patron and benefactor. Stubbornly, with a selfishness I found positively macabre, they continued to push him towards his death, determined to snatch the last few pearls from his lips before it was too late. Dr. Delpuech saw what they were doing to him, but still smiled at them and let them do it.

During his convalescence I also learned that the old doctor went far beyond his strictly medical activities, which alone might have seemed more than enough to occupy his time. He had helped his fellow citizens in many other ways, though he had never mentioned these to me, and I only learned about them from listening to the conversations with his visitors. He had founded first a farmers' guild and then a purchasing co-operative. He had even succeeded immediately after the war in setting up an association of different villages to bring electricity to the whole district.

One afternoon I found the secretary of the milk cooperative with Dr. Delpuech, holding on his knees some big account books which he had just closed up. As we were leaving the room together, the secretary, before going out, asked Dr. Delpuech: "What should we do about Albisson and Delbos?"

"Let's be patient with them once more. Perhaps you'd better send them to me, and I'll try and show them the harm they're doing us."

Often during my rounds in the country I had met on the lanes, at the same times morning and evening, the picturesque processions of little donkeys led by an old woman or a child. The animals were carrying churns, and they were going to the dairy at Peyrac or returning from it. Other smaller farms sent in a hand whose churn was specially made so that it could be attached to his back by thick straps. In the same way I learned to recognize the large dairy farms by the imposing lines of churns all down the roads on the edge of the ditches, at the entrance to the cart tracks. A truck would pass morning and evening to collect the receptacles full of milk from the last milking and substitute the previous day's receptacles, not empty (as I had thought) but filled with whey.

I knew that the headquarters of all this pastoral activity was a huge new concrete depot at the entrance to the town, the front of which read: *Peyrac Dairy Cooperative, built 1930.* I had often noticed its immense white curdling vats as I passed in front of the open doors when the tiles were being scrubbed.

While I was going downstairs with the secretary of the co-operative—"the co-op," as he called it with proud familiarity—I was staggered to learn that apart from the most modern instruments for milk collection, the trucks, the idea of these donkeys and men on foot going twice a day to Peyrac did not represent, as I had thought till then, an immemorial custom. Dr. Delpuech had launched it for the first time several years ago, following the creation of the co-op.

"And what did the farmers do with all their milk before that?" I asked.

"Not much, Doctor. They were quite contented to make a little butter and cheese from it for the needs of their own farm. Most of them had to breed stock, which they'd eventually sell to the nearest butcher or at the market, and at not much of a price, I can assure you. But now, thanks to Dr. Delpuech, even the people with small farms can be sure of selling their milk at a good price. Almost all of them have converted part of their fields from grain, which gave practically no yield, to pasture land and meadows. Besides that they can raise pigs with the whey allocated to them by the co-op. They get seven-tenths of the amount of milk they've delivered. Most of them, who used to have a very hard time of it, now live quite comfortably."

Late the next afternoon when I went to Dr. Delpuech's room at the end of my office hours, I found there the farmer Albisson, whom the secretary of the cooperative had sent to Dr. Delpuech as arranged. He was listening to the doctor with a very humble and contrite air, and seemed extremely pleased to make good his escape on my arrival.

"How difficult it is to fight selfishness!" said the old doctor after his departure, with some bitterness. "I'm not talking of simple individualism, however obstinate, the unconscious idea of 'every man for himself,' but of a far more conscious form which cheats the community more or less deliberately. It's taken me years, as you can guess, to break down the prejudices and suspicions of the people here, to bring them gradually to a spirit of cooperation. Most of them see the point now, but there are just a few who still cheat, relying on the goodwill of all the others."

"The gentleman who has just left us, for instance?"

"Yes, Albisson is one of the worst."

"What has he been doing?" I asked.

"He doesn't take all the milk from his cows, but lets his calves drink the very part which is richest in cream. Consequently the milk he brings to the co-op is of inferior quality, and so the Peyrac Co-op's good name is jeopardized by one farmer's dishonesty."

"To be frank, sir," I commented, "I think it's quite remarkable that that sort of behavior is confined to so few of them. Your co-op must have worked wonders."

"Perhaps it's only a small matter in itself," replied the old doctor, "but I see it as a sign of something more serious, part of the wasting disease which is fast depopulating the country-

274

side and destroying French agriculture. The politicians are always making fine speeches about going back to the land, but they forget, as we're all inclined to, that it's quite as important to try and keep on the land the people who are already there. When everything tends to drain them off into the towns, it's a fairly tough problem."

"And how would you set about solving it?"

"Partly by appealing to their self-interest, showing them how they can earn more money, making their work less thankless, their houses less uncomfortable, their lives less disagreeable. And we must try to see that the young do not need to regret so much the pleasures of city life."

"But won't these extra amenities only make them more selfish than ever?"

"Not if we have the spirit of cooperation I've been trying to encourage. You may be amused to hear that I'm president and founder of the local football club. I started it chiefly to encourage the team spirit in the young. Ah well, these teams and guilds and co-ops, they don't go very far, I know, they're only a small beginning."

"Even to have made such a beginning," I murmured, "seems to me a great achievement."

"Thank you, Jean," he said with a smile. "I was afraid you'd think my fifteen years' effort had borne very little fruit in the end. But you can see how humble and ambitious I've been at the same time. I never nursed any illusions, I knew the task was worth while and so I started it. But I also knew I could not hope to see the end of it, for it won't come in my lifetime."

I said nothing. The old man shivered, picking up the blanket which had slipped down a bit and pulling it over his knees again. He seemed to be collecting his thoughts, as he watched the flames dancing in the fireplace.

"But I've tried for too much," he said eventually, "I failed to see the range of the task. I forgot that I belong to a different generation of doctors which is already somewhat outdated. And another thing I forgot was that I was a widower without children or close family. I suppose I must have begun to think myself eternal, for until recently I scarcely even considered who my successor might be. When your friend Ricaud came here last night, as desperate in his loneliness as a lost child, in revolt against an existence too hard for him both morally and materially, that opened my eyes at last to the extreme urgency of the problem for thousands of young doctors, perhaps for the whole future of Medicine in the country."

He slumped back into the armchair with sudden weariness, and after a short silence said: "Even though I cannot complete all the work I have started, I would give anything to know that someone would go on with it."

"Lucien is sure to carry it on," I said gently.

"Yes, I know I can count on him. But the young man who comes in my place, what will *he* do? Will he be a real doctor, an idealist, like Ricaud? If your friend hadn't announced his decision so violently and firmly the other night, I was going to offer to take him here as my assistant. He wouldn't have had to wait long to become my successor. Where can I find another doctor willing to come and bury himself deliberately at Peyrac for all his life?"

The old doctor looked at me fixedly, and added after an imperceptible hesitation: "He may be needed any time. I pray God I may find him soon."

Immediately after saying this, he lowered his eyes, and turned them away abruptly into the big shadowy room. I could not decide whether this was because of his embarrassment over the implications of his last remark, or whether, like the break in his voice, it expressed his bitterness at dying before he had made due provision for the future of all his cherished plans.

I felt I now had a fair idea of what a country doctor's life was like. It might mean a long day spent in snow, mud and rain, saturated in complaints and miseries, impregnated with filth and stenches; followed by a whole night in some isolated hamlet on some interminable confinement case. Perhaps, groping your way back through the fog on icy roads, you would have a puncture on some windswept lane, and would have to lie on your face in the mud to fix in position a jack which would burn the numbed fingers at the touch. In such circumstances I often longed to be snug at home in a warm bed, and felt I had had more than enough of this exacting, painful and harassing existence. But at other calmer moments, when I could see things more objectively, I found something very

276

healthy and worthwhile about a life of such diversity, so many risks and responsibilities. As an additional attraction, I discovered to my surprise that I was developing a very friendly feeling for many of my patients.

Particularly when I listened to Dr. Delpuech talking to his visitors in my presence, I felt that something I had lost and forgotten for years was gradually returning to me. Long before coming to Peyrac, in my childhood I had already learned to listen and understand; and the stories the patients told me, though different in context, were strangely similar to the ones I had heard from my mother's "clients" who came to ask her advice in the back room of her tobacconist's shop in Toulouse. Their very looks were the same, I thought, as I watched Dr. Delpuech's visitors sitting very stiffly on the edge of armchairs which must be so different from their own rushbottom chairs or hard wooden benches. It was exhilarating to be reminded of this scene so familiar to my boyhood, and it came back to me now with a new vividness because I had forgotten it for so long.

I saw I had been much too quick to generalize about "peasant psychology," treating it as something rudimentary and rather sordid, and tending to write off all country people as a whole. Now when I tried to observe them better, I found amongst them characters and qualities worthy of attention and respect. Moreover, following the methods of my mother and Dr. Delpuech, I had learned how to put the nervous and shy at their ease, so that they were able to confess things they feared were absurd or shameful. I learned to put simple questions to the less intelligent, and to set one or two small traps which would catch out those who tried to take me in—including the many patients who pretended to be very poor in order to get a reduction in their fees.

It was now easy for me, once I had seen my patient, to stay for a chat with the family, to sit on a wooden bench by the fire while the wind battered fiercely against the door, the coffee pot sang, and a muddy dog thrust out his snout to sniff my shoes with interest.

Sometimes when I was delayed in a farmhouse by a long confinement or found the family at table when I arrived, I would sit down to a meal with them, and bravely partake of the famous *chabrot,* a disgusting-looking greasy mixture composed of the remains of the soup, left in the bottom of the pot for that purpose, and a bumper of red wine warmed by the heat of the plate. This was supposed to possess tonic qualities which I always took good care to acknowledge, and my hosts, who had furtively watched my reactions, would now talk to me with greater confidence after this proof of my good sense. Sometimes the farmer would quote to me with a sly smile a well-known local proverb: *Hot* chabrot *for all means the doctor won't call.* Falling in with the general good humor, I would tell them: "Oh, I don't mind losing a few patients as long as every time I come here you have *chabrot."*

Now that I knew them better, I could not possibly think men dull or stupid who could manage their own acres so skillfully, coming to terms with rain and drought, working out and balancing possibilities, exploiting opportunities, trying to see that nothing should go to waste.

These men could never have gone on living off the land unless, unconsciously or otherwise, they loved it. Constantly they had to use both brains and hands with shrewdness and skill. Indeed I came to find their activity not unlike my own as a general practitioner, based on the same combination of brainwork and hand labor, on the same absolute necessity of doing everything oneself. They and I would never be impersonal laborers, to be changed about at will, for in their job and in mine there were too many surprises and unpredictable accidents. We both had to deal with each complex individual situation that faced us, we both had to cooperate with Nature, and yield at times to chance occurrences which could not be avoided.

This parallelism often struck me forcibly when I stood in a dark alcove examining a patient half buried between three feather mattresses and a huge eiderdown, while a farmer stood by waiting for my oracular judgment. As I was determining on the treatment, establishing a prognosis, trying to obtain guidance from the patient's age and temperament and past pathology, I would suddenly perceive the similarity between my own mental processes and those of the farmer when he considered different ways of working his acres. Both of us were creatures cooperating with our Creator in new acts of creation, yet obliged, whether we were dealing with plants or animals or humans, to obey the eternal and subtle laws of sap or blood.

One evening when I returned dirty, dog-tired, and chilled to the bone, and was trying to thaw out by the fire in his room, Dr. Delpuech said to me with a friendly twinkle in his eyes: "Do you know, Jean my lad, that people here all seem to agree in finding you sympathetic and a good listener? They even say that for a Parisian you don't really seem to put on airs!"

"Who knows, perhaps after all I'm a born country doctor." I made this pronouncement with great solemnity, and then laughed heartily as at some rather farfetched joke. But a little later, just before going to sleep, I thought of my remark again, and wondered whether it was really as humorous as all that.

Chapter Fifteen

April 6–7

I HAD SETTLED down happily at Peyrac by this time, and never thought of fixing a definite date for my departure. I had almost come to feel I might be there for the rest of my life. But one evening, returning very late for dinner, I went into the dining-room and at once saw a letter propped against my glass. It had obviously come by the evening post, for the town of Peyrac was favored with two posts daily, though the environs had only one. Without really knowing why, I felt sure even before taking up the letter that it summoned me back to Paris. I was not surprised, therefore, on picking it up, to recognize on the envelope the spidery handwriting of Paul Chavasse.

Félicie had filled my soup plate, as she always did, directly she heard me close the front door. For she knew that I was usually both famished and in a great hurry when I returned in the evenings. But tonight I sat down without haste or appetite, and when she saw me opening this letter, she discreetly withdrew so I could read it alone. Paul wrote:

Dear Jean,

I dare say you'll be as startled to get a letter from me as I am to be writing it. Well, ackcherly, old boy, I'm writing chiefly as your medical next-of-kin to bring you an urgent or-else message from the hospital authorities: return within 48 hours, or else your post as dresser will be filled by A.N. Other, and with great reluctance they will be obliged to dismiss you instantly. If you come back like a good boy, I think you'll get away with a severe raspberry and no more, although they're not exactly pleased with your staying away all this time. Just shows, doesn't it, how utterly indispensable you are to the smooth running of the hospital—very flattering, I call it. Anyhow, I'd come back if I were you. I must also admit that I have an additional personal interest in your return as it will enable me to remove my own dresser's uniform for a fortnight and go home myself for a much needed holiday. I plan to leave the day after you come back, so you can see that much hangs on your return!

Sorry I've not written before, but you know how things are, or don't you? And in any case you might have written to me, we've all been dying to hear about all the people you've killed off, for the sake of good old Paris Med. Ever since you left the fold, I've been scouring the papers for news of the trial of one Jean Nérac, for unauthorized practice of black magic by the Auvergne Branch of the Incorporated Quacks and Witchdoctors Union.

Speaking of quacks, we were all very surprised when your pal, Henri Philippon, appeared on the ward the other day, a thing he hasn't done for a month at least. He spent a long time in Ste.-Madeleine Ward at Bed Number 4. When you left us, I fancy, there was a lady in this bed dying from cancer of the stomach. At present, however, it's occupied by an extremely pretty girl suffering from pneumonia, and this seems to have aroused in our good friend an acute interest in respiratory pathology.

And this brings me to a lengthy message which that lazy devil asked me to give you, though why the hell he can't write to you himself, I fail to see. However, for peace and quiet, I agreed to tell you that Vicky, who you apparently thought might be rather annoyed when you left Paris in such a hurry, seems to have consoled herself with a young painter who's arrived in Montparnasse from the Argentine with not much talent, we gather, but plenty of pesos. He's just left for Italy, but quite apart from the light it throws on feminine constancy, it means you can come back to Paris without Vicky throwing things at you.

Was there anything else I had to tell you from Henri the Horror? Oh yes, he'd been too lazy to write to you—he's telling me—but for the last week he's several times been just about to phone you concerning your protégé whose name I forget. It seems that young Adolphe Serres has obligingly written to his illustrious father, and the good Minister has already had a letter sent recommending protégé to the Chief Medical Officer for the Cantal, who was an old college friend of his. Protégé therefore, says young Serres, is pretty well bound to get the job, but would do well to present himself at Aurillac as soon as possible in case any rivals should drop a monkey wrench in the works.

Pardon me if I now return to my examination of a lady with severe abdominal rumblings. In any case I trust I shall be seeing your duly rusticated face within the next forty-eight hours—seriously, it'll be good to have you back.

Yours ever, Paul

When Félicie returned from the kitchen, she found me sitting in front of a plate of lukewarm soup, reflecting on my departure. I told her I had to go, and she clasped her hands with an air of consternation, and said sadly: "Oh dear oh dear, what on earth will the Doctor say when he hears? Everyone's got so fond of you. How empty the house will seem without you."

These sentences summed up so simply the three essential points which belonged exclusively to my life at Peyrac—the old doctor, my patients, this kindly home—that I could almost have burst out crying, like a child suddenly faced with the imminent removal of all security and all affection.

Félicie, however, active and practical as ever, had already gone back to the kitchen to fetch me some hot soup. She was back in a moment, and was now ready with her own brand of comfort. "At least they'll not be able to say in Paris that you aren't looking fit and well. Our cooking here is supposed to be too heavy, and they make fun of our braised meat and tripe and the way we put a bit of bacon in every dish. But there's just no doubt that you came here looking like a picked chicken, and now you're the picture of health."

As soon as I had finished dinner I left the table and began to climb the stairs to Dr. Delpuech's room. Whenever I was free in the evening, and especially if I had heard from Félicie that her master was alone, I had been accustomed to go eagerly up these stairs, looking forward to a chat with him. But this time I found myself unconsciously slowing down my steps as if I were carrying a heavy load; and certainly my heart was now heavy indeed.

My voice shook as I told Dr. Delpuech the news, and for a few moments he looked at me, struggling to answer but not trusting himself to speak. His emotion had for me the bitter-sweet quality of a parental kiss to a small boy returning to school. I tried to master my feelings, and noted mechanically the extreme blueness of his lips—sign of deterioration in his cardiac condition. He pulled himself together too, and on those lips I saw his wonderful friendly smile come wavering out again, and then shining with its full strength.

"Anyhow you needn't worry about me, Jean," he told me characteristically, as soon as he felt able to speak. "I'm feeling so much better that I'll be able to go down and see a few patients in my office, and I'll get Lucien to keep on the outside calls for the moment. In any case spring is coming and in a few days it'll only need a breath of good south wind to melt the last snow. In a single night after that you'll find all the orchards in blossom—a wonderful sight, and I wish you could stay to see it. But you know enough about peasant psychology by now to be quite sure that even the sick will jump out of bed and be off to the fields from then on. Which means that their poor old doctor will have something of a rest cure himself."

I suddenly remembered that Antoine did not yet know the good news Paul's letter had brought him. Since the night of the dinner party, I had not seen or spoken to him, feeling rather embarrassed about my promise, which till then I had felt almost sure was abortive. I gave Dr. Delpuech a few details about some of the cases I was dealing with at present, telling him I'd make out that evening a list of all my present patients, and leave notes about them. Then I said goodnight to him as casually as I could manage, and went downstairs to phone Antoine.

I gave him Henri's message and said it sounded almost certain that he would get the job. For a few seconds he remained dumb with incredulous joy, then he stammered hoarsely: "I'm going to get it, you say, I'm really going to g-get it?"

I could guess by his voice that he was not far from hysterical, and tried to talk very calmly myself—all these goodbyes seemed to demand considerable restraint on one's own emotions: "I've got to leave in a great hurry, Antoine, probably tomorrow morning, so I'm afraid I'll have no chance to come and bid you both *au revoir* in person. I'm so glad about the job. It sounds almost a sure thing and I do wish you both all the best, or should I say all three of you? Please write and tell me when the baby's born."

"*Au revoir*, Jean," he replied, still somewhat beside himself. "What wonderful news, and I can't thank you enough for all your help. Yes, of course I'll let you know about the baby. Thanks so much again, and from Marie too. Have a good journey back. *Au revoir*."

"*Au revoir*," I said again, and put the receiver down firmly, forestalling any repetition of his effusive thanks. My next task was even more difficult for me, and I sat for several minutes thinking about it—how to say goodbye to Lucien. By tacit agreement we had avoided each other since the night of our unhappy conversation about Marianne, and the only occasions when we had to meet were in Dr. Delpuech's room, when we only talked about patients. I could see that the strain between us had been noticed even by Félicie and certainly by Dr. Delpuech, although to my relief he had made no reference to it.

After long hesitation I telephoned and told him I was leaving and why I had to go at once, and about Dr. Delpuech's plans for dividing up future work. I said I would be leaving behind notes of all the cases he'd have to deal with on this basis, and I hoped he could manage this extra work. He thanked me noncommittally, and said he could certainly manage. "Before I leave here, Lucien," I said firmly, "there's one thing I'd like to tell you." "Go ahead," said the voice at the other end, completely neutral, indifferent.

"What I told you the other night about myself and Marianne"—the words came out with a rush—"is something I'm

283

deeply ashamed of. What you told me about your own feelings has made me realize that I've hurt you very much by hurting her. Please believe that I'm desperately sorry."

Lucien said nothing for a good minute, and then in a more friendly tone: "That's all right, Jean, I'd rather we said no more about it. I'm grateful to you for having come to help here, and I'm sorry you're going. When do you expect to catch the train?"

"Tomorrow evening," I replied.

"So to get to Aurillac, you'll have to take the bus from here at eight o'clock tomorrow morning?"

"I suppose so."

"I'll tell you what," said Lucien. "When I was at school in Aurillac I used to live with an aunt. This aunt has asked me to come and look at an ovary cyst which is giving her trouble and may need an operation. I meant to go there this week anyhow, so I can quite well fit it in tomorrow afternoon. That'll save you having to get up at seven o'clock tomorrow morning and then wasting an entire day at Aurillac waiting for your night train."

I was touched by this thoughtfulness, so characteristic of Lucien, and felt a surge of real affection for this old friend I had succeeded in alienating so badly. I wanted to express some of my feelings over the phone, but I knew that to the undemonstrative Lucien sentiment would seem out of place. My attempt at a compromise sounded unconvincing even to me, savoring of a rather forced heartiness, but it was the best I could do: "Good old Lucien, that's a fine idea. Thanks a lot."

Then it occurred to me that Antoine, being without a car, would doubtless be delighted at the chance of coming to Aurillac with us, and I went on: "I say, would you mind very much if we took Ricaud along from Montagut? He has to go in to Aurillac urgently to see the health authorities."

"All right, we'll go over there and pick him up. Only we'll have to start from here half an hour earlier. Will one o'clock suit you?"

"Will it suit me? Lucien, you're wonderful. It's extremely kind...."

While I was saying this there was a click, and I realized he had hung up. He was ready to do me good turns, like this lift into Aurillac tomorrow, but evidently preferred to accept nothing from me in return, not even thanks. My humble confession of guilt, though it had cost me some effort, had not gained my complete pardon; I was not, after all, to be let off as lightly as that. I thought of all the times I had been round the slum outside the Cité with him, acting as his assistant, and felt that if I had the chance to live and work near him at some future period I might win back his friendship.

But alas, it seemed more than probable that tomorrow was the last time I should ever see him. One of those deep friendships of youth, such as life rarely offers after one is twenty years old, had in effect come to an abrupt end when Lucien replaced the receiver. I waited several minutes before calling Antoine again to ask him whether he would like to come with us tomorrow. I had no doubts of his acceptance and prepared to listen with patience to his frantic expressions of jubilation and gratitude. But all the while I remembered that something irreplaceable had just faded miserably from my life.

I slept badly that night and woke early next morning. I rose at once so as to pack my valise before going on my last morning round. I had to go from room to room gathering together various pieces of personal property I had scattered around all over the house just as if I had been at home. Going through it for the last time I tried to think how things had looked when I first arrived. As with any scene you have only observed casually from a distance, it was far from easy to conjure up again the severe gray silent house where an old servant jealously mounted guard over the bed of a dying man, waiting to join the many tired old doctors who had died in this house before him.

But that gloomy house emerged from its lethargy very quickly and even the dead became alive to me once more: I was living and working in their place, among the fine harmonious furniture they had loved, in rooms now so familiar to me that I could have walked about in them with my eyes shut. To recall to me these dead doctors, their preoccupations and their intimate life, I had almost within reach of my hands their old books and their medical kit; by their portraits I recognized their robust faces beneath their wide-rimmed top hats. Three generations of doctors seemed to have worked, suffered, reflected, sometimes despaired perhaps, while building a temple of wisdom for my benefit, as if I had been their true heir. A serene and patient old man, looked after by a warm-hearted and devoted servant, was daily transmitting to me, as to his son, more and more of that rich heritage which could serve me faithfully throughout my life.

Every morning Félicie used to write on the pad beside the telephone the requests for me to call during the day. That morning I found on the page the names of only three patients, all in Peyrac itself. From the coatrack in the hall I took my raincoat, hanging beside Dr. Delpuech's cap, scarf, and overcoat. When I hung my hat up there on arriving the first morning, these abandoned clothes dangling there reminded me of the old rags laid out by the side of corpses in a morgue so that they can be identified. But, since then, I had grown used to them and every time I came in or went out I looked at them with affection. They no longer looked so dismal, on the contrary they seemed like trusty guardians of the hall, sharing the friendliness of this house.

I went to the postoffice, and sent a telegram to Paul Chavasse telling him I should be back at hospital tomorrow morning. Then I made my three calls without telling my patients that they were my last. As an excuse for my silence I told myself that I should be greatly embarrassed by demonstrative expressions of regret; but on reflection this seemed disingenuous. What I really dreaded was that if I did tell them, they would let me go without more than a few vague words of thanks.

Crossing the main square I noticed the red and green bottles of Mandaroux's shop. Before going away I must at least take my leave of the genial little druggist, and thank him for his help and kindness. In saying goodbye to him, I should be saying it collectively to the whole population, to whom he would doubtless pass on my expressions of regret at leaving.

His smooth cherubic face somehow managed to become deeply wrinkled in his obvious regret at my unexpected departure; I was touched and pleased to see this. "That really is bad news," he said, raising a sorrowful face towards me, "particularly as in little more than a week we could have gone out together catching vipers."

286

"What!" I exclaimed in amazement.

"Oh yes," he said, "I was greatly looking forward to it. Respect for tradition, combined with so much modern knowledge, is a very rare thing in the young. Only you always blew in and out in a tearing hurry, between calls no doubt, and I kept telling myself. 'I'll tell him all about it as soon as he's a bit less rushed, and that'll be when the fine weather comes.' And now it's too bad, you're going away just a week too soon. I'm sure I'm on the right track and we could have made some very interesting discoveries together."

"Sorry, M. Mandaroux," I said, feeling even more bewildered. "You must think me a bit dense, but I still don't see what you're talking about."

"Come and see," he replied, stopping before a cupboard, picking a key from his bunch and opening the cupboard door. The shelves inside were full of flasks and bottles, ampules and test tubes, whose labels informed me that they all contained extracts and macerations from the dried poisons of vipers. Just in front of me stood a large bottle full of snakes' heads detached from their bodies, which looked like some tame hydra pickled in alcohol. The whole was an incredible witch's cauldron before my eyes. I felt dazed, but anxious to be polite, inquired of Mandaroux: "Have you been interested in vipers a long time?"

"Oh yes," he answered, "ever since my youth. And last year I tried out injections of serum from boiled viper skins for some of Dr. Delpuech's patients; it proved extremely diuretic too. But I've got these results too late. To do as much as I'd like, I'd have needed creatures killed in April or May, and here you are going away just when we could have begun collecting them. If you'd stayed a few weeks longer perhaps the two of us might have found a cure for cancer."

I was very little attracted by the idea of scouring crumbling walls and rubble to catch vipers, but I did not confess this to Mandaroux, who was beaming at me with such pleasure on his face that it would have been cruel to dampen his enthusiasm for this unusual hobby. I began moving to the door, but as I laid my hand on it, he stopped me again and said with touching humility:

"Come back to us, Doctor. It's very unfair to the country to believe you can only make a prosperous career in Paris. You'll find good work to be done here too, and what's more, you can live a contented life. Please come back—soon—you'll see how well we'll work together. You'll have nothing to regret if you do."

We shook hands and said goodbye. He waved to me as long as I was in sight. In his emotional stress he seemed careless for once of the drafts from the square blowing mischievously down on his pink bald pate.

In honor of my last lunch Félicie had put together three or four of her most spectacular culinary successes, but alas, however hard I tried, I could not do them justice, and ate very little. In despair at her inability to stuff me with food, she made up a huge packet containing half a chicken and some little cakes, which she tied on to the handle of my valise, in case I should be in sudden danger of starving during the night's train journey.

At one o'clock exactly, just as I finished my coffee, Lucien arrived to collect me. Dr. Delpuech had insisted on leaving his room and coming downstairs. He was waiting for me in his office, sitting at his desk for the first time for many weeks, and it was there I went to say goodbye to him. Seeing me come in, he rose heavily to his feet and took a few steps towards me, saying with a smile: "Here's your relief mounting guard, still a bit weak on his pins, however."

I went up to him and he put his arm affectionately round my shoulder, as the father I had never had might have done when seeing me off to school or college. Perhaps everything would have been easier for me if at each moment of weakness in my life I could have taken new strength from some such sign of paternal affection.

He released me and handed me a file of papers which was lying on his desk, although I had never seen it there before. "If you have the time, Jean," he said, "and can't find any better subject for your thesis, you'd please me very much by running through these papers. You'll see what they are when you do. I'm a countryman's doctor, and have had the country in my blood for generations, so I've tried to put in these notes all I've learned about the hearts and minds of the men I've seen toiling around me, all I've succeeded in grasping about the social functions of the country doctor and of medicine in the service of those who work on the land."

"Thank you very much indeed, sir," I said, slipping the file into my case.

"In the old days," he told me, "there used to be a sort of scrapbook like this in many families, full of maxims and comments and advice, examples to follow, experiments which had been tried—anything which might be useful for those who came afterwards. I began to write this up for my own son, so that he could profit by my experience and start the work where I left off. But he died and I gradually stopped making further entries. I regret that now, but it's too late to start again. However, perhaps what was missing all the time was a young doctor, about your age, who will be able to go on with the book much better than I could."

"I'll do my best, sir, and thank you again for all you've taught me."

"Thanks, Jean? It's I who must thank you. And if you've not found this experience too hard"—he bent towards my ear, as if ashamed or afraid to face me with this importunate appeal—"you know, don't you, that this house will always be open to you. You know too that I'll be giving it away, not selling it. But if you do decide to come back, remember my old heart and don't leave it too long."

Then he straightened up, and looked at me firmly, holding out his hand. "I won't say goodbye, sir," I said as I took it, "but *au revoir*." We shook hands for several seconds, then we both dropped our hands. "*Au revoir,* sir," I repeated, and then turned abruptly away.

At the door of the office Félicie was sniffing tearfully, twisting her apron round her thin fingers. According to the best Auvergnat traditions, I kissed her shriveled cheeks, first the left, then the right, and then the left again. "Whatever happens," were her parting words, "don't let them starve you up there in Paris. If you find you're getting too thin, remember and come back here at once."

"I will, Félicie," I promised. "Goodbye now, and thanks for all you've done."

I went into the hall and accompanied Lucien to his car,

where he put my valise in the trunk. I climbed in, and he drove off immediately. Dr. Delpuech and Félicie were standing on the doorstep watching us go. Félicie was waving a handkerchief drawn from her quaint old corset-bodice, and Dr. Delpuech by her side raised his arm to bid me farewell. I craned my neck round to keep them in sight, but before we had even reached the first turning, one of his patients, seizing his chance, rushed towards the doctor, thrusting between us his black smock and huge round hat. Oblivious of himself, the old doctor was already back in the exacting role of patient listener which he had played all his life.

Lucien drove to Aurillac in silence, and I could not very well reopen our brief conversation of the previous night after his express declaration that he would rather not talk about it. In any case most of his attention was quite justifiably absorbed by the state of the road which the thaw had made a quagmire of slush.

Antoine was waiting for us eagerly. The car had hardly come to a standstill before he had rushed out and was opening the car door. In his anxiety to express all at once his thanks for the lift, his impatience to get to Aurillac, and his general exhilaration, he became almost inarticulate. The words would not come out fast enough. He had his windbreaker on already and was in such a hurry to leave that neither of us was even allowed to get out of the car. From the pavement he had turned to shout goodbye to his wife, and now she came out and walked towards us. She was smiling, but I found her looking very tired, with a drawn face and more dark rings under her eyes than usual. Antoine continued his flow of excited chatter, and at one point I saw her lean against the mudguard, with a grimace of pain. Unconsciously she brought a hand to her side. Lucien noticed this too, and broke into what Antoine was saying: "You are feeling all right, Madame Ricaud?" he asked. "Oh perfectly," she replied hastily, but it was obvious to me that this was not true.

Antoine turned at the question and looked at his wife with his usual affectionate smile. I felt uneasily that in his obsession with the trip to Aurillac he was not really seeing her when he looked, and had hardly heard her answer. He kissed her and advised her to lie down all afternoon, saying he would be back as soon as possible. Then he climbed into the back of the car, and as soon as we moved off again, he told us triumphantly: "So many nice things happening to me all at once. In two or three days from now I'll very likely be a father."

Thanks to Antoine, the long dreary journey to Aurillac passed cheerfully enough. At last we reached the plain. Rain was still teeming down, and the streams and ditches were overflowing with yellowish water which they emptied indiscriminately all over the road. Antoine watched eagerly for our entry into Aurillac as if it were a great capital city.

It was half past three when Lucien put us down at the door of a big café on the corner of a square. "Let's meet here about six," he said. Antoine at once asked him the way to the city hall, and on hearing that it was not far away, disappeared almost at a run. "Like to come with me to my aunt's and then to the hospital?" Lucien asked me.

"No thanks," I told him, "I think I'd rather walk around a little, and do some window shopping." He smiled and drove off.

At six o'clock I was back at our meeting place, a vast room with complicated stucco decorations and immense windows, obviously the town's main café. From the huge block of marble opposite the door which served as his desk, an opulent-looking cashier surveyed a school of waiters in black waistcoats and tight aprons who dashed between the tables with loaded trays. Everyone was shouting and smoking and playing cards, and the clatter of saucers and glasses, interspersed with the din of conversation, made an uproar which for the first minute or two left me somewhat dazed. Half the customers were hidden from view by the high backs of leather benches, and I was about to explore the place methodically when I saw Antoine beckoning me from a table in the distance, sitting next to a man who had his back to me. Antoine got up at once and came towards me beaming all over his face. "All according to plan?" I asked as he came up.

"Absolutely," he told me. "I'm with Dr. Chauvet now, my future boss, you know. He's a grand chap, former colonel in the Medical Corps, and a specialist in bacteriology. He's been all over the world, and was professor in the French University

291

at Shanghai. He's already told me some astonishing tales about China. Do come and join us."

Perhaps to proclaim to the ends of the world his unswerving local patriotism, Dr. Chauvet wore the long drooping moustache traditional to the Auvergne; it was fiery red, though now beginning to pale with age. But if the years had left a deep mark on his bronzed and weatherbeaten face, it was a face still full of intelligence and enthusiasm, and his eyes sparkled with humor.

When we reached the table he rose politely, and as soon as Antoine had introduced us, he exclaimed in a pure Cantal accent, "So it's to you, Doctor, that I owe my future assistant. Very grateful to you, I'm sure. I think he'll fill the bill splendidly."

Antoine blushed with pleasure. Then he noticed Lucien at the door straining his head through the smoke, and dashed off to fetch him. Indubitably Antoine's future "boss" was an agreeable fellow. Before my arrival he had begun giving Antoine, who seemed as ignorant on this subject as I was, some idea of his new functions as a district medical officer. As soon as Lucien had been introduced Dr. Chauvet continued this account, which staggered me by its range. It meant no less than supervising vaccinations, making official pronouncements upon epidemics, causes of death, on the supply of drinking water, domestic sanitation, cemeteries, slaughter-houses, dairies, and a lot more besides—not to mention keeping statistics on T.B., syphilis and cancer, industrial health, maternity and infant welfare, school health and assistance to old people.

"You must have a big staff to do all that," remarked Lucien, sounding equally stunned.

"For the moment I'm by myself. I can't really complain though. Twelve counties are still waiting for their first medical inspector."

"Are you given a lot of funds?"

"Not a great deal. Serres does all he can to help his Ministry, but the budget for public health is reduced a little every year."

"I suppose anyhow you've plenty of authority?"

"Not even that. I can only advise the town and county councils. All decisions are submitted for their highly incompetent approval, and as the health adviser is a tiresome fellow who would make them spend more money if they listened to him, you can guess the result. Take one example—drinking water. The law speaks only of a perimeter of protection round the sources. It has nothing whatever to say about protecting wells or keeping them away from sewers."

"Yes," sighed Antoine, "I'm in quite a good position to appreciate that."

"Possibly. But what you may *not* know is that out of forty thousand towns or villages in France there aren't ten thousand with water which is absolutely safe. I wonder which more or less civilized country you'd have to go to, to find a worse record than that."

"I hope we at least beat the Chinese," said Antoine with a smile.

Dr. Chauvet smiled too but replied: "Don't laugh at China too much, my young friend. I admit that the Chinese wouldn't think of sterilizing their drinking water any more than the good people of the Auvergne. They draw it quite calmly from streams which are full of filth and even of corpses, and to grow their vegetables they use a rich human manure which would make you sick if I described its mere smell."

"Well then?" said Antoine.

"Ah yes, but here's the point. The Chinese never drink plain water to quench their thirst. All the year round they drink tea, and tea not only tastes nicer but is made with boiled water, which in France we reserve for periods of exceptional epidemics. As to their vegetables, the Chinese always plunge them for a moment in boiling fat before serving them, just long enough to sterilize them outside without making them soggy underneath. So, Doctor, the day you and I convert our compatriots to health practices as sensible as that, we'll be able to claim, eh, that we haven't been wholly wasting our time."

An interruption came when the waiter placed glasses and saucers on the table with considerable clatter. Lucien discreetly looked at his watch, but Dr. Chauvet, probably amused by the attentive audience he had in Antoine and me, was already beginning an account of a cholera epidemic to which he had been summoned as a supposed specialist by the French missionary bishop of North China.

The inhabitants of Aurillac seemed to have very well-defined timetables. Every evening punctually at seven o'clock they must have sat down to their evening meal, for in a matter of minutes the whole café emptied, while the waiters collected the glasses and saucers, card cloths and greasy cards, then threw sawdust over the mud, cigarette ends and spit on the floor. After this they strolled between the empty tables casually correcting their alignment. Once more Lucien looked at his watch and made a move to rise.

On neighboring tables a waiter was beginning to lay out cutlery and table napkins. Anxious not to detain Lucien further, Antoine with obvious reluctance was beginning to put on his windbreaker when Dr. Chauvet made a welcome suggestion: "Since Dr. Nérac's train doesn't leave till half past nine, and if you haven't anything pressing to do in Aurillac, why can't we all stay here and have dinner together, and then all take him to the station? Of course in Aurillac you are my guests."

Antoine looked appealingly at Lucien like a boy begging not to be taken away yet from a spendid party. Lucien hesitated and then agreed a trifle brusquely to the suggestion. But all at once Antoine seemed to remember that his wife would already be waiting for him at Montagut and might soon become worried. He apologized to us and went off through the billiard room at the back of the café in search of the telephone.

He was a good while away, and by the time he returned the waiter had already brought us our soup. "Did you get on to Marie?" I asked as he sat down. "No, I didn't," he replied calmly. "I couldn't get Montagut at all. Because of the gale a branch must have cut the line between there and Farlat. It happens every time there's a storm, but these breakdowns don't last long. Anyhow, even if we left now, we wouldn't be back till about nine or ten, so if I ring again about nine o'clock, Marie won't have time to be worried."

About a quarter to nine the punctual Lucien looked at his watch again, and Antoine suddenly remembered that he had to phone. He asked the waiter to put the call through for him so as not to miss any of the stories with which Dr. Chauvet, an excellent raconteur, was at present regaling us. After a few minutes the waiter came back and told us that the line to Montagut was still out of order. Lucien now went off to try and get through to Peyrac, and when he returned Antoine and I were both laughing heartily at Dr. Chauvet's adventures on his first trip up the Yangtze.

Lucien remained standing near our table, looking at Antoine in some embarrassment. When the latter raised his eyes and saw Lucien's worried face turned towards him, the laugh died abruptly on his lips. "What's the matter?" he asked, beginning to go pale.

"Someone phoned my house from your wife about seven o'clock to see if we were back. She wasn't too well."

Antoine went dead white and got up with so abrupt a gesture that he knocked over his chair. He almost sprang at Lucien, seizing his arm and unconsciously shaking it. "What... what did they tell you, what's wrong?" he stammered excitedly, all his features contorted with suspense. "Please tell me, is it something s-serious?"

Lucien freed his arm and gently rested his powerful hand on Antoine's thin shoulder. "I assure you," he answered, "I don't know any more than that. When they didn't find us they must have called Dr. Delpuech, for apparently Félicie phoned my housekeeper to say he was leaving for Montagut. The Peyrac garage man was going to drive him there. Now don't worry too much, I'll take you back to Montagut at once, but meanwhile you can be sure that Dr. Delpuech has done all he can."

The note of absolute sincerity in his voice seemed to calm Antoine somewhat. Dr. Chauvet had already risen so as not to delay our departure. We prepared to leave at once. Lucien had left his car outside the café, and at the door he asked me: "Do you want me to drop you at the station, Jean?" But Dr. Chauvet immediately offered to take me himself, and Lucien was about to open the trunk to give me my valise when I came to an abrupt decision. "No," I said, "leave it there. I'll go back with you in case there's anything I can do. I can catch the train tomorrow evening. The hospital will have to wait."

The return trip took two hours in spite of Lucien's best efforts. The road was slippery, strewn with branches, and had rivers of mud running across it. The wind kept hurling blinding streams of water over the windshield. Lucien drove without a word, confining his attention to the bends in the road and the obstacles. There was nothing I could do to help him.

Antoine was again sitting in the back, and though it was too dark to see him, I could easily imagine him staring ahead, silently praying that all would be well and accusing himself of every crime under the sun because he had left Marie for so long in the hours when she needed him most. It was eleven o'clock when we reached Montagut and Lucien braked sharply in a vast puddle of yellowish water. Even before the car had stopped Antoine had leapt out and dashed towards the house. Lucien and I were not far behind, and though not a word had been spoken between us, I felt sure his anxiety was as great as mine, not so much for the mother and child as for Dr. Delpuech and his heart, still weak from his illness.

Most of the doors in the empty passage had been left open. We ran past the empty office and kitchen, following Antoine to the bedroom at the far end of the passage on the right. It was as poorly furnished as all the rest of the house and inadequately heated by a meager stove in one corner. In the middle of the room stood a big brass bed next to a tiny cradle with curtains closed above it. Marie Ricaud lay in the bed, even paler than usual, with dark rings round her swollen eyes. The room smelled of antiseptic and warm blood.

There were two other people in the room besides Marie Ricaud and the new-born baby presumably asleep in the cradle. One of the two was an old woman with a broom in her hand, doubtless some neighbor thrilled with the important part she was playing; the other, to my surprise, was not Dr. Delpuech but a worried-looking Bonnafy, picking up his instruments and syringes.

Antoine too must have taken in the scene in a flash. Reassured by the sight of the cradle he dashed to the bed, almost sobbing with remorse, relief, excitement and happiness. Strands of hair tumbled over his brow as he knelt at his wife's side, resting his cheek on her slender shoulder. He began pouring out a long string of passionate and distraught sentences, half entreaty, half adoration, pleading forgiveness for his desertion this evening, promising his darling Marie they would always be together from now on, and so wonderfully happy, to make up for all she had been through—and much more in this strain.

296

Marie opened her arm and hollowed her shoulder, stroked his trembling lips, tearstained eyes, and fevered brow, as she would have soothed a child in pain. For a minute or two she stayed like this, oblivious of all else beside him, fiercely protecting his weakness. But then, to take away his shame, she put herself and her child under his male protection. With a radiant smile of utter confidence in him and in the future, she pointed to the cradle and said: "Antoine, my darling, look at your son."

Rising from his knees, Antoine gently drew the curtains apart, took out a bundle of white baby clothes, lifted the bundle to kiss it, and then handed it to Marie with a smile of wonder and pride.

Bonnafy coughed and silently motioned us into the passage. "A touching sight, aren't they, those lovebirds," he whispered.

"Mother and child both all right?" I asked.

"Yes," he answered. "Nothing to worry about there, I made a check up just before you came. Her pulse is good, and she's stopped bleeding. The child's fit as a fiddle and Daddy has only had a bad scare. But next door I'm afraid we've got bad trouble."

He pointed with his finger to a door which was ajar, and Lucien exclaimed in alarm: "Dr. Delpuech?" He moved to go into the next room. Bonnafy held him back, however, and answering Lucien's question, said: "Yes, he's had a coronary. But I pumped morphia into him as soon as I got here, and for the moment he seems to be sleeping."

"How long have you been here?" asked Lucien.

"Only about two or three hours, and it's he who did all the work. Luckily a neighbor came here for a prescription about six o'clock when Madame Ricaud was beginning to bleed, and she tried to phone first to you and then to Delpuech. He arrived half an hour later, just in time, or the poor girl would have bled to death. A nasty business altogether, the sort of thing that hardly ever happens except in doctors' families. He was forced to do a Caesarean in a terrific hurry. Luckily for Madame Ricaud he only had his attack when everything was over."

"How were you brought in then?"

"Oh, that was the garage man who drove Delpuech here. He was terribly upset but he managed to get me on the phone. Luckily I'd just reached home from my rounds so I came along at top speed. When I got here the bleeding had stopped and the child was all right, but the mother had lost such a lot of blood she was almost as white as the sheets. There was blood everywhere, the towels were wringing wet with it, Delpuech's bag was open on the table as if someone had been looting it, with all the instruments in disorder and half the ampules and syringes out. Everything pointed to a tough struggle, and there was Delpuech in a corner of the room, as pale as the mother, grimacing, sweating, gasping, writhing about and groaning with pain, slumped in a chair between the garage man and the neighbor. They just stood there looking on, helpless and terrified."

"My God," I exclaimed in horror, and Lucien too looked shocked.

"Yes," said Bonnafy, "you can imagine it, can't you? A session like that for an old man with his heart in the state it was—it was plain suicide. The woman and the garage man helped me carry him at once to the bed, and I gave him a heavy dose of morphia." He paused. "Well, now you're here I think I'd better be off. I've still got a fair amount of work to do before I go to bed. But if you need me, of course, please don't hesitate to call me and I'll come round at once. In any case, whatever happens, I'll look in tomorrow morning."

He shook hands with Lucien and turned to me. I regretted not having said goodbye to Bonnafy, and even in these circumstances was glad of the chance to repair the omission. I told him I was leaving and might not be there when he called the next morning. "I hope to see you again one day," I added, "and thank you very much for all you did tonight."

"Not at all, old chap, glad I could help. And as to the hope, it's reciprocated," said the old Bonnafy. "To our meeting in Montparnasse, eh! *Au revoir*, Nérac, and good luck. I hope he recovers, but...." He shook his head sadly and walked quietly away.

As he left, Lucien gently pushed through the half open door. The room was revealed, large and full of shadow. From the door it was difficult to take in any details, for although the only electric light bulb had no proper shade, it had been three-quarters covered by a piece of cardboard to avoid disturbing the patient. You could, however, see the cracked stone floor and bare whitewashed walls; evidently the room was used as a storeroom. In a corner a small heap of potatoes was stacked against the wall. Near the door stood a few discarded armchairs minus most of their horsehair. There was a wood fire in the narrow fireplace, but it had plainly been lighted only a short while ago and had not yet dispelled the icy moisture rising from the floor and seeping through the walls. Beyond the light, apparently sleeping, Dr. Delpuech lay on an iron folding bed with blankets over him and a somewhat threadbare quilt.

Lucien approached very softly and bent over the old man sunk in his drugged sleep, trying to make a prognosis without waking him. The face was terrifyingly pale and almost unrecognizable, for pain seemed to have distorted all its features. The nostrils were pinched, hoarse gasps escaped from the half-open lips, sweat stuck the gray locks to his ash-pale brow. Even without great medical experience and the look of extreme sadness on Lucien's face, I could see that the old doctor must be dying. The new mask on his face was unfamiliar and terrible.

Lucien made no sound and neither did I, but Dr. Delpuech seemed to be conscious of our presence as we sorrowfully bent over him. He slowly opened his eyes, looked uncertainly at the room, and failed to find his bearings. He groaned as the pain returned, then lifted a hand and felt the quilt. Not recognizing the feel of his usual bedclothes, he let the hand drop clumsily down again. Finally he noticed Lucien and me, and tried to speak. But he was too weak to do much more than groan, though by bending over we just managed to catch a few stammered syllables from those parched lips. They sounded like: "Glad to see you."

Just then Antoine appeared at the door. Lucien and I were standing at the head of the narrow iron bed and the bad light in the room kept Antoine from seeing the old doctor's face and drawing the obvious conclusions. When he reached the foot of the bed he stopped abruptly, looking in a stunned way first at Dr. Delpuech, then at us. On seeing him, Dr. Delpuech tried to smile as he had done for Lucien and myself. At last, making a tremendous effort, he asked Antoine quite distinctly: "You're happy?"

I was terrified by the eager trembling look with which he hung on the answer from the young face he had seen only once before—and then the face had been set and defiant. To him the answer might contain the last significant thing in his life, the precious certainty that his death had not been wasted.

Knowing the old doctor almost as a son knows his father, sharing his anxiety about who should succeed him, I also knew his hope, momentarily cherished, to keep Antoine here in this lonely countryside. Such would have been his last wishes if he had dared to express them, I felt sure.

The young man was just about to go off to city life, and I was sure this question, asked with such anxiety, had beneath it a wider question: "Do you realize thanks to me that your duty is not to leave? Above all, have I made you happy enough to give me the right to beg you not to leave?"

When three hours earlier he had come into this house where a young mother lay bleeding, Dr. Delpuech certainly had no thought of making such a demand: it was simply his duty, despite the condition of his heart, to go where he was called when called. He liked the Ricauds, but it might just as well have been any other young mother's life in jeopardy. In the last effort from which he was dying, he had summed up in a single moment of time forty years of heroic generosity and self-sacrifice, he had done what he felt any true doctor should do.

He had risked his life many times without thought of reward, beyond the payment of a normal fee—and sometimes he had not gotten even that. (Tonight, as a matter of fact, he could not have claimed a fee for treatment to a fellow-doctor's wife.) But now the sacrifice was made, the rescue accomplished, now he knew he was certainly dying. And so the old doctor did at last hope for one reward, though even now he did not ask for it directly. He longed to believe that his death might be the means of saving more lives than just these two; he wanted to feel sure that this young doctor, who had been about to surrender on a stupid impulse, would now remain at his post.

Standing at the foot of the bed, Antoine was still bursting with masculine pride, with relief and joy rediscovered after two hours of suspense and anguish. This afternoon for the first time in six months he had stepped out of the bog of stagnation, and these first movements of escape had intoxicated him, leaving him blind to anything but his own joy. He hardly tried, I felt, to distinguish the desperate eyes appealing to him.

300

"Yes, Dr. Delpuech," he answered with a cruelty as extreme as it was unconscious, "today my happiness is complete."

Then suddenly he must have realized the callousness of this remark, for almost at once, seeing the suffering old man, he added in obvious embarrassment: "But the greatest part of it I owe to you. Without you my wife and child would both have died. I don't know how to thank you."

He spoke with increasing awkwardness. Perhaps he too now guessed the dumb pleading and would have liked to be able to explain, make excuses, defend his decision to run away, so that he did not seem despicable to the man who had just saved the lives of his wife and child.

Just before this, watching him in suspense, I had thought him cowardly and contemptible, and would like to have shouted out for him: "Yes, I'll stay on." But at once I was ashamed of this thought. Antoine had not even been asked to stay in words, though this very morning Dr. Delpuech had all but asked me outright to come back—and I had said nothing.

Between half-closed eyelids the old doctor's obstinate gaze did not leave Antoine, and now he answered in a very low voice, full of pain and exhaustion, which yet rang out with strange clarity in the bleak room: "Don't thank me. A doctor must go when a patient calls."

Lucien was evidently afraid we should tire Dr. Delpuech by staying. He made a sign to us, and we all returned to the corridor.

The neighbor must have been waiting for us. She came up with that greedy haste to hear of misfortunes so common among old people. Antoine sent her off into the kitchen, asking her if she could heat up some coffee for us, and we then made our plans for the night.

Lucien, feeling there was nothing further he could usefully do, decided to return to Peyrac, where he might be needed. He would return in the morning. Antoine and I agreed to take the rest of the night in shifts.

When we went into the kitchen, the old woman was waiting for us with the coffee. Before drinking it, she wiped her lips on an apron in our honor, and spat politely into the fire. Then, observing our distress, she took a good deal of trouble, while draining her cup, to assume the sorrowful expression she deemed suitable to the occasion. After this Antoine thanked her very much for all her help and sent her off home.

He insisted on taking the first shift. "I'll leave the door ajar," he told me, "and have a chair quite near Marie so that I can easily keep an eye on both patients at once. In any case after all the excitement I've been through tonight, I'm sure I'll never get to sleep. I'll wake you about three."

He gave me two blankets and I went into the office and lay down fully dressed on the divan. But at once I began tossing and turning restlessly. My brain too was in a ferment, and I felt I too could never get to sleep.

The rain had stopped, but a tremendous gale was now attacking the house, and seemed specially concerned to keep banging a shutter which in the evening's upheaval no one had thought of fastening back. The framework of the roof creaked all over the house and when the wind dropped momentarily, in the silence the melted snow dripping from the slates sounded like the pattering of rain. At times a whole mass of snow poured from the roof and dropped with a soft thud onto the street below.

It was still darkest night when the cold woke me up. I felt about me in the darkness. The blankets were not wide enough, and one of them had slipped to the ground. I pulled it back over me and stayed motionless for a moment waiting for something—I did not quite know what—crumpled, chilled, and dizzy. Then, realizing where I was, I considered getting up. I could not see my watch in the darkness but felt sure Antoine had omitted to wake me at the agreed time. Just then a heavy step approached on the pavement, stopped at the front door, and someone rang the bell—with such violence and insistence that I recognized at once the manner of ringing: Antoine was wanted on an emergency case.

In great haste I groped around to find and put on my shoes, meaning to go and stop the din as soon as possible; but before I was ready Antoine had reached the front door. I heard him talking to the messenger and telling him to go into the waiting room. When I opened the door of the office onto the dark passage, the light in the waiting room showed me a big rough highland farmer wearing an old felt hat and a thick sheepskin coat, mud-bespattered up to his knees. He had just finished giving a few details of the case to Antoine, who had his back to me, and was replying: "Yes, I'll come right away."

"Look, Antoine," I began, "I'll go for you, you've been up all night...."

"No," he broke in at once. "No, I must go. They're my patients." Then after a short pause he muttered wearily the words Dr. Delpuech had spoken a few hours earlier: "A doctor must go when a patient calls."

I found the switch at last and saw Antoine's face in the light. It showed all the signs of insomnia, there was a wild look in his eyes, and his mouth was set and hard. Probably to hide the convulsive trembling which had seized him, he gripped the back of a chair so violently I could see his knuckles go white. He seemed to be shuddering from cold, fever, and weariness as he announced in the same dull voice: "Dr. Delpuech died half an hour ago."

Ever since I had gotten up I had been expecting this news, and I imagined that Antoine's present stupor and tension betrayed the conflict between his new-found happiness and his distress at the terrible death which had been its price. He must be feeling guilty, too.

But suddenly his rigid lips relaxed, and he told me his secret: "I've decided to stay at Montagut," he said. There was a quaver in his voice as he made this pronouncement, and his shoulders and whole body seemed to slump despairingly. He seemed more frail and defenseless than ever, and I felt for a moment that I might have been the one doomed to bleak despair after the exhilaration of the journey to Aurillac, after the few brief hours when narrow horizons had been enlarged to take in the vista of a little happiness. He had been so close to freedom, to a return to the "civilized world." Now he had been caught and brought back to his cell. Mentally he must once more batter his head against its walls.

When I first told Dr. Delpuech that Antoine was leaving Montagut to take up a purely administrative post, the old doctor had told me, I remembered, that a person like Antoine would be miserable away from his patients and the practice of medicine. I thought of repeating this to Antoine now in an attempt to console him, but I could guess only too well how he might have answered me. I could not bear to think of the way this promise had been wrung from Antoine by the dying man, per haps with the last faltering words Dr. Delpuech ever spoke.

The messenger had stayed in the passage and now began stamping his clogs on the floor to warm his feet. This noise seemed to wake Antoine up. He straightened abruptly, and passed a hand over his face as if to wipe off dirt. When he looked at me his eyes were still full of sadness, but a steadfast unashamed sadness. I saw that in those few seconds he had made up his mind, quite definitely. He knew now what it meant to accept his destiny, to give himself to a cause; from now on he would march straight towards it. Everything was starting again just as before, but this time for his whole life.

He smiled gently at me as he passed in front of me, and said with a quiet normality: "I'll see you soon." Then I heard him putting on his leather jacket and balaclava in the passage, opening the front door, and the messenger going out with him. The door banged and I could hear the man's heavy step outside. Behind him came Antoine, hurrying to keep up with him, and for a few seconds more I could follow Antoine's lighter steps— the step of a townsman. I thought of him here in the mountains for the rest of his life, trying to rid himself of all traces of that former townsman.

By myself once more, I went to the room where the dead man was lying. I pushed the door open and gazed round the room in its sad disorder. The old doctor lay at rest on the bed. Antoine had taken from his own room the crucifix I had seen hanging above his bed, and he had folded the old man's hands over his chest, slipping the crucifix between them, and had then gently closed his eyes.

The improvised lampshade still covered the light, and I had to lean over to see Dr. Delpuech's face clearly. After watching and suffering for others so often, after bravely fighting his last battle, he had given in to death at last, in peace and at rest for ever.

For a long while I stayed kneeling at the foot of the bed, feeling the same grief as a grown-up son mourning for a father who had died. When I rose again, it was day. The light seeping in through the cracks in the shutters sketched the shape of the

ong windows which probably looked onto the garden. I felt
overpoweringly in need of fresh air. I had to escape from this
twilight of death for a few minutes. I drew the bolt, opened
he door, and was immediately dazzled by the light of dawn.

Over the whole countryside, released from winter's grip, was
he first dawn of springtime in a world renewed. On distant horizons the mountain ranges and forests and valleys had sloughed
off their soft snow and all the darkness of winter and night.
Here and there, in places where all had been dull and colorless
the day before, patches of new grass, saturated from the recent
heavy rain, were springing up fresh and green. A warm spring
breeze blew, telling of hope reborn, and high in the heavens
hung a golden cloud like the sail of a galley.

In the little garden an old plum tree was leaning over, up-
rooted by the last storm. But in the moss at the foot of the dead
tree primroses were beginning to blossom, and young violet
shoots burst up from the ground. On a branch of the shattered
old tree a bird was singing, and this bird-song, so near the voice
which had just been stilled for ever, seemed to take up the faint
cry of the new-born baby, to mingle with it, and hurl it to the
skies in a paean of triumphant hope.

Suddenly I remembered that one evening I had found Dr.
Delpuech tired out from all his visitors and had remonstrated
with him for not getting the rest he needed. "Don't worry,
Jean," he had told me, "I know I have not long to live. But
all that dies gives rise to some new life." This must indeed be
the meaning of the long night where an old man had sacrificed
himself for the birth of a child.

Part 2

FORTNIGHT IN BARRACKS

Chapter One

May 19th

Six weeks after my return from the Auvergne I began my year's military service in the Medical Corps. Our initial training took place at Val-de-Grâce, the old military hospital not far from Montparnasse. We wore small peaked caps, huge hobnailed boots, and shapeless uniforms in pale blue serge, crinkled in at the waist by leather belts.

Master Sergeant Tabureau, who was charged with teaching us the rudiments of military drill and discipline, had been detached for this purpose from a regiment of colonial infantry quartered in a neighboring barracks. Even before he entered our barrack-room on the first evening, Tabureau made his presence felt. We could hear him chasing out of the lavatories some ill-advised straggler, who returned hastily to the barrack-room, pulling up his suspenders on the way.

Paul Chavasse, who had chosen a bed nearest the door, found himself for this reason unwittingly promoted to the duties of charge of quarters. As soon as the Master Sergeant showed himself, Paul called out with would-be smartness: "Squad, eyes front!" We all sprang to attention, each in front of his bed, and in our anxiety to show due respect for military rank some of us decided to salute, even though we were not wearing our caps. The effect produced was unfortunate.

"You don't know much, do you, you sawbones? I'll have to drum the first principles of military etiquette into your thick skulls. I did hope"—Tabureau waxed sarcastic—"that having explained all this in the clearest terms this afternoon a little might stick, but it seems I was goddam well mistaken. Some of you recruits probably think a good deal of your own importance, but I can tell you straight that as far as brain goes most of you could learn a lot from the Senegalese I taught last tour of duty. I can tell you I don't much like the look of it. But never mind, we'll soon change all that," he told us somewhat menacingly.

After this he paused, and then roared out: "Now just remember this, you lot of fatheads, and especially you there"—he glared at Paul who assumed at once a suitably contrite air—"the command 'Squad, 'tenshun!' is given on the appearance of your commanding officer. 'Eyes front!' for any other officer, and 'Tenshun' "—he bellowed it, nearly knocking some of us off our balance—"for an N.C.O. in barracks. And get this once for all, you ignorant bastards: you do NOT salute unless you've got a cap or helmet on."

After this he passed rapidly in front of the beds. No one was missing at this roll call, but before abandoning us to the peace of our first night in the army, he gave us a brief final lecture beginning with: "Now you're in the army, you can all ruddy well buck your ideas up. I'm not standing for any nonsense." He concluded with: "Now you're in the army, me lads, you've got to learn to be punctual, and when I say eight o'clock sharp, it don't mean five to goddam eight and it don't mean five goddam minutes after eight either." In between the Master Sergeant traced for us in the same vigorous terms the disciplinary rules which would assure our rapid advancement in the Corps, as well as doing credit to his methods of instructing the colonial infantry.

There was a moment of somewhat constrained silence when he disappeared, during which the acting corporal in charge of the next room could be distinctly heard giving the command: "Squad, eyes front!" This might have delighted some visiting officer, but to judge from the oaths which followed, it seemed to cause Sergeant Tabureau no little displeasure.

"Oh Gawd, he's going to go on treating us as if we were all Senegalese niggers," groaned Barrière, one of the boys from Burgundy. "If this is the army," joined in Lecourt, another of the inseparable group, "all I can say is, Gawd help our sanity.

After just one day of it, coming out into the street again at five o'clock made me feel like I'd just been let out of an asylum for a few hours."

Deep gloom seemed to beset the vast room. Barrière, summing up what seemed to be the general opinion, exclaimed: "Don't know how we're going to stand this three months' hard labor."

"Oh, I don't know," protested Paul at once, "I think most of us will get used to it pretty quickly, apart from a few who don't care for any form of communal life." He looked pointedly at Henri Philippon, who was taking off his regulation boots and wriggling his toes about inside his socks, as if the heavy leather might easily have paralyzed them. He and Paul had little use for each other.

"Come off your high horse, Chav," called out Bourgeot, another of the Burgundians. "I've never noticed you show any great enthusiasm for communal life."

"Ah, but I can take it now," Paul answered, "and I believe in equality, you know, so I like thinking we're all in the same boat together, all having to do the same amount of spit and polish, all wearing the same sloppy uniform, though that may distress some people I know." Once more he threw a sardonic glance at Henri, who refused, however, to be drawn.

"Oh, I suppose it's not a bad life," remarked Bourgeot. "I shan't be exactly sorry when we get our commissions, though."

"It's a damned good life," reiterated Paul. "We're housed and fed and clothed like princes—well, more or less—I don't see what we've got to grouse about. I don't even object to our Sergeant. In the six years since we arrived at Paris, we've had a lot more difficult cases than Tabureau to deal with."

"That's true," agreed Bourgeot, "people like our late anatomy prof for instance. Do you remember how old Alliaume used to imitate him? Can you still do him, Jacques?"

Jacques Alliaume took four steps down between the beds, and then four steps back, as if he were pacing jerkily up and down in front of a blackboard. In a flash he recreated for us the solemn professorial figure, stalking about like a sick heron. In the familiar icy but emphatic accent, he performed for our benefit the professor's celebrated lecture on the anal sphincter: "Now, gentlemen, I think I may say that there is not one of you who has not seen a horse go to the men's room. . . ."

For some time he went on in this vein, and when he had finished there was a roar of laughter which seemed to lighten the general atmosphere considerably. The conversation turned to other professors and more recent exams. "I think I made quite an impression in pharmacology," Barrière informed us. "When I was asked about the function of phenolphthalein, I answered that the discovery of its laxative effect was first made in Hungary."

"You mean to say a lazy lout like you actually knew that?" exclaimed Paul in astonishment.

"Of course. A son of a Burgundian wine-grower, who'll have vineyards himself one day, has got to know things like that. A few years ago the Hungarian government ordered the addition of phenolphthalein to white wine as a preservative. But after that Hungarian white wines seemed to give everybody stomach troubles, so another chemical had to be found as preservative. This little experiment, however, provided druggists with an excellent new laxative. When I told the pharmacology prof this, he was so staggered he said: 'Thank you very much, M. Barrière. It is the first time since I have been sitting in this examination hall that I have learned something new and interesting.' Of course I tried to look as if I could tell him a lot of other interesting things if I'd wanted to."

"Like your answer in therapeutics, for instance," suggested Merlet, "to the effect that cocaine came from cocoanuts."

"One can't be expected to know *everything*," answered Barrière modestly.

After that everybody began to talk at once with increasing animation, and the air of gloom vanished completely. A fair number of barely credible stories were told, explaining the various methods which had been employed to thwart the cruel cunning of professors lying in wait for us for six years behind the green examination tables.

Henri Philippon was in the bed nearest the door in one row, and I was in the bed next to him. Disdaining the coarse garments supplied by the quartermaster, Henri had donned an elegant pair of pale blue pajamas and slipped into bed. Opposite him, in shirtsleeves, Chavasse was adroitly rolling up his puttees while continuing to talk. On his left was Barrière, and in the next beds were his Burgundian friends, Bourgeot, Robertot,

Jeannel, and Lecourt, who were starting to undress. Souléry, the poet, unwilling to brave the roughness of the sheets, was unrolling a fine linen sleeping-bag.

The conversation turned to future careers. Dubuisson was telling us about his father. "The old man's kept a detailed account of all my studies have cost him since I came to the university. Taking into account the time spent and normal interest rates, he's been working out what I'll have to earn yearly in order to get the money back and make a profit as well. He's particularly anxious to find out whether it'll be a good investment to give me another two years, so that I can specialize in something, remembering, of course, that as a specialist I'd be able to get considerably higher fees."

"Personally," Paul told us, "I'm not keen on specializing at all, it ties you down so much. I prefer to have all medicine to deal with and not just create a corner in navels or colds in the head. Oh well, perhaps I'll be a specialist in general practice. That's a good career, don't you think?"

"I don't really, Chav," protested Jeannel. "You're going right against the modern trend. Every time I come home on vacation all my friends and relations ask me: 'Well, how go the studies? Making progress, eh? What'll you be specializing in?' That's the only thing they can talk about. 'They had a specialist in . . . he went to a specialist.' In my part of the world even the most miserable small farmer has to see a specialist. Specialist in what? He hasn't an idea—but it's a word that sounds good and reassures him."

"That's true enough," Robertot confirmed. "Look at the saints even, *they've* all specialized. Where I come from, they honor St. Barbe for sudden death, St. Margaret for lumbago, St. Erasmus for stomach trouble, St. Eustace for burns. And you'd never get people praying to St. Aignan, the great saint of scalp diseases, for a sore throat."

"I've made my choice. Two years at Laennec to find out all about it, and I'll set up as phthisiologist."

"Seriously? I never realized it was as complicated as that to learn about T.B. I thought there were only two forms of that illness, the free and the paying, and that the main difficulty was to convert the former into the latter."

"And how about dermatology? That shouldn't be too much trouble."

"Oh yes, that has its points. One snag is, though, that the patient can understand what's wrong with him, and you can't get rid of him with comforting pronouncements. He'll never leave you alone till all his scabs have disappeared."

"Fair enough, old boy. But at least if you become a skin specialist you're pretty sure of not being gotten up at night."

"It'd be just right for Philippon," suggested Paul, but Henri again refused to be drawn. He was little interested anyhow in these questions of specialization and his future medical career, and he turned towards the wall and went to sleep.

How often I had heard similar discussions myself without giving them much attention! I was no longer shocked by their cynicism, and I was now quite used, for instance, to the mentality of the Burgundy group, and the way they conceived medicine as a nice paying career, and nothing more.

By the same token, after military service and his thesis, as soon as his haberdasher father had settled the profit-and-loss account, Dubuisson would either set up right away in Troyes or else spend two further years on whatever branch of medicine he might choose as his specialty—and probably make quite a respectable doctor. Bellienaz, the alcoholic, who gargled with brandy to avoid germs, would become as pathetic a figure as old Dr. Legros. Already, in fact, Bellienaz had begun to look quite like him.

As for Paul, "specialist in general practice," he already had his eye on a small flat near Montparnasse, in a block now being built which would only be completed near the end of our military service. "I'm not really cut out to work in the country, you know," he told me once. "Well, I've chosen the Avenue du Maine because it more or less divides the district—middle class one side, and workingclass the other. I'll take my chance on both." I had no fears at all for him or for his future patients.

Yes, by and large, I decided, I could pretty well say which would be the Cléments and Bonnafys and Chassagnons and Ricauds among the students of my year. But although I knew so much about *their* futures, what could I say about my own? To be honest, very little indeed. Yet six weeks earlier, getting out of the train which brought me back from the Auvergne, I had thought my own future definitely fixed. I had been lucky enough to find an empty compartment at Aurillac, and having put out the light, I began a long night of exalted plans and hopes.

Leaning my brow against the window to watch the moonlit countryside flashing by, I had recalled the last days in Peyrac, which seemed to offer me my finest examples. They showed me old Dr. Delpuech sacrificing his life so that his work should go on, and Antoine Ricaud accepting his destiny in that first dawn of spring. By comparison with such integrity and generosity and idealism, all my life in the last four years suddenly rang hollow. I could not imagine why it had not disgusted me earlier.

While the train ran on through the mountains in the clear night, I tasted a magnificent new hope. For a few weeks I had had a genuine, worthwhile life, had known a real man's work and responsibilities. This, and the old doctor's example, confirmed what he had told me one evening, that doing one's job honestly and without weakness can bring true serenity. Selfish enjoyment, sloth, and pride had at last betrayed their illusory character, and the old virtues, the ones Henri and the boys from Burgundy would scoff at, were shown at their real worth. Now I was traveling towards Paris, a different world called to me, but when I got there, I would stick to my real friends like Paul. I would work on a plan of reality completely opposed to Henri's.

In the corner of my compartment, gazing at the mountainous landscape, I had a strangely powerful sense of being reborn. I thought of Marie Ricaud and of the baby in its white cradle; so by a natural association I remembered the peak of those "other days," the period when I had been living and working side by side with Marianne in harmonious and innocent love. Then, without feeling at all diminished or in bondage, I could identify her with every moment of happiness throughout the day.

The evening I had gone to Montagut to see the little boy with tetanus I had envied the Ricauds' contentment, finding Antoine sitting working, and Marie at his side leaning affectionately towards him. I too had known an exceptional woman, who would have preferred this contentment with me to the

313

false pleasures of the town; and I had thrown away this good fortune. But suppose all was not yet lost? If Marianne in her generosity would listen to me for a few minutes, I was sure she would see for herself how sincere was my regret.

For a long while I continued on this thought: my stay at Peyrac was the first period of decent, honest, creative activity since our separation—and I could offer it wholly to Marianne. I could even offer that painful conversation with Lucien, since this had brought about my first real return to her for nearly four years, the first since the brief hours of true repentance when I had written her and she had never received the letter.

For a long time I remained motionless in the darkness, longing for her love, longing to have her lovely fair hair against my shoulder as in the old days, longing to be near her, with no one to come between us again.

Yet I knew all too well now, from many bitter experiences, that I was still weak, terribly lacking in will-power and courage. When I got out of the train, it was to Marianne I should have rushed immediately, to put myself under her protection. At that moment, had she been ready to hear me, I might have been saved. But I realized on the platform that this scene must be postponed for a short while. I dashed to my hotel room, and after a hasty wash and shave left at once for the hospital, so as not to be late on the ward that day at least.

At hospital Paul was waiting for me impatiently. He had been expecting my return the morning before and had accordingly made arrangements to travel home himself that day. He had scarcely had time to listen to my hurried apologies and explanations that the old doctor I had been working for had died. He dashed off to catch his train—a bad omen for my new start.

He and I and Marianne had worked together on the wards of the Charité, and he was therefore one of my few remaining links with a happier past. Since we had been together again, here at the Hotel Dieu, our relationship had been almost schizophrenic: in the hospital he treated me with his usual good nature as a close friend, but if I ever met him in company with Henri, Paul's attitude was contemptuous and hostile, as if Henri and I were both tarred with the same unsavory brush. I knew he failed to understand my dependence on Henri, and once or twice in earlier days he had tried to remonstrate with

314

ne about my "ignominious position as campfollower to Henri
he Horror." When these remonstrances proved without effect,
ie adopted this curious compromise. It meant that, outside
hospital, I never really knew where I was with Paul. I had
been anxious to tell him all about my Peyrac experiences, and
felt he would have shown a real interest despite his inevitable
kidding. I counted on him, in fact, to support my plans to turn
over a new leaf at Paris. So I was crestfallen to see him dash
off, and after my night on the train found work that morning
tedious.

Henri had evidently found out that I was due back the previous day and had been expecting me to ring him the evening
before to tell him I was back. In my honor he made a non-
chalant appearance in the ward about noon, and half an hour
later we left the hospital together. On the Place du Parvis, as
I was preparing to go off on my own, he asked me to come out
to lunch with him. Caught off my guard, I could not think of
any plausible grounds for refusing. It seemed too embarrassing
to tell him of my good resolutions while standing on the pavement amid a crowd of patients' relatives.

Nor did I feel able to go into it, or even talk about Peyrac,
in the smart restaurant where he took me to celebrate my return. The clientele seemed to be picking at their food with
expressions of boredom, and when they talked and laughed
they seemed to be observing rites known only to a tiny band of
initiates. Certainly the life I had just left was quite incompatible
with the artificiality of my present surroundings.

Opportunities for explaining things to Henri later were cur-
tailed by the arrival, almost immediately we had sat down, of
Denise, Henri's current girl friend, accompanied by Vicky.
Both looked very slim and fresh and chic, and we waved to
them from our table. Vicky walked down between the tables
with the studied effect of a film star negligently entering a room
at a press conference given for her benefit. When she saw me,
however, she seemed puzzled for a few seconds, and her lips
parted slightly in surprise. But on reaching our table, Denise
congratulated me on how well I was looking, and Vicky then
made some similar remark with no trace of embarrassment. To
hear her, you might have thought they were two girls running

into me unexpectedly at a party when I had just returned from a winter sports holiday.

Despite Vicky's expression of surprise, which looked genuine enough, I myself was somewhat taken aback by this meeting. Had Henri arranged it of his own accord, or invited me at Vicky's request, now that her Argentine had left her? Assisted by the waiter, Henri was busy studying the menu, and seemed completely innocent of any such stratagems. As for Vicky, deliciously fresh and pretty in a new spring dress, she was wriggling about kittenishly on her chair, pouting, throwing her head back as she gave affected little laughs, chatting away to Denise in an acidulous girlish voice, yet never failing to look around her unobtrusively to watch the effect she was producing. At the next table, an elderly gentleman, stout, balding and very flushed, was busy raising his blood pressure with a wing of chicken and a bottle of Burgundy. He stopped in mid-career to admire her. Vicky, however, did not deign to notice any such vulgar homage.

Whether or not she had planned our meeting—and I felt she probably had—now seemed a matter of no interest whatever. I had nothing further to fear. Vicky was pretty, she had a nice figure and was very well dressed, in fact better dressed than when I last saw her. The Argentine artist had evidently done very well by her before he left for Italy. But I observed with satisfaction that I could now look at her with complete indifference. None of all that really meant anything to me any longer. These artificial people were so terrified of their own emptiness that they were afraid to be alone. They could only reassure themselves by continually rubbing shoulders with each other in familiar "smart" surroundings. In their midst I experienced a moment's deep contentment, remembering Peyrac, the small deserted lanes I went through on my rounds, the remote valleys and quiet woods and all the simplicity and genuineness which life could offer out there.

Henri, finding my mind wandering, tried out stories which would normally have made me laugh, but I remained apathetic. How could I possibly have become used to this sort of life, without seeing how utterly sordid and dull it was! Certainly Henri tolerated the environment without any trouble, but then his hedonistic appetites and capacities were doubtless far greater than mine, and he was so utterly inured by now to this playboy existence that it would never have occurred to him to see anything wrong with it. To use the old cliché, true in his case, Henri was not so much immoral as merely amoral.

This unsuccessful lunch party was coming to an end. Vicky, sitting opposite me, continued to ignore the apoplectic admiration of her elderly neighbor. But at one point, at one of Henri's jokes, I felt she was making a special point of showing off her rippling girlish laugh, and the whole act of ingenuous charm which had so successfully seduced and deceived me in our early days together. For a brief moment I thought she was setting her snare for me once more. But as she threw back her head to laugh, in her usual coquettish, mock-naive manner, I was disturbed to catch her look going beyond me. I did not even need to turn round. There was a mirror behind Vicky, and in it I saw a young man by himself at a table, giving her a smug and knowing smile as he fiddled with a handsome enamel cigarette case.

We were at a table for four. Denise, sitting opposite Henri, was quite plainly his mistress. The young man with the conceited smile had certainly assumed the same relationship existed between Vicky and me. For some time now he must have been enjoying himself behind my back, and perhaps Henri and a lot of other people had caught these glances passing between him and Vicky—it made me look a complete fool. I flushed with rage, and clenched my teeth savagely. For a few seconds I felt like slapping Vicky's face, calling her a dirty little bitch, and humiliating her in front of everybody.

She must have guessed at my fury and been scared of a scene, or perhaps she had merely been trying to arouse my jealousy and was now satisfied she had done so. At any rate she cut short her laugh, and looked at me in the same submissive and enticing way as when we had first met. For fear of reprisals she was already offering herself to me, shamelessly, like a prostitute, and although I was choking with rage and wounded vanity, so that I still wanted to hurt her, yet I was uneasily stirred by the brazen look of invitation.

After several months of sexual abstinence my flesh was awake, and I felt rising within me an overpowering animal urge to see her once more naked and docile, her clothes at my feet, clasping her delicate hands with their painted nails over her breasts in a gesture of false modesty. She went on looking at me, half opening her mouth in a sensual smile which showed her fine teeth and moist lips. I could think of nothing but throwing her down, hearing her gasp in rhythm with me, and seeing my pleasure reflected again in her dilated pupils.

When we left the restaurant a few minutes later, Henri told us he and Denise were going off to Longchamps to have a close look at some horses running in a forthcoming race; did Vicky and I want to come with them? "No thanks," I told him, "I'm feeling dead tired after being in the train all night. I think if Vicky feels like it I'll go back to the hotel." "Suits me," said Vicky.

I hailed a taxi, and on the way to the hotel she let her slender body press against mine in silence, attentive to the slightest invitation. I was silent too, a little ashamed of myself. When we reached the hotel, she asked: "Do you still love me, Jean?" The memory of my recent indifference, amounting almost to disgust, kept me from giving her the answer she was expecting, and in fact I did not reply at all. Not that I was trying to put her off, though I knew it was merely physical desire which drew me to her. Merely physical desire, yes; but I could only measure the importance to me of that desire by my complete powerlessness to resist it. Breathing hard and saying nothing, I impatiently pushed her into my room like a captured beast.

"Oh no," Paul was exclaiming, "ophthalmology isn't at all difficult really. On the contrary, it's very simple: blue ointment and blue glasses for whores, yellow oxide ointment and yellow glasses for deceived husbands."

"And of course you have to strip the girls naked in order to examine their retinas," put in Lecourt.

Why was I feeling so melancholy this evening, with a vague uneasiness which stopped me laughing with the rest? All afternoon the humorous side of our new lives as soldiers had given me a good deal of quiet amusement and pleasure. Perhaps it was partly because when we were let out of barracks and I went to my room at the hotel, I found a note scribbled for me by Vicky. I had completely forgotten that she was due to return this very morning from a ten days' tour of Brittany with a reper-

318

tory company. When she left, she had been radiant at the thought of seeing her name on posters and programs. She had a very small part, which no doubt was why they had chosen her, but she already saw it as the first rung on a ladder leading to stardom. Someday her name would be in lights outside big Paris theatres. During the ten days of this tour I felt I was living as a free man again. The note I had found claimed extreme urgency, and although this was quite usual for Vicky, for some reason I found it disturbing. She told me she absolutely must see me—'must' underlined twice—the following day, and as she did not know when my military duties would leave me free, she asked me to ring her during the morning.

So once more I should have to put up with the same petty affectations and petty thoughts and petty quarrels, an intolerable mixture of vanity, obstinacy, folly, and viciousness. Tomorrow I should be back in the same old squalid rut with a vulgar and demanding girl, yet her company had become so much a habit, because of the sexual bond between us, that I felt quite powerless to break away from it.

Oh yes, I had been miserably weak and cowardly since my return from the Cantal and that first half-reluctant time of renewed intimacy with Vicky. This was certainly enough to make me feel remorseful and self-disgusted this evening, but of course it was due not only to Vicky's note: my feelings were upset by another letter I had found awaiting me at the hotel, from Antoine Ricaud. He wrote not from Montagut but from Peyrac.

I had not felt like reading this letter right away. I knew in advance how enthusiastic its tone would be, for since the contents of Dr. Delpuech's will had been made known, Antoine had been living in a sort of dream. It was six weeks already since he had moved to Peyrac, and even now, it seemed, he hardly dared believe in the reality of his good fortune.

It was natural enough that he should find this move almost miraculous, but I, having known something of Dr. Delpuech's hopes and plans, had not been very surprised, soon after my return to Paris, to receive an official letter about the will from M. Albessard, the Peyrac lawyer. This informed me that apart from a pension to Félicie the old doctor had left his house and all his money to the Peyrac Parish Council, with the proviso

319

that the house should be transformed into a sort of health center for all the population of Peyrac and district, where two or more doctors could have their headquarters and hold their consultations. The money was to pay for the building's conversion to its future use.

M. Albessard wrote to me because the will specified as an absolute condition that I should have first refusal of the position left vacant by the old doctor's death. Then, as Dr. Delpuech cannot have had many illusions about my probable choice, he directed that in case of my refusal the position be offered to Antoine. Failing either of us two, Lucien should be asked to select a doctor or doctors who would thereafter join up with him. M. Albessard informed me that for various administrative reasons there would probably be a delay of several months before the Peyrac Council had the right to accept this bequest and launch the health center.

Unfortunately, the letter went on, *although Dr. Clément remains indefatigable as ever, the district can hardly remain several months with only one doctor. So I should greatly appreciate it if you could let me have your decision as soon as possible. Without wishing to influence you either way, I should like to add a personal note as to the excellent memories the people of Peyrac seem to cherish of you.*

My heart was very full when I read of this last act of kindness towards me by Dr. Delpuech. He might so easily have told me that I figured in his will, in the hopes of keeping me in Peyrac out of gratitude; I admired his integrity in refraining from using this method. But I admired still more his refusal to tell Antoine either about the will, even when Antoine had stood there by his bed, and both had known that he was dying. Antoine's acceptance of his destiny had to be made for its own sake, a voluntary choice.

I wrote back to M. Albessard at once that before I could start in practice I had a whole year of military service to do, and that accordingly I yielded my place to Dr. Ricaud. If I had been free there and then, I should probably have hesitated a long time about accepting this offer. I was still reluctant to bury myself at Peyrac for good. The Gordian Knot was in any case cut for me by my military service, and this obstacle at once produced regrets—all the greater because they were harmless—

for the life I was going to miss. Once more in the grip of Vicky and an existence I knew to be worthless, I felt as I posted my letter to Albessard that I was losing my last chance of escape. Then I remembered that by refusing I should be handing a splendid opportunity to Antoine, and this easy generosity consoled me.

"I owe you all my happiness," Antoine had said when he came to the dying man's bed. But a little later in the night, in agreeing by that bedside to stay at Montagut all his life, Antoine too had shown generosity and heroism. His wife and child had been saved and in payment he gave up his freedom, not yet knowing that the old doctor had tried to soften as best he could the sacrifice he hoped Antoine would make for him. All was very well as it was, for as between Antoine and myself he was certainly far worthier to succeed a man like Dr. Delpuech than I.

Three days after my letter to Albessard, I had a letter from Antoine thanking me with embarrassing effusiveness for yielding him the place, and promising to hand the practice over to me at once should I reconsider my decision and wish to return to Peyrac after my year's military service. So close still to the nightmare from which he had just emerged, he seemed quite dazzled at all the wonderful things which had happened to him within a few days. Marie was now doing very well, and their son's weight was increasing at the correct pace. His parents very much hoped that I would agree to be the boy's godfather; already they were calling him Jean.

I've seen Dr. Clément, Antoine had written, *and we had a long talk. He's a splendid chap, and I think now we'll get along famously. What a stupid impression I must have made on him our first meeting, but I think he's the sort who wouldn't hold things like that against one. Anyhow we are completely agreed that the health center shall function as Dr. Delpuech hoped, just as soon as the bequest is officially accepted. We shall each have our waiting room, office, and dispensary, so that our patients won't get mixed up and need not meet each other. We'll have an X-ray apparatus in common, a laboratory, a room for minor operations, and a small maternity ward, with just enough beds and equipment to avoid taking people to Aurillac. Also we can dispense with some of the confinements*

321

done in the mother's home up till now, with all the danger and inconvenience we both know so well.

So you see, Jean, each of us will be able to keep his independence, yet we'll be living and working side by side. Félicie is staying on here, by the way,—she specially asks to be remembered to you—and she's going to help look after young Jean, while Marie is otherwise engaged. Which brings me to another bit of good news.

One of the clauses in Dr. Delpuech's will provides for a secretary-nurse attached to the Center to receive patients, make notes of outside calls, do small dressings, etc. Dr. Clément, of his own accord, suggested that Marie should take this on—isn't that a brilliant idea? I do really think she'd do it awfully well. Forgive my rambling on like this, but everything's going so well I hardly know if I'm on my head or my heels—and thank you so very much again.

A fortnight later, a second letter told me that they had moved for good to Peyrac; and the tone of this letter and those which followed made me think that in changing his address Antoine had abruptly changed his whole character. The friendly feeling towards Dr. Delpuech's own choice for his successor, Lucien at hand imperturbable and always ready to help, the emotions aroused in him by becoming a father, all that must certainly have played its part in restoring Antoine's confidence and bringing him out of his shell of self-distrust.

Of the stammering hesitant beginner there seemed to be nothing left, and I could picture him now, the assured Dr. Ricaud, crossing some farmyard with rapid decisive steps, not bothering himself at all about the dogs growling round his legs.

Chapter Two

THE FOLLOWING DAY I had to wait patiently till the lunch hour before I could go to the lodge at Val-de-Grâce to use the telephone available for hospital patients. Vicky, tired of waiting for me, had gone out, and I asked her landlady to tell her that I should be at my hotel at six o'clock.

As soon as we were off duty, Henri drove me to my hotel. Vicky had not yet arrived. While waiting for her, I took off my heavy boots and bulky uniform, and sank blissfully into pajamas. I knew this encounter would end on the divan, and as long as I had to waste my time with Vicky, I might as well take advantage of the only form of pleasure which she could still give me.

As usual she was late, and I found this long wait irritating. I wondered with some anxiety what the girl could have to say to me that was so very pressing. Eventually I recognized in the corridor the quick step for which I had so often tensely waited. She came in, laughing and at her most seductive. She kissed me, took off her hat, threw it with her handbag on the divan, sank into my one armchair and asked me for a cigarette.

While drawing the first puffs she questioned me about my new military existence. I could see, however, that she was paying very little attention to my remarks about Master Sergeant Tabureau. Incapable of sustained thought about anything except her own affairs, she plunged into a detailed account of her tour. For a short while it seemed as if she wanted me merely as an audience for her theatrical gossip, notably about the jealousy of Laura, the leading lady. At Nantes, where the company had given three performances, Vicky had found flowers each evening from an unknown admirer, and "Laura, my dear, was green with envy."

She seemed to have forgotten her urgent note, and I should

have felt a good deal more reassured if I had not seen her drawing nervously on her cigarette and watching me carefully in spite of her apparently casual chatter. Trying to surprise her, I interrupted her brusquely: "I don't really suppose you've made me come at the double all the way from the Val," I remarked, "simply to tell me about your admirers. What's so terribly important that you had to see me?"

I had been right in thinking she was on her guard, for she did not seem surprised by my question. She threw back her head, stretched out a hand towards the ashtray and stubbed out her cigarette. Then she said in the most ordinary way: "Well, darling, I believe I'm going to have a baby."

She looked at me as if the news she had just given me, even if unexpected, contained nothing to disturb me particularly. Indeed her smile suggested that she might almost have been expecting me to express delight.

I must have gone pale, and felt my knees sagging beneath me. Vicky was still watching me keenly, I could see, and I tried to pull myself together. In my stupor at this news I could only go on repeating to myself: "Keep calm, you must keep calm. She's making this up so as to see what you'll say, she wants to force you to marry her." My hand shook a little as I lit a cigarette, but while I did so, I noticed that Vicky's eyes had darkened. The anxiety she had been trying to hide from me since her arrival had forced into them a nervous gleam, and once I realized how apprehensive she was I found her much less formidable.

"A baby, eh?" I said lightly. "Doesn't show very much at present, you know. When do you think it might be due?"

Vicky pretended to ignore my facetious tone and answered: "I noticed three weeks ago." To my surprise she blushed with embarrassment to be disclosing such an intimate detail.

I looked at her, summoning up the amused and skeptical smile a doctor might give on hearing a patient's improbable diagnosis of her own case. Meanwhile I was rapidly trying to work out the possibilities. Was she telling me the truth or lying? If the latter, to find out what my reaction would be, then my decision would be simple enough. But there was no point in forcing things, as there was no immediate danger. The hypothetical baby was due to arrive in eight months, and I could easily throw her over by then, once I was sure she was lying. Indeed it would provide a good opportunity to have a final scene with her. If she was telling the truth, the matter was a good deal more serious.

I was surprised to find how skillfully I could dissimulate for purposes of self-defense, so soon after my original panic. I commented out loud: "Oh well, three weeks late, you know, that doesn't necessarily mean anything. Before definitely celebrating your future motherhood, you'd better wait a bit—if you're only three weeks overdue."

While I was speaking, an idea had occurred to me: three weeks ago, I now recalled, Vicky had gone away to her people for a few days, so she could in fact be lying quite easily. But if she really was pregnant, it might just as well be from seven weeks ago as three, and the Argentine would then be the culprit, not me. In her alarm, knowing I was coming back, she was quite cunning enough, with Denise's help, to have organized the lunch at the restaurant the day I came back from Peyrac. Had she played the usual trick on me, and instead of being on my guard and letting her leer at the young man with the cigarette case as much as she liked, had I, like a fool, fallen head first into the trap? But once I knew whether she really *was* pregnant, I could make my plans.

"Anyhow," I told her calmly, "it's very easy to be sure quite quickly. I'll give you a note to the laboratory at the City Hospital. Tomorrow morning all you have to do is take them a sample of urine, and in forty-eight hours we'll know for certain."

This was not true: to be absolutely certain would have required a further laboratory test, and meant another ten days. But while delivering this lie, I observed Vicky attentively. I knew I could judge her sincerity by the eagerness or hesitation with which she accepted this suggestion.

"You think we could be absolutely sure as soon as that?" she exclaimed, as if genuinely relieved at the prospect.

Perhaps she was still doubtful herself about her condition and hoped she might be wrong. But at least now I was sure she was not making it up. My heart was racing furiously, and I did not dare let Vicky see my face. I went over to the window. I turned round again when I was feeling a little calmer, but my legs felt so weak from shock that I had to sit down on the divan. To avoid speaking, I lit another cigarette and looked carefully at Vicky over the top of the flame. She seemed completely calm. My attitude, on hearing this disastrous news, must have given her a new hope: I had on the whole shown a neutral, and so almost a favorable, reaction.

Vicky became voluble, resuming her gossip about stage rivalries and intrigues. While she was talking ceaselessly I kept quiet, taking refuge behind the smokescreen of my cigarette, blinking my eyes as if they were smarting. I felt rather like a hunter stalking his victim.

The problem was clear: Vicky was pregnant—I felt quite sure of this even without a test. Whether by me or another man was unimportant now. I had let myself be caught, and it was on me, obviously, that she was intending to father the child. Marriage? That was quite out of the question. I would not become a public laughingstock by marrying anyone as notoriously promiscuous as Vicky. Think of spending my whole life with her! I tried to see Vicky as the wife of a country doctor, in silk dresses and high-heeled shoes, stalking scornfully along the muddy pavements of a town like Peyrac. I might as well shoot myself straight away.

Lying on the stained worn divan, where we had sprawled so often together, I felt a surge of disgust and contempt. I was afraid that Vicky might see the hatred in my eyes, and for a moment avoided looking up at her. Lucidly I began to think of ways of removing the danger. If Vicky was really pregnant, there was only one solution, to procure an abortion. At once I began thinking of ways of doing this. Of course I had never assisted at any such operation and I did not feel at all inclined to start on my own.

But Henri must have often found himself in similar circumstances, and surely he would be able to give me a good address to go to. I knew anyhow enough about minor gynecological operations to keep an eye on it and prevent its becoming too dangerous for Vicky. Even without knowing the exact technique, I did know the risks from my hospital experience. I had recently read in a medical revue that in France forty thousand women die annually from the results of abortions, whereas the deaths by T.B. for men and women combined come to only sixty thousand. Of a thousand dead bodies of women examined after inquests, a quarter bear traces of attempted abortions—this is what we were told by one of the demonstrators during a post mortem on a pregnant woman. At the hospital, seeing abortion cases in the wards, I had learned that two thirds suffer sooner or later from complications.

The evening before I should, I dare say, have been revolted if one of the boys from Burgundy had expressed out loud his plans for getting rid of an unwanted child. All that had been ceaselessly repeated to me for six years about the absolute respect a doctor should have for human life, all I had seen of the mortal risks of abortion, would have made me protest indignantly against such a crime. But when faced by the danger of being chained for life to this girl, I felt myself becoming a split personality. I could remove my last medical scruples by repeating to myself that abortions usually lead to disaster because the person who performs the operation does not pay enough attention to cleanliness, because the probe or knitting needle is infected, or the soapy water injected is not sterile. If I were present and insured a careful asepsis from the operator, the risks would be negligible.

As to respect for life, after a moment's thought I remembered having heard one evening, at my class for the dressers' exam, that it was uncertain whether the fetus in the first three months of conception could be considered as a human being, endowed, that is to say, with any spiritual consciousness. After thirty-six church congresses this point was still being debated. Was I now going to ruin my whole life for the sake of a little sack of cells and membranes, vaguely fish-shaped, which was beginning to grow larger in a corner of Vicky's womb and would perhaps die before it was really born?

Vicky began yawning, and looked at the time. After a week of separation, she must have been surprised at my amorous restraint. But then she may well have thought I wanted to respect her at least for today in the emotion of finding her pregnant. At no point did she seem to have any idea of what I was thinking of her. She would doubtless have been amazed to hear how much her body disgusted me, how a sort of superstition even inhibited me from touching her. In case she were not really pregnant, I had no wish to run the slightest risk; once bitten was indeed quite sufficient.

She yawned again and said: "I'm hungry. Denise is dining with Henri at Liberty's. Shall we go with them? I'd love to eat oysters this evening."

"Already the appetite of the expectant mother?" I said with a laugh, to show how little I was worried.

I was attracted by the idea of eating with Henri and Denise. When we had deposited the two girls, Henri and I could return to barracks together in his car, and on the way I could ask his help. I started putting on my uniform again. Vicky must have been expecting some smart officer's uniform, and seemed rather startled by what she saw. When I put on my absurd little forage cap, she had a fit of the giggles. By my expression she obviously observed the inappropriateness of this reaction, for in the street she took my arm sedately enough.

After dinner, which I found endless, Denise and Vicky decided to spend this evening of grass-widowhood in a cinema on the Champs-Elysées, where we left them. As soon as they had vanished, I told Henri about my misfortune. "A nuisance certainly," he commented. "Well, what are you going to do about it?"

"If she hasn't told me a yarn to get me to marry her..."

"Quite possible," Henri broke in.

"I'll try and get rid of the child."

He turned and looked at me in some surprise. "Doing it yourself?"

"If you'd like to do it for me, I'd appreciate it," I replied, trying to make it sound like a joke.

"Count me out, Jean," said Henri with extreme firmness. "In fact if you want my advice, don't have anything to do with it at all. With a bit of bad luck—and you've seen enough abortion cases in hospital, I dare say, to realize that you never know how that little game is going to end—it's a fine way of going to jail. I can tell you that it costs five years' imprisonment, a heavy fine, and in addition, besides getting the maximum sentence as a doctor, you may be temporarily suspended or permanently forbidden to practise. You'd do better to pay for the brat till it's weaned, it's less expensive."

My face was clammy with sweat. I pursued the discussion:

"But if she keeps the child, she'll lead me a dog's life trying to force me to marry her." I suddenly felt I had really been caught in a trap and was battering my head vainly against the door of a locked room.

"It's not to be denied," observed Henri placidly, "that you may have some disagreeable moments. But at least you've not been an utter fool, have you? You've never promised anything in the way of marriage or written anything which could be interpreted that way?"

"I damned well haven't," I told him hastily.

"That makes things easier then. As soon as you're sure of her pregnancy, tell her that this is a decision that can't be changed, however much she threatens you, that you do not intend to marry her at any price. But as you're a chivalrous sort of chap, you will be kind enough, in a pinch, to pay for her until the baby is weaned."

"How am I going to manage that?"

"Don't worry, it won't cost you much. Vicky isn't the sort to become an unmarried mother. I can't see her being very keen on washing diapers and so on. When she sees she hasn't any chance of getting you to hold the baby, literally, she'll find a way of getting rid of it. When you're with her, explaining your chivalrous decision, you might casually leave by her bag two or three thousand-franc notes, which is about the ordinary Paris rate for the job. Of course you'll have to pretend she's going to use the money to buy a new summer wardrobe or baby clothes, rather than to get rid of the infant. If you want, I can lend you the money, on condition naturally that I know nothing about the whole business, of course."

"Thank you very much, Henri," I replied, with a mixture of relief and disgust, a little touched too by his willingness to help: "I think I've got enough. It's just about what I earned from my job."

"Good. As to the operation itself, I must absolutely insist that you have nothing to do with it at any price. Let Vicky manage on her own. She knows what she wants. Don't get worked up about that side of it. You know my theory, that it's very naughty of the girl to have an affair in the first place, so it's quite fair she should be punished for it. Otherwise providence wouldn't have invented virginity and the risks of pregnancy."

We were driving along the bank of the Seine near the Tuileries gardens. It was a mild evening, and the shade which fell on the trees seemed soft and tranquil. Henri drove slowly, glancing at the girls we passed. They all looked as if they might be on their way towards love, but I did not feel like looking at them, nor at the darkening sky, where the stars were beginning to come out. All my thoughts were concentrated on a single obsession. I felt that in the last few hours my life had suddenly come to a standstill. I should only begin to live again forty-eight hours later—or perhaps never.

The next two days dragged on for me with desperate slowness. I was present in body during the training periods and lectures but I did not even listen. I went passively to roll-calls and formations, went up to put on dungarees for an exercise, and continued like this until evening, without even listening to the grousing of the Burgundians. Tabureau explained to them as a kindly Master Sergeant that these impromptu roll-calls and changes of uniform might seem completely crazy to some of us, but from a military point of view had a high educative value: they were intended, he said, to teach us discipline and lick us into shape.

With friendly understanding Henri never mentioned the subject which was obsessing me, and even invited Vicky and me to dine with him and Denise, so as not to leave me on my own with Vicky. To avoid awakening Vicky's suspicions I went, and ascribed my apathy to the unwonted expenditure of muscular energy which our Sergeant required of us the whole day long. Henri said that he too felt like a wet rag.

I had an understanding with Vicky that she would come to my hotel on the third day to bring me the result of the test, and I would wait for her there as soon as I got out of Val-de-Grâce. That evening Henri stopped his car in front of my hotel, and as I was getting out he shook hands with me energetically and repeated his instructions:

"Good luck, old man. Above all, don't come down off your high horse whatever she says. Put the money by her bag and refuse to have anything to do with her present plans. I don't suppose we can expect you for dinner this evening. This conversation will probably upset you both and for several days afterwards you won't be feeling much like eating together."

Of course the result of the test was positive. The note from the dispensary was quite definite about it. She had read it before giving it to me, and I felt she was watching me while I took cognizance of its contents. Up to the last minute I had nursed a deep irrational hope, and I found now that I was shaking. At first I could not speak, simply gazed at the letter as if the very simple technical terms it contained and the result so clearly expressed could give scope for numerous interpretations, could at least leave a little room for doubt. In the end I plunged in despairingly: "Well?" I said.

"Well what?" asked Vicky, assuming a very surprised expression.

I tried to keep my voice calm and firm. "What are you going to do?"

Vicky opened her eyes wide and looked at me with innocent astonishment marvelously simulated. More in sorrow than anger she cried: "You're asking *me* that, Jean? What do you expect me to do now?"

"It's just because I don't know that I'm asking you. You alone can decide." I spoke in a firm, businesslike, almost impersonal tone. She fluttered her eyelids and succeeded in bringing tears to her eyes. She shook her fair hair, pouting like an unhappy schoolgirl, and collapsed against my shoulder crying: "Oh Jean, how can I decide alone about *our* child?" She began to sob.

Politely I let her weep against me for a few moments, then I gently detached the arm she had slipped round my neck, led her firmly to the armchair, and forced her to sit down. Then I moved away a little so she could see how little effect her tears had on me. She must have noticed this very quickly, for almost as soon as she was seated she raised her still tearstained eyes with a look of touching submissiveness. When I merely returned her look in silence, she repeated with a new freshet of tears: "*Our* child."

"But isn't your Argentine the father?" I asked icily.

"Oh, that didn't even last a month, and only because you were so nasty to me when you went off to the Auvergne! I was just angry with you and wanted to have my revenge. But remember I returned just as soon as you were back yourself."

"None of which excludes the possibility the artist is the father."

"But the child's yours, Jean," Vicky exclaimed. "I swear it's yours."

"That might be a little difficult to prove, my girl," I answered. "If you want, we'll talk about it again later, and then, depending on the date when the baby arrives, I promise I'll help you while you're still feeding it. If it turns out to be the artist's responsibility and he hasn't come back, I'll still pay the expenses of baptism and so on, but on a purely friendly basis. Without prejudice, as the lawyers say."

"Don't be so cruel, Jean," she moaned pathetically. "You know quite well it's you I love, and together we could be so happy, darling. Don't you want to?"

"Let's talk frankly. If you're referring to marriage, count me out. In your interest as well as in my own I wouldn't dream of doing anything so stupid. I've no money, nor have you. I don't feel cut out for ten years starving in a garret, and in any case you'd drop me long before that. Far better we should stay apart and have our own lives."

"But the child?" she groaned in accents of maternal love.

"That's easy enough. For eight or nine months, if you're afraid of wearing out your breasts by feeding it, I can earn enough to pay for a wetnurse."

She must have realized that my decision was definite, for she abandoned the tortured expression of a young mother defending her baby's future. She straightened out her handkerchief, which she had nervously rolled into a ball during the scene of despair, and began to dab at her eyes carefully, so as to avoid spoiling the makeup.

Her face now depicted an innocent girl overwhelmed by fate, who might be driven to the direst straits unless I came quickly to her rescue. Shaking her head she murmured as if thinking out loud: "The poor little thing. How on earth could I bring it up all by myself? Far better it shouldn't come into the world at all...."

I said nothing, and in the end she went on: "You'll help me, won't you?"

She waited for my response eagerly, unable quite to conceal her anxiety. "No," I replied. "Count me out on that too. It's too serious. If we were caught the magistrate might show leniency towards *you,* but I as a doctor would get the maximum penalty, and it would cost me my whole career."

I knew she must have tried the marriage trick without believing in it too much. Besides, the objections I had given to our getting married were objections she herself must find reasonable enough. But ever since she had known me, she had thought of abortion, I expect, as one of the amenities I could offer should the need arise. An abortion would seem to her something quite ordinary for a medical student, one of the things they are always having to cope with. The firmness of my refusal seemed to astonish her profoundly. A disturbing gleam in her eyes gave them a brief hard brilliance, but she controlled herself. She probably thought I was trying to increase the value of my help by making her plead for it.

After a preliminary pitiful moan, subtly mixing discouragement, reproach, and hope, she returned to the irresistible argument of tears. "Oh Jean," she cried, "you're not going to throw me over. If you leave me now, where can I go?"

Collapsed in the armchair, her head between her hands, she burst into renewed sobbing. For a moment I was almost sorry for her. In self-defense I forced myself to think of the thousand schemes undoubtedly buzzing in that pretty head. I told myself over and over again that right from the start she had been using her histrionic talents to put on an act. For all her air of candor she had been lying to me all the time.

I remained impassively in front of the armchair. She slipped to her knees against me, stammering, imploring, and beginning to gulp out between her tears a long protestation of fidelity and love. But the more she pleaded and protested, the less moved I became, taking a cold and almost sadistic pleasure in my refusal to yield to her acting. Two could play at that game, and my response to each of her phrases of injured love was to debunk them as cynically as I knew how. Eventually, at one insult even uglier than the rest, Vicky all of a sudden rose to her feet as if I had just slapped her, and I saw before me an unrecognizable face in which the eyes were inflamed with rage, the thin lips were convulsed, and the brow wore an evil scowl. It

333

came to me in a flash that after all her acting only this new face, unfamiliar and hostile, showed the true Vicky.

Earlier, following Henri's instructions, I had discreetly placed three large bills beside her bag. She screwed these into a ball and tossed them into her bag, then walked furiously towards the door without even repowdering her face. She opened the door, and then swung round with her upper lip bared in a grimace of hatred which showed her white teeth. "All right," she shouted, "I'll take care of it then, but I'll see it costs you a good deal more than your dirty money." The door slammed fiercely behind her.

There was a buzzing in my ears, and I felt weak and dazed as I listened to her angry steps in the corridor dying away. It was only a vague threat uttered in a moment of fury, yet inexplicably I felt it presaged for me a certain and inevitable misfortune. Standing in the middle of the room, I drew out a handkerchief and mechanically wiped my sweating brow. Suddenly a wave of nausea came over me, so that I only just had time to rush to the bathroom and bring up everything I had eaten during the day. But in this disaster, I thought afterwards, I shall never be able to spew up enough to clear away my mortification and self-disgust.

Chapter Three

May 24–June 3

AFTER this painful scene with Vicky, I decided, as advised by Henri, to confine myself voluntarily to barracks for the next few days. I knew Henri was probably right in his prediction that Vicky would try to have an abortion performed at once. I lived in terror of being mixed up in this, should anything go wrong. My status as medical student would bring upon me the first suspicions. By not leaving Val-de-Grâce, I should establish, as Henri pointed out to me, a perfect alibi.

Still following Henri's advice, I even kept in my diary a list of those I saw each evening, although I had at first objected that such excessive precautions might seem a bit suspicious in case there was an inquiry. But I only had to explain, Henri told me, that I had been afraid Vicky might not only refuse to listen to my strong recommendations against any attempts at abortion, but might even in her fury do everything to throw suspicion on me. By deliberately shutting myself up in barracks, constantly in sight of some of my fellow trainees, at least nobody could accuse me of giving Vicky active help.

Inwardly, of course, I was ashamed of hiding away like a malefactor, and of my cowardice in driving Vicky to an operation which I knew to be dangerous. I tried continually to quiet my conscience by quoting myself dates to prove clearly that the artist might just as well be the father. Henri assured me that the lunch, on the day I returned from Peyrac, had been organized by Denise at Vicky's request, to give her a chance of making it up with me again. But I knew Henri was quite as much of a liar as Vicky herself, and in my uncertainty I started writing a letter telling her I would pay all the expenses of her confinement and also for the maintenance of the child. Henri stopped me in the middle of this, telling me: "What Vicky wanted was abortion or marriage. I guarantee she wouldn't dream of wearing out her stomach and her breasts for the satisfaction of remaining an unmarried mother. Well, you don't intend to marry her, so let her do the other thing. Your letter won't change a thing, except that for a good many years it will give her a useful weapon to blackmail you with." This too seemed sense, and I tore up the half-written letter.

By a sort of compensation, and also to try to forget the intolerable suspense, I began to work frantically hard, even at the military course. When we had completed this at the end of three months, we should become smart medical corps cadets in respectable official khaki instead of our present coarse blue serge. It also meant a rise in the weekly pay packet.

No one had ever been known to fail in this exam, and a good many of my fellow soldiers spent most of their unoccupied time in barracks evading boredom by reading, playing cards, arguing, or simply lounging about in comparatively contented idleness. For the initial mood of depression had been quickly dissipated, and the atmosphere now was of men playing at boys for the last time. Having had military service deferred till the end of our medical studies, we were all in our middle twenties, so were enjoying a splendid temporary respite, before plunging into the cares of professional life. All through the morning and afternoon we waited eagerly for the time when we would be "let out," and these long hours were redeemed by petty hopes and enjoyments, a fatigue escaped, a lecture canceled, exemption from a drill. The humblest pleasures, the shortest holiday, could give satisfaction, when one knew that these few months were really the end of youth.

I was by no means alone, however, in my new zealousness for lectures and the work of the course generally, for those who passed with the highest marks after the three months became subalterns immediately, with a substantial rise in pay. But this rank could only be given to qualified doctors, and to obtain the degree it was necessary to submit a thesis. Accordingly little parcels of proofs, smelling of fresh printers' ink, began appearing in barrack rooms and classrooms, and writers of theses could be seen correcting typographical errors with an elaborate set of symbols supplied by the printers on a separate sheet along with the proofs.

Theses had to be a certain length, and ranged from long laborious monographs, produced after conscientious research on some abstruse medical subject, full of dull statistics which it was unlikely even the judges would ever read in full, to very thin little essays, savoring all too obviously of scissors and paste, spread out over fourteen pages of foolscap, about the smallest number an author could dare to submit. The thesis, it must be admitted, was usually little but a tiresome formality, to be tossed off in a week's work with as little trouble and expenditure of energy as possible.

This at least had been my attitude until then. But if I had to be in barracks for my own greater safety, I felt I might as well get through with this chore at least, and I sought about for a subject which I could manage without having to be dashing off to libraries. Suddenly I remembered the file on Medicine in the Country, which Dr. Delpuech had given me the morning I said goodbye to him. When I reached Paris, I had put it away in a drawer with other old papers. I had completely forgotten about it, but was sure it was still in that drawer; I asked Henri

336

if he would mind calling at my hotel and trying to find it. He praised my caution in not stirring outside the Val, and brought back the file the same night. I had not, of course, confided in anyone except him why I was not going out these days, but now I had a perfect and plausible excuse.

I took out the file and undid the string with which it was tied up. Ranged under various headings I found an infinity of notes and cuttings from articles published here and there in medical revues. At first sight this jumble of papers and manuscript seemed impossible to handle, and I nearly closed the file again without reading it. But then I was ashamed of this indifference, remembering the kindness of the old man who had entrusted it to me: this work, after all, represented the experience and passionate interest of a whole lifetime. I began to skim through the papers to fulfill at least in part the promise I had made to their writer.

The more I went on reading, the more I realized that my thesis was here already, practically complete. Each sheaf of papers and notes contained material for a chapter: the countryman, his life and function; breakdown and crisis in French rural life; the need for a rural elite; the country doctor and his status; adaptation to his environment—I had only to take up my pen and edit this synthesis of forty years' experience.

A little note in manuscript slipped out of the book and fell on the floor. I picked it up, and found it was a quotation perhaps copied from some obituary: *He followed the same inner evolution as Dr. Bénassis in* Médecin de Campagne. *Having buried himself among poor farmers in the heart of the country, believing he had thrown away all his life's highest ambitions, he found his horizons enlarged instead of narrowed: above the roofs of his remote village, he found peace and came closer to the divine wisdom.* Under these words, summing up the grandeur of lifelong unselfish service, Dr. Delpuech had added: *Quoted of my friend Dr. Roger Labat, once interne in Paris, who then went to Laplume (Lot-et-Garonne), and in affection for his rustic patients stayed there contentedly all his life.*

I decided at once that my thesis should be entitled *Medicine in the Country*, and that underneath the title I would put this quotation.

I set to work enthusiastically. By putting these papers together so that they could appear publicly in print, I felt I was paying sincere homage to the old doctor's memory. But above all I found that these pages, covered with his thin firm writing, had a calming influence upon me. They began to give me a new hope, and to make my present life seem somehow less sordid.

From this time on my life in voluntary detention changed. In the first days I used to swallow hastily my meal in the mess, and then go and sit in front of the barracks door, on steps still warm with the sun. There I would chat till dusk about a thousand insignificant events of the day with the melancholy group of petty offenders, complaining acrimoniously about the rigors of army discipline, and the few provincials who stayed within military confines of an evening. Suspended idly outside the normal world, between the high walls of the Boulevard de Port-Royal and the towering dome of Val-de-Grâce lit by the setting sun, I found myself beginning to forget my troubles, and for no real reason, felt sheltered within this shell of intellectual inertia, which seemed to me peculiar to an enlisted man's uniform and barrack life.

But as soon as I started writing my thesis from Dr. Delpuech's notes and cuttings, this indolence disappeared completely. Directly I had finished dinner, I went up with my papers to a classroom smelling not of schoolboys' ink but rifle-oil from the weapons. I always found there a few enthusiasts tempted by the second lieutenant's stripes, coming to study their notes, or else learning as an extracurricular activity the complicated mechanism of the automatic pistol or the light machine gun. At our first lesson in dismantling the latter weapon, Paul, who had already tamed our Sergeant considerably, protested: "But why d'you want us to learn all that, Sarge? The Geneva Convention forbids military doctors to carry arms." "To hell with the goddam conventions," Taboureau had answered with superb indifference. "I've been told to teach you this, and teach it I will. In the army you should never try to understand, or we'd all be nuts in no time." None the less, each time a new weapon was being dismantled, Paul went on calling out: "But, Sarge, the Geneva Convention." And Taboureau would continue imperturbably with his instruction.

One evening when I was working on my thesis Paul came

into the classroom and drew me into the corridor, looking slightly embarrassed. "You know what I think, Jean," he began, "about your private life. I used to say quite a lot on that subject, but it evidently wasn't any use, so we won't go into that now. The point is that I've got a bit of news which I think might interest you."

With Vicky on my mind, I had a nasty feeling that Paul must have heard something, although he looked pleased. Good news—what could that be? "Well?" I asked.

"Well," he said, "I saw Marianne today."

"Where?" I cried eagerly.

"At the Necker. A sister of my landlady has cancer of the uterus, poor old thing, and I went to see her in the gyne ward at the Necker. Well, I found Marianne was one of the dressers on the ward. I was able to hand over my patient to her, so to speak, and she seemed quite pleased to see me. I can tell you I was damned glad to see her, but unfortunately she was very busy just then, and I only had time for a few words with her— but I thought you might like to know."

"Did she—" I hesitated. "Did she say anything about me?"

"She asked after you in a casual sort of way, and I said you were deep in your thesis and otherwise much the same, and she said 'Oh I see,' or something noncommittal like that. Then she rushed off to do a dressing."

"Thanks very much for telling me, Paul," I said. "I appreciate it more than you may think."

"Good," said Paul, "I'm glad you do. By the way, she looks just the same. It was damned good to see her," he repeated, as he walked away.

Good old Paul. I knew he had never forgiven me for my break with Marianne, and now perhaps he hoped I might come to my senses and try to make it up. I went back to the classroom, sat down before my papers, and tried hard to think.

Now that I was working on my thesis, I felt somehow worthier of Marianne, and if I had only been free I might have tried to get in touch with her. She might despise me now, and justifiably, but I could at least have written to her and told her I was sorry for all I had done. Such an expression of penitence on my part must surely be the preliminary to any revival of our love. But it simply wasn't possible now, while I was still in suspense over

339

Vicky. If Vicky had her abortion and there were no mishaps, I might have a chance of making a clean break with my past; for the moment, alas, I had no right to any relationship with Marianne whatever. If there were no trouble with Vicky, then and only then might Paul's news be of use to me.

A few days later, in the early evening, I was busy again on the thesis when Henri came into the classroom, and asked me to come out into the corridor with him. By his face, and his coming at all, I feared the worst. As soon as we were alone together, he proved my fears well justified. "Denise went to see Vicky in her room this afternoon," he informed me. "She had the job done four days ago and from what Denise told me it doesn't sound too good. Vicky is terribly anxious to see you, so I've come straight here in my car to fetch you."

I leaned against a wall in the corridor. My hands, suddenly clammy with sweat, stuck to the greasy paint. I wanted to go to sleep in a corner, so as not to have to think, only not to have to think. This whole business did not concern me any more, I felt. I was at Val-de-Grâce with my papers, my thesis work, in a place of asylum. Enemies were treacherously trying to get me involved again in this dirty business, it was unfair and intolerable. But Henri, careless of the turmoil of my thoughts, asked me a bit impatiently: "Well, what are you doing about it? Shall I take you? I have a business date at Liberty's at half past eight this evening, to sell the gray sedan, you know."

The calmness of his voice gave me a further shock. He was not involved and could afford to make light of all this. Yet on the other hand I was so distraught that I clung to this calm indifference: his head at least would be clear, and when his selfish interests weren't concerned, he was impartial enough. He could advise me. With constricted throat, I asked him: "You think I should go?"

"That's your business. But at least you aren't risking anything by going. Vicky had the abortion four days ago, and you can prove you've been right here without going out for a week or more."

"Ye-es," I said doubtfully.

"And on reflection," Henri went on, "if things turn out very nasty and you've answered the first appeal she made to you, that'll show your kindly feelings and your innocence."

I hesitated a few seconds more, but then Henri looked ostentatiously at his watch and I dashed off to get my forage cap and join him in the car.

Vicky lived in one of the big new apartment buildings in the Boulevard Victor, in the flat of a dour old woman who sublet one room. She had told Vicky on the latter's first day there that there should be no male visitors after eleven at night. But this prohibition had not worried us a great deal, for Vicky usually came to my hotel room, and the old lady had closed her eyes to Vicky's late returns and nights out, because she was fond of the theatre and Vicky could get her free seats. Thanks to this, Vicky had a very comfortable room quite cheap, with many minor advantages she would not have found at a hotel.

We rang twice at the door. The old lady was evidently not there, for it was Denise who came to let us in. The door of Vicky's room leading into the tiny hall was slightly open. I pushed it and went in first. I did not look at all at the surroundings. I knew already that the dressing table near the window was all cluttered up with makeup and grease paint, that there were pictures of theatrical stars on the walls, and invitations slipped with pretended casualness into the groove of the mirror. On a low table was a glamor-girl photo of Vicky, looking dangerously seductive.

But the face I saw in the hollow of the pillow told of a far more potent danger, of which Vicky herself seemed likely to be the victim this time. I had seen too many abortion cases at hospital not to recognize all the signs of very serious infection.

Denise bent over Vicky and said to her: "Here's Jean, my dear, so I'll leave you. I'll be back tomorrow morning to see how you're feeling." But Vicky hardly listened to her. As soon as I came into the room, she had her eyes fixed on me, and did not take them off me.

I drew up a chair to sit down near the divan, and heard the front door banging shut behind Henri and Denise. I took Vicky's wrist. Knitting her brows, she looked at me with such intensity that in my embarrassment and worry I could think of nothing to say. Under my fingers, the dry burning skin and very rapid pulse confirmed the alarming impression left by her face. I tried to smile at the drawn face strained by fever, but I understood better the obsession contracting her features when Vicky asked me imploringly: "Please, Jean, it's not serious, is it? Nothing's going to happen?"

"No, of course not. Towards the third or fourth day there's always a little fever. A few tablets of aspirin and you'll be back to normal."

I continued lying to her as best I could, and hoped I had convinced her, for she said nothing further. But suddenly she freed her wrist, and clinging to me, her eyes pale with anguish, cried: "I don't want to die!"

She sat up, flushed and gasping, in a pitiful half-delirious panic which sent a shudder through her whole body. I took her clenched fists in my hands and tried to calm her by reasoning with her gently. But instead of soothing her, my words seemed to make her even more beside herself. "You wouldn't help me, and I had to manage all on my own. If I die, it will be your fault, but I don't care, because you'll be in it too," she screamed.

She had freed her hands. I tried to take hold of them again, but she hurled me back violently, and her frenzy grew: "You think I'm feverish and making this up? Well, I'll tell you all about it. I've got rid of the baby, and you're in it up to your eyes. I've seen to that. A friend gave me an address: Madame Doupion, Mère Flytox they call her, 12 rue Casimir-Delavigne, third floor. Go and see her, you'll be quite interested. It's near the Medical School and your hotel, so you won't need to go far."

Still without taking her eyes off me, she threw her head back and burst into shrill laughter. I felt myself pale before the unknown peril approaching me. In my increasing alarm I should have liked to avoid hearing further details and yet at the same time, my heart thumping madly, I was burning to know everything.

Vicky went on laughing. She was taking her time, and seemed delighted at the chance to play with me like this, to humiliate me and keep me at her mercy. Then her laughter stopped abruptly.

"Three thousand francs—you thought you could get away

with it for three thousand francs. My life for three measly little bills. And then you'd have gone off quite happily and married some ugly horror with plenty of money. But I've got the theatre in my blood, you know, and I've put together quite a nice little scenario. Mère Flytox is perfect in her part too, you'll see. A comfortable little body, with a very ordinary face. She lives in a three-room flat smelling of cats. It couldn't be more harmless and reassuring. But I can tell you, Jean, that if I die at the end of the third act you'll make your exit with two policemen."

She paused, gasping, and looked at me fixedly for several seconds, but I said nothing. I had never seen such hatred in her eyes. She went on now in an increasingly hoarse voice:

"Mère Flytox doesn't look like it, but she knows all the tricks. She wanted to know first of all who was the father. Hell, she didn't have to ask twice. I told her right away it was a dirty little medical student named Jean Nérac. Well, she hesitated. Of course she was anxious to help me, she said, but she didn't want to get herself into trouble instead of you, so she suggested a little scheme in case of mishap, involving *you*, Jean, you the pure and incorruptible."

"Don't be a fool, Vicky," I began, trying to quiet her, but she was too full of her hysterical rage to be stopped.

"Want to hear all about it? I'm sure you must. Well, she dictated a letter to me, in which I asked her for an appointment through you. She'll take great care of this letter, and if there's an inquiry, you can be sure she'll see it's found. So you'll be the one who gave me the idea and the address, and you won't find it easy to prove the contrary before a judge. Amusing little plot, don't you think, or don't you?"

Even in the paroxysm of her hysteria she still kept looking at me slyly between her long lashes so as to miss nothing of her vengeance. But now abruptly she dropped back on the pillow, exhausted. In the dark hollows of her eyes all expression seemed to have vanished, and she lay as if dead. Sitting near her, I felt incapable of moving. I was stunned and overwhelmed. The hatred with which she had looked at me all the time was far more convincing proof even than her threats that she was inventing nothing, that I was irreparably involved. For a moment I felt like strangling her. Then this impulse faded, and I fell into a dazed stupor. My brain seemed to lose its power to focus, and inside it a few odds and ends of ideas were floating hazily: "Soon be roll-call . . . must do something . . . get her out of here . . . mustn't waste a minute. . . ." But all the while my sagging limbs seemed riveted to the spot.

At last I was able to rise, and walked across the room without looking at Vicky. "I'm going to fetch a doctor," I said with my back to her.

But as I reached the door, a great cry stopped me: "Jean!" There was a note of such panic in the voice that I turned round. Vicky had sat up again. In the grip of abject terror, she now showed only a pitifully distracted, imploring face. "Please don't leave me, Jean," she begged me. "Swear you'll come back. Please tell me you'll come back—I don't want to die." She began giving short gasping sobs.

I returned to the bed and sat on the edge of it. I wanted to force her to lie down, but she threw her arms round me, and clasped me fiercely, as if I could deliver her from all the terrifying dangers she felt rising with the darkness. Her face was convulsed with fear as she looked up at me, repeating monotonously: "I don't want to *die,* I don't want to *die.*"

She was sobbing now like a child, and at last I felt real pity for her. Even more than her words and the sobbing, I was strangely moved by the sight of the poor little face which had been so perfect, with the mascara all blotchy from her tears, the powder accumulating round her nostrils, the rouge smeared all over her lips. Forgetting myself for a moment, I suddenly felt impelled to offer her kindness and protection, to show strength and gentleness simultaneously. In her terror Vicky was now only a little girl, without courage or cunning, desperately crying for help. I spoke to her slowly, as if lulling to sleep a headstrong child, and noticed that this was making me calmer myself.

Eventually her terror seemed to abate, and I was able to free my hands, and make her lie quietly back on the pillow. I drew the sheet right up to her neck, tucked her in, and whispered to her: "I swear to you I'll come back." When I rose to my feet again, I felt slightly reassured because she gave me a look of humble confidence as she let me go.

Crossing the hall, I was surprised to see the old landlady come abruptly out of the kitchen; she had obviously been waiting for me. When had she returned, and how much of Vicky's screaming had she heard? She barred my way, and I told her politely, restraining my impatience, that Vicky had been having severe stomach pains, and had asked me to come and examine her. I was afraid I had found what seemed like an acute appendicitis, and I was now going off to find a doctor to confirm this diagnosis, which would certainly mean an urgent operation.

This lie was on the whole quite plausible, and the old lady, still standing across the doorway, seemed to accept it, and made a few sententious remarks about the way the young chased after pleasure these days even if it meant neglecting their health. But as she was opening the catch to let me out she added with a cough: "A lot of unmarried girls you hear about with acute appendicitis nowadays. Peculiar, isn't it, the way it always seems to happen to girls like Vicky?"

Outside it was still broad daylight. Noisy children were playing about on the pavement, and concierges had drawn up their chairs on the doorsteps to enjoy the mild evening air. I felt dazzled as if I were drunk. On the boulevard I saw an empty bench a few yards away. With a great effort I managed to get there, and sank onto it. My legs ached and my head was empty. Vicky's pathetic terror had made me feel calm by contrast, but all my calm had been abruptly destroyed by the landlady's innuendo. Ideas buzzed in my brain like angry wasps. I felt obscurely that time was passing and I must act quickly.

I pulled up the sleeve of my uniform to look at my watch, and found that I had to pull up my shirtsleeve too. The sweat had stuck it to my skin. It was five minutes to eight. I had no more than an hour and five minutes before the roll-call, and in my terror only one thing stood out as certain: Vicky must not be left alone in her room a single night longer. It was a question of life and death for her, and if the landlady by some miracle had not heard everything, she certainly had suspicions. In case there was a police inquiry, nothing would prevent her voicing them, and telling them I had been there.

But where could I take Vicky? To whose care could I entrust her? I was so distraught I could only think of friends who were in Val-de-Grâce with me, and who in any case, except for one or two like Paul Chavasse, would probably have wriggled out of helping me. "Who can I trust her with, good God, who can I trust her with?" I muttered out loud in my despair.

I found I had already wasted ten precious minutes on this bench, and my brain was dulled by the traffic flashing past on the boulevard two or three yards away from me, leaving behind it a stink of gasoline and dust. I became obsessed now with the idea that all was lost. I should never escape from all this, and my life was ruined. Condemned as a procurer of illegal abortions, I should never get my degree at all. My mother would die of shame and sorrow. For several years of petty pleasures and luxuries and vices I had thrown away all her sacrifice, all my future.

At last I rose, sick and trembling. I had only one last resource now: to ring at the house of some doctor in the district, tell him the gist of the story quickly, and take him to Vicky, so that he should sign an order to get her admitted to some hospital. There I would try to have a word with the interne on duty.

I walked a few yards down the boulevard, looking for a doctor's plate. Who the doctor was it really mattered very little; he was bound to keep a professional secret. At hospital too this would have some influence in case of police inquiry. But it would have been better, all the same, to know the ward interne, so I could put Vicky in his hands more or less personally. Suddenly a ray of hope came to me. I remembered Paul saying the words "women's surgical ward." Only a few days ago Paul had seen Marianne on such a ward at the Necker, and I had decided it would not be fair to get in touch with her until I could be clear of Vicky. But now I must go to her, fair or unfair. Marianne, my dearest Marianne, I *must* go to you.

Without further reflection, forgetting all the wrongs I had done her, forgetting that we were almost strangers and that I had no earthly claim on her now, I stopped a taxi, seized by a frenzied impulse of hope, hurled myself into it, calling out frantically to the driver: "To the Cité Universitaire."

My heart racing faster than ever, my legs like jellies beneath me, I dropped onto the worn upholstery and almost burst into tears of relief, like one who has narrowly escaped from some great danger and finds his nerves in shreds.

The journey up to the Parc Montsouris was very fast. I made

the driver stop outside the girls' wing of the Deutsch de la Meurthe Building, and asked him to wait for me there, then dashed up to the entrance. Only when I reached it did a terrible thought occur to me: I knew nothing at all about Marianne's present schedule. At this hour she might very well not be there, perhaps she would be dining out. There was no question of going into the hostel myself; this was quite against regulations. The tradition in such cases was to ask the first girl who happened to come out to try and find the friend you wanted. I had to wait near the door for a few long minutes before a kindly messenger appeared in the guise of a girl with glasses and a horselike face. She agreed rather primly to transmit my message, as if her own virtue might thereby be jeopardized, and I waited anxiously near the door on the very spot where I had so often waited before in certainty and joy.

I began to feel faint. I was gripped by a chilling doubt. What would Marianne say to this ghost returning, rising up after three years of forgetfulness? I had treated her unpardonably; she could not but despise me utterly. "She is good and kind," I thought in an attempt to reassure myself. But I knew too her secret pride.

With a creak the heavy door swung slightly open, and I held my breath in suspense. Directly afterwards Marianne appeared, looking for her visitor; she seemed stupefied to see this unfamiliar soldier straightening up and running towards her, embarrassingly conscious all at once of his heavy shoes and ungainly uniform. She looked at me as if she did not immediately recognize me. In a brief male glance, almost involuntary, at her body, I found her even more lovely than my memory of her. She had gained a serene and mature self-confidence, she was somehow more balanced than the Marianne I had known four years ago, still little more than a schoolgirl. We were near each other, and face to face. When she saw me properly, Marianne stiffened and stopped, standing motionless in front of the door.

She stared hard at me with what I sensed was contempt. At this I forgot all the phrases I had prepared. This time, though I dared not admit it to myself, all was irremediably lost. Without leaving Marianne time to speak, as if by main force I wanted to prevent her giving a definite clearcut refusal, I abruptly put

347

my hand on her arm to detain her. In a hoarse voice, a voice from the depths of my being, I cried out to her almost the exact words of my desperate postscript in the last real letter I ever wrote to her, the letter she never received: "I need you, Marianne. Oh Marianne, I need your help."

She took a frightened step backwards, and for a moment I thought I had said the one thing she was not expecting, the one thing which could ruin all my chances for sure. But at least I knew this appeal was utterly sincere. Perhaps because I had put into it such an accumulation of unbearable distress, the lovely dark eyes softened. I felt she was sorry for me and would not send me away without a hearing. Yet she did not answer at once. Eventually, as if forcing herself to speak, she muttered hesitantly: "What do you want?"

Very quickly, for the minutes were passing, I told her about the abortion and the immediate help only she could give me. Marianne listened, her head bent, without looking at me. When I had finished she said in a neutral voice: "I'll be with you in a minute. I must just go up to my room to get my bag and leave a note for someone—I was going out this evening."

She hurried back into the hostel, while I stayed in a daze outside the door. I watched the door fiercely, feeling that she might never come back. In fact, however, she came out again very quickly, and immediately I felt less unhappy. She held in her hand the note she had just written, but I forced my eyes away from it. Even I could not have the effrontery to be jealous of Marianne, after giving her up for three years. She left me for a few seconds to go into the porter's office, where she must have deposited the note. With a quite unexpected annoyance, I caught myself thinking that some man must be coming to fetch her at the hostel.

In the taxi Marianne took care to sit in one corner as far away from me as possible. She said nothing, and affected to be looking through the window at the people passing in the streets. I was so dazzled by the miracle of finding her and so afraid to irritate her that I dared not speak or even turn my eyes in her direction. Although her attitude seemed to be one of rigid hostility towards me, yet sitting so close to her I felt overwhelmed by all our common past, our six months' idyll of unsullied love. Never had I felt so completely mean and vile and cheap. But

348

Marianne was there, all the same. I recognized the same light perfume she always used. I felt somehow delivered by this beneficent presence near me, this presence I knew so wonderfully well.

On the staircase I looked at my watch: twenty to nine. When I rang, the old lady cautiously opened the door a few inches. Then, recognizing me, she let us in, but still barred our way. I was obliged to introduce Marianne and explain that she was a young doctor working on the surgical ward of the Necker Hospital. Marianne evidently made a good impression on the old lady, who in the end allowed us to go into Vicky's room.

Since my departure night had fallen. I went in very gently, while Marianne remained at the door. Vicky was evidently sleeping and did not move. What would she say when she saw my companion? I went over to the bed to light the little lamp, and all at once felt deeply ashamed to have involved Marianne in this squalid affair.

At last I did turn the switch, and had at once a severe shock. In three quarters of an hour Vicky's appearance had profoundly changed. Her cheeks had gone a muddy color, there were dark circles round her eyes, and her lips seemed almost blue. She painfully opened dazed eyes, smiling at me vaguely and apparently not noticing the unfamiliar person at my side. I dared not look at Marianne, thinking how she must despise me. How could I possibly have given her up for this shallow and worthless girl, whose room expressed silliness and vanity in every detail? Probably Marianne would even suppose that I had lain with Vicky on this bed.

But when I ventured to turn my eyes towards Marianne, I was reassured. Clearly she had not noticed the soft naked flesh beneath the fine lace nightdress, or the shape, under the blanket, of the pretty body which had once tempted me. This pallid face, with its vague eyes, had once been so charming to me that I had preferred it, after a long succession of others, to Marianne's. But this was not what Marianne seemed to be thinking, as she bent with keen concentration over the bed. Vicky to her was obviously not a rival but merely a patient. She, Marianne, was there in the guise of a doctor. As for me I had ceased to be alone and helpless, I had regained confidence.

On a small low table, beside an ashtray full of cigarette ends stained with lipstick, a little clock said three minutes to nine. I must leave at once. I withdrew without making any noise. Vicky, shivering with a fever which made her teeth chatter, did not even open her eyes.

Marianne followed me into the hall in silence. In a low voice I asked her: "It's very serious, don't you think, with that septicemia?"

She looked at me with a worried expression, and answered awkwardly: "Yes. It does look serious."

At the same moment the old woman came out of her kitchen. "Well," she demanded, "and how is Vicky?"

I began my story over again, trying to sound fairly assured: "We are in agreement that it's acute appendicitis. An urgent operation is required."

"Yes," added Marianne, "and since M. Nérac has to go back at once to Val-de-Grâce, it will be simplest if I take your tenant to the ward in the Necker Hospital where I'm working. I can easily get a bed for her. If you don't mind, I will telephone from here at once to ask for an ambulance. Could you please collect some toilet things, a towel and a spare nightdress, and put them in a suitcase?"

The old landlady left us to rush to the wardrobe, and we remained facing each other. There was only a rather dim lamp in the hall. I would have liked to speak, to tell Marianne something of my gratitude and my shame. I dared not. I slowly opened the front door to leave.

Marianne had remained motionless in the middle of the tiny hall, and suddenly without reflection I seized one of her hands, crushed its palm against my lips. Then without turning back, so that I should not hear her protest or read her face, I dashed down the staircase.

I promised a good tip to the taxi driver and told him that if I were late back several days' detention awaited me. He drove at a prodigious speed from the Boulevard Victor to the gate of Val-de-Grâce. Then I sprinted across the gardens, but it was already twenty past nine when I reached the door of the barrack-room. "No one missing," Paul was just saying.

"And this bed?" demanded the Master Sergeant.

"That's Nérac. I saw him just now, he must be in the lavatory."

I felt it was a good moment to show myself at the door. "Look, Sarge, there he is, you see I wasn't telling you a lie," added Paul with tranquil impudence. I blessed him again for having tamed our Sergeant to such an extent that the latter now managed to ignore just how flushed and panting I was. Such blindness must have required a real effort of goodwill, but in any case I was able to reach my bed in safety. Before Tabureau had reached the next barrack-room, our room had already burst into a joyful din, like a school dormitory when the prefect is away. Henri interrupted his undressing to inquire of me: "Well, how did it go?"

"I got in touch with an old friend who's a dresser at the Necker. She's going to get Vicky into hospital there and deal with the case."

"That's the best thing," commented Henri philosophically.

In my haste to follow Henri when he came to fetch me two or three hours earlier, I had forgotten my thesis file. Before going to bed I went to fetch it. The light was out in the room, but I did not even need to turn it on: near a window, in full moonlight, my papers formed a big white patch at my usual place.

I sat down to collect them, taking my time about it. I knew that for nearly an hour, with all the singing and shouting and conversation, I should never get to sleep in the barrack-room. It was better in this big silent room. I felt dead tired. My throat was parched and all my limbs ached. When I had collected all my papers in their folder, I bent over the table in front of the window in the gentle, almost bluish light of the moon and listened for a while to the monotonous murmur of the night breeze. Then, in immense lassitude, I dropped my weary head against my arms and longed for sleep.

For many minutes, before going back to the barrack-room, I remained there, motionless, bent over the table. How could I live through the days to come, haunted by two vital questions: what chance had Vicky of living, and did Marianne still love me?

Towards dawn I fell into a fitful sleep, to be awakened at six o'clock as usual by Tabureau coming into the room and shouting: "Show a leg there, rise and shine. Clean this place up a bit, it stinks like a pigsty."

The first days in the Val we had not been too pleased to find that our barracks smelled strongly enough to disturb a Master Sergeant of Colonial Infantry. We soon realized, however, that this manifestly unfair accusation formed part of the verbal rites with which Tabureau had inaugurated the mornings of those under him for some fifteen years. We could hardly expect him to change this magic formula just because we all took showers every day.

The working day began with a parade. The Captain did not often appear for it, and under Tabureau and the N.C.O.'s of other squads this first parade in dungarees usually started by looking like a county fair. The sergeants knew by experience that all those who were still missing a quarter of an hour after the signal for the parade must have found good medical excuses for not leaving their beds. When therefore, after patiently waiting for a quarter of an hour, they could not reasonably expect the arrival of any further latecomers, the N.C.O.'s tried to form a square out of the seething mass. By dint of much swearing, they managed to get us to form in an unstable-looking quadrilateral which conjured up only very remotely the ideal military square. But after this, like photographers unwilling to abuse their clients' patience, they sent us off at once to change into shorts and singlets, and present ourselves for instruction in P.T.

After a night of almost complete sleeplessness, I felt incapable of getting up with the rest. I felt sick and I ached all over. But then suddenly I thought of the consequences if the Captain unexpectedly arrived for this parade. Suppose I were found absent—I should probably be punished by confinement in barracks at least. At that I rose in a hurry and went through the day's routine like a robot.

At last we were free to leave barracks. Henri was going off in his car and offered to drop me at the Necker. To his surprise I refused the offer a little ungraciously, and instead went out to the boulevard and hailed a taxi. The concierge there hesitated about letting an army private into the hospital outside visiting hours, but I showed him my medical student's card, and he decided it was all right. Then I rushed to the Berthelot Wing, asking an orderly I passed where I could find the women's ward. "Bichat Ward," he told me, "under the second arch, take the staircase on the right, and it's on the first floor."

Opening the door I was seized by panic and hesitated for a few seconds, exactly as I had seen so many relatives of patients hesitate. What would they tell me? Then I made up my mind. Sister's office was near the entrance. I saw a nurse sitting in front of the table bent over a big register. I knocked and immediately explained that I was a hospital dresser myself and would like to get news of a patient who had come into hospital the night before.

"What's her name?" asked the nurse, taking up the list of patients. As soon as I told her Vicky's surname, she put the list down exclaiming, "Well I never! That girl certainly has plenty of friends to look after her. One of our dressers on this ward hasn't left her all day, and I think she must still be there. In the second cubicle on the right."

I dared not ask: "How is she?" If Marianne had been unwilling to leave her, it was surely because the case was very serious, probably desperate. I walked over unsteadily towards the cubicle the nurse had pointed out to me.

I looked through the glass. Marianne in her white coat, a big book on her knees, was reading, sitting in an easy chair with her back half turned away from me. Beside her, resting on the pillow, I saw Vicky's face. It was terrifying: the lips had turned the color of slate, and between the swollen eyelids the pupils seemed cloudy. But above all the skin had that yellowish tinge I had seen so often in abortion cases where there was serious infection.

My fears about septicemia had been obsessing me already. Knowing one of the men in my unit was specializing in gynecology and obstetrics, I had asked him at lunch what the mortality rate was in cases of septicemia following abortions. "Nearly all the statistics say it's about eighty percent," he had replied. Since then I could think of nothing but this figure, and seeing the state of semi-coma Vicky was now in, I felt a wave of horror surging over me. I hoped against hope that Marianne would say something reassuring.

Hearing me come in, she turned her head. She rose at once, making me a sign to avoid any noise. Vicky, completely prostrate, did not even open her eyes, and between her cyanosed lips

I heard her short gasping respirations. At times she seemed to be rambling in delirium.

Marianne left the cubicle and I followed her. Seeing my uniform, the patients in the main ward strained their heads curiously. "Let's go into the corridor," said Marianne.

When we were alone, in a calm composed voice such as she might have used to a patient's distraught husband, she gave me the necessary information: "She was curetted yesterday evening directly we got her in here. Everything went off all right. I stayed by her here all night. They began the anti-streptococcic serum at once."

A patient's relative would probably have been reassured, but I knew enough about the after-effects of abortions not to notice that she said nothing about the general signs.

"How about her temperature?" I asked, and Marianne answered uneasily: "Still high, I'm afraid."

"And how long has she been in this semi-coma?"

"Last night she was delirious, and she began again this evening about five o'clock. But at the beginning of the afternoon, she was quite conscious and talked to me."

"Did she talk about me?" I inquired with an effort.

"Yes," replied Marianne frankly.

I dared not ask her any more. But she must have seen such anguish in my eyes that she seemed to indulge a sudden impulse, as I had known her do in other days, by adding for my comfort:

"I didn't want to tell you, so as not to raise false hopes, but this is what's happening. A friend of the Chief's, who is head of the laboratory at the Institut Pasteur, has been experimenting with a product effective against the streptococcus in mice. Yesterday I happened to be in the Chief's office when his friend was telling the Chief about it. I remembered it last night when sitting by your—" She hesitated and then changed the phrase, "Sitting by the patient. When Thibaudet, the registrar, came this morning, I asked him if he could suggest to the Chief an immediate trial on this case. The Chief agreed and sent someone off to the Institut Pasteur to try and get some of this drug. They got it, and she was started on it at noon today."

"What's it called?"

"Oh, it's a long chemical word. I only remember the beginning, which is sulfa."

"And it's effective?" I stammered, with difficulty, so dry was my mouth.

"I've told you. They only know so far that it works on mice and guinea-pigs. That's why I didn't want to tell you about it."

"I see," I said, hardly hiding my disappointment.

"But the Chief's friend," added Marianne hastily, "declared yesterday morning that he had great confidence in this drug. In Germany they've already done a lot of research on something of the kind, but he told the Chief that his product had had far better results with laboratory animals. It's not yet been tried on a human being."

In cases of serious septicemia I had so often heard it said that the anti-streptococcic serum was almost without effect that I felt as a deliverance each word this calm, gentle, sensitive voice was saying. Suddenly, in this terrible climate of disaster, a ray of hope was shining through. My brain told me that it was dim and slender, but in my complete despair I clung to it. It was so unexpected, this glimmer of hope rising in the deathly darkness. A thrill of wonder took hold of me, and I felt like telling the whole world that Marianne was beautiful and generous, that I owed to her initiative my one and only chance.

I would have liked to take her hand and kiss it humbly, as I had done the evening before, simply to tell her that my whole life would not be long enough to ask forgiveness at her feet. But she must have guessed my intention. She took a step backwards, and as a patient in a blue dressing gown came out of the bathroom and opened the ward door, Marianne went back into the ward with her.

When, a moment later, I returned to the cubicle, Marianne had already resumed her seat in the chair by the bed. Against the partition I saw an iron chair, and I went in silently to sit in it. From this seat I saw Vicky's bosom rising and falling with a quick shallow movement. Each time she breathed in, her breath made a very slight whistling noise between her white teeth, and sometimes she stammered a few words.

At seven o'clock exactly, Marianne rose, opened a cachet, dropped the powder in a little water and gave it to Vicky, still almost unconscious. Then she said to me in a neutral voice: "I've got an errand to do. Since you're here, I may as well go and do it."

"I'd like to watch all night," I said humbly, "but I have to be back at nine at Val-de-Grâce."

"I must be back myself well before that."

"You're going to stay here tonight as well?" I asked.

"The drug has to be given every two hours, in small doses, to impregnate the organism," Marianne answered curtly, and then added, as if anxious to impress on me the exact reason for her staying: "That's why I'm not leaving her. At the Institut Pasteur they made a special point of that."

After she had gone, I left my uncomfortable seat, and moved to the armchair. I lay back heavily in it, and for a long while abandoned myself to the physical comfort it provided. Just in front of my eyes stood the bedtable. On the upper shelf were ranged various drugs, a jug of lemonade with a half empty glass, and a box of the precious sulfa-something powder. On the lower shelf Marianne had put the books she had brought with her. I recognized the back of a thick treatise on surgical pathology, which she had been reading when I came in, and by its side I saw a paper-backed book which looked like a novel.

Out of curiosity I picked it up. It was Rilke's *The Notebooks of Malte Laurids Brigge*. I began skimming idly through the pages, although too worn out and obsessed to abandon myself completely to their sumptuous poetry. But towards the end of the book a detail stopped me abruptly: in the old days I had myself passed on to Marianne one of my own long-established habits, that of marking with the fingernail or a pencil in the margin any passages which specially struck her. When we were exchanging books, we could feel in this way that we were reading them sitting next to each other. On this volume of Rilke a nail-mark went half way down one page, indicating the profound importance which Marianne, whether consciously or unconsciously, attached to it. I read quickly through the marked paragraph, but it was one of those passages full of mystery and hyperbole which do not at first yield to the mind their full sense, only drive home into the heart their main ideas. I read it through again, incredulously, with burning excitement:

Destiny loves to invent patterns and symbols. Its difficulty lies in its complexity. But Life is difficult from its very simplicity. It has only a few elements which accord with our true stature. The saint who turns away from human destiny does so for the love of God. But Woman must make the same choice in relation to Man, and it is this which calls forth the fatality in all human love: courageous and outside Destiny like one of the immortals, she stands near him as he changes and is transformed. In love Woman will always surpass Man, because Life is greater than Destiny. Her wish is to give herself without limit; therein lies her happiness. But the ineffable sadness of her love has always been this: that she is asked to limit this giving. There is all the suffering of which women have ever complained....

The darkness of evening found me dreaming without daring to move, as if by moving I feared to chase my happiness away. The miraculous evidence was there, inscribed in the margin of this page of this book. Through all my transformations Marianne still loved me, and everything had conspired patiently to bring us together again. I now understood her distant attitude: she had been hurt too much because of me, she was afraid of her fatal love, and while she still believed she had the power to do so, she tried to escape me. But when she was once again in this small room, I could easily win her back by telling her how much the man I had become in three days of ordeal despised the long series of surrenders to temptation which had so greatly changed the young Jean Nérac she had once known.

Sitting quiet and still in the soft darkness, I waited patiently for her return so that I could tell her I was sure at last of my heart's constancy and strength. An infinite serenity filled the narrow silent cubicle. Gradually I lost consciousness of time passing. In this period of restful waiting, I let myself be gripped by the certainty of a miracle. At times I felt that even Vicky, indistinct in the dusk, was breathing near me with less difficulty, that she was sleeping with more relaxation, and her slumber was thereby less frightening. Was the sulfa-drug beginning to work? It was perhaps the beginning of the second miracle, for which a day earlier I could not have dared hope.

The blind had been lowered during the afternoon, so that it was now very dark in the cubicle. The night nurse came in to refill the jug of lemonade, lit the nightlight, and pulled me out of my dreaming. I glanced at my watch. It was ten to nine. Abruptly I became alarmed. What could Marianne, usually so punctual, be doing? I stood up and looked at Vicky. She still

357

seemed to be sleeping. With a feverish arm she had pushed back the sheet, and her hand was resting, bluish, on the bright blanket. Mechanically I took the burning wrist and felt the pulse. I found it soft, hardly countable, like the pulse of one in deep intoxication. Was the heart beginning to grow weaker?

I stayed a moment doubtfully, refusing to understand, refusing with all my strength. As if trying to drive away a hallucination, I passed a hand over my face; it was moist and my fingers were trembling. I began to surrender to the evidence before me and remembering my naive hopes I began to laugh, a bitter, mirthless laugh. All was lost. For two hours I had been stupidly dreaming with my eyes open. This peace was the deceitful calm often given by imminent death. My first miracle was only a mirage, and probably the other one was too. In any case I could never talk to Marianne about love when I had helped to murder Vicky, when Vicky was dying, probably this very night.

The door of the cubicle opened again, and Marianne came in. She glanced at Vicky and then looked at me. I turned my head away. "Sorry I've been so long," she said. "Any change?"

"I'm afraid she's weaker," I muttered miserably. Marianne took Vicky's pulse and frowned.

"Don't give up hope," she said gently, again as she might have said it to a patient's relative. "I'll stay with her now, you go back to barracks. Good night."

There was no spirit left in me any more. "Good night," I said with a hopeless shrug, and walked slowly away, and out of the ward. Oh well, there was no point in being late back for the roll-call, and once again I took a taxi and arrived just in time. Not that it really mattered, I thought, nothing can make very much difference now.

Chapter Four

June 4–6

THERE WAS no news, good or bad, next day. Dashing off to the hospital in the evening as soon as we were let out, I found Marianne again at Vicky's bedside. I learned later from the night nurse that although Marianne had slept for short periods during the night she had insisted on being waked in time to give the two-hourly cachets. The drug, alas, did not seem to be working, and I believed that Vicky was gradually sinking. I was not anxious to be left alone with her in this state, and was relieved when Marianne refused my offer that she should go off duty for a spell while I was there to keep watch. She said very little to me, and with the miracle of Vicky's recovery now so remote, I began to doubt the evidence in the Rilke book for that other miracle. No, Marianne certainly could not love me still, and in any case I could not think seriously about such a thing while Vicky was dying.

The next day the agony of waiting was even greater. I had stayed awake again for most of the night, and felt utterly exhausted. On my way to the hospital I told myself anything would be better than this suspense, even hearing that the worst had happened. But when I gently opened the door of the cubicle, scarcely even looking at Marianne, I realized I had still been hoping secretly all the time to find an improvement in the patient's condition.

No such improvement was apparent. Her face was almost yellow, her half-closed, unseeing eyes were almost submerged by the dark rings surrounding them. Her hair stuck to her sweat-covered brow, and her half-open lips, blotchy with small blackish marks, emitted a rattle. All these details I took in at a single glance, and when I picked up the case-records at the foot of the bed, and saw the details of her temperature, pulse, and urine on the chart, my worst fears were confirmed as surely as if it had been written on the wall above her head: Vicky was dying.

I raised my eyes and looked wildly at Marianne in a last desperate appeal. She turned away her eyes, to arrange a pillow. Already she had done all she could; it no longer depended on her. Her eyelids were swollen, and her face was pale and drawn from weariness, which was not surprising for someone who had gone seventy-two hours with very little sleep, and that constantly interrupted. Yet she obstinately carried on with her watch, clinging to the slenderest hope that might still be left, and I felt she would only agree to rest when her patient was either out of danger or dead. I was sure, however, that this night would be the last, that the vain exhausting struggle was nearing its close.

At Val-de-Grâce our Captain had given the whole company a night's leave, so that I should only have to be back in barracks for the morning parade at seven-thirty. Sitting still and useless in a corner of the cubicle, I began a whole night of waiting in a cold terror of suspense.

When I arrived, the cubicle was already darkening with the shadows of evening, and Marianne had lit the bedside lamp. She was sitting in the armchair by the bed, a big medical textbook on her knees. Without daring to talk to her, I watched her read attentively by the narrow beam of the lamp, which formed a sort of halo over her white coat. Despite her physical tiredness, this modest figure bent over the book had a freshness and sturdy vitality which I found strangely restful and heartening. How much substance four years close to sickness and disease had given to the ingenuous girl I had seen on a ward of the Charité the first day of her first term as a medical student.

I remembered the hesitant way she had looked at me that day when I asked her to help me with a treatment, and her respectful schoolgirl answers of "Yes, sir" and "No, sir." And now I dared not rest my eyes on the Marianne of today except furtively and in silence. Since she refused to give me her friendship, let alone love me, I did not want to irritate her with my humble adoration.

I knew clearly now why she had agreed to help me. Since that distant morning when she had first come on to a hospital ward as a student, she had learned to think and work as a doctor.

360

Faced by illness and injury she felt an instinctive call, every time, to fight them. That was why she had been helping me for these three days, why she would watch this final night. For Vicky, dying through my fault, she felt a boundless pity, the response of one human being to the call of another in distress; for me she felt not even comradeship, simply the professional reflex of devotion in response to my own distress. She helped me although she despised me.

About one o'clock I noticed that Marianne, still trying to read, could hardly keep her eyes open, and sometimes, like a sleepy child, she let her head droop over the book. It was pathetic to see her in this state, and I asked her if she would not let me watch for a few hours. At first she refused, probably feeling as I did that tonight would be decisive. Finally, however, I managed to persuade her to rest a bit in the treatment room, while I stayed alone in the cubicle by the dying Vicky.

On the night table, by the lamp, I noticed the box of cachets on which for three days I had built so many vain hopes. Marianne had found out more about this drug which she could only remember at first as sulfa-something. I now knew the rest of this word, a lengthy chemical name, and I knew too that a German biologist had studied a series of compounds derived from aniline dyes and had obtained very encouraging results with streptococcic septicemia in mice and guinea-pigs. This chemical compound, which was toxic for microbes but harmless in the same dose to the cells of human tissues, might soon cause a revolution in Medicine.

For their part the biologists of the Institut Pasteur had been working on it for months, but the problem was complex. There were thousands of possible compounds in this series of aniline derivatives, enough for several generations of research-workers to be kept busy studying each one systematically, all their lives, unless some fortunate chance should come to the aid of human genius. The white powder I had in front of me on the bedtable was probably not the right one. Vicky and I were not lucky enough for that, the tragedy had come too soon. Perhaps only a month more, maybe just one short week, and the right drug might be found. Perhaps this very night, in some German hospital, the miracle was actually being performed on another dying girl. But here there was no more hope, it would have been too good to be true. Vicky had been right, our fates were too closely linked together. By dawn she would be dead, and soon afterwards I should be in prison.

I looked at the narrow cubicle. Death seemed to have shrunk the walls, could be felt prowling round the bed, coming nearer every second that passed. Incapable of moving, I heard my heart thumping furiously, and suddenly, like a murderer trying to escape from his victim, I was seized by a rush of pure panic. I wanted to run and wake up Marianne, just to have someone who could talk to me, just to stop my being alone with my terror any longer.

I got up and went out. Despite the blue nightlights I found the main ward, full of groans and snores, so dark and grim that I stopped at the first bed. I accidentally unhooked the case-records hanging at the foot of the bed, and they fell noisily. Waking up with a start, the occupant of the bed sat up with staring, startled eyes. She stammered, "What is it?" For a few seconds she stayed like this, gazing uncomprehendingly at the dark ward. Then, finding the familiar landmarks, the unmoving nightlights, her neighbors quite near her, the night nurse hurrying up at the noise, she lay down, her head between her arms like a child, and went to sleep again reassured.

Rising out of the blackness like a diver emerging from dark water, the night nurse was already near me. I knew her well by now, having seen her for three nights on the ward or in the office. In front of her I was ashamed of the panic which had made me dash for Marianne, and as she returned to her office I followed her. I stayed in the office with her for a minute or two, and when she rose to go out again, I almost asked her if she thought Vicky was going to die. But some shame held me back, for she would think I was asking out of real affection and pity for Vicky, whereas I knew the question was dictated by my own selfish terror.

I returned to the cubicle. At two o'clock I opened Vicky's mouth and pushed in the drug, punctually at the time Marianne had told me to administer it. I had said I would wake her at half past two, but was intending to let her rest till the time I had to go back to barracks, when all would probably be over. There would be no further night duty for her, and I should have plenty of sleep in prison, I thought sardonically.

But soon after two thirty I saw Marianne appear at the door of the cubicle. She still had the sleep in her eyes, and her whole face was pale with weariness. She looked at Vicky, then at me. Both our faces must have given her cause for alarm, but she said nothing. For both of us she had done everything in her power, and there was no more left for her to do except administer a few extra centigrams of the useless drug.

It was now her turn to insist that I should lie down on the bed in the treatment room. But I realized at once that despite the cool, shady silence of the little room, I should never succeed in slipping away beyond my despair and my lassitude.

Because of the heavy smell of antiseptic, I opened a window slightly. A distant clock struck three, followed by other clocks with a variety of chimes and intervals between the chimes. Last of all came the Necker's own clock, chiming on a solemn and plaintive note. Then the night relapsed into its grim silence.

Vicky and I were under siege here tonight, we had not the right to the same hours as the others, as those, for instance, whose cars I heard passing in the streets outside. Where were these people going in the cool night, so enviably free? Above the walls of the hospital I could see the upper floors of a huge apartment house, with lights burning in a few of the windows. Why, I wondered apathetically, had these people stayed up so late? For love or work, or what?

They and I already belonged to different worlds, different towns. On this side of the walls, in this niggardly bluish light, in this clinging odor of diseased bodies, the aura of pain and death cast its pall of gloom over the whole ward. Curiously enough, it was an unusually quiet night in this ward, with none of the screams and sudden crises which can make even a hardened night nurse long for the morning. It was quiet—and Vicky was dying.

In the grim silence I waited, digging my nails into my palms, utterly obsessed by my own despair, wondering if I should ever again find the bliss of sleep. In this terrible insomnia, just to stop thinking for one evening would have made a night of real peace.

I saw that I should never get to sleep before the day, so I got up and without going into the main ward went out into the corridor. Anything seemed preferable to this suffocating silence and suspense. Perhaps by walking, I should eventually become weary enough to fall on my bed like a log and forget everything.

The spring night was fresh and beautiful, but I hardly noticed it. Outside, immediately after the acrid moisture of the corridors and the wards, I was momentarily dizzied by the night air.

For a long while I walked between the big dark buildings where the only light in the windows came from the rows of blue nightlights. The Necker Hospital is extremely large, and except for a wide graveled lane nothing separates it from the Children's Hospital. My uniform might have seemed rather bizarre in the courtyards of a hospital in the middle of the night, so I avoided the lights and walked on unnoticed through solitary gardens filled with shadows. I went on dragging my heavy studded boots over the paving, until eventually a nausea of physical weariness came over me, and I had to sit on a bench. But I was soaked with sweat and almost at once began shivering. I got up again, and although my head was throbbing violently, I set out once more on my random tramping.

Gradually the night became less dark, turning to a grayish black and then to gray. With the imminence of dawn a fresh wind stirred every now and then, raising the dust in the courts. I was suddenly filled with so childish a distress, so keen a desire to rest my aching back and stop dragging forward my burning feet that tears of pain came to my eyes. I looked round me, and found I had accidentally been walking in a circle. I was in a corner of the hospital completely deserted at this time, behind the urology clinic. A few yards away I saw the chapel. Without any thought at all of praying I went inside, simply to find a refuge against the wind and a seat where I could rest.

It was not a large chapel. The faint light before the dawn, passing through the stained-glass windows, turned the bare walls to a cold gray. There was a lamp hanging in the middle of the chancel, and the burning wick projected a dim reddish glimmer, which wavered for a moment when I came in. The marble altar was flanked by two large plaster statues, the walls were adorned with pictures showing the Stations of the Cross, a few prayer-stools were arranged in front of the simple pulpit, and beyond that there were benches to the end of the chapel.

364

I staggered over to the bench nearest the door and dropped into it. There I stayed for a long while, feeling each fiber of my muscles smarting and aching, listening with futile attention to the muffled thumping of my heart. Hunched forwards, I put my head between my arms and leaned against the back of the bench in front. I must have looked like a man who was sick or drunk, and the sickness was indeed in my soul, swollen with disgust and remorse, choked by so many months of lust and selfish pleasures. My blood was dinning into my ears bitter derisory words of shame and regret and wasted effort, of vain hopes and lapses of will and mental surrenders. For many minutes I listened to the fierce unappeasable voice within me ruthlessly tormenting me. I had been blessed with a sense of vocation and a unique love. Together these should be the surest supports of a man's life, and they could have been in mine, but I had sacrificed them to all that is transient and illusory and unprofitable.

For four years I had taken every time the line of least resistance: lying to my mother, betrayal of Marianne, friendship with Henri Philippon, giving up work for the interne's exam, sloth, fickleness, the taste for money and the desire for sexual pleasure. I had indulged in the most selfish hedonism, and hypocritically excused myself by pretending I was "enjoying life." In my utter degradation I had sunk so low as to let an abortion be performed because I was too cowardly to face the consequences of my actions. I could not even accuse fate or bad luck, for if I was honest with myself I knew there had been many moments when by an effort of willpower I could have returned to the right road. But I was weak, so weak.

For a long time I stayed bent, brow between my hands, and the silence of the chapel did not seem to me too great for the voice which cried endlessly in my soul, reproaching me with leaving undone the things I ought to have done and doing what I ought not to have done.

Sometimes when I moved to stop my back hurting so much, the bench creaked with a loud noise; then silence would fall again, empty and complete. With a savage joy I told myself that this hospital chapel was not like other chapels, that nobody ever came in here with a joyful heart, that coffins were all that passed through. While Vicky was dying, and the trap she had set for me was slowly closing, this chapel of funerals was my perfect refuge, the antichamber of the void.

A little later I noticed that I was praying, but in an absurdly naive way. I might have been a small boy again praying for all the Christmas presents I most wanted. I tried this sort of prayer as a last desperate resort, repeating to myself with monotonous fervor: "Oh God, don't let Vicky die, take this threat away from me, let me stay free, oh God, let me stay free." I knew I was asking for a miracle, sometimes even demanding it. But what could I offer in exchange? In my boyish prayers at Christmas I used to recall any good marks I might have won during the year, all the good actions I had performed, and then I would solemnly make all sorts of good resolutions for the future. Now, in the same way, I began making improbable vows and absurd promises, offering a life of sacrifice, full of virtuous unselfish work.

In the windows the morning light became brighter and brighter, and time was passing. Soon it would be seven o'clock, and I should have to return to the cubicle to find there only a corpse. I shuddered. Any promise, however wild, however impossible to keep, seemed preferable to the sound of a prison door closing heavily behind me. Pressing hard against the back of the bench in front, in a new access of wild shame, I searched for something I could offer of myself which was not too ignoble, something that had been pure in my past.

All of a sudden, my mind leaped back ten years, and I remembered how ardently I had decided on my vocation, how impulsively in my teens I had chosen Medicine as a career. From that memory there was a continuous line to one evening in the late autumn, at the end of my first week in Paris.

I had spent my first days at hospital that week, and when from my window in the Cité Universitaire I saw the vast sky of Paris aglow with the setting sun, it seemed the reflection of souls in distress and bodies in torment. "All this terrible suffering," I had cried, "but *I* can help to relieve it."

I had vowed then always to show sympathy and kindness to all the patients who should come into my care, and this was perhaps the only vow to which I had not been wholly false. For even in the worst periods of my friendship with Henri Philippon, I could still think without too much shame of my mornings at hospital as a dresser. Usually late in arriving and in a hurry to leave with the last dressings or treatments barely completed, at least during the time of my actual work I had tried to be sympathetic and understanding with my patients. They must have sensed in me a latent residue of kindness, for they seemed to have confidence in me.

I recalled countless small compassionate actions, performed almost unconsciously, sprung from the humanity and considerateness that had not completely withered inside me. I was flooded with sudden joy and a wild irrational hope. It was like feeling a friendly hand on one's shoulder, unexpectedly, among a crowd of strangers. So now I thought I could hear a long-forgotten voice, which had once brought me up sharply, face to face with my conscience, at a time when I had doubted my vocation.

It was the night of the Internes' Hop, when I was starting my second year of Medicine, and I was back on one of the wards of the Charité, by the bedside of old M. Thury. I could almost feel his edema-swollen hands detaining me as they had done that night, and hear his voice gasping and breathless. "Do not resist any more," had been his message. "However long a way round it may be, everything will bring you, and has brought you, back to this same point—even in spite of yourself. Can one ever do anything except what one was chosen to do, that for which one was marked out by destiny?"

This voice linked up at once with the voice of another tired old man, which had whispered to me one evening not so many weeks back: "If at your age life sometimes seems a mere succession of lucky and unlucky chances, yet nothing happens to us in vain." But in case all this might not succeed in making me accept my destiny, that of dedicating my life to the service of others, the muffled, choking voice went on in my mind to repeat: "For us doctors the secret of happiness is simple. It lies in the unflinching performance of our daily work."

Even his death, terrible though it was, bore witness to the truth of these words which had inspired his whole life. It showed me where the only true human miracle can be found, the miracle of finding and maintaining one's serenity through unselfish service to the limits of one's strength.

So now my ideas for atonement and redemption were no

367

mere vague hysterical promises, but a very precise scheme of life brought to me by the example of Dr. Delpuech. Only my profession could save me. If Vicky recovered and I remained a free man, I would go to Peyrac and ask Lucien and Antoine for a place in their health center. I would work with them as part of a team. Struggling every hour against temptations and relapses, I would have their moral support to help me forget selfish hedonism, and accept this hard, humble, and exacting life. Since Marianne spurned my unworthy love, I would join Lucien in loving her humbly and hopelessly all my life.

A beam of sunlight, penetrating between the tall neighboring buildings and the trees, fell on the stone paving, lighting up the whole chapel with warmth and brightness, as if a mysterious hand had just split the chapel walls asunder.

My heart was beating steadily now, and all my anxiety had disappeared. This endless night of suspense, these three terrible days, my four wasted years only haunted me for a moment more by contrast with joy in the new strength which was uplifting me. I had doubted and despaired, but from this long and painful labor I had at last been reborn. Suddenly everything seemed possible once more. Life was simple, the objective was within reach, the remedy was sure.

Already I felt cleansed and full of my old enthusiasm. I was on the march towards a life which I had chosen on the impulse of my heart, and from which I should never swerve again. To live in contact with the realities of men and the land; to accomplish one's task honorably each day; to accept all the dangers and burdens and strife without sentimentality, but without ever growing hard: this was the example the old doctor had given me. The sentence I had found in his notes was inscribed in my memory in letters of flame: *Having buried himself among poor farmers in the heart of the country, believing he had thrown away all his life's highest ambitions, he found his horizons enlarged instead of narrowed: above the roofs of his remote village he found peace, and came closer to the divine wisdom.*

Now the sun was climbing higher and filled the whole chapel. I looked at my watch. It was seven o'clock. I must return to Vicky, but the obsession, which had chilled all my thoughts for three days, had vanished like a ghost beneath the gentle stream of light. Suddenly I felt with absolute certainty that the dying

368

girl was going to live. Her life was absolutely necessary to me, and now I was demanding this miracle calmly and dispassionately, with no sense of blasphemy. Not for my own sake was I demanding this life, but for all the lives I would be trying to save daily throughout my career as a doctor.

Almost lighthearted now, I straightened up on my bench. I must go back to the ward, but I had no more fears. Already I was far away from this city, ineffably detached from these surroundings. Lost in my new mountain solitudes, already with a smile I was daydreaming of humble victories which nobody else except me would ever know.

In front of the door of Bichat Ward, I hardly noticed in my haste the patients who were going off to the bathroom, towels in hand. Nor did I linger in the ward, where the night nurse was busy taking temperatures. I went straight to the cubicle, and found the door closed. Before opening the door, I looked through the glass, but without anxiety. I did not see Marianne, and for a moment I thought I must have come to the wrong cubicle, for I scarcely recognized the still face, with its eyes closed, which lay on the white pillow. Yet it was indeed Vicky, and I was on the point of crying out in amazement. I would have said she was sleeping peacefully, in her first healthy and relaxed sleep for three days. The lips were slightly open as if on the even breathing of a convalescent—but suddenly I realized that this was a delusion. Vicky was not sleeping, she was dead.

I almost collapsed. Stumbling to the corridor, I leaned against the wall, and stayed there stupidly, seeing nothing. I did not move even when a door opened near me, though I dimly registered that this was the door of the treatment room where Marianne had slept, where I was supposed to sleep, where perhaps she had come to fetch me. I scarcely recognized the vague fair-haired figure in white who was quietly smiling at me from the door. I stayed rooted to the wall while the figure came up to me, took my arm, pushed me towards the treatment room, and uttered this horrifying macabre jest: "Have you seen her, Jean? She's saved."

The nightmarish error continued. I gave a short incredulous gasp, and the voice repeated: "Yes, Jean, yes. Her temperature's dropped a lot. Thank the Lord for the sulfa-drug, it worked in the end. She's saved."

Through the ringing that filled my ears, the fog that clouded my eyes, these words still took a second or two to make their way right to my brain. But when at last I believed I had understood them, I felt I was going mad, and stammered out in a delirium of joy: "Then I'm free."

There was a suspicion of a twinkle in Marianne's eyes as she uttered a cryptic sentence: "You were never anything else but free, Jean dear."

"Jean dear!" I knew it had slipped out in her joy at Vicky's recovery, but it was an encouraging sign. It sounded as if we were at least friends again—perhaps something more. "Marianne," I began, my heart full to bursting, "how can I thank you?"

"Forget that," she interrupted me, "you haven't got much time, you know. Don't you think you'd better get back to barracks pretty quickly?"

I had forgotten. I looked at my watch. She was quite right. I must dash. "May I see you tonight?" I pleaded. "Perhaps," she said. "If I'm not here, try my hostel again. You know which it is, I dare say." And she gave me a friendly grin. "Till then," I said blissfully. *"Au revoir,* Marianne."

That evening when I came to the hospital I found Vicky alone in her cubicle. One of the nurses told me that Marianne had looked in a little while ago when the interne was making his evening round. She added that the patient was now quite out of danger, but still very weak.

I looked at Vicky through the glass door. She was sleeping peacefully, and the nurse did not want me to tire her by waking her up, so I did not go in.

A few minutes later, I was in the rue de Sèvres, reveling in the first real liberty for so many days. Before going to the Cité and seeing Marianne, there seemed one thing further to do, just to make sure that my break with Vicky could be clean. It would be a pity now to be blackmailed, and although it was not very likely in present circumstances I felt impelled to go straight away to 12 rue Casimir-Delavigne and recover my letter from Mère Flytox.

370

When I rang, that lady, less familiarly Mme. Doupion, drew the door back with some caution. When I told her my name, however, she let me in at once. On the way there I was planning to make a bit of a scene, but in Mme. Doupion's small dining room, seeing the unobtrusive short-sighted little woman Vicky had described to me, my anger dropped completely. I informed her that her client, after five days of uncertainty, was at last out of danger, and asked her quite unaggressively to return me the letter involving my person. She coughed slightly and then replied in a sugary voice: "But I no longer have that letter."

This made my temper rise again, for I thought she was trying to trick me, and I burst out angrily: "What do you mean, you haven't got it?"

"It's quite true," she told me soothingly; "a young lady came and asked me for it."

"A young lady?" I stammered in astonishment. This was the last thing I had expected.

She seemed to enjoy my dazed look and took her time before answering: "Yes, one of your medical student friends. She came about seven o'clock four or five days ago just as I was going to have dinner. She told me that the letter I had wouldn't mean very much to a magistrate, and you could always say it was planted by the other young lady as a form of revenge. So she suggested my giving her back that letter and said in return she would sign another where *she* would be the one making an appointment for . . . for my client," she concluded tactfully.

"And you accepted?" I exclaimed.

"Naturally," replied Mme. Doupion, and a sly gleam shone for a moment in her myopic eyes. "A letter like that was far better for me than the first one. She would actually have signed it, and she showed me her card too as a medical student. My profession teaches me," she added after a discreet cough, "that men are usually very selfish. All the same I told myself that in case of accident you would certainly come to her rescue. So, as you can imagine, I agreed immediately to the exchange of letters. The second girl," she commented after a short pause, "seemed most concerned about *you*."

Five minutes later the door closed behind me with a muffled sound, and I staggered down the stairs. I could easily guess what Mère Flytox had *not* told me: the first afternoon at hospital before she became delirious, Vicky had told Marianne about the letter, and in the evening while I had stayed alone for an hour or two at Vicky's bedside, Marianne had gone to call on Mme. Doupion. This time I could not be in doubt, the second miracle had happened. First there was the mark against the paragraph in the Rilke book, and then the way she had spoken to me this morning. But here was the biggest proof of all. She had been willing to free me from the consequences of my actions even at the expense of her own freedom and career. Yes, Marianne still loved me.

At the bottom of the staircase in the passage I had to stop. My legs were weak beneath me, and my heart was thumping furiously once more at this sudden revelation of my unbelievable good fortune and happiness. Mère Flytox had given me back Marianne's letter, and it lay in my breast pocket, burning into my heart.

I dashed into the street like a madman, and hailed a taxi wildly. It stopped, and I hurled myself in as if I might miss a vital train, shouting breathlessly: "The Cité Universitaire, the Deutsch de la Meurthe Building, as fast as you can go."

Epilogue

Late June

SIX CANDIDATES submitted their theses together. The other five raised one hand towards the statue of Hippocrates, while I pronounced for all of us the traditional oath of healing:

"In the presence of the Masters of this School and of my dear fellow disciples, facing the effigy of Hippocrates, I promise and swear to be faithful to the laws of honesty and probity in the Practice of Medicine. I will give treatment free to the indigent, and I will never demand a fee in excess of my work. Admitted into the homes of my patients, my eyes shall not see what is done there, and my tongue shall keep silent whatever secrets are confided to me. My position shall not be used to corrupt morals or encourage crime.

"May men grant me their respect if I am faithful to my promises. May I be covered with the opprobrium and contempt of my colleagues if I fail to keep them...."

Now there were six new doctors to be inscribed on the Medical School register. Already the members of the jury, draped in their solemn black gowns with scarlet satin hoods, had risen with dignity, taking up their ceremonial caps from the big horseshoe table. After a discreet glance at their watches they hurried off towards the robing room, thinking probably of the afternoon's patients who would be coming to their consulting rooms. We let them pass with deference, and as soon as they had gone through the door of the professorial quarters, we followed them in order to perform a few last administrative formalities. I had also to return the black gown I was made to put on before pronouncing the Oath. It had been useful in concealing the coppery tone of my uniform.

The door of the robing room opened on to a corridor near the hall, where a crowd of students were waiting for an exam. From their midst several curious heads peeped discreetly for-

373

ward. They appeared much amused by the sight of their professors getting out of their ceremonial robes and preparing to reappear in mufti, while a beadle was putting back their official caps in green hatboxes with all the solemnity of a trained valet. I remembered having laughed myself a year earlier when I was taking the same exam and saw the same disrobing process and the disorder in the room. A professor who was then getting entangled in the folds of his gown might perhaps, a quarter of an hour later, be marking my papers and flunking me. In anticipation I secretly used my one possibility of reprisal, a sarcastic laugh.

But in these few minutes the era of examinations and being flunked had come to an end, and I no longer felt like smiling. Like a child who grows suddenly taller and no longer needs to look upwards at adults, so I watched this very ordinary spectacle from almost the same level as these professors, and no longer found in it anything funny.

Seeing the hilarious students massed on the doorstep, I was assailed by a touch of melancholy. As I walked through these clusters of noisy onlookers, a few of them were still anxiously skimming through books which I recognized as being texts on therapeutics. They must therefore be waiting for their written therapeutics exam, so I knew they were all in their last year. A few months separated us, and like them my hair had not yet thinned, my face was still almost unlined. Nothing, I felt, would distinguish me physically from the youngest among them. Had I grown so much older mentally that I could find these senior students so childish? My time at the medical school was over, but had I also left behind my real youth? Were those magical years so soon to be buried in the past?

I noticed a mirror hanging between two cupboards, and brought my eyes up to it anxiously, hoping to discover signs of my maturity on cheeks and brow and eyelids. I was reassured almost at once. Here was no longer the easygoing carefree look of adolescence, but something different, richer in steadiness, sensitivity, and assurance. I was twenty-six years old, and my face showed clearly, for my private vision at least, the result of the slow unconscious transformation which had brought me to manhood, to the age of practising a noble profession, the age of realizing a mature love.

374

From now on I was a doctor. I had just pronounced the ancient oath of Hippocrates, so charged with wisdom that it had served as a guide to doctors for over two thousand years. I had only to observe it scrupulously, to stick to my task, and as Dr. Delpuech had promised, peace and happiness would be added unto me. To find my other source of strength and inspiration, I had only to push open the oak door of the thesis-room, where Marianne was waiting for me.

It was a vast hall with a monumental fireplace, dark paneling on walls and ceilings, and all round the room portraits, statues, and busts of medical men. It was ill-lit by the June sun filtering in through the thick velvet curtains. Marianne herself had been sitting on a bench almost directly under one of the statues, a lowering marble figure with a mighty brow, an aquiline nose, and an aggressive jaw between debonair mutton-chop whiskers. Several times during the ceremony I had turned towards the patch of brightness that was her dress and fair hair. When I went in now, she was still sitting on the same bench, and we two were alone in the room. Paul and my other friends had been prevented from coming by the demands of their military training, and the other candidates, along with a few friends who had been providing some of them with moral support in this harmless ceremony, had already left, eager to celebrate their new estate with suitable revelry.

At the entrance I stopped, wanting to take it all in once more, this impressive scene of my metamorphosis, so as never to forget it. The vague circumstantial remarks on the importance of Medicine in the country, which the presiding judge had pronounced without great conviction, were already slipping from my memory. The President's rhetoric had less force than the plain words of old Dr. Delpuech and the destiny he had lived out in his native mountains. In fact, from the whole of that purely formal ceremony, I felt I should later remember only the decisive minute when I had recited aloud the Hippocratic Oath.

When she saw me, Marianne rose. She ran towards me, smiling, to kiss the new doctor. Against the solemn background of brown paneling, old portraits, and statues, I watched her coming towards me radiant as a young goddess—a gentle, modest, generous goddess, full of energy and grace. What a perfect

375

doctor's wife she'll make, I thought in my vast and dazzling joy, and how my mother will love her. Close to Marianne, I need have no more fears about building our bright home of the future. From now on I possessed the two happy certainties: a true vocation and an enduring love.